PISTACHIO

JEANIE DOYLE SINGLER

authorHOUSE®

AuthorHouse™
1663 Liberty Drive
Bloomington, IN 47403
www.authorhouse.com
Phone: 1 (800) 839-8640

This book is a work of fiction. People, places, events and situations are the product of the author's imagination or are used fictitiously. Any resemblance to actual persons living or dead, or historical events is purely coincidental. The story and setting are not meant to represent any events or property that now or ever has existed.

No part of this book may be reproduced, stored in a retrieval system, or transmitted by any means without the written permission of the author.

Published by AuthorHouse 03/23/2017

ISBN: 978-1-5246-8465-5 (sc)
ISBN: 978-1-5246-8463-1 (hc)
ISBN: 978-1-5246-8464-8 (e)

Library of Congress Control Number: 2017904283

Print information available on the last page.

Any people depicted in stock imagery provided by Thinkstock are models, and such images are being used for illustrative purposes only. Certain stock imagery © Thinkstock.

This book is printed on acid-free paper.

Because of the dynamic nature of the Internet, any web addresses or links contained in this book may have changed since publication and may no longer be valid. The views expressed in this work are solely those of the author and do not necessarily reflect the views of the publisher, and the publisher hereby disclaims any responsibility for them.

To the Tuesday Morning Writers Group
for their helpful suggestions regarding this story.

CAST OF CHARACTERS

PISTACHIO, the band

Annmarie Erving Hamilton (deceased) – Organizing member of Pistachio, also played guitar and sang
Preston Erving (deceased) – Organizing member of Pistachio, composer, and guitar player
Marcella Damarios (deceased) – Lead female singer
Brett Hadleigh –Lead male singer
John Hanson – Drummer
Sunny Damasi – Keyboard player
Philippe Jenaro – Guitar player
Roberto Lopez – Horn player

Other Characters:

Atlanta Gabriel – Brett Hadleigh's first cousin
Enrique Pedro Damarios – Marcella's brother
Robert J Hamilton – Annmarie's husband and Wharton's uncle
Wharton Forde – Annmarie's nephew, an attorney
Sylvia Erving Nelson – Preston's daughter and Wharton's cousin
Kitty Kentish – Wharton's sister
Aaron Kentish – Wharton's brother-in-law
Kelley Forde Bugati – Wharton's daughter
Fredee Nitsah – Atlanta's girlfriend
Georgiana Kong – Atlanta's girlfriend

Sherry Jarvis – Atlanta's girlfriend
Drina Faron – Atlanta's neighbor
Lucille Maginnis – Accountant at Stadium Music Company
Ramona Merz Hadleigh Silvatrin – Brett Hadleigh's former wife

ABOUT THE AUTHOR

This is the fifth mystery novel by Jeanie Doyle Singler, a lifelong mystery fan, set in the Pacific Northwest where she lives with her family. Other books include: SIMON'S REUNION, LOUISA BLUE, and JET AND BLAST CASTLE.

PROLOGUE

Spokane Coliseum, October 18, 1967, a date and place immortalized in Atlanta Gabriel's memory. It could have been the end, but in fact it was the beginning.

A teen-ager at her first rock concert, Atlanta bounced with excitement as the group performed its last piece before intermission. Her cousin, Brett Hadleigh, leaned toward his microphone. Turning to Marcella Damarios, the female lead singer, he serenaded her with emotion so intense Atlanta lost herself in romantic fantasies. For that moment in time it could have been her to whom he sang.

Returning Brett's gaze, Marcella echoed his words in descant while the band provided background harmony. Without stepping away from her microphone Marcella swayed rhythmically, her long cherry-red dress swaying from the movement of her shoulders while she swirled designs in the air with a black chiffon scarf she slid from her shoulders.

With a crash of cymbals the piece ended and the auditorium was plunged into darkness. The crowd exploded in thunderous applause. As the house lights gradually brightened the applause ceased, leaving a hushed silence. Then conversation erupted throughout the coliseum.

Atlanta turned to her friend Mary. "When did your mom say she was picking us up?"

"Outside the entrance at 11:30."

"I hope we have enough time to see Brett. My mom arranged for us to meet him backstage."

"Ooh, cool." Mary wiggled her delight.

When fading house lights signaled resumption of the concert Atlanta sprang to her feet with the rest of the audience as spotlights roamed the stage in search of the musicians.

A generic radio voice boomed into the obscurity, "Welcome back to the stage, Pistachio!"

As the crowd roared, spotlights caught figures moving to claim microphones and instruments. Atlanta positioned the miniature binoculars she had borrowed from her brother to watch the faces of individual performers. She caught the expression on her cousin's face as he grabbed his microphone, checking the position of the others while looking with concern toward the edge of the platform. Atlanta moved the glasses to where she saw the stagehand lift his arms in a motion of uncertainty and shake his head. Scanning the group, she realized Marcella was not there.

Brett sprang to action motioning to the performers who commenced a piece featuring his voice for the solo. Atlanta kept watch on the stage wings searching for the female lead.

When the song ended Brett announced, "Let me take this time to introduce the individuals that make up Pistachio."

The band as a whole began the arrangement, the stage fully lit. Then the spotlight focused on the lead guitarist, a skinny youth with a shock of thick dark hair, whose instrument became the center of attention as other sounds receded into the background.

Brett declared, "Philippe Jenaro, lead guitar."

Applause thundered as the spotlight moved to another musician and Brett announced, "Preston Erving, rhythm guitar." Again applause and the keyboard player, a tall black athlete introduced as Sunny Damisi, played his solo.

Atlanta noticed Brett repeatedly checking the wings as he introduced the performers. Annmarie Erving also played guitar, moving to perform duets with each of the others. The spotlight picked out the horn player, introduced as Roberto Lopez, a handsome young Hispanic.

Atlanta began to feel anxious noting Marcella had not yet appeared and the spotlight had reached the drummer, John Hanson.

As the piece wound to its explosive finale, the stagehand ran to speak to Brett. A hush fell over the audience as the man moved back to the wings. Brett announced that Marcella had taken ill and would be unable to continue the performance. Annmarie moved forward to claim her microphone and the concert continued leaving out numbers specifically belonging to the absent vocalist.

Atlanta knew Marcella's dedication to performing even when she didn't feel her best. With no indication of illness during the first half of the concert, Atlanta felt something had happened. She focused on the continual movement in the offstage area where the stagehand still stood at the edge of the platform. A man in business dress near there was questioning him.

As clearly as if she had heard it spoken out loud Atlanta saw the stagehand mouth the word "Dead". The man made a run for the exit door near stage left.

Atlanta suspended her thinking. Due to her relationship to Brett she knew the performers. Her parents had allowed her time to stay late and see her cousin. However, as that moment approached she felt apprehensive. Bringing her girlfriend along, she moved from her seat in the side section to the floor. They walked to a door that opened into the backstage area and its long hall. A crowd had gathered there occupying the attention of the door guard. As they paused next to the wall Atlanta searched the gathering for a sign of Brett, noticing that next to a door marked "Men" another door stood open. At either side of it a uniformed policeman refused entry to anyone who approached, pointing toward the auditorium.

Alarmed, Atlanta watched the scene, certain something dreadful had happened to Marcella. A young man scuffled with the police attempting to enter the guarded room but was pulled away by a couple members of coliseum security. Then Atlanta spotted Brett standing with others from the band on the far side of the door being defended by the police. Annmarie Erving stood beside him comforting him while he sobbed into his hands.

"Come on," Atlanta said to her girlfriend. "I see Brett." She led the way skirting police and guards, moving unobtrusively through the crowd until they reached the group.

"Atlanta, what are you doing here?" It was Preston Erving.

"What happened?"

He shook his head.

Brett had regained control. "Atlanta, you shouldn't be here now."

"What's going on?"

His gaze held the shock and horror of someone who had been struck a fatal blow. "Marcella is dead."

"What happened to her?"

Annmarie, still beside Brett, shook her head. "We don't know."

"My mom's going to be here," Atlanta's girlfriend tugged at her sleeve.

"You'd better go," Brett said. "I'll talk to you later."

Turning to leave Atlanta spotted the emergency medical team guiding a blanket draped body on a gurney out the door at the end of the hall into the black night. In spite of the horror she felt her eyes were drawn to the door from which the medics had come. In a glimpse as she and her girlfriend passed on their way out she saw men mopping up what appeared to be blood from the floor of the ladies room.

CHAPTER ONE

Wharton Forde swung his cream-colored Mercedes into the vacant parking place in front of the Barnes and Noble Booksellers, wondering why such an advantageous spot was available at ten o'clock. As he locked the car his uncle's comment attacked him. "You should've got black. More impressive."

"It's bad enough being a lawyer without looking like the Mafia," Wharton grumbled at the thought.

Acknowledging his uncle near the bookshelves in the corner of the in-house café, Wharton continued to the counter where he ordered his customary hazelnut latte with an extra shot. He passed a table of ladies staring at him with varying expressions of curiosity and intrigue. He felt as if he were the luncheon special, a delicious entrée. Vanity, his internal cynic accused, think you're hot stuff.

"Never been hot stuff," Wharton barked back at the Accuser.

Less than a month since his Uncle RJ Hamilton's wife, Annmarie, had died, Wharton could see the toll her death had taken. RJ's face sagged. His normally brilliant blue eyes stared blankly. The defeated hunch of his shoulders made him look older than his seventy-one years, as if the weight of the world were vanquishing him.

As soon as Wharton was seated RJ pushed an envelope across the table.

Wharton frowned. "What's this?" The return address indicated it came from the medical examiner's office.

"Autopsy, the official explanation of Annmarie's death."

Wharton opened the envelope and spread out its contents. He perused the sheet of paper. "Circulatory failure due to CNS depression indicative of overdose. What does that mean?"

1

RJ grimaced. "Annmarie took a beta blocker for high blood pressure and to prevent another heart attack."

Wharton turned the paper over. "So what's the problem?"

"They intimate she died of my medication combined with hers."

"What's yours?" Wharton searched for the description on the report.

"An ACE inhibitor, also for high blood pressure." RJ's voice dropped. "Together with hers a deadly combination."

"They?" Wharton grumbled, the all-knowing, all-powerful who plagued one incessantly with rash judgments, severe criticism, and unrelenting expectations.

"Police."

"Police?" Wharton scowled. "Are they questioning Annmarie's death?"

"Wouldn't you?" The pain in RJ's eyes belied his wry smile. He shrugged. "Just a lot of questions. . . suggestive questions."

"Like what?"

"Was I aware of the danger of her medication?" He folded his hands and placed them on the table. "How much insurance did she have? Was she alone when she died?"

How could one ever explain to the police the dedication a man had for his wife and how little money would mean without her? "What do you think about it?"

"I can't believe she'd have accidentally taken too much medication or that she'd have taken any of mine. She knew the dangers." RJ met Wharton's eyes. "And no, she had no death wish."

"I know that, RJ." Annmarie was Wharton's favorite aunt, a bubbly, hi-energy, people connector and community leader. Annmarie Optimism Hamilton, Wharton called her. She warmed a room just walking into it.

"You want to know the truth?"

Wharton fired a reproving glance at his uncle. He always wanted to know the truth. He had no use for prevarication, exaggeration, or hypocrisy. Truth led him down many precarious paths, but he pursued it relentlessly.

"I think something was fishy about her death, too. If I were them I'd question me." A determined light appeared in his eyes. "Only I know I didn't do anything to cause it."

"But who . . . ?" Wharton's mind raced down paths of conjecture.

"Who else could have?" RJ finished Wharton's question.

"And why would they?" Wharton continued. "Everyone loved Annmarie."

"Well, not everyone." RJ sighed. "Speaking one's mind always ticks off a few people."

"True," Wharton conceded, "but not someone who'd want her dead."

"No, not want her dead." RJ stared at his folded hands.

Silence fell between them. Wharton sipped his latte, glancing at the café entrance where two older gentlemen surveyed the room.

RJ broke the silence. "What I was wondering, Wharton," he raised pleading eyes to his nephew's. "Could you look into it? I need someone on my side."

Wharton widened his eyes. "Cowboy, I'm an attorney, not a detective."

"I know, but you have connections. You could find out things."

Wharton stared across the room at the two older men taking a table in the corner. What kind of buckaroo did his uncle think he was? Attorneys don't round up culprits; they covered their posteriors.

"Undoubtedly the police will continue to harass me, but I'm innocent. I need someone to pursue the real solution."

"It's highly doubtful I could find anything." Even as he protested, Wharton's mind charged through possibilities for obtaining information.

"It would mean a lot to me if you'd try."

Wharton sighed. "Give me some time to poke around." He fixed his uncle with a penetrating stare. "You're convinced it wasn't an accident."

RJ met his eyes with determination, nodding. "You know I'm not an alarmist. It'd be easy to stick my head in the sand and ignore this. But," his voice cracked, "it's Annmarie." He took a deep breath. "Besides," he grimaced, "the police are all over me. It's hard to be in denial with all their questions. And their questions deserve answers, even I can see that."

In the background Barry Manilow sang *Copacabana*. At the entrance to the café a chunky brown-haired woman with gray roots smiled, waving to the table of ladies then sashayed across the room doing a combination funky chicken and samba to the Latin beat. Wharton smiled in spite of himself. Annmarie would have jumped up to join her. She would have had the baristas joining them. No, he couldn't let the situation pass. If someone had prematurely ended her life, even if he could accomplish nothing in the end, he still had to make the attempt.

——————— ✦✦✦✦✦✦ ———————

Atlanta Gabriel pulled open the large wooden door of the Barnes and Noble Booksellers and stepped inside. A whoosh of warmth accompanied by the scent of fresh roasted coffee rushed her. She inhaled the essence of this, her happy place where she could always find books, pleasant conversation, and tea. She had a lot of friends here, not all of them were people.

Following the aroma of warm cinnamon scones to the café, she searched for her girlfriends, who were hard to miss given the racket they made. Besides them Atlanta noticed three tables of older men. At a table near the bookcases, a white-haired gentleman sat with someone she couldn't quite see due to the display of tea tins in the way. A dark-haired man sat alone at a table for four near her girlfriends, absorbed in the newspaper.

Moving toward her friends Atlanta cast another glance at the corner table where two men sat in companionable detachment, each engrossed in a book. If she wasn't mistaken the black man was Sunny Damisi, former keyboard player for the musical group Pistachio. Her cousin Brett Hadleigh had been a member of the group.

Georgiana Kong moved her knock-off Coach bag from the extra chair and patted the seat without looking away from their girlfriend, Fredee Nitsah, whose hand gestures indicated she was telling another tale of adventure from her personal repertoire. Atlanta moved to the indicated seat, nodding to the ladies.

"Fredee's back in the soup again," Georgiana whispered, tossing Atlanta a glance from around a wedge of her Oriental black hair. In spite of her age, she still had little gray, unlike Atlanta who had been disguising her silver threads for years.

"Imagine that." Atlanta flashed Georgiana a smile. Fredee never lacked for a tale of adventure. "I'm going to get tea."

Leaving her sewing bag Atlanta moved to the beverage line and ordered a hot Cinnamon Sunset tea. She continued to the condiment bar where the man she believed to be part of Pistachio poured himself a glass of water. "Say," she accosted him, "would you by any chance be Sunny Damisi?"

He turned his teddy-bear face and big dark eyes on her. She would have to stifle her Renoir blush if he wasn't. "Imagine being recognized after all this time." His voice had the deep resonance of a consummate baritone.

"Brett Hadleigh is my cousin." Atlanta, at 5'9", felt like a pixie next to the six and a half foot man with grizzled hair.

"How about that." His smile widened. "How is Brett doing?"

Atlanta noted the touch of concern on Sunny's face. Brett had struggled with bouts of depression ever since Marcella Damarios died, ending the group Pistachio. "He'll be here on Friday for a visit." Both excited and apprehensive about it, Atlanta doubted her Dr. Brothers' qualifications in dealing with his morose disposition.

Sunny nodded in the direction of his companion. "Philippe and I come in often. You'll have to tell Brett. It'd be great to see him again."

"Philippe?" Atlanta turned the direction Sunny indicated. She had paid no attention to the little white-haired man with him.

"Philippe Jenaro," Sunny explained. "You remember him?"

"Of course." Philippe was Pistachio's lead guitarist. It had been years since she had seen him. "Is that Philippe?" Amazing what age did to rock stars.

Sunny laughed. "He's becoming an intellectual." Picking up two plastic glasses of water, he beckoned toward the corner. "Come and say hello."

Atlanta followed to where Philippe sat with a mug of tea, engrossed in a book on managing wealth. He looked up at their approach.

"This is Brett Hadleigh's cousin, Atlanta," Sunny introduced her in a raised tone of voice, alerting her that Philippe must be hard of hearing.

Swathed in a camel coat, white silk scarf and golfing hat, he dazzled her with an expansive smile. Rising, he held out his hand into which Atlanta placed hers. "A pleasure to meet such a lovely lady." He bowed formally, brushing a gentle kiss across the back of her hand. Age had reduced Philippe's trim body to a petite version of his former self.

Atlanta laughed at his dashing gallantry. She had kept her figure and her abundant crop of hair, regardless of its color, and her love of dramatic fashion. However, she had never been petite or pretty. Her features were too striking, her bones too angular, her manner too intense. She had a great desire to please people, but couldn't get her act together. The emotional traitor inside always pushed her in an unpopular direction.

Retaining Atlanta's hand, Philippe patted it kindly. "You know Preston Erving and his sister Annmarie are both dead now?" He shook his bushy mane of silver hair.

Atlanta frowned. "I heard Preston died a year or so ago."

Sunny gave his head a mournful wag. "Annmarie died a couple weeks ago."

"Some say her death was suspicious," Philippe added.

"So besides you two, Brett is the only one of the group left?" Atlanta felt an ache for the endless dwindling of family and friends. Life was knocking them over like dominos.

Sunny sighed. "The drummer's still alive in an Alzheimer's home out on the peninsula."

"Join us?" Philippe reached for a vacant chair at the adjacent table.

"Thank you." Atlanta raised her voice for his benefit. "But I'm with the ladies over there." She waved a hand in their direction.

"The sewing club?" Philippe cocked his head, winking at her.

Sunny said, "When Brett comes, you bring him over."

"We always appreciate the company of a pretty lady," Philippe added.

Atlanta laughed, promising she would. As she moved to rejoin her coffee klatsch the man sitting alone stood, obstructing her path.

"Were those two men part of Pistachio?" His chestnut eyes possessed a polar glint, but his voice was mellow.

Experiencing a vague sense of familiarity, she nodded. "Why do you ask?"

"I thought I recognized them." He stood about her height, a distinguished splash of gray in his coal black hair.

"Do you know them?" Hispanic she thought, wondering why he seemed familiar.

"I did once. I don't think they'd remember me."

"Why don't you go over and see?"

The man backed up a step. "Some other time."

"Who was that?" Georgiana demanded as Atlanta reclaimed her chair. She shook her head. "He asked about the men in the corner."

"I mean," Georgiana continued, "who are the men in the corner?"

"Members of the band Brett belonged to."

"Pistachio?" Sherry Jarvis turned her pseudo blonde head, fastening her attention on Atlanta.

"That's right." Atlanta had known Sherry from the time they were young basketball moms.

"I saw an article in the paper about a member of the band who died recently." Sherry kept her finger on gossip's pulse. "Annmarie Hamilton."

"That's what Sunny said." Atlanta grimaced. "What happened?" In spite of growing up in the newspaper generation, she paid little attention to the news media, a lot of depressing faulty information.

"Something about conflicting medications." Sherry folded her many ringed fingers and pursed her lips.

"Was it suspicious?" A twang of disquiet had seized Atlanta when Sunny mentioned Annmarie's death.

Sherry shot her a well-you-must-know look. "They thought one of the medications belonged to her husband."

Catching up to the conversation, Fredee added, "I read the article. Her brother died about a year ago, another medical mistake." Running her hand through her gray roots, she left her cropped brown hair standing on end to match her upswept eyebrows.

"Haven't there been rumors associated with Pistachio ever since Marcella died?" Sherry tilted her head, causing her dangling earrings to swing.

Atlanta was beset again with the old malaise regarding Marcella's death. "I always wondered what really happened that night."

Wiggling a finger in the air to attract attention, Fredee demanded, "Who is Marcella?"

"She and Atlanta's cousin Brett were the lead singers," Sherry explained in a how-can-you-be-so-ignorant voice.

Indifferent to Sherry's rebuke, Fredee continued her questions. "What happened to her?"

A good question, one to which Atlanta would appreciate the answer. Would it make a difference to Brett if he knew what actually happened? She wondered what he did know that caused him so much anguish.

"Died all of a sudden during the intermission of a performance," all-knowing Sherry supplied.

Atlanta figured that was the result, not what happened, it didn't explain the cause.

"Of what?" Fredee persisted.

Sherry shrugged.

Atlanta shook her head. "According to reports at the time a hemorrhage of unknown origin. They called it natural causes."

"Maybe not so natural after all." Georgiana wiggled her eyebrows.

The other three stared at her.

Atlanta sighed. "I always thought what happened to Marcella was suspicious."

"How many are left besides Brett?" Sherry asked.

"The two over there." Atlanta beckoned to where Sunny and Philippe sat. "They played keyboards and guitar. The drummer is in an Alzheimer's institution. There was a horn player, too, but I don't know what happened to him."

Fredee stuck her hand in the air again. "When did Marcella die?"

Sherry contemplated the coffee shop mural over the service counter. "Over forty years ago."

"Forty-five," Atlanta added.

"Whoa," Fredee commented, "that's ancient history."

"Sometimes the past casts a long shadow," Atlanta murmured packing her thread and scissors. Conversation moved from frustrations of aging to current sewing projects then to gossip and community news.

The others also packed their materials, making preparations to leave.

As Atlanta moved toward the cafe entrance, the two men near the bookcase rose and came her direction, carrying their paper cups. She stopped cold. "Wharton," she breathed as she met the gray-eyed gaze of the younger of the two.

"Atlanta." He paused returning her startled gaze. "How are you?"

A parade of replies tore through her mind. The ghost of years past hanging around for Halloween. The last rose of summer trying to keep my petals intact. She took a deep breath and stifled her sarcasm. "Great . . . and you?" Aside from the silver in his bushy brown hair and the squint lines around his eyes he appeared to have changed little.

"Good. Are you still counseling?" Wharton held the door of the garbage receptacle open for her.

Although in heels Atlanta was eye-level with Wharton, he always made her feel small. "I've retired except for special cases from time to time. You're still practicing law?" She managed a smile as she deposited her cup in the trash then held it open for him.

"The same as you, just special cases. Do you come here often?"

Atlanta shrugged. "A couple times a week."

"We should have coffee." His voice sounded tentative.

Was he just being polite? "Sure," Atlanta agreed. She had nothing to lose. In all probability it was a meaningless proposal anyway.

Catching his breath, Wharton felt the blood rush to his face. Atlanta. He stared into her clear brown eyes. Years had slipped away since he had last seen her. Now that his wife had passed away he recalled his longing to pursue a deeper relationship, limited then by his bonds of matrimony. However, Atlanta's reproachful expression inhibited him. Suggesting coffee with bashful schoolboy hesitancy, he permitted her to escape with an undefined appointment. Something he regretted the moment she favored him with her Mona Lisa smile and moved to exit the café.

While accompanying RJ to his car Wharton considered the undertaking to which he had agreed. "Give me a few days and I'll get hold of you."

"Thanks, Wharton. I'll appreciate anything you can do."

So, big shot, how are you going to handle this? Wharton's internal cynic began a litany of recriminations. As a man of boldness and purpose, he seldom gave in to anxiety or dismay. However, as he advanced in years a scornful cynic had taken up residence in the corner of his mind, plaguing him with contemptuous questions, undermining his native confidence.

Having taken RJ's letter regarding Annmarie's autopsy, Wharton noted the address, figuring no advantage accrued from procrastination. It was less than a thirty-minute trip from the bookstore to the medical examiner's office.

The autumn interlude, having descended on the Pacific Northwest with a high-pressure system keeping the ocean's storms at bay, bolstered Wharton's confidence.

Parking his car on the side street he approached the medical examiner's building from the south. At the information desk he requested the doctor who prepared the report on Annmarie's death and was directed to a partially glass enclosed office with Dr. Ralph Carson, M.D. PhD. etched on the door.

Since it was open Wharton stepped inside where he found a man searching the file cabinet located against the wall behind the door. "Dr. Carson?"

The man turned his small dark eyes on Wharton with a question that sent his heavy black eyebrows shooting to his overhanging hairline. If the man had a beard his face would be lost to the observer. "What do you want?"

Wharton detected a fellow New Yorker in the man's gruff response. "Some information on an autopsy."

"Give me a minute here."

As he waited Wharton examined the doctor's office, furnished with file cabinets and flat surfaces covered with paperwork. A lab coat hung on a hook in the corner beside a bright blue Columbia parka. Plaques on the wall testified to the doctor's education and credentials.

Returning to his desk, he beckoned Wharton to the extra chair. "You got a case number?"

Opening his mouth to protest, Wharton recalled the letter. Unfolding it, he looked for the number, which he gave the doctor.

After putting it in the computer, the man scanned the screen. "What do you want to know?"

"An explanation of Mrs. Hamilton's autopsy, in layman's terms?"

The doctor focused on Wharton. "Circulatory failure."

Wharton balked at the succinctness of the man's replies. He could have used a chatty fellow. "How does that cause death?"

"Fails to provide body tissues with enough blood to function." The man leaned back in his chair, folding his arms across his chest. "Effectively shuts the body down."

"How did that happen?"

The doctor raised an eyebrow. "What's your interest in the deceased?"

"I'm her nephew." Wharton figured it would eventually come to that. "My uncle is being questioned as if he were guilty of overdosing her on his medication."

Doctor Carson registered no expression, but his tone lightened. "Evidence indicates an overdose of blood pressure lowering medication."

Was that what this was all about? "And that was your conclusion?" Wharton emphasized "your".

"She died of circulatory failure. Since she had a beta blocker prescription it would be reasonable to conclude either she made a mistake or someone else did.

"What kind of mistake?" Wharton was skeptical.

"Increased dosage or an additional drug." Interest had shown up in the doctor's eyes.

"Were other drugs involved?"

"A cyclobenzaprine for which she also had a prescription."

"What's that?"

"A muscle relaxant." Dr. Carson sighed as if in resignation. "But that wouldn't have affected her blood pressure." His leaned toward his computer. "The toxicology report indicates presence of a monoamine oxidase inhibitor."

Wharton shook his head at all the medical mumbo jumbo. "What does that do?"

"It's an anti-depressant that would react badly with the cyclobenzaprine."

Wharton found the concept incredible. "Enough to kill someone?"

"I can tell you how she died and what drugs were present in her body, but which did the killing . . ." Dr. Carson shrugged. "I could hypothesize, but to pinpoint it exactly. . ." He grimaced.

Wharton didn't know what to ask. He didn't know what he was looking for beyond some way to get RJ off the hanger. "Did you find any other anomaly?"

"A bruise on her head."

"From what?"

The doctor contemplated Wharton. "Hard to say."

"Could she have fallen?"

"Not to produce that bruise."

Did that mean something? The doctor had not been at the scene of death. Undoubtedly Wharton needed to examine that before he went any further.

CHAPTER TWO

Friday checked in sooner than Atlanta expected. Brett's plane was due into Sea-Tac International at 1:00 p.m. Her drive from Tacoma was exhilarating on a cloudless day fall snatched from summer with temperatures in the high 70s. A touch of burgundy and gold on the deciduous trees hinted at their forthcoming demise.

Encountering Wharton Forde at Barnes and Noble had jolted her out of her emotional rose garden, tossing her into a weedy patch of vulnerability. More than ten years had expired since her last brush with him, allowing her a new viewpoint on their relationship.

She had successfully disengaged from the wistful memory that bound her to the time they had shared. The essence of their involvement had floated off like so many petals on a summer breeze, having never been tangible anyway. Time and distance had reduced her pain to self-recrimination for believing in illusions and swept away any hope she retained. The moment had come to abandon romantic fantasies spun from misinterpreted glances and phrases to the relics of adolescence.

As a young woman she had believed in romance and love, the kind vocalists sang about and the Bible described. Naively she married believing in that. However, the first "I love you" to which she surrendered had become "I love you and you and you". Faithfulness had not been his gift, nor was honesty.

However this experience failed to end her dreams. She married again. This time to a kind, faithful, responsible man whom she believed truly did love her. Sadly his concept of romance was a period in literature and his passion was reserved for finance. Somewhere along the way her dream of love had become entangled in cynicism and the determination to face reality. Love and romance made great theories, but in truth were simply beautiful illusions.

Having endured rejection and disappointment she could withstand a brush-off without shedding a tear. Nonetheless, emotional fatigue had persuaded her there were better ways to spend her life than dreaming of the impossible. She refused to spend any more time thinking about Wharton Forde.

She parked her plum-colored PT Cruiser in the short-term parking and continued to the main terminal where she noted Brett's flight was arriving on schedule. A British Airways nonstop from London made Atlanta expect it would take him time to clear immigration and customs before being available.

Her self-imposed conscientiousness in arriving early allowed her time to get coffee and a roll. After paying for her purchase, Atlanta noticed the ballroom dance instructor from her classes at the community center approaching.

"We're back in town," Susie Bramwell hailed Atlanta in her enthusiastic voice. "We'll be having class this evening as usual."

Classes had been suspended for a month while the instructors were on vacation.

"My cousin will be with me for a while," Atlanta explained, stepping back from the young lady who reminded her of the Bionic Woman, healthy, strong and perfectly put together.

"Bring him along." Susie swung her dark pageboy, speaking over her shoulder as she moved to make her purchase. "Kitty is bringing extras with her this evening."

Atlanta flashed a big smile then headed to baggage claim where she had agreed to meet Brett. Besides him the family in England had dwindled to a few distant cousins and their offspring. Five years earlier when Atlanta's husband had died she spent six months with Brett, pursuing their childhood memories, looking up distant relatives, and giving Atlanta a greater connection to her English heritage. The time there had allowed her to experience Brett's isolation, loneliness, and depression. It was then she invited him to spend time with her. In spite of her concern regarding his psychological downs Atlanta looked forward to his company.

Ghosts of the past had materialized in Atlanta's conversation with her friends earlier in the week. While she was in high school the group Pistachio had been popular with a number of hit albums and appearances across the northwest. Atlanta adored Brett. He had such promise as a young man, with movie star looks and a strong tenor voice. Although she had spent time with him at family gatherings, he was busy, in demand, and traveling much of the time. No one questioned his rocketing projection to stardom, nor had anyone seen the abrupt end coming. She often wondered now if he had been depressed even before Marcella's death, or had that been the beginning.

When Atlanta spotted him across from the escalator, he appeared more light-hearted than she had expected, laughing as he spoke to someone nearby. The years had been kind for he still possessed his trim build and his hair, although striped now with gray. He wore a small mustache, wire-rimmed spectacles, and a tweed newsboy cap. Smiling, he waved as Atlanta approached then reached out to hug her.

"Long trip?"

"The captain kept his interruptions to a minimum. I managed to get some sleep." Brett pulled a roll-on and carried a suit bag over one arm.

Atlanta led the way to her car. "I ran into Sunny Damisi and Philippe Jenaro earlier this week."

"Are they living here?" Brett helped her open the back of the Cruiser and deposit his bags.

"I assume so. They said they get together regularly at the bookstore and for you to come in and see them."

Brett smiled, "I'd like to do that."

Spinning down the circular exit from the parking garage, Atlanta informed him, "Annmarie Erving, Hamilton I think her married name is, died a couple weeks ago." She grimaced. "There's something suspicious about it apparently."

Brett adjusted his seatbelt. "Ramona told me Preston died about a year ago."

Atlanta shook her head. "Ramona?"

"She rings me up from time to time."

Atlanta rolled her eyes. After negotiating the merge onto the freeway, she asked, "Where is she now?"

Brett sighed. "Portland."

"Are you thinking of seeing her while you're here?" If Atlanta had difficulty letting go, Brett carried his past around like a money clip.

"Not if I can help it."

Atlanta wished she could believe him. "Has she been a problem?"

"She wouldn't know how to be anything else."

Noting the bitterness in his voice, Atlanta asked, "What did she do, figure out you're not broke after all?"

Brett flashed an impish grin. "Serves her right for being so quick to toss me aside."

The family had never appreciated Ramona Merz Hadleigh Whoever-she-was-now, Brett's ex-wife, instantly spotted as a money miner by everyone except Brett.

Transferring to southbound I-5 where the pace of traffic picked up, Atlanta directed her cruiser toward home.

Brett cast a bleak look. "If this were forty-five years ago when Marcella died, I'd think someone had it in for Pistachio."

Although semi-retired, Wharton still handled cases for his law business, operated now by his son, Carson Forde, and his daughter, Kelley Forde Bugati. This occupied him for a couple days, leaving no time to pursue his commitment to RJ.

When it came to the scene of the crime, Wharton was well acquainted with the home of his aunt and uncle. What he needed was the scene at the moment Annmarie was found dead. To this end he contacted a friend in the Sheriff's office.

"Sarkis," the brusque lieutenant barked into his phone.

Wharton identified himself and stated his request.

"Let me check the file and see if there are pictures. Should be if everyone was doing their job."

Wharton waited in silence, listening to keys clicking on the lieutenant's computer.

"What do you want to know?"

"To be honest I'm not sure." Wharton explained his mission for RJ. "Do you happen to know anything about that investigation?"

"Not specifically," the lieutenant confessed. "We could trade information if you want to come and take a look at these pictures."

As soon as Wharton had arranged to stop by the Sheriff's office his cell phone jingled again.

"How about dinner with us tonight?" his sister, Kitty Kentish, offered.

"Do I ever refuse a home cooked meal?"

"There's a condition," Kitty added, keeping her voice light and cheerful.

Instantly suspicious, Wharton asked, "What's that?"

"You need to come to dance class with us." She made it sound like fifty-yard line seats at a Seahawks game.

"Dance class. Are you kidding? With my coordination getting across the street can be a challenge."

She assumed her scolding voice. "You don't have to be good; you just have to be there."

A dozen dancing experiences flipped through Wharton's mind, none of them encouraging. "I think I'll pass."

"Come on Wharton, be a sport."

"No."

"We'll have roasted pork chops and ooh la la potatoes," Kitty wheedled.

It had been a months since Wharton had had his favorite meal. Kitty really knew how to get to him. He hesitated.

"Coconut cream pie," she added in a breathless seductive voice.

"Extortion. I'll sue."

"Go ahead, but come to dance class with us."

Okay, he figured, something was up. "Who are you trying to fix me up with?"

"Wharton, I wouldn't wish you on some poor unsuspecting woman." Kitty even sounded sincere.

"Thanks, just for that I should come."

"Five thirty sharp."

Trapped, he thought, putting away the phone.

Returning to his Mercedes, he contemplated why he felt he had stumbled into a snare. In truth he couldn't think of anything he would rather do than find some wonderful woman with whom to spend his remaining years, but it wasn't that easy. Ever since his wife, Linda, had passed away he had met a lot of ladies, nice, interesting, attractive ladies, but it just wouldn't work. His wayward heart clung adamantly to its stubborn fixation with Atlanta Gabriel.

He had met her on a law case in which his client had been accused of misconduct regarding fees for services. Atlanta had been a consultant. The case had mushroomed from a simple civil suit to a courtroom drama involving felony charges. For six months he had worked with her, developing a personal as well as professional relationship. Before completing the case he discovered he was in love with her, impossibly hog-tied in a no-win situation. Both of them were married and faithfully committed to their marriage vows. When the case ended, he said, "I love you" and "good-by" almost in the same breath then walked away. That was twelve years ago. He had plunged himself into his work. Time had dulled the pain. Several years later his wife had died of cancer.

Then, like stepping off a log into the raging river, he had walked into the Barnes and Noble where seeing Atlanta again revived the whirlpool of emotions he thought he had escaped.

After so many years of differed emotion, walking with his wife through her battle with cancer, he should have gotten over this passionate attachment. His wife's cancer had pushed Atlanta out of his brain as he concentrated on the day-to-day ups and downs accompanying Linda's struggle. When she passed away it had been years since he had seen Atlanta, making it possible to move on with only occasional thoughts of her.

However, he had neither forgotten nor eradicated those feelings, evident the moment he saw her again. She had changed little; more lines on her face, more intensity to her abundant red hair, but the impish sparkle of humor still lit her copper-colored eyes. Without a word her expressive enthusiasm was evident in her energetic demeanor, still creating a romantic intoxication that drew him like a magnet.

Wharton's angular cedar home sat high on the hill overlooking the Port of Tacoma. Its location made it a swift trip to the center of the city and the Sheriff's office. The sun glinting off the lolling waters of Puget Sound couldn't fool him into believing they would get a reprieve from the approaching bad weather. The forecast confirmed a line of storms advancing one upon another headed for the sound.

Lieutenant Davy Sarkis sat staring at his open doorway when Wharton arrived. The lost-in-thought look in his bright brown eyes transformed into a welcoming spark as he rose to his full six-foot-five inches and greeted Wharton.

"Here's what you're after." The lieutenant slid a pile of glossy photos to the edge of his desk as Wharton parked in one of his side chairs. "I can't let you take them, but use all the time you want to study them."

Wharton leafed through the photos. At first glance he couldn't see they had much to offer. "What should I see here that I'm not?"

Davy observed Wharton over the edge of his wire-rimmed spectacles. "The position of the body struck me first."

Wharton studied the picture showing Annmarie lying as she was found.

"The supposition was she had heart failure and fell, hitting that end table." The lieutenant pointed to a spot on the photo. "Don't you think that's an awkward position for her to have landed in? Especially so perfectly?"

Wharton examined it again. "What would you have expected?"

"That she'd have fallen forward, crumpling up, maybe to the side, but flat back like that?" Davy spread his hands.

Wharton noted Annmarie's position, lying flat on her back next to the marble topped table with her arms at her sides, her knees bent to keep from her feet from reaching the sofa.

"It looks like her body has been arranged."

Wharton frowned. "The pathologist mentioned a bump on her head. He didn't seem to think she'd have gotten it in a fall." The way the scene was shaping up offered little comfort.

Davy stroked his chin. "You can see what made the investigator suspicious, especially once the pathology report came in."

"So what conclusion are they drawing?" Wharton figured he might as well know what he was up against.

"Someone overdosed her then arranged her body to appear as if it was a sudden heart attack and she fell." Davy's bright eyes speared Wharton.

"She fell after she died, or after the attack, is that what it's supposed to look like?"

"Correct." Davy leaned back in his chair.

"Is that consistent with the injury?"

Davy shook his head. "What did the pathologist say?"

"He'd agree with you." Wharton sighed.

"The autopsy suggests she was hit before she died." The lieutenant paused then went on, "Which isn't necessarily inconsistent with having a heart attack, falling, then dying."

That was RJ's problem. The wound made it appear possible she was murdered.

The lieutenant pressed his lips together and frowned. "Brings up some interesting questions though."

Wharton grimaced. Like the ones the police were asking RJ. "Her husband wouldn't need to hit her over the head to get her to do anything."

"That's supposition," the lieutenant warned then shrugged.

"It still leaves room for someone besides RJ to end her life."

CHAPTER THREE

Once Atlanta reached her Victorian home overlooking the Town of Steilacoom and the evergreen islands conspicuous in the sound, she escorted Brett to the guest bedroom, tucked away at the back.

Leaving him to unpack, Atlanta did the early dinner preparations then sat in her striped wingback chair and fell asleep. The sound of Brett's footsteps in the hall woke her.

He slid into the matching chair where sunshine from the leaded-glass windows lit the silver in his hair.

"Does Ramona know you're here?"

"I didn't tell her." Resting his head against the back of the chair he stretched his legs on the footstool in front of him.

"You say that as if she has you bugged." Atlanta would just as soon see Ramona off on an extended cruise to the Outer Hebrides.

He snorted at his former wife's ability to track him.

"I have dancing class tonight. Would you be interested?"

"I've not been dancing for a long time."

"The instructors deal with whatever level you're at," Atlanta encouraged him.

He shrugged. "Sure, couldn't hurt me."

Atlanta contemplated Brett's serene expression. "You seem more . . . well . . . lighthearted."

"I guess I've finally faced reality." Brett sighed, looking sheepish. "Marcella isn't coming back to life. I need to move on without her."

Atlanta gaped at him, surprised by his admission.

"I've been locked in the past." He examined his long fingers. "I've judged every woman I meet, every relationship, with her."

"I didn't realize you'd spent that much time together." Atlanta had been a worshipful teenager then working to get her handsome cousin's attention.

He frowned. "Not so much length of time," he lifted his shoulders, "as quality."

She was skeptical. "You're not just romanticizing her memory?" Atlanta had done that, idealizing the men in her life, Brett included.

"Oh, probably." He grinned. "Nonetheless, our relationship was real. Marcella and I cared about each other in a way I don't see much of anymore, it wasn't just physical attraction."

Unconvinced, Atlanta considered Brett. He certainly appeared to have reached a degree of mental peace however he rationalized it. She almost envied him. Although she was resolved to leave romantic fantasies behind she couldn't say that she found any peace in the decision.

Brett pinned her with his hazel-eyed gaze. "You never found your dream then lost that person?"

"Apparently not." Wharton Forde flickered across Atlanta's mental screen. She switched channels. Just another heartache on Loneliness Road, a little more difficult to relinquish when the time came, as it always did. A little more painful to recall as she had never met anyone quite like him, before or since.

She watched Brett's gaze wander to the golden-hued wall across the room as if capturing visions she couldn't see. She took a deep breath. "I've become cynical instead."

Compassion appeared in his eyes. "Maybe that's the difference."

"But you were so young," Atlanta protested. "How could you attach all your dreams to Marcella?"

He laughed bitterly. "A little of your romanticism?"

Atlanta fought a sudden impulse to tears. "I've never known anyone with more than superficial interest in me, even my husbands. They objected to anything more than skin-deep . . . accused me of picking on them."

"So you've given up?" It sounded like an accusation.

"It's not that I believe real romantic love doesn't exist. I know it does . . . for some people. It's like being beautiful, or talented, or rich, it happens to some people, just not to me." Atlanta sighed. "I suspect if my dream actually materialized it would scare me." She stood up. "It's time we have dinner if we want to make it to dance class."

Returning home after meeting with Lieutenant Sarkis, Wharton felt rankled at having gotten sucked into his sister's trap. However, it wouldn't kill him. He had no better plan for the evening. Checking his reflection in the closet's mirror-laminated door, he noted the gray wool sport coat reflected the touch of gray in his bushy brown hair. The black slacks and burgundy shirt were as in-between as he could find in his wardrobe. He wasn't looking to be voted most eligible bachelor anyway.

Aaron and Kitty Kentish owned a rambling multi-level in an affluent development on the north end of Steilacoom with lush landscaping, flaunting its vibrant fall colors. A volunteer big leaf maple tossed huge gold leaves onto the lawn adjacent to the driveway where Wharton parked his car.

Aaron, statuesque and academic, opened the door for him with the pained expression of one who feared he would shortly need to apologize. "It's really not that bad," he anticipated Wharton's frustration. "She's really not trying to fix you up."

Wharton shrugged.

His brother-in-law was as monochromatic as his sister was vibrant. Both were real estate agents who owned their own brokerage. Aaron had abandoned sales in favor of management and Kitty, relishing interaction with people, continued in marketing.

Aaron led the way from the earth-toned foyer down slate steps into the family room where a cozy fire burned in a miniature gas stove seated on a marble platform. Sitting in overstuffed chairs they discussed the weather, a beautiful fall afternoon, the stock market, down again for the fourth day, and the approaching political election. Kitty served gourmet cheese and breadsticks with a Ste. Michelle Pinot Noir.

Bringing her wine, she perched on the edge of the plaid sofa next to Wharton. "I understand RJ spoke to you about Annmarie." Her thick bristling hair looked as though she had just stepped out of a windstorm.

Wharton wondered what his sister had heard. "The police are implying he killed her."

Kitty had good instincts when it came to people and her feet were solidly planted on the ground, a little too solidly at times. She never appreciated Wharton's sensitive side.

She narrowed her dark eyes. "Impossible, if they knew RJ." She set her wine glass down. "Do you think you can help him?"

"Jupiter, Kitty, I do corporate law. I'm not even a trial lawyer, just a paper pusher. I don't know what I can do." He sighed. "You talked to Annmarie. Did she ever say anything to suggest someone with a motive?"

Kitty turned to Aaron who followed the conversation with his pale blue eyes.

He frowned at the glass of wine in his hand. "Anything against her would be so petty it'd amount to a motive only if the person were deranged."

Wharton hadn't thought of that. "Do you know if she associated with someone deranged?"

"She was on the school board. Those people go off the deep end at times, but deranged . . ?" Kitty shook her head.

"She was also on the jury for that big shopping center lawsuit," Aaron put in.

"Same kind of thing." Kitty rose, picking up her wine.

"I told RJ I'd look into it." Wharton explained his trip to the medical examiner.

Aaron leaned forward. "He thought it was suspicious?"

"I got that impression."

Kitty returned to the kitchen, from where she shortly called them to dinner. The meal was everything Wharton could have hoped for. As they finished the doorbell rang. Aaron went to the foyer and brought back a short plump woman with an engaging smile, brown hair, and kind eyes he introduced as Mabel Robertson.

While Kitty chatted with Mabel, Aaron cleared the table, confiding to Wharton, "She was one of Annmarie's friends."

At this Wharton rose, directing his attention to Ms. Robertson with greater interest.

"Mabel is coming to dance class with us," Kitty informed them, giving Wharton a warning frown.

What's that supposed to mean? Wharton frowned back. Turning to the lady, he charged into the conversation. "I understand you were a friend of Annmarie Hamilton." No sense wasting any time.

She raised her eyebrows and took a step back. "Yes, I was."

Wharton tempered the abruptness of his tone. "Do you know if she had any enemies?"

"Enemies?" Mabel looked confused.

A number of sarcastic comments rose to mind. Wharton adjusted his attitude. "Someone who didn't like her, objected to her opinions."

"Actually she was amused by people she annoyed." A hint of doubt appeared in Mabel's eyes. "I don't think she took them serious."

Wharton retreated into silence contemplating a question that would elicit information without alarming or getting the usual fluff.

Mabel saved him the trouble. "A couple times she had a strange visitor. Well, not strange, except people don't usually go door to door selling things anymore."

"Who was it?" Wharton demanded.

"I don't know." Mabel grimaced. "She mentioned buying illustrated manuals from someone selling rare or special books."

"Did you see them?"

Mabel shook her head. "From what she said they were decorating or fashion books."

Wharton wondered if RJ knew about this visitor. He made a mental note to check as Aaron announced it was time to go to dance class.

CHAPTER FOUR

Atlanta backed her Cruiser out then waited for Brett to get in. Although the Steilacoom Town Hall was only a few blocks away and downhill, it would be uphill all the way back. Besides, the Bionic Woman and her young muscle man would give the class a workout. Dancing was not a pursuit for the wimpy and out of shape.

Atlanta had changed into a long purple and orange skirt that whirled when she turned. Half dancing's fun was making her skirt whirl. She tied a matching scarf around her throat and tossed the ends over her back. Brett wore a cardigan sweater with his dress shirt, looking elegant and handsome.

The Town Hall's federalist style facade evidenced Steilacoom's official historical heritage, claiming to be the oldest incorporated town in the State of Washington. Golden light glowed from the tall mullioned windows and Engelbert Humperdink crooned *The Last Waltz* as Atlanta and Brett approached, putting a match to the coals of her romantic imagination. She shook her head to eject the sensation and signed in for them.

Besides the instructors, Susie and Charlie Bramwell, only two couples arrived before them, younger people in their late forties. The Bionic Woman in a short ruffled skirt and her Terpsichore in slim slacks and a long sleeve polo whirled around the polished oak floor doing a progression of graceful waltz steps, while the others sat in chairs along the edge of the room changing into dancing shoes.

Atlanta introduced Brett to the dance instructors while other couples continued to arrive. With an electrifying shock Atlanta noticed Wharton Forde among the new arrivals. Her fight-or-flight mechanism urged escape. However, she fought it back. He couldn't hurt her any more. Having survived the loss of her illusion, she no longer entertained expectations.

In fact the only expectation she had ever cherished was continuing their friendship, but he hadn't even considered that. "I love you," he had said. Just so many words as things turned out.

Once the dancers signed in and took seats along the walnut-paneled walls, fair-haired Charlie with his boyish smile greeted them, noting the newcomers. Hosts were asked to present their guests. Atlanta heard Kitty Kentish introduce Wharton as her brother. Besides dance class Atlanta encountered Kitty and Aaron at other community affairs. She hadn't been aware of their relationship.

From the doorway, Fredee Nitsah, late as usual, waved to Atlanta then signed in, jabbering her apologies to Susie. Approaching Atlanta as she changed shoes, Fredee stopped suddenly to stare at Brett. Glancing at him, Atlanta realized he also recognized Fredee.

Putting her finger to her temple, Fredee declared with an ah-ha look on her face, "The computer class at TCC."

Brett laughed. "That's right. A long time ago."

Puzzled by the exchange Atlanta looked from one to the other.

"Ten, twelve years ago, if you remember, I took a computer class at the community college," Brett informed her.

"I was in the same class," Fredee added with a delighted ta-da step.

Charlie addressed the class. "I'd like everyone to line up, men in one line and women in the other, facing each other."

The group of a dozen couples obliged the instructor.

"We're going to start with the foxtrot. To be sure we're all on the same page we'll go through the basic step for the newcomers." The instructors demonstrated between the two lines. Then facing each other they coaxed the group to follow until everyone had succeeded in getting down the basic pattern and tempo.

Fredee latched onto Brett, lining up opposite him, leaving Atlanta on the end beside her. Atlanta noted Wharton abandon his sister, coming to the end of the men's line facing her. Time to put on her breastplate and take up her shield. She had no intention of engaging in friendly negotiations with Wharton Forde.

"Okay," Charlie declared, "get together with your partner and assume dancing position."

Brett gave Atlanta an apologetic smile as Fredee grabbed his arm. The man with whom Atlanta normally danced was absent. As she stood waiting to see who ended up without a partner, Wharton approached.

"And Juliet said to Romeo." Wharton shaded his eyes and made a visual search of the room. 'Wherefore art thou Romeo?'"

Atlanta blushed, feeling mocked. In spite of her determination to avoid an encounter and feeling insulted, when he held out his hand she placed hers in his, adding tartly, "As long as you understand I'll leave you as soon as Romeo shows up." She noted the flush that swept across his face and the regret in his eyes.

"Okay, everyone, let's try the basic step."

As Wharton stepped toward Atlanta to assume dancing position, his foot whacked her ankle. "I'm about as good with my feet as I am with my mouth."

After a number of awkward starts and stops, they managed to safely make a turn around the floor staying marginally within the slow, slow, quick, quick framework. Concentrating on their steps, staying in time and position occupied their attention for the next half hour until the instructors announced a break.

Wharton followed Atlanta to chairs lining the wall, taking the seat next to hers. Removing a package of mints from his pocket he offered her one. "How are you?"

She met his eyes with defiance. "I'm good."

"And James?" Having spotted Atlanta the moment he arrived, Wharton noted she was with an elderly gentleman. Introductions satisfied his curiosity when she introduced her cousin. However, he failed to find anyone resembling his recollection of her husband.

Atlanta favored him with an indulgent smile. "He's dead."

"I'm sorry." Although Wharton flushed, hope gave him a high five. "Long?"

"Five years." Atlanta still dazzled him with her eyes.

"Linda died of cancer about nine years ago."

"Oh, I'm sorry." The sympathetic expression on Atlanta's face gave Wharton a prick of guilt. Her comment seemed much more sincere than his. "I didn't realize Kitty had a brother," she continued in her elegant British accent.

Wharton found her refined articulate voice a charming contrast to her bright eyes and intense expression. "She keeps me in the wings until it suits her plans." He noted Atlanta's cousin engaged with the noisy woman from the bookstore.

"And you oblige?" Atlanta's abundant red hair drifted in different directions, rebelling against the clamp she used to hold it back. Her colorful outfit gave her the look of a gangling gypsy, all arms and legs and swirling fabric.

"Gallant and amiable, that's me." Wharton noted her skeptical expression.

Fredee addressed Atlanta as she and Brett moved their direction, "Where have you been hiding this lovely man?"

"In England."

Fredee turned to Brett. "What do you do in England?"

He smiled affably. "Count money."

"Ooooh, I like him even better." She hooked her arm through his.

He gave her an admonishing grin. "Other people's."

Placing her hand on her hip, Fredee challenged him. "You must make money from the Pistachio recordings?"

"Pistachio?" Wharton jumped on the opening. "You knew Annmarie Erving?"

"Preston and Annmarie?" Brett raised his eyebrows. "Why do you ask?"

Before Wharton could respond the dance instructors called everyone back to the floor. "Let's line up again, men here, women there."

Wharton and Atlanta resumed their positions in line. Once he had succeeded in getting around the floor and through a couple pieces without stepping on his lady's foot, he took the opportunity to clarify what had come up at break. "Brett was a member of Pistachio?"

"That's right." Atlanta studied him with curiosity in the lift of her golden eyebrows.

"Then you knew Preston and Annmarie Erving?" Wharton missed a step putting them out of synch.

"By sight," Atlanta replied as they stopped to reengage the beat. "We didn't see a lot of Brett then."

"So you wouldn't have known Annmarie recently?"

Atlanta shook her head. "Once the group broke up I never saw any of them accept in videos of their performances."

He had hoped for more. "How about your cousin?" The waltz had ended and couples stood waiting for the next piece to begin. Wondering what he should do with his hands, Wharton shoved them into his pockets.

"He may have seen her once in a while or kept in touch." Atlanta appeared puzzled by all the questions.

Realizing his interrogation hardly qualified him for Mr. Romantic Lead, Wharton tossed Atlanta a brief glance searching for a sign she still cared. "It's been a long time. I wasn't aware James had passed away." Propelled by emotional forces he could not have explained, he had maneuvered his way into being her partner, considering neither what he hoped to accomplish nor what he placed at risk.

Although she gave him a big smile her eyes flashed a fiery spark. "I retired from counseling when James became ill."

Wharton understood what that was all about. "My kids run the law business, although I keep up an office for special cases." He took a deep breath. "I miss working with you."

She laughed with a touch of scorn and changed the subject. "Why all the interest in Annmarie Erving?"

"I promised her husband, RJ, I'd look into her death. The police think there's something suspicious about it."

The next piece of music began and even Wharton could recognize the pronounced rhythm in *The Tennessee Waltz*. They resumed dance position.

"Do you know what was suspect about it?" Atlanta asked.

Wharton missed a step as he considered his answer.

She laughed as they recounted and resumed the dance.

He explained the drug interaction and the bump on Annmarie's head.

Atlanta frowned. "Do you know what happened to her brother, Preston?"

"He died of heart failure."

"But do you know the particular cause?" she emphasized "particular".

A touch of apprehension seized Wharton as he realized the implication.

"I heard there was something unexplained about that, too."

"I think I dismissed it as gossip." Here may be something he needed to follow-up. Wharton tried to recall what had been said at the time of Preston's death. "I should have paid more attention it seems."

"There may be no connection," she shrugged. "It all feels like ghosts of the past to me," she murmured, almost too low for him to hear.

"Ghosts?"

She shook her head. "I was just thinking of Marcella."

Marcella? Wharton's brain raced through his memories. The name sounded familiar.

Strains of *Fascination* filled the hall. The instructors announced they would be playing pieces, allowing the group to determine which dance step would be appropriate. Horrible idea, Wharton thought. How the heck would he know?

Noting his expression, Atlanta smiled. "I can probably figure out which one we need."

Grateful for her musical insight, Wharton listened as she counted the beat and informed him which step was appropriate. His brain still tossed the name Marcella around, attempting to locate the memory connected to it. When the instructors announced the end of class for the evening he asked Atlanta, "Who is Marcella?"

"Was," Atlanta corrected then explained the connection to Preston and Annmarie. "But she's been dead for forty-five years. I'm sure it has nothing to do with this."

Wharton sighed, feeling as though he had wandered in a maze, finding his way out purely by chance.

"Brett is staying with me for a while. You're welcome to come and talk with him."

"I'd appreciate that." Wharton made a mental note to take advantage of her offer.

"Let's go to Benny's for dessert?" Kitty suggested as the group took their places in the car.

Aaron negotiated his luxury sedan through Steilacoom to the point of the boulevard where it made a Y. A coffee shop specializing in gourmet desserts resided there.

Low in the sky the moon masqueraded as a misplaced street light. The wind, winding its way through the trees, made them shudder with warning of impending storm. In spite of this the soft, warm night was an exquisite left over of summer. As the group got out of the car, Wharton felt a twinge of regret at summer's passing, as if it were more personal than a change in weather patterns.

In the café's library atmosphere with dark paneled walls and brass fixtures, they found a table for four in front of the gas-burning fireplace where they ordered dessert and coffee.

Participating in the dance post mortem, Wharton remained uncharacteristically polite, patiently awaiting an opportunity to question Kitty. A lull in the conversation allowed him to charge in. "Do you know the particulars of Preston's death?"

She contemplated him shifting focus. "As I understand he died of complications from his health problems and medications."

That sounded suspicious. "Was there an autopsy?"

She turned to Aaron who said, "I believe there was."

"Where do you suppose it was done?"

"He'd been taken to Tacoma General," Aaron said, "and declared dead on arrival." He grimaced. "But if he wasn't dead before, he died in the ambulance."

Wharton said to Kitty who stared at her cheesecake frowning. "Atlanta suggested something was suspicious about his death, too."

"What are you saying, Wharton?" Kitty's tone accused, but her expression was concerned.

"I'm not saying anything." His conversation with Atlanta still haunted him. "What do you know about someone named Marcella?"

"Preston and Annmarie talked about her." Aaron stirred his chocolate brownie in the melting ice cream.

"She was the lead singer in their group." Kitty sighed. "Probably the one with the most talent and promise."

"What happened to her?"

Kitty exchanged a glance with Aaron. "She died during a performance at the Spokane Coliseum."

"Of what?"

Aaron shrugged. "No one really knows."

"Did no one see the death certificate?"

Kitty shook her head.

"Come on," Wharton chided, "don't tell me the newspapers didn't follow that doctor around and get the scoop."

Kitty continued to shake her head. "Look it up for yourself."

He scowled. "You don't think Preston or Annmarie ever knew?"

Aaron wagged his head.

Wharton poured himself more coffee from the communal pot, mulling over what he had learned.

"A shame what happened." Aaron had a wistful expression. "Who knows where they'd have gone had she lived?"

Wharton refused to let it go. "Was there gossip about them?"

"That was before the whole drug scandal scene in popular music culture." Kitty explained.

"If I've got it right the tabloids alleged the lead male and female singers were having an affair," Aaron put in.

"And the male lead singer is the fellow I met tonight?"

Kitty widened her eyes. "Is that right? I never saw him before."

"Was either of them married?"

Mabel spoke up, bringing all eyes to her. "I believe Brett Hadleigh had been married before the group got started and divorced about that time. I was at the university in Portland when they met and got started. He was older than the others, a graduate student, I believe."

"Did you know them?" Wharton seized the opportunity.

"I had classes with Marcella."

My new best friend. "What was she like?" he asked before realizing what a stupid question it was.

Mabel gazed at the fireplace's gas flame. "A lot of contradictions, very outgoing, but insecure. Always performing, the center of attention, but never thought people cared about her. When she talked about herself, you had the feeling she was talking about someone you didn't know."

Wharton gaped at Mabel, attempting to picture Marcella.

"I've seen pictures of her." Kitty stirred her tea. "Was she really that tall?"

"She was a large girl, big boned, not fat . . . and tall. Just about as tall as the guys in the group. And they weren't short."

"Did you know any of the others?" Wharton still struggled to determine what he most needed to know. In the end he'd probably not figure it out until too late.

"I could recognize them on campus because I saw them perform. Marcella and Annmarie were the only ones I knew because I had classes with them." Mabel pushed her empty plate to the side.

"Was she a good student?" Aaron the intellectual asked.

"Actually she was. Very bright, but confused." Mabel shook her head. "I always had the feeling she was headed for trouble." Then with a quick glance at Wharton she added, "But not what happened."

"What do you think happened?" He pinned his gaze on her.

Leaning back in her chair as if to distance herself, Mabel shook her head.

Kitty emptied her tea cup and glanced at Aaron.

"Time we get going, I think." Aaron stacked his cup on top of his dessert plate.

CHAPTER FIVE

Monday morning Atlanta detected a slump in Brett's disposition, not unwarranted given the wind besieged the house with driving rain, flinging tree branches around. Debating borderline dangerous weather with the possibility of prolonged gloom, she concluded a trip to the bookstore wasn't necessarily taking their lives in her hands.

The aroma of warm cookies and espresso infused her with thankfulness she hadn't given in to the ominous climate. Apparently not alone in her conclusion she noted a number of regulars, among them her friend Georgiana Kong and her husband Yves. When she and Brett had given in to the temptation of warm cookies and tea Atlanta introduced him to her friends.

Georgiana peered at him through oversized reading glasses, smiling amiably. "I don't see your friends yet." She nodded toward the corner where Philippe and Sunny had sat the week before. "But there's the man you talked to last week." She beckoned toward the table where a dark-haired, dark-complexioned man stared at Brett with an expression of interest.

"He looks familiar." Atlanta frowned. "But I don't think I know him."

While gazing that direction, Atlanta noted Philippe and Sunny heading toward the café. He waved a greeting as the two made for the coffee line. In spite of his stoop and the cane Philippe walked with the grandeur of a statesman.

"Why don't you ask them to join us?" Georgiana suggested.

Once they had secured beverages Atlanta beckoned to them.

Philippe bowed graciously, doffing his brown wool cap.

Sunny offered his hand, agreeing to join them. Brett rose to shake hands as they moved tables together then explained his trip to Tacoma.

"Philippe is studying wealth management," Sunny declared with a broad grin.

"Or mismanagement," he grumbled.

"Rich big shot?" Yves squinted at him.

"Apartment owners are always rich," Philippe informed Yves with a straight face. "At least according to their tenants."

"Philippe bought apartments with his money. Gives him an income for his old age and lots of headaches to go along." Sunny shifted his chair back from the table to give his feet more room.

"Sunny gives his money to his grandchildren and they supply him with headaches." Philippe winked at Atlanta.

Sunny explained. "Philippe's apartments are all in this area. He's lived here for quite a while. I just moved from California. My daughter and son both live here."

"And his grandchildren," Philippe added with a sage smile.

As the conversation moved to other topics Atlanta noticed the storm had acquired greater intensity. The slender trees lining the parking lot bent nearly in half. At the café entrance she observed Wharton Forde with the same elderly man as the week before. The older gentleman took a table near the windows while Wharton, without acknowledging her presence, joined the line for coffee. Atlanta assumed he was unaware or uninterested, behavior with which she had become familiar.

Occasionally after the law case had ended, Atlanta encountered Wharton in public places. Although his eyes flashed recognition, he treated her as a stranger, never making contact. Devastated she kept her distance. In private she sobbed out her broken heart, but in public maintained her poise. After the time they had spent together, the trial and the depth of their friendship the least he could do was say good morning. He should have trusted her enough to realize she would not embarrass him. His behavior made no sense in light of his declaration of love. Must regret it she figured and was doing what he could to erase the significance. He had succeeded. She did not believe he loved her then, now or ever.

"Where is Roberto?" Brett asked. "Atlanta said John was in a home out on the peninsula."

Sunny nodded. "He's mostly oblivious now. I went to see him a couple times when he was moved there. In the beginning he knew me, now I'd not be certain."

"And Roberto?" Brett raised his eyebrows.

"I believe he is in Oregon." Philippe said, staring at his coffee cup. "He grew up there, you know."

Sunny leaned back in his chair, tapping a rhythm on the edge of the table. "After the band broke up he played with other bands for a while. Drummers are always in demand."

Philippe added, "I think he sold insurance, at least for a while."

"Will you be around home later?" A familiar voice made Atlanta turn as Wharton stopped by the table.

Recovering from her astonishment, she replied, "Yes, we will."

"Would you mind if I stopped by for a chat?"

"Why don't you come for dinner?" The words popped unexpectedly out of her mouth.

Wharton looked surprised, but recovered quick enough to accept the invitation. As he moved to his table, Atlanta wondered why she had been so rash as to propose fixing dinner.

With the promised storm under way, whipping power lines and swaying streetlights, Wharton traveled Pacific Avenue south to make another call on the medical examiner.

When RJ approached him the week before, Wharton had no idea Annmarie's death was suspicious. Now not only was it Annmarie but Preston too. Suspicious of any Delphic oracle and not given to negative imagery, Wharton had difficulty assimilating his relatives as murder victims. He huffed his scorn at the thought, grumbling under his breath as he returned to Dr. Carson's office.

The doctor's dark eyebrows disappeared into his hovering hairline and his face registered uncertain recognition as he greeted Wharton, beckoning him to the empty chair in front of his desk.

"I need another autopsy explained." Irrational guilt attacked Wharton. He hoped this would be the last death he would have to research.

"Number?" The doctor drew his keyboard closer.

"I don't have a number. The name is Preston Erving."

Dr. Carson tapped a few keys and scrutinized his monitor. "Deceased November 2011?" The doctor leaned back facing Wharton. "What do you want to know?"

"Explain the cause of death?"

He considered the screen for a few moments. "Heart failure."

"What caused it?" Wharton wasn't sure how to obtain the information he wanted.

Fastening his gaze back on Wharton, the doctor added, "There was evidence of drugs for treating hypertension and abnormal heart rhythms, a beta blocker and an anti-arrhythmic. The combination could have caused a severe drop in blood pressure or an arrhythmia."

Wharton groaned. "Are they usually prescribed together?"

Dr. Carson relaxed his rigid jaw line. "Under certain circumstances."

"Are you saying he took an overdose?"

"Possibly."

Wharton had a vision; he was the dentist pulling the doctor's teeth so fast it would make his head spin. "You have doubts?"

Dr. Carson folded his hands, narrowing his eyes. "There was trace evidence of an antidepressant, a monoamine oxidase inhibitor."

Wharton's internal computer threatened to crash. "Could you write those down for me?

He sensed suspicion when the doctor asked, "What's the problem?"

"You tell me. Would it be usual for someone taking the first two to take the anti-depressant?"

Dr. Carson inhaled audibly, shaking his head. "That anti-depressant is used when the safer ones won't work. It's rarely prescribed these days."

"What is it used for?"

"Cocaine addiction, bulimia, night terrors, post-traumatic stress disorder, symptoms of multiple sclerosis, depression that doesn't respond to other anti-depressants."

Things Wharton didn't want to know anything about.

The doctor picked up a notepad and scribbled a few lines on it.

Wharton plunged forward. "What was the conclusion of the autopsy?"

"Death due to heart failure as a result of toxicity. The police ruled it accidental."

"Accidental?"

"Apparently." The doctor's eyebrows drew together. "The drug information was given to them for investigation."

"I'm confused why this was ruled accidental and Annmarie Hamilton's considered suspicious."

Dr. Carson shrugged and shook his head. "I can't help you there."

Wharton rose, thanking Dr. Carson for his assistance and departed, thinking he would need to make another visit to Davy Sarkis. But first a chat with RJ who might know why Preston's death should be handled differently than Annmarie's.

Returning to his car, Wharton used his cell phone fingering the contact number for his uncle.

"How about coffee at Barnes & Noble?" he suggested when RJ responded.

RJ welcomed the invitation, declaring he would see him there in half an hour. The rain was blinding. Wharton negotiated the side streets and parked alongsidethe building just as RJ pulled his Camry in a couple spaces away.

Wharton spotted Atlanta the moment they stepped into the café. Elated to discover she was a free woman, although disconcerted he had not known of it sooner, he had been pleased to encounter her at dancing class, even to learn of her connection to Annmarie. However, he was confused by her aloofness. For all the warmth she lavished on him he could be a Rocky Mountain shotgun recluse.

While approaching the order line he considered the extras at Atlanta's table. Once he had secured beverages, figuring suspension of the confab wouldn't be a death sentence for the group, he stopped to arrange a chat with her cousin. Most accommodating, Atlanta even invited him to dinner. To his dismay he still detected no tenderness or passion only her typical gracious hospitality.

Returning to his uncle's table Wharton declared, "I have some questions."

RJ appeared more animated than previously with purpose to the set of his shoulders and spark in his blue eyes again.

"What do you know about Preston's death?"

RJ widened his eyes.

"Apparently it was a bad drug combination." Wharton observed his uncle's expression. "You didn't know?"

RJ shook his head.

"Do you know what health problems he had?"

"High blood pressure." RJ grimaced "Seems to run in the family. Also heart rhythms I think."

Wharton nodded. "They found medication for those. What about depression?"

"Not to my knowledge." RJ frowned.

"He wouldn't have had a prescription for a big time anti-depressant." Wharton lifted his eyebrows.

Lines appeared between RJ's eyes. "Anti-depressants and heart medications are dangerous."

"Exactly."

RJ's voice registered alarm. "What are you saying?"

"Annmarie might not be the only one to die questionably. Something else, do you know of a visitor she had around the time she died? A man?"

"Annmarie always had visitors. She collected people like stamps." RJ paused, "Why?"

Wharton scowled. "Were you the one who found her?"

His uncle nodded, staring at his coffee cup. "I came home after my monthly men's Bible study."

"Where was she?"

"Lying on the floor in front of the chair where I usually sit."

"Now think about this." Wharton leaned across the table. "What was your first thought when you saw her?"

RJ narrowed his eyes. "She looked like she had lain down to take a nap."

"On her back with her arms at her sides?" Wharton raised his eyebrows, "Is that something she'd have done?"

RJ appeared confused then his eyes lit with a flash of enlightenment. "No. She usually curled up in the corner of the sofa."

"Did she look like she was arranged?"

RJ shrugged.

"Did you know she had a bump on her head?"

RJ shook his head.

"They found it in the autopsy. She didn't have it before that day, or earlier?"

"Not to my knowledge."

Wharton took out his cell phone. "I'm going to call Lieutenant Sarkis and see what I can find out about Preston."

Alarm sprang into RJ's eyes. "Will the police think I killed him too?"

Wharton halted his move to dial. "I don't think so, RJ, but if we're going to find out what actually happened, things might get worse before they get better."

RJ nodded his assent, but his eyes expressed his apprehension.

The rigorous storm persisted as Wharton bade his uncle farewell then headed for the County-City Building in downtown Tacoma. Rain bounced off the concrete and ran in little rivers to the drain grates, accumulating debris along the curbs. He parked on a side street, heading into the wind as he walked to the government seat. Rain assaulted him, hurling its precipitation horizontally.

When he arrived Davy Sarkis was not in his office, but had telephoned to say he was on his way. Wharton ambushed the lieutenant as he came through the door. "I have a few more questions."

Davy paused to greet Wharton then led him to his office. "Regarding the Hamilton woman?"

"No. Regarding her brother Preston Erving."

The lieutenant spun his chair to face Wharton and sunk into it. "What about him?"

"I want to know what the police concluded from that autopsy." Wharton took the chair facing Davy.

Frowning, Davy turned to his computer where he typed for a few moments. "The police report labeled it heart failure due to accidental toxicity".

"Just how did they determine it was accidental?" Wharton crossed his arms over his chest.

After studying the report the lieutenant sighed. "Must have assumed that to be the case."

"Are you kidding? Without questioning a combination of heart medications and an anti-depressant?"

Davy narrowed his eyes. "Are you implying something?"

"If the police want to corral Annmarie's husband regarding her death because of drug medleys then why not apply the same rules to her brother's death?"

"What if your uncle is charged with both deaths?" Lieutenant Sarkis raised an eyebrow, pinpointing Wharton with his bright eyes.

"I know RJ wouldn't harm his wife or her brother." Wharton faced the lieutenant squarely. "The best way to exonerate him is to determine what exactly did happen."

Davy flung open his hands. "I can't help you on either end as things stand. I won't stop the investigation of your uncle and I can't do anything now regarding his brother-in-law." He sighed. "But I'll do what I can if you find something positively pointing in one direction or another."

Perplexed, Wharton left the lieutenant's office wondering what triggered one investigation and let the other slide. Could the difference just be the people who handled it? Who would have worked closely with Preston?

Returning to his car Wharton called Kitty. "Who knew Preston really well?" he asked the moment her voice came on line.

"Lucille Maginnis, the accountant at his store."

"She still works there?"

"To my knowledge. She's a little younger than he was and a widow."

Although no musician Wharton had a lifetime love of music. He was gratified to discover Stadium Music Company, devoted to the sale of instruments, sheet music, and the associated accoutrements was still in business. Long established, it resided in an elderly building typical of the north end.

Good fortune rode along permitting Wharton a parking spot directly in front of the glass-faced store. A bell attached to the door jingled as he stepped into the shop, which turned out to be nearer barn-size than the slim stall it appeared at first glance. Wharton waited while a thin-voiced soprano described a vocal score to the young man behind the counter.

Once he got his chance with the clerk Wharton was directed to the loft where a short, stocky woman with salt and pepper hair greeted him with a terse nod. "C-can I h-help you?" she stuttered.

"Lucille Maginnis?"

Abandoning the paperwork in front of her, she gave him another brisk bob of her head.

Wharton explained his mission, winning her assent to his inquiry. "Did Preston suffer from depression?"

Her dark eyes questioned Wharton's premise. "Most m-m-musicians and c-c-composers suffer from d-d-depression. Preston some, not a lot."

"Did he take anything for it?"

She shook her head. "Too d-d-dangerous with his heart m-m-medications."

"So he understood the danger of anti-depressants?"

"He used m-m-music and quiet t-time instead." As she became involved in the subject Lucille lost her stutter. "Sometimes he rearranged the shelves or cleaned a cupboard."

"Did he have any enemies?" Somehow the question seemed stupid, trite.

Lucille widened her eyes.

He explained about the autopsy and combination of medicines. "He wouldn't commit suicide?"

Pressing her lips together she gave a vigorous shake of her head.

After thanking her Wharton returned to his car. Where should he go from here? The first direction the police would head was after the one who benefited from Preston and Annmarie's death. Undoubtedly RJ would have inherited all of Annmarie's worldly goods, but he had them anyway. What about the amount of insurance involved? A quick call to RJ would tell him about Annmarie's, but who would know about Preston's?

Before reaching his car Wharton realized the best option was Lucille. Returning to the music store he continued up the stairs to her office where he found her dabbing her eyes with a tissue.

She cleared her throat when he put the question to her. "A q-q-quarter of a m-m-million."

"Who was the beneficiary?" That much money might mean something to someone.

Lucille stared down at the papers on the desk in front of her. "I am."

Wharton gaped at her, managing to prevent the "you're kidding" from escaping his lips.

"It wasn't for m-m-me," she explained. "It was for the b-b-business."

"But you were the beneficiary?"

She inclined her head.

Who would make such a risky bequest? "Were there stipulations? Conditions?"

"Not in writing." She sighed. "I knew what I was s-s-supposed to do with it."

Here was someone in whom Preston had invested significant trust. Was she worthy of it? Her presence at the business and straightforward answers made a case for her virtue. "But you could have done anything you wanted?"

"I suppose." She met his eyes with defiance.

Although inclined to accept the loyalty of her character, Wharton made a mental note to check her veracity. "Did he have other insurance or anything he left to someone else?"

"A p-p-policy from the store for $100,000."

"Were you also the beneficiary on that?"

She shook her head. "His d-d-daughter."

Wharton recalled Preston had both a daughter and a son. If he was not mistaken the son had died quite some time ago. "Do you know what her name is now? Where she is?"

"I can give you what is on file here." Lucille rose and crossed to a cabinet near the door. From it she extracted a manila folder. "Sylvia N-N-Nelson. Pennsylvania."

Wharton watched Lucille take a scratch pad and write a few lines on it. "Did she come for the funeral?"

She bobbed her head, staring at Wharton with a concerned expression.

His mind juggled ideas. Was she someone he should suspect or confide in? Preston had trusted her and perceptible evidence supported that trust. "Did you ever question the conclusion regarding Preston's death?"

Her reply came slowly. "He wouldn't have m-m-mistaken his m-m-medication. He had a system." She returned the manila folder to the cabinet then crossed the room to a desk in the corner where she opened the middle drawer and removed an oblong plastic box. This she handed to Wharton. "He kept his pills in this."

Wharton examined the box containing fourteen small compartments above which were raised letter abbreviations for the days of the week. The sections for Sunday, Monday and Tuesday were empty, in addition to the top one for Wednesday. "What day of the week did he die?"

"Wednesday."

"Did he die here?"

"The s-s-store's cleaning p-p-people found him and called 911."

Wharton recalled what Aaron had said about his being declared dead on arrival at the hospital. "Can I take this with me?"

Lucille frowned, but nodded.

CHAPTER SIX

After the giddy moment of altruistic insanity in which she invited Wharton Forde to dinner, Atlanta's me, myself, and I carried on a panel discussion arguing the why and wherefore of her impulsive decision. Not one of the group could furnish an explanation she was willing to accept.

As the hour for his arrival approached pixies in high-wire slippers ran up and down her nerves. Why couldn't he have just told her he made a mistake telling her he loved her? She could forgive him or resent it and snub him. As things stood she felt neither able to return to the closeness of the past, nor justified in rebuking him. Even ignoring his existence was precluded. The best she could manage was to dismiss the past and treat him as an acquaintance.

Once dinner was set, to quell the pixies she retired to the living room where Brett perused her music collection. He had aligned all her Pistachio albums along her green and gold sofa.

He grinned at her. "It looks like you have them all."

"Of course, what would you expect?" As the lead male singer's adoring teen-age cousin she had collected every possible scrap of memorabilia, every word written about them, every picture, and obviously all their recordings.

He shrugged. "That some might have been destroyed or lost, or you'd have gotten tired of the space they occupy."

Atlanta shook her head. "I guard them ferociously."

"You even have the old LPs and their jackets." Brett held up one. In the cover picture the group posed among the rocks along the Oregon coast with the surf splashing below.

"Do you remember that picture?" She noted the wistful expression on Brett's face. "You look like the photographer caught you by surprise."

"I was probably looking away and he called me back to attention."

"Marcella looks like she doesn't feel well." Atlanta observed her awkward stance and the way her lips were pressed together.

Brett tipped the cover to examine it closer. "She was ill some then. Stomach flu, I think."

"She didn't drink or do drugs?" Atlanta had never heard that with respect to Pistachio.

Brett flipped the album over where more shots of the group ran along the border. "She did some drinking when we first met, but later quit all of that."

"Was that picture from earlier or later?" Atlanta retrieved her reading glasses from the end table to focus on the smaller shots. In one of them, Marcella reclined in a chaise, one hand on her abdomen and the other shading her eyes.

"Later."

"Could her stomach problems have related to her death?" Would the album pictures provide a clue?

Brett flinched but shook his head. "I don't think so."

Interrupted by the doorbell Atlanta glanced at the mantel clock. The hour had arrived. A piquant chill grabbed her. Wind and rain blasted into the room when she opened the door allowing a wet and windblown Wharton into the house. He gave her a tentative smile as she took his coat and ushered him into the living room where she reacquainted him with Brett.

Once the men were engaged in conversation she returned to the kitchen and prepared a tray of shrimp and crackers with dipping sauce plus three glasses of Shiraz. She returned to the living room and placed her tray on the gild-edged coffee table. Brett was sharing Atlanta's collection of Pistachio recordings with Wharton.

"How did you meet Preston and Annmarie?" He asked Brett.

Atlanta wondered if Wharton would see something in the photos she and Brett had missed.

"In a college variety show." Brett sat in one of the candy-striped easy chairs. "I used to sing in a quartet. Preston and Annmarie performed as a duo. They invited me to do some singing with them."

As Atlanta handed Wharton a glass of wine he captured her gaze arresting it with a questioning lift of his brows. Averting her eyes she handed a goblet to Brett.

Wharton moved to the sofa facing him. "When was the last time you saw either of them?"

"Four years ago when I visited Atlanta. I stopped in at the music store and chatted with Preston."

Wharton helped himself to crackers and shrimp. "Have you ever met Preston's son or daughter?"

"I met his daughter once at her brother's funeral. Neither of them had any interest in music, which I think was a disappointment to Preston."

Wharton glanced at Atlanta then asked, "Did he ever talk about Marcella?"

Brett's gaze drifted across the room. "When I saw him that last time he talked about how he had pressured Marcella regarding her performances. He felt she was the key to the group's success."

"Did he think he pushed her too far?" Wharton asked.

Brett shrugged. "He may have." He took a deep breath. "He seemed regretful, but didn't elaborate."

Absorbed in the conversation, Atlanta suddenly realized it was time to put the finishing touches on the meal. Afterward she announced dinner, leading the men through a narrow passage into the golden-hued dining room where leaded glass windows reflected the brass chandelier.

As they took places at the formally set table, a loud clattering on the roof stopped them.

"Tree branches," Atlanta explained. "It happens whenever we have a wind storm."

After everyone was served, Atlanta brought up Annmarie. "Do you believe something was suspicious about her death?"

Wharton sighed. "I'm not sure I've gotten to the believing point, but something appears fishy." He explained what he had learned about Preston. "None of it makes any sense. What motive would anyone have to do away with a couple of old musicians?"

"Inheritance?" Brett suggested.

"Or insurance?" Atlanta put in.

"I'm checking those. Her brother had a couple large policies, but I'm skeptical it'll lead to anything." Wharton cast a pointed glance at Brett. "What about you? Do you have a big insurance policy that will benefit someone?"

Atlanta paused, her fork in the air. "Do you think something could happen to Brett?"

Wharton laughed, minimizing the effect of his question. But now the idea had been introduced, Atlanta could not dismiss it. "Do you think it's possible someone is getting rid of the group?"

"Possible is one thing." Wharton shrugged. "Probable another."

When Atlanta rose to clear the table, a loud creaking, cracking noise stopped her in mid-action. The guys looked to her with raised eyebrows. She shook her head as she heard the sound of the wind buffeting the house. As she turned to take the load of plates to the kitchen, a crashing boom shook the entire building, causing the crystal in the wood-carved breakfront to rattle and the floor to reverberate.

Wharton jumped up, "What was that?"

Alarm widened Brett's eyes as he looked at Atlanta.

Her heart leaped to her throat as she croaked, "It sounded like it came from the rear of the house." She set her plates back on the table and followed the men as they rushed back through the narrow hall. Stepping into the living room they were met with a burst of cold air. Passing into the back hall they could see the streetlight on the avenue above Atlanta's house through a gaping hole in the roof of the farthest bedroom. The bushy boughs of a tree lay across the bed.

Horrified at the sight, she worked to believe her eyes.

"Come on," Wharton beckoned to Brett, "let's go see what happened."

Atlanta followed them out the back door. In the yard she could see a tree had fallen from the neighbor's property up the hill behind her house. The wind still whipped, pelting them with rain.

"Do you know your neighbor?" Wharton asked as they stared at the damage.

"Only to say hello." Atlanta wasn't sure she even knew the name.

Ignoring the wind and rain, the three walked from the yard to the alley, where they had a better view. The tree, reinforced by its position on the hill above Atlanta's house exercised considerable force in its fall, plowing through the roof and making a valley across the support beams. The damage was extensive and dangerous.

Shock suspended Atlanta's thinking as denial took over. She could not believe such destruction could be accomplished in one fell swoop.

Wharton turned to her with a grimace of concern.

"What should I do?" Where was the list of things to do when a tree falls on your house?

"Call your insurance company." He handed her his cell phone.

"Right now?"

"That would be a good idea." He raised his eyebrows as if she was being stupid.

Maybe he should have a tree fall on his house, Atlanta thought ungraciously. "Do insurance companies answer the phone at night?"

He frowned at her. "Call and find out."

Although the boisterous storm continued the rain had declined to mist propelled by the wind. She took Wharton's phone into the house to look up her insurance company's number.

A modest cluster of spectators had gathered giving open-mouthed scrutiny to the disfigured roof. Wharton walked to where Brett stood with the sightseers.

"It's a good thing it was dinner time and not bedtime." Brett's tone was breezy.

Wharton detected a degree of apprehension beyond the windstorm's damage. "Are you feeling paranoid?"

Brett laughed with his voice, but his eyes failed to share the amusement.

Atlanta approached, swinging a camel colored cape over her shoulders and holding out Wharton's cell phone. "Apparently I'm not the only one with a problem. I left a message and my phone number."

From the group gathered along the street a woman moved toward them. "I own the house behind," she said, "and the tree." She wore a raincoat, holding it together with her arms wrapped around herself, her silvery hair blowing in the wind.

Atlanta greeted her neighbor.

"I'm sorry about the damage," the woman put her hand on Atlanta's arm.

Sighing, Atlanta shook her head. "I still can't believe it."

"Why don't you ladies get in out of the cold?" Wharton urged them.

"Come up to my house. The least I can do is offer you a cup of tea and a warm place to stay."

When Atlanta had gone, Wharton chatted with one of the onlookers who informed him the best alternative was to call the fire department. They had the equipment to do the emergency service. Wharton found the number with his cell phone then talked with a fireman who informed him they could remove the tree from the alley and cover the open portion of the house with a tarpaulin. After the fire team succeeded in temporarily securing her house and sealing off the interior from further water damage, Wharton and Brett climbed the hill to a light colored Cape Cod with a partial brick facade.

Making the trek Wharton noticed Atlanta's house was not yet out of danger. Other trees in her neighbor's yard were equally good candidates for toppling onto her roof. The ferocious wind had stopped to take a breath, no longer swirling loose branches in midair; although the tops of the evergreens still swayed ominously.

Atlanta's neighbor greeted them at the door then led them to where she sat on a bronze brocade loveseat. The room was filled with amber glass bowls, vases, and picture frames containing photographs of individuals of Hispanic descent. A crucifix hung above a dark-stained credenza in a niche off the living room.

She offered tea and coffee.

"I'll have coffee." Wharton made a restless turn through the small room, noting the Italian artwork in black metal frames before perching on a straight-backed chair.

Brett accepted tea and sat down beside Atlanta.

"I really thought if one of those trees came down it would be on my house." The woman handed mugs to the men. "The wind usually comes from the northwest."

"Unfortunately, your trees are still whipping around." Wharton grumbled. "However, they're so close to the descent they're more apt to fall on Atlanta's house regardless of the wind's direction."

"I guess I'll have to have the others taken down so this doesn't happen again. By the way, I'm Drina Faron." She offered her hand to Wharton who introduced himself.

Atlanta said. "This is my cousin Brett Hadleigh."

"Brett Hadleigh?" Drina repeated the name frowning. "That sounds familiar."

"Old rock star," Brett said with a crooked grin.

"He was one of the lead singers in the sixties group Pistachio," Atlanta explained.

Drina's face drained of color as she stared at Brett with shock in her expression. Recovering, she hurried on to talk about the weather. "These storms are so dangerous."

Having detected the quick mood change and shift in topic, Wharton glanced at Atlanta wondering if she had noticed.

Although participating in the conversation, Atlanta's mind ran on a double track, assessing her situation. Would it still be safe to stay in her house? If not, where could they go?

When the conversation turned back to the weather, Atlanta voiced her misgivings. "Do you think the house is okay to stay in?"

"Not tonight," Wharton declared without hesitation. "You should at least wait until your insurance company has cleared it."

"We can go to an inn," Brett suggested.

"I have two extra bedrooms," Wharton offered. "You can stay with me."

No! No! No! screamed the alarmist in Atlanta's head. No way did she want to stay with Wharton, or anywhere near him. She had enough problems.

"It's no problem," he assured her.

Some other way, she prayed silently. *Another option, please Lord.* Atlanta considered her options. It may be too late to presume upon a friend but surely not to get a hotel.

"I still need to have my chat with Brett," Wharton encouraged her.

Atlanta glanced at Brett, whose expression was noncommittal.

"Let's go to your house and get what you need for a couple nights. Then you can follow me to mine." Wharton rose as if the decision were made.

Brett rose also, leaving Atlanta still struggling for a better plan. She stood, thanked Drina for her hospitality, then followed the other two trekking to her house, where lights remained on and the side door unlocked.

First they went to where the tree had come through the roof. Tarpaulin covered the gaping hole, flapping as the wind puffed at it. Although the tree remained, its broken branches and debris from the roof covering the bedspread, the tarpaulin provided respite from the wind and rain. From the hole in the top of the back bedroom they could see the attic. The tree had also punctured the roof over the second bedroom and clipped the corner of the bathroom. The entire back portion of Atlanta's house had been damaged.

The rear of the house joined the front by means of an open archway, leaving no simple way to close off the ravaged portion. Cold air reached them, which the furnace seemed unable to overcome, albeit closing the bedroom and bath doors provided some respite.

Since only the front portion of the house had a second story, Atlanta figured she had better check her bedroom and bath upstairs for damage. The two men followed her.

Here the top of the tree had put a hole in the wall just above the window in Atlanta's bedroom breaking it. The fire crew had also covered this with tarpaulin, However, her room was filled with cold air.

Atlanta realized with a sinking feeling she couldn't expect Brett to stay the night, nor should she either. She felt numb with shock.

"Why don't you pack a few things, plus anything of significant value," Wharton suggested.

"I need to clean up the dining room and kitchen." Atlanta's mind focused on the mess she had left when the tree fell.

"We're not in any rush," Wharton assured her.

Atlanta stood frozen in the middle of the room. The broken window had torn the embroidered sheer covering it and knocked over the Victorian lamp. It had scattered glass across the walnut nightstand and a corner of the lavender spread on her bed. She moved across the room to pick up the lamp, which she observed with thankfulness was still in one piece.

She glanced at her closet. "I think I'll clean up downstairs first." She regarded Wharton. "You're sure this isn't a problem for you."

He gazed at her with an expression she could not understand. "Not at all. I'll help Brett move some of the debris out of the house."

Downstairs, Atlanta carried the dinner remains to the kitchen, loaded the dishwasher and put away the food. She replaced the dining table lace tablecloth, then wondered at her foolishness. Control, she thought, taking hold of things that had gotten completely out of hand.

Afterward she went to her bedroom where she packed enough personal items for a couple days, including her box of precious jewelry and her laptop computer. Her other valuables were either too large to bring or of sentimental rather than monetary value. She and Brett took her PT Cruiser and followed Wharton's Mercedes out of Steilacoom, heading to I-5. Atlanta managed, in spite of traffic, to keep his car in sight. With Steilacoom on the Tacoma's Southwest corner and Wharton's home on the Northeast it took more than half an hour to reach their destination.

In spite of misgivings, stepping into Wharton's one-level cedar home infused her with a sense of peace and comfort. The damage to her house had robbed it of its tranquility. Although Wharton's home hardly qualified as homey, it was tidy and comfortable. Characterized by bulky, heavily cushioned sofas and chairs, jumbo tables, credenzas, and imposing pieces of artwork it offered protection.

All this she took in as they entered through tall double doors into a wide foyer that transitioned easily into a formal dining room. A wall separated this from the living room. An archway opened into a short hall where Wharton led them to the two extra bedrooms, between which was a bath.

Glancing at his watch, he commented on the time and with a lingering concerned expression urged them to get some rest. Atlanta's brain had shifted into neutral. She nodded, murmuring her thanks, and gratefully closed the door on the room she had been assigned. Alone for the first time in hours, she admitted to extreme fatigue. Taking a tissue from the box on the nightstand, she sat in the leather chair and quietly wept.

CHAPTER SEVEN

The moment Wharton's eyes opened his memory served notice he had invited two people to enjoy his hospitality, which presented a problem. Cooking wasn't one of his accomplishments. He mooched home cooked meals off relatives and friends. What was he going to do about breakfast? Since he knew how to make coffee he accomplished that as soon as he was dressed. Then he figured a trip to the local grocery store bakery was in order.

When he returned he found Brett in the sunlit family room reading the local newspaper. Inviting him into the kitchen, Wharton set out his rolls and offered him a cup of coffee.

"Looks like the storm caused a lot of problems," Brett observed. "Thousands lost electricity."

"Happens every time we get one of these windstorms." Wharton set out two mugs of coffee and the carton of milk. "I'd appreciate it if you'd tell me about Pistachio." Wharton stirred milk into his coffee.

Brett refolded the paper, drawing his eyebrows into a "v" over his nose. "Marcella was the heart of the group. Before she came along, Preston and Annmarie were just a couple of good musicians who played for small get-togethers, a coffee shop, or the university SUB, no pizzazz, no following, no particular name."

Wharton took an apple fritter and sniffed the cinnamon. "Don't be bashful," he admonished his guest, "have a roll. What about when you joined the group?"

"We were just a trio with a vocalist. I added a little dimension, but we still did the small jobs."

"What made Marcella so special?"

Eying the plate of rolls as if he couldn't make up his mind, Brett finally chose a maple bar. "Everything about Marcella was special. She had energy like a magnetic aura. She attracted people like gravity."

The intensity in Brett's tone triggered Wharton's skepticism."Was she talented?"

"Exquisitely. She had a sensational voice, strong and melodic with a wide vocal range. Not only that, she was a born performer. She loved playing to an audience. We arranged songs around her voice then filled in the harmony and background."

Brett could have pitched Marcella to a promoter with his passionate declamation. Obviously she was more to him than a fellow musician. "Were there more than the four of you in the band?"

"Preston and Annmarie played keyboards. Annmarie also played violin. Preston composed and arranged music. We developed a strong harmony and a folksy style that became popular. Then we added a drummer, a horn player, a guitar player, and another keyboard player. As time went on Annmarie played guitar too."

"When did you break out of the small get-togethers?"

Closing his eyes Brett considered. "I had completed graduate school and Preston had finished his undergraduate degree. Marcella decided she was tired of the university thing and quit. Annmarie had another year to go. So it was more or less as we finished school."

"How long before you made it out of Portland?" The album covers Wharton had seen at Atlanta's house revealed a wide range of appearances including San Francisco, Sacramento, Seattle, and Vancouver.

"The first big hit we had was *Just To Love You*. That got us invitations to appear beyond Oregon. We were invited to do intros for other touring groups."

"Your appearance at the Spokane Coliseum – when was that in the progression of your group's success?"

"Effectively the end." Brett sighed.

"Had it not been the end where do you think it would have fallen?"

He frowned. "By then we had three substantial hits, one LP out, and another just about ready. We were able to do our own shows instead of leads for someone else, but we hadn't made the big circuit yet. We were still confined to the Pacific Northwest and Northern California."

Wharton leaned back in his chair. "Did you have any hint Marcella was ill?"

Shifting his gaze away from Wharton, Brett muttered, "That's something you think about when you're sixty, not when you're twenty-five. All of life was ahead of us then."

"So you had no idea?" Wharton detected some evasiveness in Brett's demeanor.

"I'm not sure she was. Atlanta's remark the other night made me think about it – but even then I couldn't say she was ill."

At the mention of her name Atlanta appeared in the doorway.

Atlanta's first sensation on opening her eyes had been appreciation for the sun, shining with childlike innocence, belying the parade of images bombarding her with the previous night's calamity. She found it difficult to lift her head from the pillow considering the enormous responsibility ahead. How would she even begin?

Picking her gold watch off the oak bedside table, she had noted the time, 8:30. Pierced with guilt for sleeping in, she forced herself to rise. Procrastination wouldn't make problems disappear. Grabbing her toilet articles she had ventured into the hall where she heard male voices from another part of the house.

Adding to her dismay she figured in the evening's chaos she must have stuck her wits in the dishwasher with the dinner plates and shrunk them. The blue sweater she had packed clashed with the olive slacks. The purple silk shirt wasn't any better. She had forgotten to bring socks and hairspray. She felt like crying, but that would just cause her makeup to run.

Joining the men in the breakfast room, she figured she'd make a good addition to the ugly house advertisement. It took inner fortitude just to say, "Good morning."

Wharton rose. "Coffee?" He grabbed the pot and a mug. Indicating his bakery specials, he added, "I'm famous for my rolls."

Atlanta rolled her eyes laughing then took the chair next to Brett. "What are we going to do?" she asked as he wiped maple frosting off his mustache.

Wharton set a mug of coffee in front of her. "Did your insurance company get back to you?"

Atlanta's mind backtracked through the previous night's events. "I don't know. I'll have to check my messages."

"Once you get hold of them, they'll have a plan of action." Wharton gave her an encouraging smile.

After retrieving her cell phone from the bedroom she checked, finding two messages. The first was from the insurance company informing her the restoration company, Lewis Brothers, would contact her for an appointment to assess the damage. The second left her bewildered. She scowled at Brett. "How did Ramona get my cell phone number?"

"Ramona?" Brett's expression resembled a groundhog blinking in the blinding sun.

Atlanta pinned him with her gaze. "Did you give it to her?"

He shook his head.

She had never trusted Ramona and where Ramona was concerned she didn't trust Brett either. "She wants you to call her." Atlanta found Brett's passive attitude annoying. Since Ramona obtained the divorce Atlanta feared she could run him over like a brakeless city bus on the Union Avenue hill.

Abashed, Brett asked, "Did she say what she wants?"

"Does she ever say what she wants?" And if she did, Atlanta thought, would it mean anything?

Brett glanced apologetically at Wharton who observed the exchange with interest. "My ex-wife."

Wharton's expression lit hopefully, "Was she acquainted with Preston and Annmarie?"

Brett grimaced. "Just barely."

"How about Marcella?"

He made a raucous sound. "She hated Marcella? I dated her after Ramona and I were divorced."

Wharton held up the coffee pot to which Brett nodded.

"She wasn't counting on Brett making any money from his music." Atlanta pushed her cup closer to Wharton.

"And when he did, she was sorry to have given him up?"

"It appears that way." Brett laughed.

Passing the milk and sugar, Wharton asked, "She never married?"

"Oh, on the contrary," Brett gave Atlanta an uncomfortable glance. "She married at least three times."

Atlanta stirred milk into her coffee wondering how Brett knew all this. She addressed Wharton, "Why do you ask?"

"I'm looking for any clues to who might have killed Preston and Annmarie."

"Ramona is too flighty to plan anything so complicated." Atlanta hated to shoot down his speculation. "Even if she wanted to do away with Marcella."

"Would there have been enough royalties to make it worthwhile?"

"You couldn't live on it." Brett sighed. "Although the music was much more popular after the group disbanded than before."

"It was the beginning of a trend," Atlanta added. However, Ramona's interest in Brett may go beyond just his royalties.

"Are they passed down to heirs?" Wharton inquired.

"If the copyrights are still in effect."

"So if Ramona succeeded in remarrying you she could get hold of your royalties."

Brett shrugged. "Theoretically."

Bach's *Minuet* announced a call on Atlanta's cell phone.

"This is Daniel Lewis," the deep voice informed her. "I understand you've had tree fall through your roof."

Atlanta explained what had occurred the night before.

"How about I meet you there at 10:30?"

She glanced at her watch. "I can do that." She turned to Brett and explained.

"I'll come with you." He picked up his coffee cup and took it to the sink.

"Why don't you two plan to spend at least another night?"

Atlanta considered Wharton with a sigh, wishing she didn't have to think about it. "I'll let you know later. Thank you."

"Cheer up." Wharton placed a hand on her shoulder. "Someday this will be one of those amusing experiences you tell your friends about."

Atlanta stepped away from his reach, doubting she would ever arrive at that stage.

CHAPTER EIGHT

After Atlanta and Brett left, Wharton's daughter called requesting he sign some paperwork. Winding his way into the Port of Tacoma, he juggled ideas from the morning's conversation. Did Preston and Annmarie's Pistachio connection contribute to their deaths? How much did they receive in royalties?

Wharton's daughter, Kelley, had taken her father's genes, making her short and chunky, with fluffy light brown hair and a take-charge air of efficiency. Her brother, Carson, resembled Wharton's wife, Linda, tall, thin, and sensitive. Kelley got things done with speed and competency; Carson did it with inspiration and brilliance. Both were significant assets to his law practice. Their participation allowed him freedom to semi-retire in his late fifties.

"What do you know about music royalties?" Wharton asked as Kelley handed him papers to sign.

She lifted her eyebrows. "Composer?"

"And recording artist."

She shrugged. "Not much, but I could find out."

"Would you? Find out how much money might be involved and what happens when the artist dies."

Wharton spent the morning handling documents until Kelley stuck her head in announcing she was going to lunch. Consulting his list of questions, he determined to learn more about Lucille Maginnis and Sylvia Nelson.

He called his sister's cell phone.

"What can I do for you?" Kitty asked in her realtor's voice.

"Have lunch with me and answer a few questions." She had more connection to Preston's relationships than he did.

"Answers are the price of lunch." Kitty verified his offer.

"Sure if you can't afford your own."

They agreed to meet at the grill in Tacoma's downtown hotel. Kitty arrived first, securing a table by the window. The restaurant's subdued colors were enhanced by the sunlit view of autumn's bright splash on the trees.

Once they had ordered Kitty demanded to know the price of lunch.

"What do you know about Lucille Maginnis?" In Wharton's experience women always had a better fix on people's involvement than men.

"She was with Preston for over thirty years." Kitty rearranged her silverware. "I believe she was in love with him."

Wharton frowned. "Did he reciprocate?"

Kitty grimaced. "Preston loved his wife and children. How he felt about Lucille, I don't know, beyond trusting her completely."

"How did she feel about his wife and children?" What Preston felt probably wasn't the issue.

"You ask a lot of hard questions, Wharton." She flashed him a scowl.

"It's going to take answers to hard questions to get RJ off the hook." Did she think he was gossiping?

"All I can give you is my personal opinion." Kitty sighed, narrowing her eyes. "I don't think Lucille was brokenhearted when Susan died. I believe she expected things to change between her and Preston, but they never did. She may have hoped for more, but she lived with the way it was."

The waiter brought their salads and refilled their water glasses.

"How did she feel about Preston's kids?"

"She was friends with his son." Kitty poured dressing on her salad and began tossing it. "But I don't think she got along with Sylvia."

"Relationship jealousy?" Wharton could imagine the daughter and beloved secretary vying for Preston's attention.

Kitty grimaced. "Sylvia wasn't particularly easy to get along with."

"The son died some time ago." Wharton tried to recall what he had heard. "Before or after his mother?"

"Before." Kitty eyed Wharton with disapproval.

"It's not that I don't know any of this," Wharton defended himself. "I just don't have the specifics down pat."

"You're memory is that bad?"

Wharton frowned at his sister. She looked as if she were serious. "Do you know who handled Preston's financial affairs?"

"I don't remember the name, but they're in that complex of cottage looking offices on the north end." Kitty made some descriptive hand motions.

He spent a few minutes concentrating on his salad. "How about calling Sylvia, have a friendly girl to girl chat?"

"What for?" Kitty regarded him with suspicion.

"Find out about Preston's financial affairs and his relationship with Lucille. What made Sylvia antagonistic? Was someone a threat to him?"

Kitty tipped her head, considering Wharton. "I really don't know her."

"When did that ever stop you?"

She went back to her salad, ignoring him. He let her think about it.

"Do you really think someone killed Preston?" she asked.

"It's as likely as someone killing Annmarie and the police are investigating that."

After lunch he called RJ. "Has Annmarie's will been probated yet?"

"It's still in the process." RJ sounded discouraged.

"What about Preston's?"

RJ sighed audibly. "Annmarie inherited some musical stuff from him."

"I think I'll get a copy. It might give us some ideas."

At the public records office Wharton obtained a copy of the probated will then headed home.

Gazing at her house from the street above made the damage to Atlanta's house appear much greater than from inside. Swinging into the lane behind, she parked her Cruiser on the concrete slab beside the garage.

As she and Brett tread the brick sidewalk to the back door she noticed a green pickup at the side street curb with Lewis Construction LLC–Restoration Contractors painted on the door panel. A short trim man dressed in khaki slacks and a bomber jacket got out and approached them.

"Ms. Gabriel?" He had dark brown eyes, black hair and a nose appropriate to a much larger man.

"That's right."

"Kent Lewis." He held out his hand.

Atlanta accepted his firm handshake figuring he looked more like a Zorba or Stephenopolis.

They continued to the back door, which she unlocked. Stepping inside, they were met by the cold air of an empty house and the smell of evergreens, almost like Christmas. She could think of a better way to get a tree.

Atlanta led the contractor to the back bedroom where the most visible damage had occurred. Using a flat square box with a meter gauge on it, he made an inspectionof the ceiling and walls. Atlanta noted the meter's red line moved erratically between the far left and degrees from center to right. Completing his assessment of the bedroom, he moved his investigation to other areas of the house.

When finished he returned to the living room where Brett sat in the easy chair. Atlanta perched on the edge of the sofa.

"First we'll get the tree out of your roof and line up a roofing contractor. Mr. Lewis smiled encouragingly. "Then I'll have the water damage specialists come in and dry the place well. We don't want mold or mildew hidden in the walls."

"Is it safe to stay here?" Atlanta asked him.

"Best stay somewhere else for a couple days. Once we get the tree out and roof covered, it'll be much safer . . .and warmer. While the roofers are here, you might want to be away during the day until they get the base done."

"How long before you'll have someone here to remove the tree?"

"Should be later today. I have to submit the damage report and restoration plan to the insurance company for approval before I can line up contractors."

Atlanta nodded.

"We'll need to put on a lock box for workers to get into the house when you're gone, if that's okay?"

Sure, why not. Atlanta grimaced.

"They're insured and bonded, but if you have items of significant value, it would be advisable to remove them."

Atlanta sighed. It made her tired just thinking about it.

Mr. Lewis gave her an encouraging smile. "It'll all be over before you know it."

"Thank you." Atlanta thought what a sweet liar he was.

When she had closed the door on him, Atlanta turned to Brett. "Some holiday you're going to have."

"A real adventure." Brett grinned.

"I'll call Wharton and warn him he's stuck with us for a few more days."

"I'd better give Ramona a call and see what she wants."

Atlanta frowned. That sounded like a crummy idea, but Brett was the one who had to deal with her.

After leaving a message on Wharton's answering machine, Atlanta made a visual tour of her house, searching for items to remove. She took a couple jeweled picture frames she had received as gifts, locked the drawer with the family silver in it and put the key in her handbag. In her bedroom she packed the cosmetics she had forgotten the night before and some more suitable clothes.

When she returned to the living room, Brett was standing by the front room windows with the phone at his ear. "We're not staying at the house right now."

Noting the stack of album covers resting on the credenza, she turned back to him.

He raised his eyebrows and rolled his eyes. "I don't think that's a good idea."

Although there probably wasn't any financial significance to the albums, they were priceless to her and Brett. Since he remained occupied with the phone, she motioned her question.

He nodded emphatically.

She located a shopping bag with handles and put the records in it. She took a signed lithograph from the wall, wrapped it in a towel and placed it in another shopping bag.

"Okay, how about the Barnes and Nobles in Lakewood?" Brett looked at Atlanta with a question on his face.

She shrugged and nodded.

He held up the wrist with his watch on it. Atlanta looked at hers. "Noon? We could do lunch."

Brett communicated this information then ended the call.

CHAPTER NINE

The Barnes and Noble Café was sparsely populated when they arrived. Atlanta inhaled the aroma of fresh espresso and relaxed. They took table for four near the floor-to-ceiling windows and Brett offered to buy lunch.

"She's late as usual," he declared, bringing two ceramic cups of tea to the table. "She's visiting her third husband's son's family from a first marriage."

Atlanta raised her eyebrows. "It's surprising she can keep them straight."

Brett grimaced. "I don't think she does."

When a confused Ramona scrambling relationships flashed into her mind, Atlanta laughed. Although she could imagine Ramona's long term goal, a share of Brett's fortune, what did she want in the short run?

"There she is." Brett indicated a short, plump woman with bright orange hair pausing at the café's entrance.

"It's *sooo* good to see you," she coed to Brett. Then to Atlanta she said, "It's such a long time since I've seen *you*."

Not long enough, I'm sure. Atlanta greeted her, "How are you?"

"I have this awful problem." She set her large, shiny handbag in one chair then took the one next to it. "My car's worn out so I have to get another one."

Atlanta could think of worse problems.

Ramona went on talking. "I have such a dreadful time getting those salesmen to understand what I want." She dropped a wad of keys into her handbag.

"What do you want?" Brett placed his folded hands on the table.

"One of those big cars that ride real smooth, but get good gas mileage." She turned her pale green eyes on him.

"Like a Toyota Camry?" he suggested.

She looked shocked. "Oh, no, not a Toyota."

"Cadillac?" Atlanta was relatively certain she knew what tree Ramona was barking at.

"Oh, yes, exactly." Ramona smiled sweetly then her eyebrows drew together. "But they don't have one that gets good mileage."

The barista announced their order was ready.

Brett rose. "Can I get you something?"

"One of those fluffy things with the whipped cream."

"Frappuccino?"

Ramona nodded. "And a bowl of soup and a pretzel."

Obviously she's not on a diet. "Is that what you're doing here?" Atlanta asked.

"I came to find a new car." Ramona sighed.

"They don't have new cars in Oregon?" Atlanta mumbled under her breath as Brett returned with two bowls of soup.

"But it's hard to afford a new one."

"You could get a low mileage used one."

"It'd help to have a man go with me. They take men more seriously."

That's it, she wants Brett to help her buy a car, step one, anyway.

"Can't you have your car fixed?" Brett asked.

Ramona shook her head. "But you could go with and help me find a good car." She gazed at him with puppy-dog eyes.

Brett hesitated, casting Atlanta a troubled glance.

She had no intention of getting involved. Brett had to make his own decisions and live with the consequences.

The barista called the order ready and Brett went to pick it up.

"You had a tree fall on your house?" Ramona raised a highly arched eyebrow. "Where are you staying?"

"At a friend's." Here it comes, Atlanta thought.

Brett placed Ramona's order in front of her.

"Why not come stay with me while Atlanta's house is being repaired?" Ramona's voice was full of sugar and cinnamon as her eyes pleaded with him.

"I'm helping Atlanta out." Brett retook his seat.

"Won't the insurance company do that?"

"That's right." Atlanta answered for Brett then scolded herself for clearing Ramona's way. "But it may take two of us to be available for the contractors to get into the house." She noticed her friends Fredee and Georgiana heading to the coffee counter. "Excuse me a moment." She picked up her tea and went to join them.

Fredee did a little jig of pleasure, greeting Atlanta while Georgiana smiled gravely, rolling her eyes.

"I had to get away or stick my foot in my mouth."

"Oh, tell me. I can swallow my foot and not even get a lump in my throat." Fredee planted herself in take-off position.

Atlanta explained both the damage to her house and Brett's situation with Ramona while the ladies ordered and received their coffees.

Georgiana patted her arm. "Trouble seems to come in heaps."

"Well he can't leave you in the lurch. Besides that I'm sweet on him," Fredee declared. "Let's go get rid of that woman."

Atlanta hesitated as Fredee turned toward their table, knowing she was as good as her word.

"Down, Fredee, down," Georgiana cautioned her. "Let's not get Atlanta in trouble."

"Sounds like she already is." Fredee turned to her. "Where are you staying now?"

"You remember the man I danced with at class last week?"

She nodded.

"He was having dinner with us when the tree fell and invited us to stay with him."

"Oooo, good job." Fredee cooed her approval.

Blushing, Atlanta frowned at Fredee who had already headed off to Atlanta's table. She and Georgiana followed.

Fredee placed a proprietary hand on Brett's shoulder. "And who is this woman, honey?"

Brett grinned, introducing Ramona who eyed Fredee with an unfriendly glint, her lips pressed together.

Atlanta introduced her friends to Ramona while Brett helped them move extra chairs to the table.

"What tree fell on your house?" Georgiana asked.

"One from the house across the alley behind me."

Fredee scooted her chair closer to Brett. "Do you know who lives there?"

Atlanta noted Ramona's frown. "Only to say hello. It's a widow named Drina Faron."

"Drina Faron?" Fredee frowned then stuck her finger in the air. "I know her. She's a nurse at my doctor's office. She was an illegal alien from Mexico. Her family worked the iterant labor circuit in Yakima and Wenatchee. She lived for a while in Spokane."

Atlanta's cell phone rang.

"This is Kent Lewis. I need that house key from you for the lockbox. Can you meet me there at 2:30?"

After arriving home Wharton checked his answering machine and retrieved the message from Atlanta indicating they would be staying another night. Cheered by the news, he fought off the sensation something was remiss in their relationship.

He heated the leftover coffee then took a cup to his family room where he settled into the leather easy chair, placing his feet on the ottoman. He opened the manila folder with copies of Preston's settlement and read. To his credit the will had been updated after his wife and son's deaths leaving the bulk of his estate to his daughter, Sylvia. He had made a special bequest to Annmarie of his Pistachio collection and rights to his royalties.

The sound of a key in Wharton's front door startled him until he recalled giving one to Atlanta. "Your cousin's not with you?" he asked, meeting her at the door.

Her grimace indicated she could gladly strangle Brett. Her auburn hair blew around her face as the breeze off the bay flew in the open door and her dark eyes glowed with frustration. She reminded him of the wild horses he had seen in Montana during his college years, tossing their heads and galloping off, manes flying in the wind.

"What's the word on your house?"

"They were removing the tree when I left."

Wharton sympathized with her, knowing what the restoration process was like. "There's leftover coffee."

She followed him to the kitchen where he poured her a cup and reheated it. "Will Brett be here for dinner?"

"Hard to say," she huffed.

"I took a package of steaks from the freezer."

"Let me fix dinner?" she offered.

"That'd be great." It might fan the heat off her frustration and he could virtuously escape fixing a meal.

In the family room, Wharton picked up the probate papers and secured them in his desk. When he returned to the kitchen Atlanta was examining the steaks, having fashioned an apron out of a kitchen towel and a bag clamp.

"I'll set the table first?" she said. "It only takes a few minutes to cook steaks."

"I'll set it. You take care of cooking."

She located potatoes in the refrigerator drawer, plus a bag of salad greens, a tomato, green onions, and a cucumber. In addition she found a bag of frozen broccoli in the freezer section.

"Do you still eat your steak medium rare?" Atlanta found the cutting board and a glass bowl.

Wharton perched on a stool across the counter from her. "You remembered." That was encouraging.

She shot him a warning glance as she cleaned vegetables and arranged greens in a bowl.

What did he do now? Heaven knows one was always on a slippery slope with a woman. He watched her put together the salad. "You ever think about marrying again?"

He had often sat on the same stool, chatting with his wife while she prepared dinner. Their relationship had been pleasant, comfortable and easy. However, it had lacked some vital ingredient leaving him hungering for a deeper connection. Working on the law case with Atlanta had tested his self-control, his faith, and his commitment as he explored that greater depth. Sitting on the stool watching her filled him with impassioned hopefulness, longing to experience that interaction again.

"Not really." She grimaced. "I've already been married twice."

That was a slap in the ego. Figuring she had experienced the same fulfillment in their bond he had, he anticipated now they found each other again, free from prior commitments, they could renew their relationship.

She opened cupboard doors, searching until she found a small casserole dish into which she placed the frozen broccoli. "You're looking forward to marrying again?"

Recalling his commitment to set the table, Wharton stood. "I'd like to spend the rest of my life with someone I deeply loved." He captured Atlanta's dark-eyed gaze and held it a moment. However, the glint in her eyes was skeptical.

She turned away to place the potatoes in the microwave. "I no longer believe that's possible for me."

As Wharton took plates from the cupboard and grabbed the silverware from a drawer near Atlanta he considered her comment. "What's impossible? Marrying someone you love?"

She gave a sardonic hack. "Being loved by someone I love." Opening the refrigerator she searched the crisper drawers until she located an onion.

Her comment left Wharton bewildered. What did she mean? Was she in love with someone who didn't reciprocate?

She shaved a few slices off of the onion and placed it in the fry pan with a dab of cooking oil.

"How about a glass of wine?" He examined his rack for a suitable choice. "Cabernet?"

"If you'll pour me a little in this?" She held out a measuring cup.

He uncorked the wine and poured what Atlanta requested. From his formal dining room he brought placemats and two stem glasses.

While Atlanta sautéed onions Wharton set the table then returned to his perch on the stool. "Are you in love with someone who doesn't reciprocate?" He was no coward, might as well face the demon head on.

"I'm no longer in love," she emphasized the word "in". "Although I do care for him." After adding steak to the pan she turned an interrogative frown on Wharton.

Her expression made him feel obtuse. Was there hope for him if she were no longer in love? Although the fact she still cared could present problems. Wharton watched her heat frozen broccoli in the microwave, then melt butter and add lemon juice to it. What experience had put the cynical bite in her words?

"You haven't found someone to love?" Atlanta placed finishing touches on the salad then poured lemon butter over the broccoli. After removing the steak from the fry pan she added wine and Worcestershire sauce, heating and stirring for a few minutes before she poured it over the steak.

Bewildered at the turn the conversation had taken Wharton frowned. He had told her he loved her; she had said she loved him. What happened? Had she forgotten? Had something occurred to change her? While moving dinner from the kitchen to the table, he searched for some way to understand. Obviously starting where they left off wasn't an option.

Once they were seated and she had allowed him to say grace, he determined a trip into the past might give him a clue. "When did you retire from counseling?"

Her cocoa-colored eyes appraised him with reproachful doubt then lit with amusement. She removed her makeshift apron and placed it in her lap. "When James became ill and needed someone to be with him continually."

"How long was he ill before he passed away?"

"Altogether about a year."

It had been close to twelve years since they had worked together. "So you still counseled for several years after the law case?"

She nodded. "How about you?"

"I've just begun retiring, moving gradually and allowing the kids to take over the majority of cases. Some clients will only deal with me. Old duffers generally."

"I have some special people I've worked with for years I continue to see regularly. Otherwise I only consult, like the law case."

Maybe she worked on another case after theirs. "Do you work with an attorney?"

"Sometimes. Sometimes with the schools or a business."

Wharton had difficulty finding anything to explain the change in her attitude.

Wharton insisted on clearing after dinner which Atlanta appreciated. Her energy had fizzled like a stuck balloon. After they retired to the family room to watch a television mystery movie, the doorbell sounded.

Wharton frowned as he got up to answer the door. "I'd forgotten about you." He stepped back allowing Brett to enter.

Atlanta noted his frazzled look as he followed Wharton into the family room. "How'd it go? Did you get Ramona a car?"

"No," he growled. "She can't afford what she wants and she doesn't want what she can afford."

Undoubtedly Ramona's lunacy would entice Brett safely down the slippery path to her intended goal. No sense raising the warning flag. If one hasn't figured out how to handle his ex after this long, it's probably hopeless.

A brief glance at Wharton causing their eyes to meet told Atlanta he wondered what was going on. She flashed him an exaggerated smile.

Brett caught the exchange and explained. "She's a pushover for salesmen."

"You didn't offer to do anything for her?" How Ramona planned to trap Brett, Atlanta didn't know, but little doubted she had a plan.

Brett shook his head. "I've learned that much by now."

"Is she going back to Oregon?" One can always hope.

"No. She's staying with a stepson in University Place. She wants me to go back to Oregon with her."

Figures, Atlanta grimaced.

Brett sat on the leather sofa beside her. "I ran into Sunny and Philippe before we left the bookstore. John Hanson died." The flash of anxiety on Brett's face said more than words to explain his dejection.

"The drummer for Pistachio?"

Brett nodded. "Over the weekend."

Wharton stood at attention, observing the conversation. "Will there be a service?"

"I expect so." Brett's expression questioned Wharton's interest.

Atlanta sighed, people die, especially those who are ill. It didn't necessarily mean anything. "Did he have family?"

"In Sequim, I think they said." Brett ran a hand through his hair.

"Sunny and Philippe said he was living in a facility. Where was that?"

"Port Angeles."

Atlanta met Brett's eyes. "Do you want to go if we can find out when the service is?"

"Yes." He sighed. "I'd like to do that."

Wharton followed the discussion. "Would you mind if I tagged along?"

His interest brought on a feeling of foreboding. Did he connect this death to that of Preston and Annmarie?

Wharton moved to his leather chair. "Any indication what he died of?"

Atlanta turned to Brett. "I assumed his illness. Didn't Sunny say he was in a nursing home?"

Brett frowned. "I think it was a special place for people with Alzheimer's and dementia."

Wharton shook his head. "That wouldn't mean he was dying, just that he couldn't live by himself."

The concern that leaped into Wharton's eyes troubled Atlanta. "People can live fairly long with Alzheimer's." Even as she said it she realized the implications. Surely it didn't mean anything. "Did Sunny and Philippe say if they were going to the service?"

"I gathered they would if they could find out where it was."

"Let me check the Internet and see what I can find." Wharton moved to his computer.

Brett and Atlanta became absorbed in the mystery movie. Part way through, Wharton returned to his chair and watched with them. When it was over, he said, "Thursday afternoon in Port Angeles."

Atlanta calculated. She couldn't be around her house with the repair work going on. It could be a good break for Brett, if he didn't decide to go to Portland with Ramona.

"How about we all drive up together?" Wharton suggested.

Atlanta glanced at Brett, who nodded his agreement.

CHAPTER TEN

The moment Wharton opened his eyes an idea tagged him an airhead. What about Stadium Music Company? Who inherited that? He made a mental note to recheck Preston's will.

The Pistachio drummer's death opened up an unexpected avenue of inquiry. The possible connection to Preston and Annmarie had crossed Wharton's mind. Had there been an autopsy? Probably not. So whatever he could have learned, whether or not it applied, he would never know.

Once he was dressed he took another run to the bakery for rolls. When he returned Atlanta was unloading the dishwasher. Brett sat at the kitchen table with the newspaper and a cup of coffee.

"What are your plans?" Wharton got out a plate for the rolls.

"I have to meet the contractor at 10:00." Atlanta heated a cup of water in the microwave then scrounged through his cupboards for tea bags.

Wharton put three plates and forks on the table. "I think I'll check with RJ. Maybe he'd like to go with us."

"Where did you get the information?" Atlanta sat beside Brett who was still absorbed in the paper.

"The obituary was on the Internet." Wharton doctored a cup of coffee and sat down.

"Did it mention cause of death?"

Wharton shook his head. "I think that'll be hard to find without the death certificate."

"Can a person get that?" Brett abandoned the paper.

"Eventually. I doubt it's filed yet."

When Atlanta and Brett had left Wharton called RJ. The Hamilton home, an expansive brick rancher at Tacoma's northwest edge overlooking The Narrows, was so meticulously manicured it looked like an ad from a real estate magazine. However, when RJ opened the door to admit Wharton, he noted the interior lacked its usual polish. RJ had both a yard and cleaning service, but the credenza in the hall was covered with paper, envelopes, and magazines, a scattering of dishes near the living room recliner, a pillow and throw lying on the sofa, a pile of clothes in the hall next to the laundry room proclaimed Annmarie's absence.

Wharton stared at the spot where she had been found while informing RJ of John Hanson's death.

"We're all getting old." RJ rubbed his chin. "I'm not sure you can expect anything else."

"How old would he have been?"

RJ calculated. "Late sixties." He beckoned Wharton to a seat in the living room.

"That's not old. Not these days. Even for someone with Alzheimer's." Wharton perched on the edge of the sofa.

RJ frowned. "You think his death is suspicious?"

Wharton lifted his shoulders. "Brett Hadleigh is visiting his cousin in Steilacoom. We've decided to go to the service. Do you want to come?"

RJ readily agreed. "I've thought about a stranger coming when Annmarie was here. The only one I can think of is a bookseller who came door to door while I was at Bible study a couple times."

"Did she buy anything?"

"A couple decorating books, I think, or fashion."

"Where are they now?" Wharton noted the periodicals spread on the coffee table. All of which were news magazines.

RJ glanced around the room as if expecting a "here we are" call. "I'll look for them."

"Do you think this person went to the neighbors too?"

RJ tipped his head. "Maybe. I can ask."

Another thought seized Wharton. "Do you have videos of the Pistachio performances?"

"Annmarie had some. I'd have to hunt them down."

"Do that, too, would you?" Recalling the photographs at Lieutenant Sarkis' office Wharton observed the room's arrangement of furniture. He realized how unlikely for Annmarie to fall asleep where she was found. Nor would she have toppled into that position. Although a sizeable room, the crowd of furniture made the conclusion illogical. More likely she would have hit a sofa or chair than the end table. Neither would have produced a fatal bang on the head. To take a nap there she would have to be curled, unless she was a whole lot shorter than Wharton remembered. "Did you see the police shots of this room when they found Annmarie?"

RJ looked up sharply. "I didn't want to. Should I have?"

Wharton regarded RJ's dejected expression. "If it becomes important I'll take you to Sarkis' office." He noted the relief on his uncle's face. "Something occurred to me this morning. Who inherited Stadium Music Company?"

"Preston had a business partner who owned forty percent of the stock. After his son died Preston divided his holdings between Annmarie, Sylvia, himself and his son's wife. At the death of any of Preston's shareholders, those shares would be distributed among the remaining, preventing the business from escaping the family through inheritance."

"Except for spouses," Wharton added.

RJ's brows drew together. "Right."

Pushing the throw aside Wharton slid back on the sofa. "What if someone decided to sell their shares?"

RJ shook his head. "They could only do that with 100% agreement of the others."

"Who is the partner?"

"I never knew." RJ grimaced. "He was a silent partner."

That certainly warranted investigation. Would it have provided a motive to want Preston dead?

Even from outside Atlanta detected a substantial difference in her house. The tree was gone. A darker heavier tarpaulin replaced the former, more tightly secured.

A burst of air rushed her as she opened the front door. Half a dozen commercial fans puffed hot air drying the dampened roof and walls while industrial dehumidifiers added to the deafening roar. Electrical cords running over the floors constituted an elaborate obstacle course.

Atlanta and Brett paused in the foyer gaping at the sight. Brett's gloomy expression reflected her dejection. The reconstruction monster had invaded her refuge, spreading its tentacles throughout her personal space.

Brett grimaced. "Makes you want to slap the next person who tells you how much worse it could be."

Atlanta laughed, taking a broad step to avoid stumbling over a heavy-duty electrical cord.

The doorbell rang. Kent Lewis, clipboard and pen in hand, took them on a tour detailing the work that would be done to reconstruct. "It'll take a week to get the roofers in; with all the storm damage they're backlogged."

Atlanta wanted to protest, but realized the pointlessness. "What about the bedroom walls?"

"We have to make sure everything is dry before we do any reconstruction. I've a carpenter lined up when the time comes. He'll take care of the back bedroom and the one upstairs."

Atlanta accepted a copy of the insurance proposal paperwork thanking Kent Lewis for his time. He reiterated the fact neither she nor Brett needed to be present for the contractors to complete their work.

Before she could decide what to do next, the doorbell rang again.

"Victoria Station," Brett commented as she opened the door to Drina Faron.

Although having seen her neighbor from a distance frequently, Atlanta rarely met her face to face. With so much on her mind the night of the storm she had paid little attention. Now gazing into Drina's face, she realized the woman was much older than she had thought. Her face resembled a charcoal print with a chalky complexion and heavily shadowed eyes.

"I wanted you to know I have a tree service coming to take down the other two big trees on the ledge behind my house." she held together her bulky cable-knit sweater.

"Come in," Atlanta invited. "I appreciate it, although I wish it weren't a good idea."

"I'm almost glad to get rid of them." Drina looked around. "They create so much trash all the time."

"Would you care for tea?"

She looked over Atlanta's shoulder. "Sure, that would be nice."

Atlanta led the way to the kitchen where she offered Drina a chair at the small café table in the windowed corner. Setting the old metal teakettle on the stove, she took cups and saucers out of the cupboard.

"I've often thought we should get better acquainted."

Atlanta put out milk, sugar, and tea bags. "We seem to go crashing through life at such a pace it's hard to stop long enough."

Brett entered the kitchen stuffing his cell phone into his pocket. Drina studied him with obvious curiosity.

Probably talking to Ramona, Atlanta reflected with chagrin. "Tea?" she inquired as he took a chair beside Drina. To her guest Atlanta said, "One of my friends mentioned she knew you from her doctor's office."

"Who is that?"

Atlanta noted a curtain of caution draw across Drina's expression. "Fredericka Nitsah."

The curtain reopened as Drina smiled. "We chat some when she comes in for her appointments."

"I understand you lived in Spokane?" Brett ventured.

Bobbing her head Drina concentrated on her teabag. "We were stationed there in the military. When my husband retired he managed an assignment to this area. Since a couple of the kids live here we stayed."

Taking cookies from a blue tin on the counter, Atlanta arranged them on a glass plate. "Did you also work in Spokane?" Something in Drina's demeanor put her on alert.

"Yes, for a cleaning service contractor."

"Commercial?" Brett put milk and sugar in his tea.

Drina focused on his movements. "Large buildings, public places like the community theater, library, the Coliseum." Her voice became softer with each phrase.

Atlanta set the cookies on the table and took a chair. "A member of Brett's band died at the Coliseum years ago."

Drina glanced quickly at Brett then directed her attention to her tea and cookie.

"It was the official end of our group," Brett added.

"This cookie is really good. I'd like to get the recipe." Drina spoke with a trace of self-consciousness, adding, "I noticed you weren't staying here."

Atlanta nodded. "I think we should be able to come back pretty soon."

For a time they chatted about the storm and changes in the Town of Steilacoom then Drina declared she needed to get home.

"What are your plans today?" Atlanta asked Brett after closing the door on her neighbor.

"Ramona wanted to me to help her look for cars again."

"Do you really think she's going to buy a car?"

Brett raised his eyebrows. "What do you think she's doing?"

Atlanta shot him a you've-got-to-be-kidding look. "Trying to hook up with you again."

He frowned. "I feel I owe her something."

"Like what?" Atlanta shook her head in dismay. "And why?" Didn't he see trouble coming? Undoubtedly Ramona fed his feelings of obligation.

Traveling to the Barnes and Noble Atlanta's traitorous psyche wondered if Wharton would be there. Confused by their conversation the previous night, she felt he attempted to communicate something. However it blew past her. He appeared disturbed by her answers to his questions. What did he want from her?

CHAPTER ELEVEN

Wharton offered to drive the group to the Olympic Peninsula. The previous afternoon Atlanta removed what she and Brett had left in his guest rooms, letting him know her house was safe now. He arranged to pick them up at 8:00 a.m. prior to stopping by for RJ.

Atlanta resembled the flame-tinted splendor of nature as he followed her to his car. He was attacked by his impassioned tenderness for her, bringing memories of times they had spent together in a coffee shop arguing the law suit. A smile flitted across her face as he opened the door for her, but the depth of her dark eyes held a question, reminding him some enigma had inserted itself into their relationship.

As Brett stowed his suit jacket in the trunk he addressed Atlanta. "That neighbor of yours acted strange every time Pistachio was mentioned."

Atlanta turned to him as he got in the backseat. "Do you think it means something?"

Wharton glanced at Brett in the rearview mirror as he started the car. "She was pretty vague about what she did in Spokane."

Wharton turned to Atlanta.

She answered his unspoken question. "The lady in the house behind me," she explained Drina's visit. "She seemed curious about Brett and his connection to Pistachio, but became defensive when we noted her interest."

"Was there anything connecting her to the group?"

Atlanta looked over her shoulder at Brett.

"She cleaned the Spokane Coliseum at some time or other."

"Including the time when your group performed there?"

Brett's "Ah . . ." indicated the thought had not occurred to him.

They traveled Chambers Creek Road, winding alongPuget Sound's rippling waters reflecting the deep evergreen and royal blue of the islands floating there. When they reached University Place RJ was ready to join them, adding his jacket to the trunk and getting into the backseat beside Brett.

Wharton formally introduced them.

Brett expressed his condolences regarding both Preston and Annmarie. "It makes me wish I'd seen more of them."

RJ nodded with a sigh then turned to Wharton. "I found those videos you wanted."

"Great." What he hoped to discover he wasn't sure. It seemed farfetched believing all the deaths related to the group. However, eliminating possibilities before exploring them was counterproductive.

A few brave sailboats whipped along in the breeze as they crossed the Tacoma Narrows Bridge, high over the waterway, to the Kitsap Peninsula. Following Highway 16 northwest through lush evergreen jungle they intersected Highway 3 between Port Orchard and Bremerton. Moderate traffic allowed a snappy pace as they traveled north past the naval shipyard and submarine station to reach the Hood Canal Bridge. The snow frosted peaks of the Olympic Mountain Range beckoned as they continued on Highway 104 then the Pacific Coast Highway 101 south of Discovery Bay. Following the coastline along the Strait of Juan de Fuca they reached Port Angeles, hovering on the edge facing Vancouver Island, Canada.

By the time they reached the small port it was after noon. Wharton engaged his GPS to guide them to the Funeral Home where the service would be held. He parked in the lot for the Mortuary, a dark wood structure of northwest design, occupied now by a couple cars.

"What do you want to do?" Wharton shut off the engine. "It's early yet."

"Stretch my legs or I won't be able to walk," RJ declared.

The four got out and moved to a paver patio surrounding a fountain where they perched on the concrete benches. It made a strategic location for observing other attendees arrive.

A procession of four vehicles parked together along the sidewalk in front of the mortuary. An assortment of people, young and old, men and women, gathered outside the autos. For a time they stood conversing, then gradually broke into smaller groups, a couple of which went into the mortuary, another remained talking and another moved toward the outdoor seating area.

Three people about the age of Wharton's son and daughter approached engaged in conversation, ceasing as they reached the sitting area.

The young gentleman held out his hand, introducing himself as John Hanson's great-nephew then beckoned to the two young women with him. "These are my cousins, John's great-nieces."

Wharton shot Brett a meaningful glance. Taking the hint Brett introduced himself. "I used to be in the band with John, years ago."

"Really." The young man scrutinized him with a degree of awe. "When he got older he talked more about the band. I never heard him play."

"He was a great drummer." Brett introduced Wharton and Atlanta.

The nephew greeted them, his smile producing deep dimples in his lean face. "You always wish you knew someone better – after they're gone."

Grabbing the opportunity, Wharton demanded, "What caused his death?"

"He had Alzheimer's," the tall willowy niece declared, her frank gaze challenging.

Wharton wasn't sure that answered his question. "How long?"

She turned to her companions.

"Only a few years that we knew about," said the shorter girl with dollar size eyes and a pug nose. Her tone indicated doubt regarding the conclusion. "But someone told me it takes longer than a few years to die of Alzheimer's."

"He may have had it longer than we knew," her companion countered, tossing her long brown hair over her shoulder.

Wharton detected a contradictory undercurrent. "Was his death sudden?"

Big eyes consulted her companion with a glance. "My mother thought so."

"Who is your mother?"

"Carrie Wilson, his sister."

"Is she here today?" Wharton glanced at the group still gathered near the cars.

"She got here earlier."

Wharton made a mental note to hunt her down.

As more cars entered the parking lot the various groups moved toward the mortuary entrance. "We'd better go in."

———————— ✦✦✦✦✦ ————————

Accustomed to a triumphant Christian service, celebrating the life of the deceased and his ascension to the presence of God, Atlanta was unprepared for the stark ceremony at the funeral parlor. Although it covered the appropriate bases, offering mainstream hymns and readings it lacked the assumption of exultation present in her house of worship. She felt more inclined to weep here than for her compatriots who had passed on recently. She knew they had ascended to everlasting life and she would see them again. Given this service's generalities and platitudes, it seemed unlikely John was having a tête-à-tête with God. However, since God's RSVP list was known only to Himself, one couldn't say with certainty where John was. Nonetheless, Atlanta experienced sadness for him and those he left behind.

At the end the gathering of about forty mourners received an invitation to the home of a sprightly sixty-ish woman. A sheet with address and map was on a podium at the back of the chapel.

The service was conducted with an open coffin, attendees invited to pass by as they were ushered out. Observing the deceased's face Atlanta searched her memory for a picture of John when she had last seen him. She had difficulty associating the vibrant young drummer with the bony, aged face in the coffin.

Ahead of the others, she paused outside to wait for them. As people exited Atlanta noticed a number of familiar faces. Wharton, RJ, and Brett joined her. When Brett waved Atlanta looked to see Sunny and Philippe with a dark-haired Hispanic stepping out of the chapel. He paused to speak with a red-headed woman who was turned away from them.

Sunny flashed a smile, heading their direction, followed by Philippe who doffed his wool cap in their honor. His face remained sober, but his eyes twinkled.

"Are you going to the reception?" Brett asked the pair.

"I think we will," Sunny declared glancing at Philippe.

Wharton scanned his passengers. RJ waved a piece of paper. "I grabbed the directions."

Agreeing to meet at the reception, Sunny and Philippe left while Atlanta followed to Wharton's car. Their destination turned out to be a two story bungalow on the east side of Port Angeles outside the city limits with a spectacular view of the Strait. They wound up a graveled driveway to the rambling house perched on the hilltop with a wide veranda surrounding it. Encompassing more than the standard city lot, the property allowed parking for a dozen or so cars. Sunny and Philippe arrived directly behind Wharton's group and they all entered the house together.

Atlanta noted that though the exterior originated earlier in the twentieth century it had been resided. However, they had maintained the home's antique appearance. Inside extensive remodeling overcame the sense of antiquity. The interior gave clues indicating it had once been a collection of many rooms now converted to a great room, functionally divided into a sizeable living room, formal dining area, and open kitchen space.

Floral bouquets from the service had been pressed into service to decorate the dining table and living room coffee table. Beverages were available on the kitchen island where the largest group of people had gathered.

One of the women came forward to meet them, introducing herself as John Hanson's sister Amanda. Trim-figured with youthful energetic movements, she had dark brown hair, undoubtedly enhanced to disguise the age her face gave away.

Taking charge Wharton introduced their group, explaining their connection to the deceased.

"You'll want to look in the garden room," Amanda encouraged them. "John's drums are there with pictures of Pistachio."

"Where is that?" Wharton glanced around.

She pointed to an open door at the edge of the kitchen. Through the screen door Atlanta could see a covered walkway leading to another building.

Gratefully noting the cold buffet arranged on the dining table, Atlanta headed that direction. It had been long time since breakfast.

After taking advantage of the refreshments, chatting briefly with John's local friends and relatives, Atlanta accompanied Wharton. They crossed a breezeway through which the northwest sea breeze sailed briskly, lifting her hair and giving it a whirl.

The other building was a capacious garage and workshop partially converted to a garden shed and commandeered for the reception as a memorial to John. His drum set was stationed in the corner along with a table of pictures and Pistachio souvenirs. Another table displayed photographs and mementos of his family life, including his years growing up and the later years of his life and career.

Atlanta and Wharton fastened on the table of Pistachio memorabilia.

"Are you looking for something in particular?" Atlanta noted a group of pictures she had not seen before.

He shrugged. "I would be if I knew what to look for."

She picked up a photo of the group, attempting to place it in time.

Wharton peered over her shoulder. "What do you see?"

She lifted it for him to view. "Something about it bothers me." Taken during a performance it caught the drummer placed on the left side of the stage. However, it was not the drummer that caught Atlanta's attention.

"This is the famous Marcella?" Wharton pointed to the woman.

Atlanta nodded. She had never seen a picture of the vocalists from this angle. Brett was on the far side turned toward Marcella as if singing to her. Marcella's figure was perfectly outlined in profile, the fitted upper portion of her dress smoothly transitioned into a flowing skirt. As Brett had said, she was a large woman, tall and broad, but not without a figure. From this point of view she appeared much trimmer than Atlanta remembered her from other photos.

RJ, Brett, Sunny and Philippe joined them in the garden shed. They were a noisy bunch, debating with whoops of laughter the photographs and memorabilia to which their background gave them greater connection.

RJ approached Wharton and Atlanta. "I met one of the nurses at the facility where John died."

Atlanta noticed Wharton's instant attentiveness.

RJ included Atlanta in his gaze. "She said his death was a shock."

"Why is that?" Wharton snapped.

"She didn't think there was any reason for him to die now." RJ's expression echoed Wharton's.

"Was she suspicious?"

RJ shook his head. "Perplexed, I'd say."

"What's her name?" Wharton asked then continued without giving RJ a chance to reply. "Where is she?"

"Nancy Johnson, she's in the other building."

Returning to the main house Wharton was on a mission again. RJ provided sufficient description of Nancy Johnson to eliminate most of those gathered since they were not tall, brown haired and well-endowed. In the kitchen a woman who met the description was chatting with a Hispanic man. Wharton unobtrusively moved near the pair.

"Was there any warning?" the man asked.

The tall wedge-shaped woman shook her head. "He'd been behaving normally." She glanced at Wharton. "For a person with Alzheimer's."

"Did they do an autopsy?"

"No." The woman studied her interrogator. "It's rare they autopsy one of our patients. There'd have to be something obviously suspicious."

The man smiled at her, glancing briefly at Wharton. Checking his watch, he declared, "I need to get going."

When he had gone, Wharton asked, "Nancy Johnson?"

She turned warm brown eyes on him. "That's right."

"Do I understand correctly John's death was the normal course of his illness?"

Nancy leaned against the counter, crossing her arms over her bosom. "I had no reason to think he'd die any time soon."

"So what happened?"

She sighed. "I don't know. I checked the nurse's notes on his chart. He received all his customary medications at the designated times in the appropriate way."

"Does that mean something unusual occurred?" Wharton didn't like the sound of another suspicious death? Too much coincidence denied coincidence.

"In my opinion," she raised her eyebrows, scrutinizing Wharton, "he behaved as though he had an overdose."

Wharton detected doubt in her voice. "But you don't think he did?"

"I not only checked his chart and with the nurses who took care of him, but I checked the quantities of that medication on hand." She brushed her short unruly hair away from her face. "I verified in every way I could he hadn't been given extra medication."

"What is the medication?" Not that it would mean anything to Wharton.

"A cholinesterase inhibitor." After a glance at Wharton's face, she added, "It increases the level of acetylcholine in the brain, which is what the brain uses to transmit impulses from one neuron to another. Lack of acetylcholine contributes to Alzheimer's."

"But it's dangerous like any other drug."

"Exactly. An overdose is extremely dangerous, deadly." She took a deep breath. "On the other hand, his symptoms weren't far outside the normal range of the drug's side effects."

Wharton pressed his lips together. "So his death will be attributed to natural causes and no one will ever know the difference." He put a hand on her shoulder. "I'm sure you did everything you could."

Returning to the garden shed Wharton considered the conversation. Who was going around eliminating old folks? Wharton was certain Nancy Johnson felt something was wrong with John's death and he was inclined to agree with her. He expressed his opinion to RJ when he found the group still examining mementos. Noting the stricken look on Atlanta's face as she listened, he figured her knowledge would warn Brett who hailed RJ attracting him away to one of the displays.

Wharton said to her. "You realize what this means?"

"Others may be in danger, including Brett."

"Sunny and Philippe." Wharton grimaced. "Do you think I should warn them?"

"It's only fair." Atlanta bobbed her head. "They can take or leave your warning, but they should be cautioned."

"I wish we could find out exactly what happened to John." He noted others had joined the three band members at the Pistachio memorabilia and were questioning them.

Gradually the reception broke up. People reclaimed their cars and drifted away. Wharton gathered his group for the return trip, launching into his advisory as they walked toward the car. He explained to Sunny and Philippe his investigation into the deaths of Annmarie and Preston, and his sense that John's death may not have been as innocent as it appeared. "I think all of you from Pistachio need to consider someone may be trying to eliminate you."

Wharton wondered as he spoke if Sunny and Philippe could be guilty of the deaths. However, their expressions as they attended the story belied their involvement. Sunny's large eyes widened in astonishment. Philippe tipped his head, narrowing his eyes in concentration as his hearing loss made astute attention necessary.

"But what would anyone have to gain?" Sunny shoved his hands in his pockets and hunched his shoulders.

"I was hoping one of you could give me a clue." Wharton stopped. "What about money? Royalties?"

Philippe shook his head. "For Brett and Preston who wrote the music it would make more sense. Sunny and I were merely performers."

Wharton sighed. "So that wouldn't mean much where John and Annmarie were concerned?"

"It may depend on how they handled the money we initially earned performing and recording," Brett put in. "That's when we made big money. If they were successful investors it could mean a lot of money."

"But the ongoing stream of payments wouldn't be that great?" Wharton pinned down each assumption. "If we're not looking at a financial motive, what else might there be?"

Philippe adjusted his cap to prevent the wind from taking off with it. "Love."

"Love?" Wharton huffed.

Philippe's candid blue eyes twinkled. "Isn't that a prime motive for murder?"

Atlanta thought love was the wrong word. Love wasn't a motive for murder.

"Along with revenge." Sunny added, his expression still skeptical.

"Revenge?" Wharton scowled. Obviously that hadn't occurred to him.

Atlanta laughed, realizing Wharton thought it would be simple. She noted the flush on Brett's face. What was he thinking?

Glimpses of the strait's shimmering waters gave way to long shadows playing hide and seek in the trees as they retraced their route to Tacoma. A delightful end to the late fall afternoon brought out first car lights then streetlights and residential lights, bright spots in the shade. Wharton dropped RJ off in University Place then took Atlanta and Brett to Steilacoom. "How about we take a look at what the contractor's have done in your house?"

Frowning, Atlanta invited him in, noting the huge dumpster sitting in her yard. The contractor had warned her it would be there to handle trash from replacing the roof.

Met by a rush of warm air and the background hum of fans and dehumidifiers, they proceeded to the back of the house where the day's reconstruction was readily discernible. The back bedroom walls had been sheet-rocked and taped. The second story was no longer visible. Atlanta figured now she needed to choose paint colors. Upstairs her damaged wall had been mended and the wallboard replaced. So much progress lifted her spirits.

"Looks like an adequate job," Wharton commented as they returned to the main floor.

Atlanta huffed, figuring it was more than adequate.

"Is there dancing tomorrow night?" he asked, heading for the door.

"I believe so." Atlanta stopped in the middle of the living room.

Wharton turned back to her. "Will you be there?"

"If Brett wants to go." She met Wharton's eyes.

Raising his eyebrows, he grinned. "Come anyway, Brett can take care of himself."

Wharton's bossiness was becoming annoying.

"How about I pick you up?"

"That's not necessary. I'll see you there – if we come."

CHAPTER TWELVE

When Atlanta opened her eyes, the reconstructed wall in her bedroom hovered over her, demanding a place on her agenda. As she showered and dressed she determined to make a trip to the local decorating shop for inspiration. The timing was right for a revamp. Since Sherry Jarvis was her decorating guru Atlanta invited her along.

She also called Fredee. Ever since Drina stopped in Atlanta had been plagued by her manner regarding Spokane and Pistachio. Thinking Fredee might shed light on it she invited her out to lunch.

In the living room she found Brett ready to spend another day with Ramona hunting for a car. They stopped first in Lakewood to pick up Sherry then continued to Barnes and Noble to deposit Brett.

As Atlanta pulled out of the parking lot Sherry turned to her abruptly, rocking the dangling bells on her ears. "I thought he was divorced from that woman."

"Don't get me started," Atlanta warned as they headed to the big box home store.

"Did you hear the police took R.J. Hamilton in for questioning?"

"No." Atlanta felt a stab of alarm. "When?"

"This morning according to my nephew." Sherry adjusted her narrow square sunglasses, assuming her you-must-know voice. "Perhaps they found something to make them think he's involved."

"But they questioned him already."

"Maybe they have new information."

"Wharton won't like that." Atlanta shook her head.

"What's with you and him these days?"

Fortunately they had reached the store. Atlanta ignored Sherry's question, while parking and locking the car.

Once inside Sherry's attention was diverted to Atlanta's rejuvenation project. They wandered the isles, gathering samples and brochures, studying the paint displays, wallpaper, carpeting, and light fixtures.

"How big a change do you want to make?" Sherry asked.

"Depends on how much it costs."

"Given what's going on in your house it would be cheaper to do it now than later, not to mention less hassle."

Atlanta grimaced, less hassle always appealed to her.

At the interior decorators shop they checked out fabric samples for upholstery, drapes, and soft accents.

"Purple is making a comeback," Sherry suggested. "It would perk up your lavender bedroom."

Taking Sherry's advice, Atlanta collected a selection of fabrics to take home and consider.

"Fredee's meeting me for lunch if you want to join us," Atlanta offered. "Mexican."

They continued to a petite Mexican restaurant in Lakewood. As soon as Atlanta parked, Fredee came rocketing toward them from the opposite side of the lot.

"You didn't bring that lovely man with you?" she complained.

"He's meeting his ex-wife again."

"We're going to have to do something about that."

"I wish," Atlanta sighed.

Basically cheap fast food, the restaurant was nonetheless authentic Mexican. After placing orders they chose a table in a secluded corner behind a phony palm plant. The place was busy and the hum of conversation added to their privacy.

"You said you had questions." Fredee managed in spite of her mouthful of food.

"Remember I asked you about Drina Faron?"

"From my doctor's office?" Fredee bobbed her head.

Atlanta stirred salsa, sour cream and guacamole into her salad while explaining about Drina to Sherry. "How much do you know about her and her life in Spokane?"

Fredee shrugged. "She worked for a cleaning service that had the contract for the Coliseum there."

"Did she ever talk about Pistachio?"

Fredee paused with her fork in the air. "As I recall, she said she had a particularly bad experience one night during a concert and quit working then."

"What kind of experience?"

Fredee shook her head.

"Did she say who the concert was?"

"Nope."

Atlanta grimaced. "I wonder what it would take to get her to talk about it."

Fredee leaned forward. "Bribery? Truth serum? Excruciating torture?"

Atlanta laughed. "I was thinking of something less dramatic."

While parting after lunch, Fredee agreed to ask Drina strategic questions.

Once back in the car, Sherry returned to her question about Wharton. "You never answered," she accused Atlanta.

"Nothing is going on." Atlanta shot Sherry a warning glance.

Ignoring her, Sherry continued, "You've been seeing a lot of him recently."

"Purely circumstantial." Atlanta explained the storm and damage to her house.

Sherry peered over her sunglasses at Atlanta. "Are you sure you can handle it?"

"I'm never sure I can handle anything." Atlanta swung the car into Sherry's driveway with a laugh.

Returning home, Atlanta was revisited by her recent conversations with Wharton. His questions as she had prepared dinner confused her, not to mention his penetrating glances. What was on his mind? He also seemed particularly adamant she be at dance class. His past behavior made it clear he had no romantic interest in her. Undoubtedly he wanted to pick her brain regarding the mystery. She wished something was in it for him to pick instead of loose ends rattling around.

Her emotional traitor suggested she may be wrong about Wharton's not caring for her, offering enticing scenarios to explain his conduct. Pushing aside these unwelcome thoughts, she desired to see things with an unclouded eye. Wishful thinking would place her back on the romantic trail she had traveled before only to be thrown from her charger and left brokenhearted. She had had enough heartbreak for one lifetime. She had better ways to spend her time.

Approaching her house, she noticed the contractor's truck in front of it. This might be the time to arrange additional changes.

When Wharton arrived home the night before, he found a phone message from Kelley. He returned the call after breakfast, agreeing to meet her at the office.

"What are you up to, Dad?" she questioned him when he arrived.

He managed an innocent expression.

"Carson said you were in Port Angeles yesterday."

"Ah, that." Wharton explained as he headed down the hall to his office.

Kelley placed a stack of paper on his desk that he signed while she took a seat in his side chair.

"I looked up royalties." Insight flashed across her countenance. "So that's what this is about. You're interested in the band's royalties."

"What did you find out?"

"It's complicated. I expect it's not just royalties but copyrights you need to understand."

"Can they be passed down in a will?"

She held up her hand. "Regarding music royalties there are layers of rights, print, mechanical, performance, digital and synchronization."

Wharton sighed, leaning back in his chair. "So explain."

"The first thing to establish is whether or not they had copyrights and had them registered. Then did they renew them at the appropriate time?"

"Let's assume that's the case." Kelley was so thorough at times it frustrated Wharton.

"Okay. Then it makes a difference if a person is the composer of the music, writer of the lyrics, or merely a performer."

"Composer/writer?" Apparently Preston was both, although Annmarie was neither.

"That person has the most rights. They share in the rights regarding whatever else is done with the music."

"What about the performer alone?"

"Performers receive royalties on the sale of CD, tapes, records, and digital rights."

"What about music played on the radio or in the movies?"

"That's "mechanical rights", essentially the publisher's rights. Now a performer or a composer may be the publisher and hold all the print, mechanical and performance rights, or at least a portion of them." Kelley brushed her curly hair away from her face. "It's very complicated and rules are being continually modified."

"Do you have any idea what kind of money we're talking about?" As far as Wharton could see that was still the point.

She shook her head. "Information I found gave some basic means of calculating, but it directly related to the particular licensing agreement in effect. Even then it depends on how many sales, performances, or uses each piece had. Only someone actually in that business could answer those questions for you."

Wharton sighed. He wasn't sure he wanted to know but he didn't see anyway around it. "Back to will-ability."

"As best I can determine, a copyright or licensing agreement legally kept in effect should be passed down with the estate."

Wharton grimaced. "I guess if the copyright is legal to pass down I need to find out from the people involved whether or not it was in effect and what kind of return it gives them."

When Kelley left he contemplated where he was in his investigation. If the composers were the greatest royalty beneficiaries that left only Brett since Preston was dead. He wondered if Lucille knew anything about Preston's royalties. Then he recalled Preston's will had mentioned bequeathing Annmarie his Pistachio collection and royalties, leaving both Annmarie and Brett with the most significant interest in the group. He'd have to ask R.J. about it.

Wharton recalled his decision to attend dance class. Should he just show up on his own or would it be better to check with Kitty? Something else occurred to him. Would Kitty know who the silent partner was?

He pushed his quick dial for Kitty.

"You want to go to dance class again, right?" Kitty said the moment she answered.

"You think you're a mind reader?" His sister was downright annoying.

"So what do you want? I don't imagine you're calling to inquire about my health."

"Is something wrong with your health?"

"No."

Wharton reverted to his other reason for calling. "Do you know who the silent partner in Stadium Music Company is?" He explained what R.J. had told him.

"Not offhand, but let me ask Aaron."

"I'd appreciate it." As annoying as she could be Kitty was always ready to help.

"So, are you coming to dance class?"

"Are you offering dinner?" Might as well make the most of the opportunity.

"If you're going to dance class, you can come to dinner, too."

"What time?"

"Five-thirty sharp."

Leaving his office Wharton stopped by accounting and spoke to the lady in accounts receivable, a heavy-set woman with shrewd dark eyes.

"I need a credit check on Lucille Maginnis and Sylvia Nelson."

She arched a heavy eyebrow at him.

"I'll get addresses for you."

CHAPTER THIRTEEN

Just before six o'clock Ramona dropped off a frazzled Brett. Atlanta had to bite her lip to keep from laughing, he seemed so worn out and frustrated.

Sinking into the easy chair he leaned his head against the back, closing his eyes. "She may have left me, but if I'd stayed with her any longer I'd have left her."

"Did you find a car?"

"Hmmmph!"

Not sure what that meant, Atlanta left him in peace while she finished preparing the meal. They ate in silence.

Brett did answer her question. "No, we didn't find a car."

"Does her car really need to be replaced?"

He shrugged.

"I'm going to dance class tonight. Are you interested?"

"I'm interested, but my body isn't."

Atlanta laughed.

While changing into a whirling batik skirt with streaks of evergreen and purple in it, she considered staying home. However, she figured Brett could use time alone in peace and quiet.

A trace of fog created a hushed fall evening with a haze around streetlights and muffled sound waves, reminding her of an English horror movie. The Anderson Island ferry's hoot sounded like a forest animal, although she could see its golden lights approaching the wooden dock.

She parked across the street from the town hall where its lights cast a bright glow on sidewalk and shrubbery. She noticed Wharton's Mercedes farther up the block. The lively swing notes of *In The Mood* welcomed her as she stepped into the foyer. She greeted Charlie, standing near the stereo equipment arranging CDs, and Susie, chatting with new arrivals. Atlanta exchanged remarks with her fellow dancers about the weather and swift approach of Halloween.

"How about being my partner again?" Wharton approached as she changed into dancing shoes.

"I didn't tromp hard enough on your feet last time?"

"Lead feet," he quipped, "didn't feel a thing."

Charlie stood in the middle of the polished wood floor and called for the dancers to line up, men opposite the women. "We're going to begin with the east coast swing." He demonstrated the step. Then with Susie did an exhibition in promenade position after which they led the group through the sequence.

"Forced to learn jitterbug in high school gym class," Wharton replied when Atlanta quizzed his swing skill.

This dance required more energy leaving everyone eager for the break when Susie announced it. Kitty and Aaron joined Wharton and Atlanta as they munched salted nuts another dancer had furnished.

"Did you attend your cousin's concerts?" Kitty inquired of Atlanta.

"Only a couple of them. I was still in high school."

"But you knew the other band members?"

"Sort of. I met them at family get-togethers."

"What did you think of Marcella?" Kitty fired questions like an automatic bean shooter disabling Atlanta's response mechanism. "Were she and Brett a couple?"

Atlanta took a deep breath stepping backward. "They dated some."

"Nothing serious?"

The dance music started up again, rescuing Atlanta from Kitty. She frowned at Wharton wondering if he had suggested the interrogation.

He shook his head. "That was her idea. Apparently she heard tabloid gossip about Brett and Marcella having an affair. I couldn't answer her questions."

Charlie announced they would be reviewing the foxtrot and for everyone to warm up on steps they already knew.

"I'm not sure I could either." Atlanta explained as they assumed dancing position, "Brett never got over Marcella, but I don't know if they had an affair. They met just after Brett's divorce, but hung out in the group most of the time."

Wharton cocked his head and sent Atlanta a reproving glance.

She frowned concentrating on her footwork. "You're probably right."

While they stumbled through the basic steps of the foxtrot and variations they had learned, Atlanta considered Brett and Marcella's relationship. In retrospect she realized an affair made more sense than her naïve supposition. But did it make any difference?

———————— ✦✦✦✦✦ ————————

Wharton observed Atlanta's mental scrimmage regarding her cousin's relationship. Impressed by her willingness to withhold judgment, he was the Doubting Thomas of platonic relationships.

He made progress keeping his feet under control as they added to their foxtrot repertoire. However it took all of his concentration. When Charlie announced the last dance and dimmed the lights, he was amazed how quickly time had gone. As he guided Atlanta around the floor for the ending piece, craving sufficient mastery of his footwork to be romantic, he realized he wasn't ready to part from her company.

"How about coffee?" he suggested when Andy Williams had finished exulting *April in Paris.*

Atlanta's expression gave him the impression he'd been speaking Hangeul.

"I'm sure Brett can manage without you a little while longer." Wharton figured that was the trigger behind her reluctance. A wisp of uncertainty challenged his self-confidence but he refused to consider she may not want to spend time with him. "You can help me sort things out." He leveraged his offer in view of her hesitation.

A frown flickered across her face. "Where?"

"The little coffee shop on Steilacoom Boulevard. Why don't you take your car home and I'll follow you?"

She agreed with all the enthusiasm of a hostile witness.

Making an illegal U-turn in the middle of Lafayette, Wharton followed her. She parked in the garage as he pulled his Mercedes behind.

Lights glowing from the house windows looked like a Thomas Kincade painting. A lady walked her dog on the side street while a dark colored sedan crossed the intersection below them. Traveling uphill to Starling Street, Wharton arrived at the intersection with Steilacoom Boulevard just behind the raven sedan, continuing to the wedge-shaped coffee shop he had gone the week before with Kitty and Aaron.

Marine fog obliterated any sign of moon and stars. An other-worldliness about the night attacked Wharton's assurance as they entered the incandescent building. However, the oppressive feeling disappeared in the face of golden lights and the hum of conversation. Locating an empty table for two in a corner away from the windows, they ordered tea and dessert.

"Could someone have been jealous of Marcella and Brett?" Wharton squeezed lemon into his tea.

Atlanta chewed her thumbnail. "I hadn't thought of their relationship like that. It lasted such a short time."

Wharton managed to keep his expression from showing reproof.

"I should have put two and two together." She sighed. "Brett has mourned Marcella most of his life. It's illogical a simple friendship should have caused him so much pain."

"I don't know," Wharton countered. "It's the emotional not physical that makes a person difficult to forget."

Atlanta's ebony eyes dissected Wharton's expression, making him wonder if she could see his nerve endings and brain waves.

"I don't think I've ever heard a man say that."

"You don't believe me?"

She smiled, arching an eyebrow. "That would be presumptuous, wouldn't it?"

He laughed. He could think of plenty of presumptuous women . . . and men. Maybe he was one of them. "It's been five years since your husband died?" Wharton's genius flair never included tact and subtlety. His gift was firing fast and hitting the bull's-eye. An invisible shield descended between them. He recognized it too late to stop the words. "You married only once?" Curiosity always won out over discretion.

Atlanta concentrated on spreading whipped cream over her berry torte. With some defiance she said, "I married really young. In my early thirties he died. My first husband is the father of my children."

Wharton watched fascinated while she divided her dessert into equal sections. "I take it you have regrets."

She appeared surprised by his question. "Regarding my marriages?"

He nodded.

She took a bite of dessert before answering. "I wish I could have had the marriage I dreamed about when I was young. But without my first husband I wouldn't have my children, whom I love dearly. My second husband was good to me. We had a good time."

Feeling like the prosecuting attorney didn't stop Wharton. "But something was missing?" Suddenly he caught a glimpse of the precipice ahead.

Atlanta tossed her head and laughed. "Intimacy." His question must have registered in his expression for she continued, "Not physical."

"Isn't sex the ultimate of intimacy?" Control of the conversation was fluttering out of his grasp.

Atlanta challenged. "If you look up the definition of intimacy you won't find sex mentioned."

He made a mental note to do that. "How about companionship?"

"Companionship is nice, but not necessarily intimate."

Wharton felt like a dumb school boy. "Then what do you mean by intimacy?"

Her gaze traveled across the room resting on the fireplace flames. "I think it's sharing with someone private, personal, high risk things you generally keep to yourself and being able to trust that person, feeling cherished and safe from judgment or criticism."

Harboring doubt intimacy had ever been an issue for him, Wharton longed for someone with sufficient intellectual capacity to discuss theoretical issues and enter into conflict. Linda had been kind, patient and understanding, but mentally drifted away when he became philosophical and totally disappeared in the face of conflict. Atlanta's perceptiveness and her willingness to stand her ground had always attracted him. In fact just as the push-pull in dance made it possible to travel the floor synchronized, the push-pull of their psychological relationship held him as emotionally bound as the beauty of her face. "I guess I should get you back to your cousin."

Atlanta gave him a perceptive smile, which he found outrageously irritating.

CHAPTER FOURTEEN

When they reached Atlanta's house, Wharton insisted on walking her to the door, making her feel like an awkward teenager on her first date. Wharton smiled with a trace of tenderness, threatening to disarm her defenses. She offered her hand in businesslike fashion. "Thank you."

Taking her hand, he held it a moment as if he had something he wanted to say. Instead he murmured, "My pleasure," and stepped backward.

Atlanta removed the keys from her miniature handbag, unlocked the door, entered, then closed it behind her. From the foyer she could hear the sports reporter declaring winners and losers on the television. She could see Brett's foot extended in front of him. A sour odor reached her nostrils producing a flash of illogic leaving her ill of ease. Two quick strides brought her into the room where Brett sat propped in her wing back chair, quivering spasmodically. His face was flushed and his breath shallow and rapid.

Alarm messages flew through her brain. Rushing back to the doorstep she saw Wharton close the door on his sedan. Waving her arms she dashed toward the car shouting his name.

Getting out, he called, "What's the matter?"

"Something's wrong with Brett."

Without a word Wharton followed her back into the house. When they stepped into the living room, she turned back to him for his reaction as he took out his cell phone.

Atlanta went to Brett and touched him. His skin was hot and the area around his eyes appeared yellowish. Evidence of nausea left her confused. What was wrong? What had happened?

While she knelt beside Brett, Wharton paced like a caged lion.

In less than five minutes the parade arrived, a Police officer, the fire department and the emergency medical team. The officer questioned Wharton. The medical people interrogated Atlanta while checking Brett's vital signs.

"Does he have any health conditions?" the young black man asked as he put the blood pressure cuff in place.

"Not to my knowledge." She noted the empty plate on the end table beside Brett's chair.

"Does he take any medications?"

Atlanta felt remiss. "I don't know. Shall I look in his room?"

"That would be a good idea." The short stocky medic with bushy blonde hair gave her it-took-you-this-long-to-think-of-that glance.

In her guestroom Atlanta found evidence of a neurotically tidy man with garments hung in the closet by style and shirts neatly folded and stacked in the dresser. Even his toiletries were lined up in order by size. Atlanta detected nothing resembling a medical prescription. A bottle of aspirin, one of daily vitamins, and a container of glucosamine tablets lined up next to his shaving lotion. However, in the vanity top drawer she found a small plastic box with five compartments, three containing one capsule each. She examined one of the capsules, Prozac, the anti-depressant. She should have realized.

Carrying it, she returned to the medics who prepared to move Brett to the gurney.

"I found these." She handed the box to the blonde EMT.

"Did he have a problem with depression?" the black man pinned her with his gaze.

Atlanta felt a pang of guilt. "Yes, he did." Had she ignored some sign? "But I didn't realize he took medication."

As the medical people positioned Brett on the gurney the police officer came to question Atlanta.

"He was here alone?"

"That's right," Atlanta said. "I went to dance class at the town hall. He was too tired to join us." She realized the signs pointed to attempted suicide, but she couldn't accept that.

"We went for coffee after that." Wharton came up behind her.

"He was okay when you left?"

"He was fine. A little frustrated with his ex-wife."

The officer raised an eyebrow. "Has he been depressed recently?"

"No, he hasn't. He's been in excellent spirits." Better than expected, she thought, but she hadn't known about the Prozac. Had that made the difference?

"Do you know how he spent the day?"

"With his ex-wife looking for a car."

"Are you his next of kin?"

Technically Atlanta wasn't sure, but she nodded. For the time being she was his next of kin. "Where are you taking him?"

"St. Clare's."

The moment the door closed behind the medical people, Wharton asked, "Was there any sign of break-in?"

Atlanta stared at him in disbelief. "What are you saying?"

"Do you think this was some kind of accident?"

She opened her mouth but nothing came out.

"Don't be a fool, Atlanta. We saw this coming."

"What do you mean?"

Wharton scowled at her. "This is the fourth member of Pistachio . . ."

His thinking finally caught up to her. "You think someone tried to murder Brett?"

"What's your explanation?" Wharton challenged her.

"I don't have one," she snapped, "but I'm not jumping off the bridge without looking first." She didn't necessarily disagree, but couldn't there be other explanations? "I need to go to the hospital."

"Take a look around here first for anything out of place."

Would she even recognize something out of order?

"Come on." He pointed toward the kitchen. "Let's have a look."

Atlanta preceded him into the foyer. Glancing into the dining room, which opened off the hall, she determined everything was just as she left it. She examined the kitchen more carefully. A tall glass tumbler sat on the counter next to the sink. She picked it up and observed a trace of dark colored liquid in the bottom. Probably cola, she thought and checked the refrigerator. A one-liter bottle of coke, about a third of the way full, sat on the top shelf. Brett probably had a glass after dinner.

While Atlanta examined the kitchen, Wharton checked the side door to the back yard. The concentration with which he pursued his examination attracted her attention. "Did you find something?"

"Do you keep this door locked?" He knelt to examine the slot for the key.

"Usually."

"Would it have been locked when you went to dance class?"

"As far as I know."

"It's not now." He stood and with the side of his finger gently pushed down on the lever handle, demonstrating his conclusion.

Atlanta reached for the handle.

"Don't touch." He modified his tone. "We may need the fingerprints."

"What do we do?" Life had not prepared her for this.

"If you'll trust me, I'll call a detective I know and find out."

"Okay." She sighed, removing a key from the small rack of hooks inside a cabinet by the back door. "Here's a house key."

As soon as Atlanta left for the hospital Wharton dialed Lieutenant Sarkis, figuring important evidence could be lost by delay. The sheriff's department answering service indicated if this were an emergency to call 911. A sudden inspiration brought Dark Ansgreth, Wharton's pastor, to mind. The lieutenant and the pastor were friends. After Dark provided Davy's cell phone number Wharton called the lieutenant.

Anticipating Davy's brusque response, Wharton was surprised by the mellow voice that answered.

"Something's happened."

"Which is?" The lieutenant's voice was noncommittal.

"My aunt and uncle's rock band has taken another hit. I believe someone tried to kill another of them. I want this house investigated before possible evidence disappears."

"Where are you?" Davy's abrupt attitude returned.

Wharton explained.

"Was it reported to the police?"

"An officer was with the paramedics." Although Wharton didn't have the impression there would be an investigation. "They're treating it as a self-administered overdose."

"I can't do anything official."

"What about unofficial?"

Davy heaved a long sigh.

Wharton reached into his bag of positive affirmations. "Good deeds pay off. You never know when you'll need the information later."

Davy huffed. "Give me the address and half an hour to get there."

Wharton roamed the house while he waited, creating a mental picture of someone overdosing Brett. Someone he knew? Examination of the front door indicated no tampering. The unlocked side door could indicate something, but what?

Beside Brett's chair were the daily papers, folded and set aside. An empty plate with crumbs on it indicated something to eat. But there was no glass. Was the one in the kitchen Brett's? If so, why was it not with his plate?

When the musical doorbell chimed Wharton admitted the lieutenant in jeans, tee shirt and a windbreaker.

"So what happened?" Lieutenant Sarkis demanded the moment he stepped into the room.

"That's what I'd like to know." Wharton explained how Atlanta found Brett after returning from dancing class.

Davy sniffed. "What's the odor?"

"Apparently he was nauseated." Wharton figured that was evidence of something.

"Was he on medication like the others?" Davy moved to Brett's chair.

"Atlanta found Prozac."

The lieutenant walked around the chair. "So why don't you think he took too many?"

"Some were still left in the box and he's the fourth member of Pistachio to die or have his life threatened by misuse of medication."

Davy frowned.

"Most of these people died of something that reacts badly with the medication they're taking."

"Which would indicate familiarity with what they're taking." The lieutenant approached the front door, examining it visually.

"What would react badly with an antidepressant?" Wharton realized even if he knew what medication a person took he wouldn't have any idea what would cause a fatal reaction.

"Alcohol is the usual culprit."

Recalling the glass in the kitchen, Wharton led Davy to the other room. While the lieutenant observed, Wharton sniffed the glass, careful not to touch it. He frowned. It smelled like some kind of dessert.

Davy did the same thing. "Cinnamon? Let me get my briefcase."

When the lieutenant returned he put on a pair of plastic gloves, took the glass and placed it in a plastic bag. Then he examined the cupboards. When he reached the one containing condiments and spices, he studied them, carefully moving a couple to reach others. He removed an eight-inch tall, dark brown glass bottle. The label indicated it was "pure vanilla". This he placed in another plastic bag.

Lieutenant Sarkis continued searching the kitchen. He opened the refrigerator and inspected the contents. Wharton noted the bottle of cola sitting on the shelf. Davy also took this and placed it in a bag. From the kitchen he went to the dining room where he opened the doors on the china hutch and buffet. In a door on the lower right of the buffet was a small supply of liquor, Kahlua, Crème de Menthe, Dry Sherry, Framboise, Vermouth, Baileys Irish Cream, a bottle of red wine with a decorative stopper in it. The lieutenant frowned, rechecking the supply. He removed the Vermouth and dry sherry, placing them in another plastic bag.

After scanning glassware on the upper shelves in the hutch he returned to the kitchen cupboards. He counted the glasses of the same size and shape as the one that he had placed in the plastic bag.

"Ask this woman how many of these she owns," Davy instructed Wharton.

Wharton directed the lieutenant's attention to the back door. "This was unlocked. Atlanta said that's not usually the case."

Davy studied it then flipping on the light switch to the side yard, surveyed the area. "Is this the back entrance to the house?"

"I don't believe so. There's another door down the back hall off the living room."

The lieutenant took off that direction with Wharton following. That door had a lock on the knob as well as a dead bolt, both engaged. Davy pressed his lips together and shook his head. Returning to the living room he took in the scene left by the medics.

Wharton had not moved the plate or newspaper he found. "Well, it doesn't look the scene of an attempted suicide."

Wharton sighed, never having seriously considered that.

Pausing in the middle of the floor, Lieutenant Sarkis turned to Wharton. "Is this scene likely to be disturbed in the next twelve hours or so?"

"Atlanta is at the hospital right now. I assume she'll be home later."

"Encourage her not to disturb anything here until I get back to you?"

Wharton nodded. "What are you going to do?"

"I'll talk to a friend of mine in forensics and see what options we have. Is there something I could use to eliminate her fingerprints from others we find?"

"I have something in the car if you'll wait a moment."

Wharton proceeded to the Mercedes. On the console was an advertisement Atlanta had picked up at the coffee shop and forgotten to take with her. Wharton gave it to the lieutenant.

"I'll get back to you as soon as I have anything."

CHAPTER FIFTEEN

Wharton parked his car next to Atlanta's Cruiser at St. Clare Hospital's emergency entrance. He found the waiting area swarming with anxiety-ridden folks. The triage receptionist, a queen-size blonde with sympathetic brown eyes was taking information from a Hispanic couple with a listless child and an elderly woman sat at the station beyond answering questions for an unseen attendant. There was no sign of Atlanta. The black security officer eyed Wharton as he stood at the door visually searching the room.

When the couple had completed their interview, Wharton approached the receptionist to inquire about Atlanta and Brett.

After checking her computer, the colossal blonde asked. "Are you a relative?"

Tempted to bluff, Wharton hesitated before shaking his head. "Is there any way I can speak with Atlanta?"

With an empathetic smile the receptionist said. "I can tell her you're here." She moved away from the computer. "What's your name?"

After giving his name Wharton took a chair in the waiting room. In a few moments Atlanta appeared. Her willful hair had escaped its restraints, poking out in artistic poufs while her face sagged with anxiety. White face paint and red lips would have made her the sad clown. However, her eyes lit on spotting him, which plucked his heartstring.

"How's it going?" He stood, beckoning her to the chair beside his.

"You couldn't fill a one-inch post-it with what they tell you." She folded her hands and took a deep breath. "They're treating him as an overdose."

"Self-administered?"

"Presumably. The questions they ask make me feel they think I overdosed him." She shot Wharton a rueful smile. "But I suppose it's just the information they need."

"How does it look for Brett?"

Atlanta lifted her shoulders. "I can't tell. They make general comments about doing everything they can. At least he's still alive."

"Is he conscious?" It might help if they could learn something right away.

"I can't tell. He's restless and babbles, but I don't think he's conscious."

Wharton described Lieutenant Sarkis' scrutiny of her house. "You need to be careful about doing anything to change things there until I hear from him."

Atlanta frowned. "How can I do that?"

"Use my guest room." He grinned.

"That may have worked with Brett, but now . . . " she threw her hands in the air.

Wharton aimed an accusing glance at her. "You don't trust me?"

"What will people think?"

"News flash!" He leaned toward her. "People don't think and if they do it's just about themselves."

Atlanta laughed then grimaced. "What if someone tried to kill Brett and knows he didn't succeed, will he try again?"

That's a good question. "We'd better not let anyone know he survived."

"How?"

Wharton pursed his lips. "If we had police assistance, but on our own . . ." he shook his head.

"What about your lieutenant?" Atlanta raised her eyebrows.

"He might help if he finds something indicating a murder attempt." Wharton recalled the lieutenant's assignment. "By the way, how many of those tall glasses like the one left on the counter do you have?"

"Originally eight, I broke one, so there should be seven."

Wharton put a note on his mental scratch pad then shifted gears. "I need to know how much royalties Brett got from his Pistachio music."

Atlanta moved her gaze to the ceiling. "I don't know and if he doesn't recover, I don't know how we'd find out."

"Who inherits from him?"

"I told them I was next of kin, but I'm not sure that's the case."

"He had no children?"

She shook her head.

"Brothers, sisters?" Wharton ticked off possibilities.

"His sisters have passed away and his parents are dead."

"Who would he leave things to?" Difficulties promenaded through his mind as obstacles occurred to him. "How about his ex-wife?"

Atlanta bit her lip. "I hope not, but you never know. I'm sure she has her wishing cap on and is doing her cabala dance."

"She wouldn't be guilty of his death?" Wives, ex-wives made good candidates for getting rid of a husband.

Atlanta's brows drew together. "That would be hard to believe, she's such a nitwit."

"You think she's incapable?"

"Oh, I suppose not." Atlanta focused on her hands then cast him a sheepish glance. "I just don't like her much."

Wharton grinned. "That might be a problem if she were overdosed."

Atlanta giggled. "I do have difficulty seeing her as a murderer though."

"I think we should keep her on the list, stay open minded." Something else occurred to Wharton. "Do you know if he had life insurance?"

Anxiety and grief returned to Atlanta's face. "No. I don't and I don't know how to find out if something happens to him."

"Did the medical people entrust you with his personal items?"

"Everything but his clothes." Atlanta stood up. "I'd better get back."

"Remember, you have a place to stay." Wharton extracted his wallet and a key. "In fact, here is the extra key you returned."

In the wee hours of the morning Brett's doctor, a small fair-haired man with protruding brown eyes and exquisite eyelashes, entered the intensive care unit where Brett had been moved from emergency. He informed Atlanta he was cautiously optimistic about Brett's recovery. He told her to go home and get some rest.

She wanted to know what happened. Maybe they could avoid a repeat.

"Serotonin syndrome."

"What's that?"

The doctor tipped his head and frowned. "A condition resulting from too high a level of serotonin in the brain."

That seemed obvious from the name, but didn't explain anything. She noted the skepticism in the doctor's expression. He didn't think she would understand, but she refused to be left hanging. "What causes that?"

"Combining SSRI anti-depressants with an MAOI for one."

"What is Prozac?"

The doctor sighed. "An SSRI."

"Then what is an MAOI?"

"Another anti-depressant."

"How would he have gotten that?"

The doctor raised his eyebrows, nodding as if she would be better at answering that.

"The only thing he had was Prozac."

"You don't have anything like that?" Was the doctor actually suspicious of her?

Atlanta shook her head. "I've never taken any kind of anti-depressant."

The doctor had the I've-bad-news-for-you look on his face. Had she been his patient she would have expected to be told she was terminal. "Those drugs are difficult to get without a prescription."

She was in no mood for hide and seek. "What are you saying?"

"No doctor would prescribe those two contra indicating medications together." He aimed his reproving frown at her. "We'll have to report this to the police."

Atlanta smiled. "Great!"

He gaped at her.

"Then we can get an investigation." That would solve one problem. "There've been too many deaths among Brett's friends, but we haven't been able to get the police involved."

The doctor offered a bewildered reflection of her smile.

"What we really need is for no one to know Brett survived. If someone tried to kill him and knows he didn't succeed he may try again. Is it possible to keep it quiet?"

Stroking his chin, the doctor sighed. "Let me see what we can do."

Atlanta watched him depart, gliding quietly out of the room with a preoccupied expression. She turned back to Brett lying rock still, his eyes closed. Watching the monitor screen, she noted the rapid heart rate. But all she could think was *"Thank you, Lord, he's still alive".*

Returning to her car she debated whether to go home or to Wharton's house. Another drug combination boondoggle, making it even more probable someone had tried to kill Brett. Rather than interfere with finding the guilty person, Atlanta made only a quick stop at home, getting what she needed to stay the night away.

As she drove across town, the empathetic expression in Wharton's gray eyes flashed into her head. Relying on that expression was a straight shot to heartbreak. Logic and Emotion batted the ball back and forth. Some men are everything a person could want in empathy and sincere concern, even willing to be placed at risk to help, but not to help her, at least not without ulterior motives.

Tranquility reigned in Wharton's neighborhood when she arrived. Recalling he kept his Mercedes in the left half of his double garage, she parked her Cruiser on the driveway behind the right hand door. Using the key he had given her she let herself into the silent house. A torch lamp lit the foyer allowing her to see the way to the bedroom she had used previously.

With Brett absent the house felt different. Wharton was right; no one she knew would suspect her of inappropriate behavior. In fact, her friends would whoop it up teasing her, which she would just as soon avoid. However, it would do her reputation no harm. Perhaps if she zipped her lip no one would know.

In spite of emotional exhaustion and the late hour sleep dodged her. Images of Brett popped into her head the moment she closed her eyes. One by one she analyzed his acquaintances, examining any motive for wanting him dead. But she came up blank. It made no sense. Perhaps this was a mass killer who used medical prescriptions to do away with people. However, the connections to Pistachio fought that concept.

CHAPTER SIXTEEN

As invasive as a peeping tom, the sun glared with crystal brightness, prying Wharton's eyelids open. Although his bones didn't creak with elderly stiffness he was not so young anymore he leaped out of bed with energy to spare. Plus his head felt like a caffeine hangover.

While attending it, he allowed his mind to travel back to Atlanta's house the night before. If someone tried to kill Brett, what ruse had he used to get in? How had he successfully overdosed him? Wharton continually reverted to the same conclusion. Brett must have let the person in. Would that mean he could say who the trespasser was? Had this interloper caused the other three deaths?

After sticking his feet into leather slippers Wharton headed for the kitchen, noting the closed door on the spare bedroom. He hadn't heard Atlanta come in.

His resident cynic offered a jarring hint as he examined the glass pot, determining the remaining coffee wasn't fit to drink. What a pleasure not to be alone. He shoved the thought aside with a stab of melancholy. Inhaling the fragrance of ground coffee, he prepped the machine then returned to his bedroom to shower and dress.

As he returned to the kitchen his cell phone rang.

"Got the results on the glass," Lieutenant Sarkis informed him.

"What was in it?"

"Besides Coke, vanilla, vermouth, and tranlcypromine sulfate."

More technical gibberish, one needed to be a chemist. "So what's that?"

The lieutenant sighed. "Anti-depressant. The lab is supposed to have more information to me later."

"What about finger prints?"

"We're still working on that."

"Atlanta is concerned if someone tried to kill Brett and failed, he'll try again."

"If someone is determined to kill him," the lieutenant agreed.

"Can we protect him?" Wharton figured waiting to find out didn't make sense.

"For the time being you're going to have to get the hospital staff's cooperation."

Juggling options for throwing his weight around at the hospital, Wharton encountered Atlanta in his wide foyer. She looked dangerously determined in claret cut-offs and tall cinnamon boots. Only the fatigue in her dark eyes and droop around her mouth testified to the previous night's adventure and her agonizing knowledge. She explained her conversation with the emergency doctor.

"They're going to investigate?" That was an unexpected blessing.

"He didn't say investigate," Atlanta corrected with a huff. "Just file a report."

He patted her shoulder. "Buck up, that's something."

She rolled her eyes then shot him an impish grin. "He seemed to think I'd be upset having it reported as if I'd overdosed Brett."

Wharton noted the injured expression behind her smile. "No one is going to think you'd kill anyone."

She looked away redoing the knot in her scarf. "I'm going back to the hospital."

He was puzzled by her reaction. "How about we go together?"

"I might be there a while." She removed the keys from her handbag.

"I can work around that."

She squinted at him. "I can take care of myself."

"I know. I'll bring you back to get your car, if it becomes necessary."

Atlanta shrugged. "Okay."

A brisk breeze off Puget Sound made Wharton glad he had grabbed his wool jacket before leaving. Saturday's mid-morning traffic was light, making for a swift trip to Lakewood. The medical personnel moved with hushed efficiency ignoring Wharton and Atlanta as they made their way to Brett's room. However, a nurse at the station nearby stopped them to answer questions. Although she remained cautious she allowed them to enter, leaving the door open and remaining in the hall.

"That's encouraging," Wharton whispered.

Atlanta nodded, but her eyes were on Brett who appeared peacefully asleep although still attached to the monitors, which registered an even pattern of heart rhythm. "Do you think he regained consciousness?"

Wharton shrugged. "I'll ask the nurse."

Young, with an athletic build and air of competency, the woman in the hall regarded Wharton as if assessing his right to the information. "I was told he had brief moments of consciousness during the night."

"Did he say anything about what happened?"

"Apparently he was disoriented and had difficulty comprehending where he was or why." With a sympathetic grimace she continued, "He'll recover, but it'll take time to get the drugs out of his system."

"How long will he be kept here?"

She shifted her gaze to the patient's monitors. "He needs to be stabilized. Then it's possible he'll be moved to a psychiatric ward at Tacoma General."

Reentering Brett's room, Wharton passed on the information.

"Do you think he'll remember what happened?" Atlanta's eyes gave away her uncertainty.

"That, my dear, is the $64,000 question."

After an hour Wharton told Atlanta he would be back at noon. In route to his office he received a call from his sister.

"Roberto Lopez," she said when he answered.

"The horn player?"

"He was Preston's silent partner."

That was unexpected. "Where did he get the money to support Preston's venture?"

"You didn't ask me to locate his financial assets," Kitty reminded Wharton with asperity.

"It was a rhetorical question," Wharton huffed. "Do you have an address?"

"Portland, Oregon," Kitty declared, then gave him the street address.

Wharton explained the events of the previous evening. When he reached his office several pieces of information awaited his inspection. Two of them were the credit checks on Lucille Maginnis and Sylvia Erving Nelson.

Lucille's data was just as he expected, conscientious maintenance of a high quality rating, little debt and payments made on time. Sylvia's rating was a different story, but consistent with her age and cultural conditioning. She carried a large mortgage, significant credit card debt, and several department store accounts. Wharton wondered what kind of income she pulled in to handle such a financial load. And what did she do with the insurance she inherited from her father? With no other benefit, that had been a hefty sum.

However, did that put him any closer to finding out who was picking off members of Pistachio? To his knowledge Sylvia was somewhere in the east, nowhere near the death scene. Although verifying that would be wise.

On his desk he also found a note from Kelley with the formula for figuring royalties. He stuck it in his pocket realizing it was time to return to the hospital.

On reaching Brett's room he was surprised to find Lieutenant Sarkis. Atlanta was explaining what the nurse had told them earlier. Brett still slept.

Lieutenant Sarkis turned to Wharton. "Can I see you outside?"

Wharton followed him to the waiting room.

"We didn't find any fingerprints."

"On the glass?"

"On anything."

"Not even Atlanta's?"

The lieutenant shook his head. "Hers were on the bottle of cola, the vanilla, and the vermouth, but that's all, no one else's."

"And you infer?" Wharton didn't like the insinuation.

Davy shrugged. "It's her house; obviously her prints would be there."

"But that means no one wiped things clean." Disappointment attacked Wharton. He had hoped for a more enlightening outcome.

Lieutenant Sarkis bobbed his head. "And no one left additional prints."

"What does it mean?"

The lieutenant ran his hand through his already windblown hair, making him look like a surprised wildcat. "Brett Hadleigh took an overdose. His cousin administered the overdose, intentionally or by mistake. Someone came with the overdose and administered it wearing gloves or without touching anything."

"No prints on the doorknobs either?"

"Nope. Other than Atlanta and her cousin's. The prints on the side door were smeared, which you could have done examining it or showing it to me."

"So there'll be no investigation?"

"Not necessarily."

Wharton recalled Atlanta's words. "The doctor said he has to report the overdose. Does that mean they'll investigate?"

The lieutenant shook his head. "They'll examine the report."

When the lieutenant left, Wharton returned to Brett's room. "How about lunch?"

He could see Atlanta's protest coming. "You're at my mercy, I'm the one with the car."

"That sounds like a threat?"

"I promised to take care of you, so we're having lunch."

<hr />

On the way to his car Wharton detailed his conversation with the lieutenant.

"But they still may investigate?" Atlanta seized the morsel of hope.

"Supposedly." Wharton maneuvered his vehicle out of the parking lot and onto Bridgeport.

Pushing through the marine layer, the sun gave Atlanta's spirits a lift.

"Would Brett have let a stranger into your house?"

She frowned. Affable and refined, Brett made an unsuspecting target. "It depends on the pitch he used."

"Or she."

Atlanta discounted women as murderers, undoubtedly naïve. "Ramona's the only woman in Brett's life and I don't think killing him would suit her purposes."

"Which brings up another woman."

"Marcella? She's been dead forty-five years."

"Could something connected with her have lived on?"

Atlanta shrugged. "Her life and death are both a mystery."

"Does Brett know anything about her past?"

"Brett never discusses Marcella's past, her family, or her background." As far as Atlanta knew Marcella's existence consummated on her arrival at the university in Portland. "But I can ask."

"We need to turn over every rock. Never know where the rattlesnakes are hiding." Wharton swung his Mercedes into the Goodwill parking lot and shot Atlanta a crooked grin.

She glanced at him sidewise. "We're having pre-owned lunch?"

After opening her door he wagged his head toward the small Greek restaurant residing at an angle to the parking lot. The tiny establishment had a blue and white interior touched with black filigree, pictures of the Greek Isles, and a collection of small tables covered with white linen.

Pausing near the door, Wharton asked, "Is there anything you particularly dislike?"

"Greek food."

"You'll like this."

Atlanta determined less hassle outweighed making her own choice. Nodding her assent she found a table while Wharton placed their order. The charming restaurant combined fine dining accoutrements with fast food service.

He returned with two diet cokes. "I figured it was too early for wine."

She laughed. "If you don't want to push me around in a stroller."

"Would Sunny and Philippe know anything about Marcella?"

Atlanta had discounted what other members of the group knew, thinking Brett knew Marcella best. However, she could be wrong. "They might."

"Can you get hold of them?"

"Only showing up at the bookstore."

The waitress delivered two large Greek salads, a plate of deep fried calamari, pita bread with marinara dip, and tzatziki.

After testing the meal Wharton said, "My sister told me Roberto Lopez was the silent partner in my Uncle Preston's music store."

Atlanta dipped her pita in marinara sauce. "I didn't think anyone had heard from him in years."

"I'm not sure anyone has."

As they returned to the car he suggested, "Why don't we stop at the bookstore before going back to the hospital?"

The Barnes and Noble represented a friendly face. Even before they pulled open the large wooden doors, she recognized Sunny and Philippe at their customary table. She also noticed Fredee and Sherry at a table across the room and immediately perceived a problem. Fredee waved fit to flag down the Queen Mary, making an aside to Sherry who peered over her reading glasses at Wharton. Atlanta gave a finger wave of acknowledgement as she followed him to where the two men sat.

They greeted Wharton and Atlanta with questions about Brett. Atlanta explained while Wharton filled in details after cautioning them regarding the danger.

At Sunny's invitation Wharton snagged chairs from an adjacent table. He presented his request for emergency contact information. Both willingly provided addresses and phone numbers. "What do either of you know about Marcella's past?"

The question elicited a parade of doubtful expressions.

"Where did she grow up?" Atlanta asked.

Sunny's dark eyes consulted Philippe. "Ashland, Oregon, I believe."

Philippe regarded Atlanta sympathetically. "I think her father was retired military. Her mother may have been dead when we knew her."

"Is her father still alive?" Wharton asked.

Sunny shrugged and Philippe wagged his head.

"What did he do in the military?" Atlanta asked. "Anything medical?"

Philippe fingered his petite mustache with a look of concentration. "Signal core, I believe."

"All these deaths suggest some medical knowledge," she explained.

"Or a working knowledge of chemistry," Wharton added.

Sunny shot Philippe a cheesy grin. "Philippe's degree was in biochemistry. He worked in a medical lab."

Philippe returned Sunny's grin with a smirk. "And Sunny served as an Army medic."

Wharton tossed Atlanta an astonished glance and rose. "Shall we return to the hospital?"

"I'd better say hello to my friends before we leave." she indicated Fredee and Sherry. As Wharton and Atlanta approached she noticed Sherry give Fredee a warning look and a few quiet words. She silently thanked Sherry for taming Fredee's tongue.

"Now what did you do with that lovely cousin of yours?" Fredee queried the moment Atlanta reached them.

She gave a vague reply finding it difficult not to confide in her friends, but the less people who knew about Brett the better.

Returning to his car, Wharton asked, "Did you know Sunny and Philippe had medical backgrounds?"

Atlanta shook her head. "Do you suspect them?" She studied his expression wondering if he were seriously suspicious.

"We can't eliminate anyone based on personal prejudice."

Another thought occurred to her. "My neighbor Drina who feigns lack of interest in Pistachio works in Fredee's doctor's office."

"You need to get better acquainted with her."

Atlanta needed to do that regardless. She felt remiss the night of the storm to acknowledge she hardly knew her neighbor.

As Wharton opened the car door for her, she realized how comforting his companionship, assistance, and support had been while she dealt with her recent challenges. Suddenly she visualized the emptiness of her life once it returned to normal. The thought paralyzed her momentarily. She took a deep breath.

"Something wrong?" Wharton eyed her suspiciously.

She shook her head.

CHAPTER SEVENTEEN

Wharton wasn't buying. As he closed Atlanta's door and got into the driver's seat their conversation about intimacy roared back into his head. "I thought real relationships were built on sharing." He turned to her without starting the car.

Her dark eyes widened as she met his.

"Or perhaps you don't want a real relationship." He baited the trap.

She still hesitated. Then with a mischievous grin she said, "It just occurred to me when this is over I'll miss your bossy interference."

He laughed. "What makes you think I'll quit being bossy and interfering?"

She glanced at him sideways. "That wasn't what I thought you'd quit."

Did she expect him to disappear? How could she think that? Now he had found her again, now that they were free from other commitments, why would he leave her? "You think I'm that easy to get rid of?"

Her copper eyes challenged. "What do you think you are?"

Wharton placed his hand on his chest. "Doggedly faithful, perennially loyal, persistently committed."

"Wow." She laughed.

"You don't believe me?"

She did not respond, but stared out the window with a remote expression.

She didn't believe him, he realized. Had she never believed him or had something changed her mind? When he told her he loved her, she said she loved him too. Had that changed? His feelings had not altered, had hers?

"Caught," he said quietly.

Atlanta turned to him with a frown.

"Assuming." Wharton leaned his head against the car's side window. "I have a question."

"What's that?"

"What happened?"

Double lines appeared between her eyes. "To what?"

"Your feelings for me."

She put her fingers to her lips, contemplating him with a look of compassionate sadness.

He awaited her response with growing apprehension, his confidence tiptoeing farther and farther away. It never occurred to him she would forget or her love would die. "You no longer care for me?" The words would hardly come out.

"I care for you," Atlanta responded. "That's not it." She took a deep breath. "It no longer matters if you care for me."

"But I do."

She lifted her shoulders. "It doesn't matter anymore."

What did that mean? How could it not matter? It mattered to him. Wharton felt he had won the contest but lost the prize.

Bowing her head she studied her hands.

He reiterated his question. "What happened?"

When she looked at him there was fire in her eyes. "You abandoned me."

His voice squeaked. "Abandoned you?"

"You said you loved me, that we were friends, then you walked out of my life and never spoke to me again."

"I thought we agreed our relationship was impossible as things were."

She sighed. "We could still have been friends."

"And we weren't?" Wharton challenged her, but she remained reticent. "And you think I'll walk out on you again?"

She shook her head, lifting her shoulders. "It doesn't matter anymore."

"How can it not matter?"

"I don't know, but it doesn't." Atlanta turned back to the window, withdrawing into silence.

After a few moments, Wharton started the engine, shifted into reverse and eased the car out of its parking spot. He maneuvered the Mercedes into traffic and headed for the hospital. It was a short drive and when he had tucked the car into a parking spot he turned to Atlanta with raised eyebrows. "What do you mean you don't know?"

She raised her eyebrows and grimaced.

He got out of the car and opened her door. "I'll be back in a couple hours."

As he watched her move resolutely toward the hospital entrance he felt the vibration of his cell phone.

"I just talked to my neighbor," R.J. informed him. "He recalls seeing someone he didn't recognize come to the house a couple times."

"When Annmarie was alive."

"Right."

Perhaps they would get a break. "Do you think he'd talk to me?"

"He said he would."

When Wharton reached his uncle's house, he found R.J. in the yard clearing away leaves from his flowering plum tree. Fall's brisk clarity had given way to a mellow sunny afternoon.

Wharton followed him to a group of chairs in the covered area at the front of the house. "Which neighbor?"

R.J. pointed left across the street. The house sat at an angle to R.J.'s with a clear view from a front room window. "He'll be over in a minute."

"Who is he?"

"Retired military officer. Dabbles in real estate. I didn't think about people across the street when you said to check with the neighbors." R.J. grimaced sheepishly. "You see why I need you."

Wharton watched a short, trim man of average build and erect posture stride toward them. His neat appearance and clipped haircut spoke of his military years. As he took the third chair R.J. introduced him as William Borden.

R.J. introduced Wharton and explained their relationship.

"Why don't you tell me about the stranger you saw?"

"I was reading the newspaper." William pointed to his house. "The windows you see are in the living room. When I looked up I caught sight of a man going up the walk."

"Can you describe him?"

"I can, but it won't do you any good. I saw him from the back." The man's dark hazel eyes assessed Wharton. "He was average height, medium build, dark hair, nothing distinctive."

"What was he wearing?"

Mr. Borden considered for a moment. "Jeans, sweatshirt, dark shoes. Nothing distinctive."

Just the luck, Wharton thought, someone who could help, but lacked the necessary information. "When did you see him relative to Annmarie's death?"

"Six weeks before it. August 30." The answer came without hesitation.

"How do you recall that?" Wharton frowned at the man.

"It was the day before we left on a Labor Day trip."

"Did you ever see him around here again?"

William nodded. "About a month later I saw him walking down the street away from R.J.'s house." He pointed to their right.

"How do you know it was the same man?"

Mr. Borden paused, staring across the street. "Something in the way he walked. He didn't exactly limp, but he had a slight shuffle, as if he'd overcome an injury."

Wharton grimaced. "Did you see him on the day Annmarie died?"

"I wasn't here that day. My wife had an appointment in Seattle. We were gone the whole day."

Wharton remained chatting with the two men for some time before returning to the hospital.

When Wharton picked Atlanta up at the hospital she begged off dinner, anxious to return home after the day's stress. He sympathized, although apprehension regarding their conversation still plagued him.

He grabbed a frozen meal and stuck it in the microwave. From his study he brought a tablet to the kitchen counter and made notes on his investigation. Perusing the list he figured he would have been one up never to accept the challenge. Now instead of Annmarie's death and his uncle's implicated guilt there were three deaths and an attempted murder. Would the authorities put all that at R.J.'s feet? Wharton felt he was digging a hole that might bury all of them.

Tempted to abandon the project he recalled his words to R.J. "It might get worse before it gets better." He hadn't realized the truth in that statement. Practicing what he preached became an additional dare.

Exhausted, he failed to set an alarm and overslept. Sidetracked by recent events he had lost track of the day. A TV evangelist clued him in; it was Sunday. The clock informed him he still had time to make his church service. He grabbed his corduroy blazer, got out the car and headed across town.

Sliding into the pew beside Aaron just as the organist finished the prelude, Wharton cast Kitty a don't-ask glance. Pastor Ansgreth came to the head of the aisle to greet his congregation. Rumor had it he was dating a young woman who recently joined the congregation. He had been a widower since his wife was killed three years before. Congregational consensus held he should marry the lady before she got away.

"Thy will be done on earth as it is in heaven," the pastor stated a portion of the Lord's Prayer. "What are we asking for in this petition?"

Wharton snorted. It had taken him years to come to terms with God's will. Even now he regressed at times demanding his own way and fighting God for control. In his heart he knew what God wanted was best, but outward appearances were so deceiving. Wharton was a take-charge kind of person. Allowing God to lead the way down a trail heading he knew not where was almost more than he could stomach.

"Sleep in?" Kitty asked with dancing eyebrows as she passed the collection plate.

Wharton scowled at her.

After the service Aaron invited him to join them for brunch. However, Wharton was anxious to find out how Atlanta and Brett faired, explaining to Kitty and Aaron what had happened. "Any suggestions for keeping Brett safe once he's out of the hospital?"

Kitty's glance consulted Aaron who spoke, "He can stay with us. We have no connection to the group."

Not a bad idea. It certainly beat leaving Brett a penned goose at Atlanta's house.

After leaving them, Wharton drove to the hospital where he found Lieutenant Sarkis scrutinizing Brett, whose eyes were open. However, his expression registered confusion.

"You don't remember *anything*?" The lieutenant verified.

Brett glanced at Atlanta then back at the lieutenant. "No."

Great, thought Wharton, just what they didn't need.

"What's the last you do remember?"

Brett's gaze moved about the room. "Ramona was looking for a car."

Davy glanced at Atlanta, who nodded.

"The nurse said more of his memory would return in time."

Which doesn't help us now, Wharton thought ruefully.

"Give me a call later," Davy Sarkis said to Wharton as he turned to the door.

Wharton noted the drawn look on Atlanta's face. How long had she been here? He could see Brett was operating in a twilight zone and would soon be asleep again. "How about brunch?"

She turned to Wharton with a look of refusal on her face.

"You need to keep up your strength or you'll be no good to him."

"Who are you the diet doctor?"

"Just someone concerned about your welfare. Besides we need to talk about what to do with him once he gets out of here."

She shrugged and gave in.

"Is it better or worse Brett doesn't remember what happened?" Atlanta expressed her misgivings as she followed Wharton to his car.

"Worse." He shot her a sharp glance. "Lack of memory might have a short-run advantage, but someone trying to kill him won't count on that. He'd want to finish the job."

Sliding onto the smooth leather seat Atlanta felt like weeping but took a deep breath. They needed to focus on solving the murder attempt not weeping about it. "Do you think his lack of memory is significant?"

"Of what?"

"Brain damage, traumatic shock, fear phobia?" An endless parade of potential effects of an anti-depressant overdose assaulted her.

"I don't know," Wharton huffed. "I'm no doc."

Startled by his sharp retort she retreated to silence.

Wharton chose a Mexican restaurant. Since they had missed both breakfast and brunch they each ordered a fajita salad and soda then munched chips and salsa while waiting.

"Have you considered what to do with Brett when he gets out?"

A sinking feeling seized her. She shook her head.

"Kitty suggested he stay with them. They have no connection to Pistachio, or you, or Brett."

Atlanta sighed. She wasn't sure she was up to making Brett's decisions. Anyway, he wasn't out of the hospital yet. "I'll mention it to him."

"Am I pushing you?" Wharton gave her a sympathetic once over.

She met his eyes, dark gray in the restaurant's lamp lighting. "Making decisions isn't my strong suit."

When he dropped her off at St. Clare's she continued to Brett's room. She found him sitting up in bed watching television, much improved. "How are you feeling?"

His complexion had lost its red flush and his eyes were clear. "Not bad, considering." He watched her remove her jacket and slide the guest chair closer to his bed. "What happened?"

Frustration seized Atlanta. "You're supposed to tell me that."

"The last I recall is coming home from car shopping with Ramona."

Atlanta noted his apprehensive expression. "What about my asking you to dance class?"

His countenance brightened. "Yes, I decided not to go."

"What you did do after I left?" At least his memory wasn't a total loss.

"Fell asleep in the chair. Unfortunately since I woke up here I'm not even sure about that." His dejection reappeared.

The nurse was probably right, more of Brett's memory would return with time. He had already made progress.

She recalled her assignment. "What do you know about Marcella's family?"

"Marcella?" He frowned.

Atlanta shot him an analytical glance, concerned for his long-term memory, but he seemed puzzled. "What do you know about her family?"

"Not much." Brett switched off the television.

"It looks as if someone is eliminating members of Pistachio. What happened to her has always been a mystery. Maybe it's connected?"

He took a deep breath, leaning against the raised portion of his bed.

Atlanta detected resistance. "Do you know something you haven't told us?"

"I probably know a lot of things, but would they mean anything?" His blue eyes acquired a defensive gleam.

"I'm not sure you should be the judge of that." She found his protectiveness irritating. He was always shielding some woman. "Do you know anything about her family since she died?"

"At the funeral they were in shock since to anyone's knowledge she wasn't ill. The doctor who signed the death certificate was vague. No one was straight with us, but nothing we did could bring her back." Brett raised his hands in a gesture of despair. "It was best for everyone to let it go and move on."

Atlanta wasn't buying. "Do you think her family felt that way?"

"They couldn't be expected to." Brett gave a shake of his head. "They asked a lot of questions but got no answers either."

"Did they blame you for her death?"

He looked like he had been hit by the door. "How could they?"

"It doesn't have to be logical. They could blame you because they had no explanation and you were around her at the time."

He nodded, a faraway look in his eyes.

"What are you not telling me?" Atlanta knew what Brett didn't say often meant more than what he did.

"Nothing," he declared, but would not meet her eyes.

He was holding something back, but she had pushed him as far as she could. They watched television until he fell asleep again.

Just as she rose to find a cup of coffee the nurse came to check on him. While she attended to his monitors, checked his blood pressure, and made notations on his chart, Atlanta questioned her.

"He is scheduled for psychiatric evaluation tomorrow. If that's okay, he should be able to go home."

"Is his blood clear of the drugs now?"

The nurse shook her head. "It'll take at least a month for those drugs to clear his system."

That stunned Atlanta. "Did they report it to the police?"

"You'd have to ask the doctor." The nurse appeared uncomfortable.

"When will he be here?"

"Tomorrow before they do the evaluation." She moved to the door. "Then again afterward."

Atlanta made a mental note to arrive in time to talk to him. What would Brett's release mean? Would it be easier to keep him safe at home?

There might be more people to watch out for him in the hospital, but he would be up for grabs like a cooling pie. Out of it he would be a shifting mark, a tossup at best. How could she possibly handle the responsibility of keeping someone safe from a murderer? Just the thought was overwhelming.

She felt sure Brett knew something regarding Marcella he refused to share. He could surmise it made no difference, but Atlanta felt any tidbit might be helpful. After all this time why would he shield her? Atlanta understood protecting her memory but in the face of his own or his friends' deaths? Unless, an idea attacked Atlanta, his reticence was self-protective. Who else might know what Brett could be hiding? Would Sunny or Philippe? Either what Brett wouldn't talk about or Marcella's family? Maybe she should see what she could find on the name Damarios.

Just considering the possibilities created anxiety and emotional strain, leaving her exhausted. Wharton's involvement was a blessing in spite of their difficulties.

She struggled with their conversation the day before. Wharton acted as though the ten years of separation didn't exist. That it didn't matter he had not spoken to her in all that time. Men are so ridiculously obtuse. How could she explain to him what she struggled to understand herself?

She had told him the truth. She still cared for him, but was no longer concerned whether he cared for her. She did not fear his rejection, had no expectations. She could appreciate his company and leave it at that. Even now, she could look forward to his return and sharing some of her questions, but be content not to see him again.

She could not believe his feelings were any different. Would he have abandoned her for all those years without a word if he cared the way she had believed he did? She had no doubt he could still walk away without looking back; abandon her with no regret.

CHAPTER EIGHTEEN

Monday morning meeting Brett's doctor was Atlanta's top priority. When she called the nurse informed her the doctor had an emergency, postponing the examination until afternoon. Atlanta told Brett she would come at 12:30.

As soon as she had completed her call, the company supplying the industrial fans and dehumidifiers arrived to retrieve them. When they had gone, she experienced the deafening roar of silence. With Brett in the hospital and her home under construction she felt abandoned and disconnected. She almost succumbed to the temptation to call Wharton. However, with a stack of projects needing completion, she could do without his domineering presence.

With the drying equipment gone she might soon be required to produce her redecorating plan. With that in mind she brought her supply of samples and brochures to the dining table. Before she could sit down to organize them her doorbell rang.

She was surprised to find her neighbor there.

Although Drina's expression betrayed uncertainty she smiled. "I need to discuss something with you."

Atlanta invited her in. "How about tea?" While preparing it she asked, "What did you need to discuss?" She placed scones, butter and jam on the kitchen table then poured two cups of tea.

"The tree service said if they took down those trees and removed the stumps the ground there might slide down the hill in heavy rain. It might also undermine the stability of the house."

Visions of Drina's yard sliding into her own seized Atlanta's imagination. "He was a real good news man."

Drina smiled. "I can't say I was happy to hear it. He proposed a retaining wall."

"That's a good idea, right?" Atlanta sliced her scone in half then put butter and jam on it.

"Not to mention expensive," Drina lamented. "And the actual retaining wall would be on your property. The trees are on mine, but the property line runs between the trees and the descent to your house."

"So you're telling me I need to put in a retaining wall."

"I suggest we make it a joint project and share expenses."

Atlanta sighed. It wasn't what she most wanted to spend her extra money on. "I'd want to talk to the contractors."

"Of course. In fact, you should hire them." Noting Atlanta's despairing expression, Drina added, "The tree service made a couple recommendations."

Atlanta took the contractor's names, telling Drina she would get in touch. When her neighbor left she found she had lost the spirit for decorating decisions. It was time to leave for the hospital.

Brett had just returned from his examination when Atlanta arrived. Liberated from his monitors, he sat in the bedside chair dressed.

"Have they released you?"

"Not officially."

She noted his languid expression, although his coloring was good and his eyes clear.

The nurse Atlanta saw the night Brett was admitted entered accompanied by a tall thin man in business dress she introduced as Dr. John Coventry, Brett's attending psychiatrist. Just as they finished introductions, Dr. David Sanderson, his internist, entered. Atlanta retreated to a chair by the window while the doctors conversed.

"I find nothing to indicate attempted suicide." Dr. Coventry addressed the internist, turning kindly eyes on Atlanta. "Brett explained recent occurrences. Combining an MAOI and Prozac could result in death. It's not impossible for someone to have tried to overdose him."

Dr. Sanderson gave Atlanta an extended stare. He probably still thought she was the guilty party.

"Brett assured me Mrs. Gabriel could not possibly be guilty." A twist of humor accompanied the doctor's smile. "At least he is willing to take his chances with her."

Atlanta believed Dr. Sanderson felt much less magnanimous as he drew his thin eyebrows together over his large round eyes. "It'll take time to get the drugs out of your system. You need to avoid anything containing tyramine, caffeine, and tryptophan." The doctor handed him a sheet of paper. "Here is a list of foods and drugs to avoid for the next month. These are dangerous with an MAOI."

"What about the Prozac?" Brett spoke for the first time.

Dr. Sanderson grimaced. "You need to stay off of that for the time being also." He turned to Atlanta handing her another sheet of paper. "These are symptoms you need to watch out for. If any of these occur call me or Dr. Coventry immediately."

———————— ✦✦✦✦✦✦ ————————

Atlanta had raised credible questions the night before. Did Brett know something regarding Marcella he wouldn't discuss? Without discounting her concerns, Wharton felt more relevant issues needed tracking down first, locating the silent partner for one. A trip to Stadium Music Company moved to the top of his agenda.

Morning brought with it the Pineapple Express, pattering on his roof and pouring over the gutters. Awash in heavy rain, Tacoma possessed a misty surreal quality as he wound down the steep hill into the port. A small tugboat guided a huge freighter toward the unloading docks and an army of orange cranes removed boxcars from anchored ships. Traffic whizzed along as Wharton took the 509 bridge into downtown and Ninth Street to Tacoma Avenue. The spires and turrets of Stadium High School were just visible in the background as he approached the music shop searching for a parking space. Fortunately he caught someone backing out as he approached.

Waiting for the car to leave he noticed a familiar looking man exit the music store and get in an SUV a couple spots from where he sat. He also noticed a woman waiting in the vehicle.

Tranquility reigned when Wharton entered the shop. A young man behind the old wooden counter removing stacks of sheet music from a carton looked up briefly as Wharton headed for the mezzanine stairs. Lucille sat in her customary spot focused on her computer screen.

Wharton's greeting disturbed her concentration, but she smiled demurely. "What can I do for you?" She stammered less than in the past.

He took the chair facing her desk. "Do you know how to get hold of Roberto Lopez?"

Without hesitation she removed a small notebook from her desk drawer and read off an address in Portland.

"How long since you've seen or heard from him?"

"Nine, ten months. He c-comes for the annual stockholders meeting. I c-contact him in January with financials and t-tax information."

Lucille's point-blank reply rendered Wharton speechless. He hadn't expected it to be so straightforward.

"R-Roberto's popular today." She flashed him a smile aware she surprised him. "You're the second p-person to ask."

Wharton seized on that. "Who else?"

Lucille shook her head. "Dale came up and said someone here wanted R-Roberto's address."

"How long ago?"

Lucille glanced at the violin shaped wall clock. "About ten minutes."

Wharton's mind dashed back to the man leaving as he arrived. Discovering why he was familiar rose in importance.

He hesitated briefly before plunging into matters he would otherwise have considered none of his business. "Was Roberto a wealthy man?"

Lucille considered. "Comfortable."

"Because of his investment here?"

She bobbed her head. "And royalties. Preston said R-Roberto became financially r-responsible quicker than the others."

"Including himself?" Wharton failed to consider the group's youthful inexperience might have kept them from making the most of their financial opportunity.

"He r-regretted the time he took to r-realize Pistachio wouldn't pay his way through life."

About to rise, Wharton recalled another question. "Do you know what Sylvia Erving does for employment?"

Lucille regarded him with a lifted eyebrow. "Works for the ATF."

"Alcohol, Tobacco and Firearms?" He was shocked. "Doing what?"

"Accounting I believe. She's not in the field."

Wharton frowned. "Would you think she made a lot of money?"

Lucille smiled in conspiratorial fashion. "Spent money like she d-did. Preston c-complained she didn't know the value of a d-dollar."

"Then you'd expect her to be in debt?"

She shrugged. "Probably. I d-didn't get the idea s-she saved or invested."

"But you never heard she was in trouble financially?" The debt on Sylvia's credit report must be significant of something.

"The m-money she got after P-Preston's death should've p-paid off any problems."

Wharton couldn't help but wonder about their relationship. "When was the last time she was here before Preston died?"

Lucille paused to consider. "She usually came in the s-summer, but I think she came t-twice that year, once early and once later."

"Later when?"

Sighing, Lucille said, "I don't know, but I could find out."

"Preston died in November. It wasn't then?"

"Not exactly, but not far off. She c-came here. They had a huge argument and she s-stomped out."

Wharton raised his eyebrows. "Do you know what it was about?"

"He just said, 'She'll get over it.'"

"Do you think she did?"

Lucille grimaced. "Well . . . she was here for his memorial service and seemed okay."

"If you find out exactly when she was here the last time before Preston died, let me know."

Wharton left Stadium Music Company mulling over the information he had received. What did it mean, if anything?

While Brett's discharge paperwork and instructions were managed, Atlanta called Wharton. "Is it dangerous for me to take him home?"

Wharton sighed. "It would be well to make him effectively disappear. Kitty and Aaron are more than happy for him stay with them."

"How long are we talking about? Who knows when we'll figure this mess out? He can't stay there forever or even until he returns to England." How had her cousin's pleasant visit arrived at this point?

"There's no reason though why he couldn't stay with Kitty for a while."

Technically, Atlanta thought. "But we can't just lock him up in a house."

Wharton must have detected her frustration. His voice mollified. "We can until he is fully recovered from this overdose. That would give us time to figure out what to do."

She sighed.

"Let me come get him and deliver him to Kitty's? You go home as if he's still in the hospital and you were visiting."

The implication in Wharton's suggestion alarmed Atlanta. "Do you think someone is watching us?"

"Danged if I know. But it's better to take precautions than get caught unaware."

Obviously, she thought. "Is there a way to find out?"

"We need to talk about that. I'll come right away and get Brett."

Atlanta conveyed to Brett their plans for his immediate future. He frowned but made no objection. Wharton arrived in twenty minutes, entering the room in his take-charge fashion. "I'll take Brett to my car in the emergency area. You leave the way you normally do when visiting. I'll meet you at your house as soon as I've delivered Brett."

Too unsure to argue Atlanta nodded, watching as Wharton and Brett left his hospital room.

When she arrived home, the restoration contractor was walking through with the finish carpenter. "He needs to know what paints or wallpaper you want."

She beckoned to her table of samples in the dining room. "I'm working on it."

Kent consulted his clipboard. "The roofer called. They'll be here tomorrow to begin their work."

Atlanta considered how Brett's situation affected her restoration project. "How much access to the house will the roofer need?"

"None, they bring everything with them."

After agreeing to prepare her list of wall finishes and paint colors she ushered the contractors out, noting Wharton's Mercedes arrive at the curb. He nodded to the men then proceeded into her house as if he owned the place. Annoyed at his take-for-granted attitude Atlanta doubted he had listened to her before.

"Is Brett okay?"

"He's fine," Wharton reassured her with a big grin. "Kitty will plump him up like a feather pillow."

"Would she have any success getting him to talk about Marcella? I get nowhere. He clams up like it's an obscure abysmal secret."

"I'll tag her."

By this time it was late in the afternoon and Atlanta was feeling hunger pangs. "Would you like to have dinner?"

"We could go out," Wharton made the considerate offer.

"I'd rather be home." Atlanta went to the kitchen and opened her refrigerator. "I can come up with something quick if you'd care to stay for dinner."

"My pleasure." Wharton grinned. "We do have to make some plans for the future."

CHAPTER NINETEEN

After tucking Brett under Kitty's protective wing, Wharton called Lieutenant Sarkis outlining his anxiety regarding Brett's safety. The lieutenant offered a number of suggestions.

While Atlanta fixed dinner he sat at her kitchen table with a notepad making a list of matters for consideration. "We have more than one problem."

She stopped her activity to ask, "For instance?"

"As you so aptly pointed out, we can't keep Brett locked up forever, protect him the rest of his life or even while he's in the U.S. We have to determine who is trying to take him out."

Atlanta huffed, "If we did that we wouldn't need to protect him."

"Why don't we use him as bait to find out who is doing this."

Her dark eyes grew wide with alarm.

"Give me a better plan," He challenged. He didn't discount her concerns, but offense was preferable to defense. "I'm not suggesting we make him a sitting target."

A touch of color rose to her cheeks. "What are you suggesting?"

"Fix it so whoever comes near him will be identified."

Atlanta's eyebrows drew together.

"Lieutenant Sarkis suggested we put up surveillance cameras."

"Here?"

"Where else?"

She returned her attention to the meal she was fixing.

Did anyone question the outcome of Brett's overdose? Was the administrator of the extra anti-depressant satisfied with a job well done? Or was he aware Brett survived and looking for another opportunity? Was someone watching the house, following Atlanta, attempting to reach Brett?

A camera could show whether anyone approached the house or Brett. Even a modest security system could help.

Atlanta brought plates and silverware to the table. "How would we do that?"

"Let's check out the Internet and see what we can find? My law firm has access to investigators who do surveillance for support in law cases. Perhaps I can get one of them." Although he wasn't a trial lawyer, Wharton still managed the acquaintance of people with specialized talents.

"Won't we arouse suspicion if someone sees us putting in security devices?"

Wharton flashed a big grin. "Very conveniently you're having your house restored. Contractors come and go regularly. I think we could manage it without attracting attention."

She placed a bowl of salad on the table and then brought a dish with pasta, chicken, and asparagus tossed in a creamy sauce. Wharton inhaled the aroma and smiled at her. "I might get used to this and want Brett to stay in trouble."

She scowled at him. "I'm perfectly happy to have you come to dinner without threatening Brett's well being."

"Point well taken." Wharton requested the opportunity to ask the blessing and prayed for Brett's safety in the process.

"What about your sister's house?" Atlanta asked.

"Hopefully no one knows he's there."

"Shouldn't she also have a surveillance system?"

"Let's get the equipment put in here and bring Brett back."

After dinner Wharton helped clear the table then followed her to the room where she kept the computer.

Sitting in the rolling office chair while she sat beside him on a wooden one, he typed "surveillance equipment" into the search box. A list of possible sites appeared. He searched for a generic website providing information as opposed to a sales pitch. He located one advertising comparison of video surveillance equipment. He printed equipment descriptions, pricing, and issues for consideration. He also went to a web address representing spy tools for serious surveillance and retrieved information depicting assorted hidden cameras, recording equipment and spy gadgets. When he had acquired a stack he suggested they move to a table and examine it.

Atlanta led him back to the dining room where she pushed aside her redecorating swatches. Sitting together they sorted and arranged the material. For some time they sat in silence reading, exchanging sheets from time to time.

"So what do you think?" he asked when they had finished.

Atlanta laughed. "It makes me think I'm trying to play spy. I've a hard time taking it seriously." Her expression darkened with apprehension. "One question, how many locations do we want surveyed?"

He considered. "The front door, side door, and back door for certain."

"And inside?"

"Brett should have one on his person."

"We'd need to talk to him about that." Atlanta sighed glancing at her pile of decorator paraphernalia. "It's awfully pricey. I've already put a pile into repairs. Not to mention my neighbor is taking down her trees and I have to put up a retaining wall."

"Maybe we can borrow the equipment for a while."

In the morning as Atlanta descended the stairs her phone rang.

"This is Kitty Kentish. I wanted to let you know your cousin is okay. However, he's concerned about you. I thought it would help if you came for lunch."

Atlanta felt a wave of relief, realizing she probably hadn't relaxed since Brett got out of the hospital.

They agreed on 11:30.

The phone call helped focus Atlanta's attention and energy, inspiring her to complete her decorating plans. After producing a tentative layout with her first choice colors she stacked the samples for meeting with the contractor.

Questions regarding Marcella continued to plague her. Since Brett wasn't the only one who knew her, Atlanta determined a trip to the Barnes and Noble could prove fortuitous.

The Pineapple Express had moved on, leaving behind a clear chilling sunshine. A brisk breeze sent white caps running along the waves on the sound. Making her way to Lakewood Atlanta noted ripples in the standing water on the streets. In spite of the wintry signs, she felt renewed hope.

At the bookstore all her friends were there. Sunny and Philippe sat engaged in an animated discussion. Philippe shook his head as Sunny elucidated his points stabbing the table with his forefinger. Sherry, Georgiana and Fredee sat with their heads together so engrossed they failed to notice Atlanta's arrival. She took the opportunity to order tea and approach the men.

Philippe stood, doffing his cap. He pulled a chair over from an adjacent table. His smile was sweet, warming Atlanta's soul.

Sunny asked about Brett and Atlanta brought them up to date.

"We're discussing Roberto Lopez."

Atlanta raised her eyebrows, recalling the scene. "It looked like you were having an argument."

"I figure Roberto knew Marcella before they came to Portland." Philippe scowled at Sunny.

"Maybe he should have," Sunny conceded with an unperturbed shrug, "but I don't think he did."

"What difference does it make?" Atlanta was puzzled.

Sunny grimaced. "We're discussing reasons someone might want to get rid of Pistachio."

"And you think it might have something to do with Marcella?" This was the first anyone besides Atlanta had even considered the possibility.

"She's the only one about whom there is any mystery?" Philippe put in.

"What do you think Brett knows about her he won't discuss?"

Philippe stroked his chin. "They'd been in love for some time but were trying to keep it from the group."

Sunny shot Philippe a frown. "What makes you think that?"

Philippe tipped his head to the side and gave Sunny a you've-got-to-be-kidding look. "It was obvious to everyone . . . except you, I guess."

Sunny leaned back in his chair with a frustrated expression.

"Was someone else interested in her?" Why would they keep their relationship a secret?

"I think she'd had a relationship with Roberto before she came to Portland." Philippe nodded at Sunny.

Sunny shook his head.

"There's something about Marcella Brett won't discuss. I've tried, but he claims anything he knows wouldn't have anything to do with what's happening now."

Sunny grimaced and Philippe shrugged.

"Do you know anything about her family or who inherited her royalties?"

"I presume her family did. I never heard anything to the contrary."

After additional unanswered questions, Atlanta excused herself and joined her girlfriends.

As she approached they ceased discussion and greeted her with artificially innocent smiles. Something about the pervasive air of innocuous virtue made Atlanta suspicious. However, since she, too, preferred avoiding certain topics, she tolerated their feigned naiveté.

They chatted about the weather, plans for Halloween, and their physical ailments. Atlanta explained the progress on her house and plans for redecorating.

Eventually a lull in the conversation arrayed the three ladies in a pose of expectant inquisitiveness staring at Atlanta as if they awaited her explanation. She glanced at each of them puzzled by the silence.

"So . . . are you dating him?" Fredee finally burst out with the question that appeared to be on their minds.

"Who?" Atlanta frowned.

"Who!" Fredee exploded. "Who do you think?"

Atlanta shook her head.

"The man you were here with the other day." Sherry made it sound perfectly obvious.

"Wharton?" Why would they think that?

"Every time we see you you're with him." Georgiana explained.

"He's helping me out. He was at the house the night the tree fell on it." A lame explanation, but Atlanta's brain wasn't up to a better one. She couldn't go into Brett's situation and she was definitely not dating Wharton. In fact her friend's conclusion annoyed her.

The trio tipped their heads in unison, gazing at her with varying degrees of disbelief. Time to go home, she thought. She wasn't up to the inquisition she saw coming.

CHAPTER TWENTY

Wharton made up his mind to drop in on an acquaintance he made during an industrial piracy case he had handled for his law practice. The office door declared "Discreet Investigations, Luke Tsukimoto, E.M.S.PS".

No one occupied the small anteroom when Wharton stepped in.

"Ah, Mr. Forde, attorney-at-large." A compact Asian came through the open door to Wharton's right, extending his hand.

"Tsukimoto," Wharton greeted the dark-haired, dark-eyed man grinning at him with a row of straight white teeth. "What do all those letters behind your name mean?"

"Lots of letters, you look wise and educated." Luke Tsukimoto giggled like a teen-ager. "Experienced Master Sleuth, Professional Services." He bowed. "At your service."

Wharton laughed.

"You need some sleuthing?"

"I need some surveillance equipment for a while."

As Luke led him into his office, Wharton explained what he figured Atlanta needed. Attached to corkboard on Luke's office wall was an assortment of spy gadgets similar to pictures they had perused the night before. Wharton wandered along visually examining the apparatuses.

"What you describe sounds simple enough. I think we come to an agreement. Three outdoor, something like this." Luke pointed to a pair of wireless security cameras. "You need it to pan, tilt and zoom?"

Wharton shrugged. "What do you think?"

"If you just want to know if someone tries to get in the house not observe what he's doing a static one will work."

"We need to identify the person."

141

Tsukimoto nodded. "You can still do that with a good static camera."

"We also need something to identify anyone approaching Brett."

Tsukimoto's eyes lit as he raised a finger in the air. "I have just the thing, a micro camcorder in a pen."

He opened a drawer in his desk and withdrew a pen then demonstrated the working recorder for Wharton.

"Amazing." Wharton realized, not only its suitability for his project, but its danger in the hands of the unscrupulous.

He arranged for rental of the security cameras, the digital recorder, the pen camcorder and to have them discreetly installed in Atlanta's home. All that remained was to break the news to her.

But before he did that he ought to check with Kitty. See how the prisoner was fairing.

"I'm no nurse, Wharton. He's safe and comfortable. What more can I tell you?"

"If you really want to know, you can get him to talk about his relationship with Marcella."

"Is there something particular you want to know?"

"He seems reluctant to talk about her. Atlanta thinks he's hiding something that may help us figure out what's going on."

Wharton could hear Kitty's mental calculator running.

"Atlanta's coming to lunch, you could join us."

Wharton never refused a free meal. He still had time to check in at his office, which was quiet with both Carson and Kelley out with clients. He handled some paperwork Kelley left then leaned back in his chair contemplating a means to determine where Sylvia Erving was the fall her father died. Would R.J. know?

What did she do with the money from Preston's insurance? Wharton spent half an hour examining Sylvia's credit report, the high and remaining balances, ratings, and date sequences related to her debts attempting to locate the missing one hundred thousand. One entry under the heading "public record" caught his attention. It read, "Judgment, $175,000, 7-15-2011, Smithson, Bernard, and Company." The rest of her debts rose and fell apart from any influx of wealth. The large debt raised questions but failed to explain the missing hundred k. Would knowing make any difference or was Atlanta right, the mystery hinged on the mysterious Marcella?

Thinking of Atlanta brought up the "i" word, intimacy. How could she say it had nothing to do with sex? Wharton grabbed his dictionary and looked up the definition.

"1 a: INTRINSIC, ESSENTIAL b: belonging to or characterizing one's deepest nature 2: marked by very close association, contact or familiarity <-knowledge of the law> 3 a: marked by a warm friendship developing through long association b: suggesting informal warmth or privacy <-clubs> 4: of a very personal or private nature".

Unfortunately for him she was right, no mention of or even allusion to sex. He considered his marriage to Linda. They had been happy with a close association, contact and familiarity, a warm friendship developed through long association. However, something was missing; he had never been able to share his "deepest nature". Whenever he tried to discuss those deeply personal thoughts, concerns, or wonderings, he met a wall of incomprehension coupled with self-protective dismissal. Frustrated, he had concluded the problem lie in the difference between men and women. A female didn't think philosophically or wonder about abstracts. He accepted his relationship with Linda but shared his abstract opinions with his male friends. However, although those relationships allowed discussion of philosophical issues it was necessarily without emotional interpretation or inference.

Everything changed when he met Atlanta. She comprehended his deepest nature, both the intellectual and emotional. She was the personification of his most treasured dreams.

What happened? Had he failed her somehow? She loved him, but didn't care if he loved her. What did that mean? Wharton's thoughts made him restless. He hardly comprehended his questions, much less the answers. He resented Atlanta for igniting his doubts.

Was he so obtuse he didn't know what intimacy amounted to? And if that were true, was he willing to learn or was his pride so great he'd rather fend off anything contrary to his preconceived ideas?

He stood, shaking off his mental oppression. He was becoming morose in his old age. He always swore he wasn't going to become one of those melancholy old people lost in the past. He was a man of action, right? Time to go to lunch.

Wharton's car was in the Kentish driveway when Atlanta arrived. She hadn't been aware he would be there. Not that it mattered.

Kitty opened the door and invited her into the family room where a small fire burned in the petite wood stove. Wharton and Brett sat at right angles chatting. Both smiled as Atlanta took a seat beside Brett.

"How are you feeling?" She examined him, noting his pale face. But his eyes were bright and clear.

"Like an airhead."

She frowned.

"He said he felt light-headed this morning," Kitty clarified.

"We need to put a bug on you." Wharton pulled a small package from his shirt pocket. "This is a micro camcorder." He held up the black and silver pen. After explaining how it operated he demonstrated how Brett should keep it.

"What do I accomplish with this?" Brett examined the pen before placing it in his pocket as instructed.

"We're hoping to identify who tried to put you out." Wharton's glance consulted Atlanta. "Keep someone from trying it again. Unless you want to stay locked up at Kitty's."

Brett smiled at her. "It's very pleasant here, but I'd rather move freely."

Wharton turned to Atlanta. "I've arranged for security cameras for your house on loan from an acquaintance in the business. We can meet him after lunch."

Atlanta was torn between feeling foolish at so much falderal and fearful it wouldn't be sufficient.

"Lunch is ready," Kitty announced. Her dining room table was set in honor of Halloween. Orange plates, black mugs, dark brown soup bowls filled with a creamy soup with flecks of parsley floating on top, and paper napkins with autumn leaves. A large leaf-shaped platter held sandwiches.

"Are you sorry your musical group broke up so soon after you became popular?" Kitty addressed Brett.

Atlanta noted his defensive expression.

Kitty frowned at him. "Wasn't it crushing to have it end so abruptly?"

"The end left us dumbfounded." Brett concentrated on his soup. "Not to mention brokenhearted."

Kitty dunked her sandwich in her soup. "Were you and Marcella planning to be married?"

Guilt made a quick trip across Brett's face. "Not really," he mumbled.

"Your relationship wasn't that serious?"

"It was for me. Marcella was more interested in performing."

"You don't think she'd have married you?"

Brett shrugged. "She refused a number of times."

Atlanta realized how naïve she had been. Not only had she failed to realize they were physically involved, she wasn't even aware Brett wanted to marry Marcella. What other obvious circumstance was she ignoring? Even as the thought passed through her conscious she felt a twinge, a whispering voice pointing out something she failed to acknowledge.

Recalling her conversation with Sunny and Philippe, Atlanta asked, "Did Marcella know Roberto Lopez before she went to school?"

Wharton's eyebrows shot up, but Brett eyed Atlanta suspiciously. "I think so but she never talked about it."

"Didn't they grow up fairly close to each other?"

Brett considered. "They were both from Ashland, Oregon."

"I have Preston and Annmarie's videos of Pistachio performances," Wharton spoke to Atlanta. "We should get together and take a look at them."

"I wouldn't mind seeing those," Brett said. "We could invite Sunny and Philippe."

"Good plan," Wharton jumped on the idea. "How about tonight at my house?"

Atlanta couldn't let go of her fear. "Will Brett be safe there?"

"We'll have all the surveillance equipment set up at your house. Give our intruder an opportunity to show himself."

"Besides, I have this." Brett pulled the pen out of his pocket with a big grin.

Atlanta was a bundle of anxiety, but reacting in fear wouldn't help matters. "What time?"

"I'll have my theatre set up at eight. Brett can stay with Kitty until you pick him up on your way over."

Far from convinced, Atlanta put up no argument.

CHAPTER TWENTY-ONE

Atlanta's house resembled a contractor convention. A long red crew-cab with Evergreen Roofing imprinted on the door sat in front of Kent Lewis' pickup along the sidewalk. A white van sat behind bringing to mind Atlanta's interior contractor, but the black SUV behind had the Paradise Design logo on the side returning her attention to the van. Was that the security people?

The hubbub inside made Atlanta feel like an intruder in her own home. A couple of men she didn't recognize wandered along the periphery of the exterior. The racket the roofers made tearing up the old roof and tossing it into the dumpster at the back of the house outdid the fans and dehumidifiers that had been removed. Kent Lewis sat at the dining room table with the finish carpenter.

"What's with the security guy?" Kent looked annoyed. "You didn't say anything about that."

"It's on loan and temporary," Atlanta explained. "Although I should have a permanent one installed."

"You might want to do that while the house is being redone." The carpenter folded his arms over his chest.

"I'm not sure I can afford all that now." She explained the retaining wall she needed and asked Kent for a recommendation.

After noting his suggestions on a pad she spent the next half hour explaining her decorating plans. Just as they finished the doorbell rang. Wharton waited patiently in the living room, studying the Pistachio album covers while Atlanta concluded with the contractors.

"I'll show you where the cameras are." He led her to the front window and pointed to a camera attached to the carriage lamp at the side of the house near the front door. It was hidden beneath the light fixture's upper metal cap, unnoticeable to a casual observer. "That should catch anyone on the walk or at the front door, also anything in the periphery at the front of the house."

Then Wharton took her to the back and showed her the camera situated on the garage, aimed at the house and back yard. Another one had been installed at the side door, taking in the portion of yard missed by the others.

"So the only area not covered is the north side?"

"No entry into the house from that direction makes it unlikely someone would be there." Wharton raised his eyebrows observing her expression.

The whole thing made her uncomfortable, but what could she do?

From there he took her to the back bedroom where she kept her computer and pointed out the cameras' receiver.

Returning to the living room Atlanta silently wished for a return to normalcy. She had lost control of her life, losing her sense of self in the process.

At the door Kent Lewis and the finish contractor were ready to leave, indicating they would be back when the roofers finished. Atlanta noted the white security van had also gone, leaving only the roofers who were putting away their equipment.

"Will surveillance equipment really make a difference?" She vacillated between fear of failure to protect Brett and the sense they had reached overkill.

"If someone is watching this place still trying to take him out."

"It seems so surreal. I can't decide what's my life and what's a dreadful nightmare."

"Right now your life might be a dreadful nightmare. Don't lose heart." Wharton patted her shoulder. "I'd better get going. I've things to do before everyone shows up." He paused as if reluctant to leave her, opening his mouth to say something then seeming to think better of it.

Atlanta was looking for comfort. However, Wharton wasn't one from whom to seek solace. Maybe when Brett returned things would be more normal again.

Leaving Atlanta's house Wharton headed downhill to Lafayette Avenue. The panoramic view of Puget Sound with Anderson and McNeil Islands against the backdrop of the Olympic Mountains inspired his imagination. He pictured ferry rides, ocean resorts, and mountain retreats. However all of them included Atlanta, a vaguely disquieting realization.

Pushing these thoughts aside he concentrated on questions he needed answered. At R.J.'s the lawn service truck and trailer were just pulling away, leaving a neatly manicured landscape.

R.J. greeted him with obvious pleasure, inviting him into the kitchen where he offered hot coffee and cookies his neighbor had brought.

"Softening you up for seduction?" Wharton inspected the array before selecting one with chocolate chips.

R.J. snorted. "What brings you here?"

"Did you know Roberto Lopez is the silent partner in Stadium Music Company, lives in Oregon, and comes here every year for corporate meetings?"

R.J. regarded Wharton with a look of amazement.

"Obviously the company didn't bank with you." Wharton plunked himself down on one of R.J.'s kitchen chairs.

"No, they didn't. One thing I did know, Roberto was better at finances than the rest early on."

"How was Marcella at finances?"

"I never knew her. My impression, she didn't spend money like wild but she didn't make great investments either." R.J. poured himself a cup of coffee and joined Wharton at the table.

"Were her royalties transferred to her family after her death?"

R.J. shrugged. "One would assume."

Wharton studied the house across the street. He thought he saw the man who had seen the stranger standing at the window. "You inherited Annmarie's?"

R.J. nodded. "And Preston's after his death?"

"What if something happened to you? Who would get them?"

Surprise flashed across R.J.'s face. "Sylvia, I guess."

"You don't know?" Wharton frowned.

"Since Annmarie and I had no children and Sylvia's brother is dead she inherits everything. I just don't know about Stadium Music Company."

"You inherited Annmarie's share of the music company?"

"Right, but if something happens to me it reverts to the other shareholders."

Wharton focused on R.J. "Were the copyrights kept in effect?"

"To my knowledge all legal matters are up to date. The group had sharp legal representation that remained with them through the years."

Wharton leaned across the table. "How much of a motive would that give you?" Catching a look of disbelief on R.J.'s face, Wharton amended his question. "From the perspective of the law?"

"I had it all anyway. Preston died before Annmarie, so she had his and in effect so did I."

Wharton snagged another cookie. "What do you know about Sylvia?"

"Not much recently. We never hear from her except at Christmas."

"Could she have resented the fact she wouldn't inherit music company stock or that Annmarie got Preston's royalties?"

"If she did, I didn't know about it."

"Any idea how she got a $175,000 judgment against her?"

R.J.'s eyes widened as he shook his head. "But Lucille might."

Before leaving Wharton invited R.J. to join the video gathering. On his way home he stopped at the grocery store to pick up soda and popcorn then a hamburger at Wendy's.

Back at his house he sorted the videos, realizing they were labeled with dates of specific performances. He wondered why they weren't more archaic. Perhaps they had been transcribed from the original format. Back in the 60s he didn't think they had VCRs and certainly not DVDs.

He wasn't sure what could be gained from watching them. If the mystery was definitely connected to Pistachio, or the enigmatic Marcella, they would have more significance.

He considered Brett Hadleigh's fixation with Marcella, attempting to even remember women from his twenties. Maturing later than his youthful compatriots, he had dated in college, had a good time, but nothing serious. He met Linda in graduate school, but even then it had taken time to develop a serious interest in her. They decided to get married his last year of school, but waited until he had his law degree.

When Linda died, he mourned her loss, his loneliness without her, the happy times they had shared. However, he could not even imagine mourning the way Brett had done, a period of fifty years or more. However, he had neither forgotten Atlanta in the twelve years they were separated nor ceased to think of her. But it was not mourning, since she was neither dead, nor entirely out of reach.

However, something had happened to Atlanta that made her distrusting, distant and, if he wasn't mistaken, angry. To his recollection they had parted on the best of terms. What happened? He ran into her a few times just after the lawsuit concluded. For both their sakes he had been careful, acknowledging her presence, but making no contact, presuming she would be just as anxious as he to forestall gossip. He didn't want to hurt Linda. She had been jealous of the time he spent with Atlanta on the law case. Once the suit concluded he could no longer justify that time, but things were different now.

He struggled to understand what happened. His modus operandi was to face problems squarely. Yet with Atlanta he felt reluctant. What did he fear? She might run away?

CHAPTER TWENTY-TWO

Backing her vehicle out of the garage, Atlanta lamented the deep darkness. Once October came daylight made only brief sojourns into day and her life took on some of winter's dimness.

On the drive to Wharton's house, she stopped by the Kentish home for Brett. Both hopeful and skeptical regarding the videos, she looked forward to gaining information while fearful of unrealistic optimism. If nothing else the get-together provided a safe, companionable diversion from recent predicaments.

Wharton's house radiated warmth from a blaze of lighted windows. When he opened the door the smell of popcorn enveloped them.

He had assembled the group in his den with the videos primed on his wide screen television. "I've tried to arrange these by date, beginning with the earliest." He brought glasses of soda to Atlanta and Brett who sat together on the sofa.

A quick knock grabbed Wharton's attention. He opened the door for R.J. dangling a bag of cookies. While Wharton dumped the cookies onto a plate R.J. took a chair with Philippe and Sunny.

"I didn't recall we had many videos in the beginning." Sunny commented.

"Most of these are from later dates." Wharton took the chair closest the hall entry. "The label on the first indicates a performance at the university in the spring of 1964." He pushed the remote button bringing the television to life.

Crude by twenty-first century standards, the images lacked the clarity of digital or even recent videotape. The photographer, obviously an amateur, had failed to capture either the ensemble or the individual performer in clear detail with obscure shots from oblique angles. Nonetheless, the group's overall performance, style, and animation manifested itself admirably. Atlanta watched with fascination people she knew as they were over forty years earlier. How incredibly young they all looked. Brett had changed less than others. Although white, his hair was thick. His face sagged with lines of aging, but he still possessed his trim build. She was not a good judge of the changes life had brought to Annmarie and Preston, not having seen them in their older years. Watching them sing and dance seemed more like watching her children than her contemporaries. Sunny had matured from the skinny youth in the video to a broad built man with crisp gray curls. However, his face remained essentially the same, not having as many lines of aging as did Brett. On the other hand, Philippe was unrecognizable. The short skinny youth with the head of thick black hair and big eyes was lost in the bent man with white hair and lined face.

Brett, Sunny and Philippe sat transfixed, watching. Atlanta could imagine the mesmerizing affect of seeing oneself more than forty years in the past. Would a person remember his thoughts at the time? Atlanta wondered if it was possible to analyze one's attitude from afar and recognize the consequences.

Then there was Marcella so young and vibrant on the screen. She was tall, taller than Philippe and Annmarie, about the same height as Preston. Large built, but with a curving figure and youthful bones visible in the flesh of her arms and legs, she performed as if she were one with both the group and the audience, a conduit of emotion from one to the other. Sunny, Philippe, Roberto and John watched her carefully, but for cues rather than like Brett with adoration. Undoubtedly their romantic give and take enhanced the emotional quality of the music.

When the video ceased and Wharton rose to change the cartridge, Philippe declared, "I wished I'd known how handsome I was."

Sunny snorted. "What makes you think you were handsome?"

Philippe admonished Sunny. "Just look at that profile, those eyes. If I'd been aware I'd have mesmerized the girls."

Sunny groaned and Brett laughed.

Philippe winked at Atlanta.

"Did it tell you anything?" Wharton questioned Atlanta.

She shrugged. "I'm reserving judgment."

Wharton inserted the next tape. "This is the university again in the fall of the same year."

They watched performances from the fall and winter of 1964. In 1965 Pistachio's performances were confined to small venues in the vicinity of Portland, expanding to public arenas in Portland, Spokane, Tacoma, Seattle, and Vancouver in 1966. They moved up a notch to do intro performances for major touring groups in larger facilities by 1967, which included better quality video recordings.

When they reached performances recorded in 1967 Atlanta noted Marcella had gained weight. Studying her as she moved through her rhythmic gyrations, Atlanta looked for signs of illness. Shadows under her eyes were apparent at times, but most of the noticeable changes were mid-torso weight gain and puffiness in her face. Atlanta noticed at times when the music became mostly instrumental Marcella disappeared from the stage to return in moments and resume her performance. Moving into later 1967, Marcella stopped disappearing during the act, but had slowed her gyrations, taking on a swaying motion in place of the bouncing, dance routine.

Wharton stood to exchange videos. "The one I most want to see doesn't appear to be here." He glanced at R.J. who looked bewildered. "There is no sign of the final performance in Spokane."

Everyone turned to Brett.

"I'm not sure one was ever available. I don't even remember hearing about it."

"Surely someone would have wanted it." Wharton inserted a cartridge into the VCR and resumed his chair.

"Do you want to see any of them over?" Wharton had stacked the tapes in groups by year.

"Rerun the later ones from '67." Atlanta pointed to his largest stack.

Wharton reset the VCR and put the tape in motion. Casting a quizzical glance at her, he wondered what she had seen she wanted to review. Refocusing on the television screen with greater intensity, he concentrated on shots of the audience. Several people showed up in more than one.

During a break to reset the tape he queried the group. "Did groupies follow your performances?"

Sunny, Philippe and Brett consulted one another.

Sunny laughed, "I married one of them."

Wharton had noted the exuberant black girl spending considerable time at the foot of the stage.

"She usually had a friend with her," Philippe added.

While watching the next performance, Wharton concentrated on the audience gathered at the foot of the stage. He located the black girl and her friend, also a young Hispanic, whose attention was often divided between the performers and their fans.

Wharton paused the video. "Do you know who that is?" He pointed to the young man.

Philippe squinted at the screen.

Brett grimaced but remained silent.

"You up for a trip to Oregon?" Wharton turned to Atlanta. "We should visit Roberto. Have him fill in some of the gaps."

After he changed the tape they watched the last of the performances for which R.J. had recordings, one from very early 1967. Perusing the audience again, Wharton located the young Hispanic having a good time. Shifting his gaze back to the performers, Wharton noticed Marcella lacked the animation she had exhibited in previous videos, moving heavily as if she had gained an enormous amount of weight. Although heavier than earlier, she mostly seemed to lack energy.

When Linda was diagnosed with cancer she complained of fatigue, and in radiation and chemotherapy her fatigue grew even greater. Was it possible Marcella had been ill, perhaps with cancer?

After everyone had seen enough of the videos, Sunny and Philippe took their leave. Soon after, R.J. also headed home.

"I'm serious," Wharton declared. "I think we should make a trip to Oregon."

Atlanta and Brett regarded him without comment.

"Would you be interested?"

"I could use a trip to Oregon. Get away from here a while. What do you think, Atlanta?"

"I think I'm outnumbered."

Wharton went to his desk and retrieved his planner. "How about this week-end?"

Atlanta shrugged.

When all his guests had gone, Wharton felt if he put together all he had seen recently he would have a chunk of the puzzle. But he couldn't get it together. Nothing seemed to connect.

He wondered if Atlanta had seen anything significant. He noted her interest in later videos and the intentness with which she had watched them. If they put their heads together could they come up with an answer? Would the trip to Oregon make any difference or be just another blind alley.

Somehow he kept running into blind alleys and dead ends. During the evening Atlanta had been polite and distant. He just couldn't figure it out. She acted as though they had never been in love. Had she changed her mind? She said she still loved him. How could she love him and be so distant?

Now that he had found her again and they were free, it was time to renew their relationship. But nothing in Atlanta's demeanor indicated any such interest. He was tempted to ask Kitty if she wouldn't give him a bad time. He still might do that if he could figure out an anonymous approach. However, it would have to be good or Kitty would see through it.

CHAPTER TWENTY-THREE

All night Atlanta watched Pistachio videos in her dreams. The performers took on enormous proportions and distorted images, changing from youths in the actual videos to aged musicians. Brett with his silver hair sang to a fat Marcella with the Hispanic face of the groupie. Philippe hunched over his guitar with his shriveled body and banged on the instrument with stiff elderly movements. Sunny plunked on the keyboards with long bony fingers his grizzled head bobbing rhythmically. The drummer was a ghostly skeleton and the horn player had no face.

At six o'clock she got out of bed and went to the kitchen for a glass of water. Unwilling to return to her dreams she sat at the table making a list of the things she needed to get done before making the trip with Wharton.

Her spirit voted against the journey. Wharton didn't need her; he could handle it by himself. All that prevented her from pulling out was the thought of Brett out of circulation. Relaxing had been a challenge ever since the attempt on his life. Continually looking over her shoulder she wondered if someone stalked them. As much as she disliked the surveillance equipment she recognized its necessity.

Mentally reviewing the videos she realized something was there she couldn't identify. Some clue filed away in her cerebral archives hinted at the mystery. She still wondered what Brett wouldn't talk about. Perhaps between her and Wharton they could break down his reserve, alone making the trip worthwhile.

Since she was up and sleep seemed distant she showered and dressed then returned to the kitchen to fix breakfast. She prepped the coffee pot, got out the ingredients for scrambling eggs and bacon, and set the kitchen table. Just as she completed the task Brett arrived.

"I really appreciate a good morning these days." He laughed lightly. "Realizing I could not be waking up any more."

Atlanta grimaced. "You still remember nothing?"

He ran his hand through his hair. "Nothing specific for sure." He sat on the nook's padded bench.

Atlanta poured coffee and stirred the eggs. "I didn't realize you were taking Prozac."

"I still have problems with depression." He dumped milk into his coffee. "My counselor thinks spending more time in a sunny climate might help."

"Lack of Vitamin D?"

Brett shrugged.

Once the eggs were done she brought them and a plate of buttered toast to the table and they abandoned the mystery.

"I detect some tension between you and Wharton," Brett said with delicate tact.

Atlanta sighed. She didn't want to discuss Wharton.

"You've known him for some time?" Brett continued poking.

"We worked on a case together about twelve years ago."

"I thought it was more than that." Brett's expression was skeptical. "He looks like he's in love with you."

Atlanta cocked her head eying her cousin. "I didn't realize you were that perceptive."

"I'm not." He grinned. "It's just real obvious."

Prepared to argue, Atlanta took a deep breath. "Perhaps I'm obtuse."

Brett laughed. "Or in denial."

Time to change the subject. "How do you feel about going to Oregon?"

"It couldn't hurt."

"I need to settle things with the contractors first. What are you going to do?"

"Dodge Ramona."

"You've been successfully out of the way ever since you went to the hospital."

"That's right." The idea seemed to surprise him. "I wonder what she thinks."

To my knowledge she doesn't, Atlanta thought uncharitably, but said, "No one told her anything."

"You haven't seen her?" Brett sounded incredulous. He probably gave Ramona more credit than she had due.

Previously preoccupied Atlanta hadn't given Ramona any thought. However, now the issue was before them, it was odd she hadn't tried to get hold of Brett or questioned his absences. So unusual in fact it was almost suspicious.

"Maybe she went back to Oregon," Atlanta suggested hopefully.

Brett shrugged.

"If she isn't questioning where you are, maybe it's best to leave well enough alone."

Brett's lack of response convinced Atlanta some way or other he would make contact; even if it just caused more problems.

One more try, "We've made it look like you didn't survive the attempt on your life or that you might still be in the hospital."

The concept seemed to capture his attention. Was there hope yet?

"It wouldn't hurt to go to Oregon and not tell her."

Why he felt he should keep Ramona informed was beyond Atlanta's comprehension. Maybe he still cared for her.

✦✦✦✦✦✦

As soon as he had dressed and downed a cup of coffee, Wharton called his daughter at the office. "I'm going out of town for a few days."

"No problem here. Your administrative assistant said she had the information you requested."

"Okay, I'll stop by and pick it up." When he had ended the call Wharton put in Atlanta's number. "You still up for Oregon?" Best not assume as was his habit.

"I guess so." She didn't sound like she was standing at the curb waiting for him.

"I need to check your surveillance video, too."

A pregnant pause ensued. "When?"

"In an hour or so?"

"Okay. If I'm not here, Brett should be."

Mist hung heavy over the bay as Wharton left his home for his office. It could mean clouds were gathering and a storm was on the way, or even more likely the sun would burn it off and be out in all its glory. October was an unpredictable month.

In order to make the Oregon trip profitable he needed some information on Marcella's family there, requiring a stop at Stadium Music.

Parking irritated him, not as available as previous. A group of people discussing sheet music on the main floor paid no heed as he climbed the stairs in search of Lucille Maginnis.

Looking up from her work, she greeted him with a smile.

"I have more questions." Wharton perched on the chair across from her.

"Okay." She radiated a cheerfulness that had been absent the first time he came.

"We're going to Oregon to see Roberto Lopez. I wondered if you'd have information on the whereabouts of Marcella Demarios' family."

She gazed at him a moment processing. Bobbing her head she pecked on her computer keys then took out a memo slip, wrote on it and handed it to Wharton. It was an address and phone number. He tucked it into his wallet.

"I b-believe," Lucille said, "Marcella's f-father lived in Portland. That's his address."

"Is he still alive?"

"I think P-Preston said her f-father had died, but she did have other family."

"Thanks for the help." Wharton stood up then sat down again. "If you don't mind my asking what exactly did you do with the insurance money you received when Preston died?"

She stared as if she hadn't understood the question. He feared he had offended her. "Since the b-business had no n-need then of the funds I invested them in the name of the c-company."

Wharton raised his eyebrows, impressed with her integrity. "I could use such a loyal employee."

She smiled.

"Any idea what Sylvia did with hers? Or how she'd get a $175,000 judgment against her?"

"Oooo, $175,000." Lucille shook her head. "But I m-might be able to find out."

"That would be great." Wharton was gratified he had asked. "How are you doing?"

"F-fine." Lucille smiled at him. "I'm g-glad you're checking this."

Wharton took out a business card and handed it to her. "If you find out anything give me a call."

She nodded.

Leaving Stadium Music he wondered if Marcella's father's death would reduce the effectiveness of the Oregon trip. Since effectiveness was up in the air anyway no point in waving a black flag.

His office stop was quick. Kelley had put the paperwork from their secretary with her research on his desk. He checked his messages, glanced at his email and taking the paperwork with him left for Atlanta's, hoping to get there while she was available.

Proceeding up her walk he took notice of the surveillance equipment, wondering if anything helpful would be on the recording.

"Just in time for lunch," Atlanta declared when she opened the door.

"I'll go for that," Wharton agreed.

She led the way through the hall into her cheerful yellow kitchen. Brett sat in the corner with a cup of coffee, a plate of sandwiches and a basket of chips in front of him.

Wharton took a chair. "When can you leave for Oregon?"

Atlanta poured coffee. "After I take care of a few details here." She handed him the cup and a plate. Sitting on the bench at right angles to Brett, she asked. "When did you want to go?"

"Tomorrow?" Wharton removed Lucille's notes from his pocket and set them on the table. "I got some addresses that should help us."

Atlanta gazed at his notes. "I'm not sure I can get everything under control by then."

"Give me a call when you've decided for certain." He took a sandwich off the plate.

After lunch Atlanta led him back to the surveillance recorder in her study.

Brett followed, standing in the doorway as Atlanta pulled out her desk chair for Wharton. "What are you looking for?"

"Anyone hanging around your house." He managed to get the video to register on the monitor.

The three watched in silence as it went through the days since installation. They saw the paper delivered, the garbage truck pickup, and one of Atlanta's neighbor boys soliciting for school. A man came to read the meter from Town of Steilacoom. However, no one who looked suspicious.

Wharton frowned.

Atlanta sighed as if relieved and glanced at Brett who also wore an expression of relief.

"You know," Wharton warned them, "It'd be better if someone showed up and we could get resolution."

Atlanta grimaced and Brett nodded.

Wharton wished he could offer her some encouragement or relief from concern, but he didn't have any answers and he didn't want to offer false hope. They needed to stay on their toes. He doubted whoever was mixing medications had given up the plan.

When Wharton had gone, Atlanta tidied the kitchen and made calls regarding her restoration project. The interior contractor agreed to her instructions although he informed her they would not be working on it until the following week. Afterward she found Brett in the living room with a novel.

"I feel guilty leaving Ramona in mid-stream." He stuck an envelope in the book to mark his place.

"For heaven's sake why?" Atlanta figured his anxiety regarding his ex-wife was over the top.

Brett shrugged. "Old habit?" He lifted an eyebrow inquiring if she'd accept that.

"If you get hold of her you'll undo everything we've done to protect you."

"You think Ramona is involved in this?" His tone was skeptical.

"No," Atlanta said. "I don't think she's sharp enough for that. She doesn't need an overdose to hook you into her plans. She just needs to play the helpless female."

"You make me sound like an idiot," he objected.

"All men are idiots," Atlanta declared. "So what is a person to do? For that matter so are all women in one way or another."

Brett grinned. "Are you having a bad day?"

Atlanta shot him a frustrated glance, then realizing her negative attitude laughed, shaking her head. "Am I the sausage calling the hot dog fat?"

"You know," Brett rubbed his chin, "I have this feeling I should know what happened that night."

"Is your memory returning?" She sat on the end of the sofa.

He shook his head. "Not really. It's just a feeling." He frowned. "Why can't I remember?"

"Aren't traumatic events like that?"

Brett stared at the painting over Atlanta's shoulder. "But it wasn't traumatic when it happened, only afterward."

He had a point. If he didn't know he was being poisoned, it wouldn't be traumatic until after. "Maybe it's an effect of the drug he gave you."

"Or she?" He lifted a teasing eyebrow.

Even feelings were hopeful, sounding like progress to her. Thinking about the night Marcella died, such a long time ago, with her memory enhanced and compromised by time and things she learned since then, Atlanta worked to separate what she had actually heard and seen from additional information given to her after the fact. One thing Brett said that night came back to her. "Do you remember the night Marcella died you said you would explain later?"

Brett had the tenant-at-the-wrong-address expression.

Obviously not. "What should you have told me?"

He studied his hands.

Was he trying to remember? Decide what to tell her? Atlanta couldn't decide if the decades had dimmed his memory or if he was keeping secrets. She wasn't sure what made her think he had secrets, but she knew he wasn't being upfront.

With a deep sigh he said, "I'd been trying to get Marcella to marry me for some time." His gaze traveled out the window. "I thought once she may be pregnant."

"Did you ask her?"

"Yes."

"She denied it?"

Brett nodded. "She said her monthly periods were normal."

"You know some women still have them when they're pregnant."

"Really?" His eyes widened.

Recalling her glimpse of the ladies' room at the coliseum Atlanta asked, "Could she have had a miscarriage?"

"Do women die from miscarriages?"

"Not usually." Atlanta sighed. "But I suppose it's possible."

"It would account for a diagnosis of natural causes."

"But wouldn't someone have said something, at least to her parents." It made no sense to Atlanta if that's what happened why no one said so. Although, given the culture then perhaps . . . .

"I don't think her parents knew what happened to her." Brett was back to studying his hands. "If nothing else they should have been angry with me if that were the case."

"Did they know about your relationship?"

"Not particularly. But I don't think there was anyone else at the time they could have blamed it on."

Atlanta raised her eyebrows. Ramona always fooled Brett. Who could say Marcella had not done the same thing to him.

He shook his head as if he had read her mind. "I can't believe there was someone else."

"Did she have relationships before you?"

Brett stared past Atlanta at the antique painting. "Oh, probably, high school things, maybe even college, but nothing that lasted a long time."

"It wouldn't have had to last a long time." Who else might know? Atlanta's mind traveled through people who might have been in Marcella's confidence. Annmarie, the only other woman in the group, was dead. Atlanta would have been too young then to know the groupies who hung around. Hadn't Sunny married one?

Atlanta looked at her watch. If she stopped by the bookstore café her girlfriends might be there. Even better she might catch Sunny. Did she dare leave Brett? Would he do something stupid and endanger himself?

Concluding if Brett refused to be self-protective Atlanta could do little to prevent him from becoming a casualty of his own myopia. If he called Ramona, it was only sort of awful. Atlanta didn't figure Ramona was poisoning Pistachio. Consequently, she bade him a pleasant afternoon and left for the bookstore.

Surprised her girlfriends weren't there she glanced at her watch, realizing they generally came earlier in the day. However, to her gratification Sunny and Philippe sat in their usual corner.

After purchasing tea from the espresso bar she approached them.

"Ah, the lovely lady," Philippe stood, performed his romantic bow and pulled over an extra chair.

"Brett didn't come with you?" Sunny asked.

"No, he's worrying about his ex-wife again."

Sunny grimaced. "Maybe he should've stayed married to her."

Atlanta laughed. "He wasn't given the choice."

Philippe nodded sagely.

"Can we do something for you?" Sunny astutely assessed the situation.

"Brett and I were discussing the night Marcella died, wondering if she had anyone in her life besides him."

Sunny and Philippe exchanged a glance. Philippe shook his head.

"Not that I was aware of," Sunny added.

"I wasn't always certain how devoted to Brett she was, but there was no one else." Philippe regarded Atlanta with regret.

"How about groupies?" she persisted.

"Most of them were women," Sunny put in.

"No men?" Atlanta wasn't ready to give up.

"Oh, a few young guys ogled her from the footlights."

"Generally those guys were trying to attract the female groupies," Philippe said.

Atlanta felt deflated when she left the bookstore. She hadn't learned much. However, it might help to find Marcella's family in Portland if they could.

An exquisite fall afternoon, the sky a clear baby-blue, with a light breeze causing the many-colored leaves to shimmer as sunlight hit them. However, like a lot of things in life it looked much warmer than it was.

The bright sun failed to diminish fall's cold bite; just as her momentary tranquility failed to mask the underlying danger still threatening.

Arriving home, she was so relieved to find Brett had taken a nap, neither calling anyone nor going out, she could have waltzed him around the room.

While fixing dinner she noted a car stop along the side street farther up the hill toward her neighbor's home. Three people got out, a woman, a man and a young boy. They stood for a time talking and gesturing toward the houses on the block, Atlanta's in particular. After which they proceeded up the hill to Drina Faron's home.

"Who is it?" Brett asked coming to stand beside her.

"Someone looking for Drina Faron," Atlanta replied. "She looked familiar for some reason. Could be Drina's daughter I suppose."

Brett narrowed his eyes thoughtfully, but said nothing.

Atlanta returned to her dinner preparations, remarking, "I think I'll let Wharton know we can make the Portland trip with him."

"I was trying to recall the last time I saw Roberto."

"Have you seen him since the group broke up?"

"We got together a couple times to talk about putting another band together."

Atlanta paused in setting the table. "Without Marcella?"

Brett nodded.

She found it hard to imagine Pistachio without Marcella. "Did you want to make a go of it without her?"

Brett shook his head. "It took me a long time to want to do anything without her."

Atlanta recalled Brett's depression, his loss of interest in life after the singer's death. "Did others?"

"Philippe and Roberto both figured we could still be successful. Even John Hanson was willing to give it a try."

"But not Preston and Annmarie?"

Brett's gaze traveled out the window. "They seemed pretty neutral about it. They neither pressed to continue nor objected to the idea."

"Why do you suppose that was?"

"After Marcella died they each found someone who they eventually married. Their lives went a different direction." Brett sighed, leaning back in his chair.

"Would anyone have resented that?"

He raised his eyebrows. "You mean enough to be killing people forty years later."

Atlanta realized the stupidity of her idea and smiled apologetically. "I suppose not. I'm catching at straws."

CHAPTER TWENTY-FOUR

After tossing his roll-on into the trunk of the Mercedes, Wharton checked the mailbox and locked his house. Fog lay in a frosty white layer over the Port of Tacoma, making his neighborhood appear an island in the sky. The morning's hushed stillness made him feel as if he floated somewhere out in space unconnected to reality. Wharton wasn't a fanciful person. He found the feeling foreboding.

Eagerly anticipating the Portland trip with Atlanta, he feared it may be impetuous goose hunting. He had no confidence they could discover anything and wasn't even certain what they sought. Attempting to shrink his misgivings he told himself it was good to get away now and then. Brett and Atlanta made good company. Not to mention whisking Brett away may rescue his life from extermination.

Often lately Wharton found himself vacillating between anxiety regarding the two of them while enduring his inner antagonist's chiding for presumptive concerns. Should he just turn the whole problem over to Lieutenant Sarkis and forget it? No matter how sensible he couldn't do that. He had no faith the police saw the danger threatening the lives of people he cared about. When considering his concern overrated, he recalled finding Brett and the fact both his aunt and uncle were dead with thin explanations for cause.

Buck up, fella, you've committed yourself. There's no point in backing down now. It's not you in danger and you could very well save the life of someone who is.

Brett and Atlanta were ready when he reached her house. They loaded suitcases into his trunk then took places in the car, Atlanta in front with him and Brett behind. After preliminary chatter about the weather, the group retired to silence as they headed south on I-5 through Olympia, Centralia, and Chehalis.

Intermittently driving into and out of the fog they cruised I-5 as the morning mist gave way to brilliant sun. The resplendent green hills were scattered with burgundy and orange touches of fall. The Columbia River shimmered in the sun as they crossed from Vancouver, Washington into Portland, Oregon. The city spread before them nestled in the trees, ablaze with fall colors.

"I'm going to take the Rose Quarter exit. To my understanding Roberto's address is in the historic neighborhood near there."

"Maybe we could invite him out to lunch," Atlanta suggested.

Wharton looked at his watch. She was right. It was nearly noon and not a good idea to starve his companions. "Maybe we should have it first."

"Why don't we at least try to find where he lives?"

Wharton handed Atlanta his phone on which he had brought up the GPS directions. "We're on Weidler now."

"You need to take a left at 17th."

Wharton made the left and crossed through the light on Broadway into a predominantly residential area populated with massive older homes.

"There's the address." Atlanta pointed to a large lavender and white frame house occupying the corner of a block. "It's a Bed and Breakfast," Atlanta informed him as he parked the car along the street in front. "I wouldn't think he'd live in an inn."

"Maybe he rents an apartment there," Brett put in from the back seat.

"Why don't you check to see if he's there," Wharton addressed Brett.

"No!" Atlanta objected. "Brett can't go."

Wharton had forgotten the danger. "Sorry. Let me go."

He got out of the car, climbed the stairs to the ground level of the house then continued up the porch stairs. He rang the doorbell.

After a few moments a woman with dark hair pulled into a rooster tail at the back of her head and sympathetic brown eyes opened the door with a welcoming smile and invited him in. "Did you have reservations?"

Wharton shook his head. "I was looking for Roberto Lopez. According to the address I have, he lives here."

Regret, anxiety and a trace of amusement raced across her face. "Roberto is my uncle. He owns the Bed and Breakfast and lives here, too. My husband and I operate it for him."

"My friends and I wanted to visit him regarding some very old times."

A wary expression drew her brows together. "I'm sorry but he's in the hospital."

"What happened?" Wharton was instantly suspicious.

"An accident."

"What sort of accident?"

She grimaced. "Well, not an accident really. He apparently got his medications mixed up and took too much."

Not good news. "Where is he now?"

Roberto's niece took a step back. "Legacy Good Samaritan Hospital. He went into convulsions and we called 911. He's still under observation to be sure he's okay before coming home."

Wharton fired another question. "Is he conscious?"

"Yes. They caught it before he went into a coma." She backed up another step. "He's diabetic."

"How long is he expected to be there?"

She hesitated, eying Wharton suspiciously.

Suddenly aware of his presumptuousness, he said, "My name is Wharton Forde. My Aunt Annmarie and Uncle Preston were part of the band Pistachio with Roberto. I have Brett Hadleigh who was one of the singers in the car with me and his cousin Atlanta." Wharton removed his wallet and produced his identification.

"I'm going to see him this afternoon."

"Would it be possible for us to accompany you? We probably all need to have a chat."

She opened her mouth, but no words came out.

"I'm sorry if I alarm you, but some strange things have happened to members of the band all in the same vein as Roberto."

Her eyes widened. "Strange things?"

"It would be better to explain from the beginning to both you and him."

"I don't want to alarm him."

Wharton grimaced. Alarm wasn't the worst thing that could happen to Roberto. "We need information from him, too, to help solve this problem."

She still hesitated appearing torn between disbelief and anxiety.

"Why don't you join us for lunch? We can explain and you can decide how best to handle it with Roberto."

She glanced at her watch. "Okay. Things are taken care of here for the time being."

"Maybe you could suggest a place in the neighborhood."

At this she smiled. "Sure there's a great pasta place on Broadway. Let me get my jacket and I'll join you."

Brett and Atlanta waited in silence observing the door through which Wharton had disappeared. *Victorian Lace Bed and Breakfast* read the wooden sign identifying the business, painted the same lavender and white as the building. With its turrets and gingerbread trim the house could have made the cover of *Victorian Homes*.

When Wharton emerged accompanied by a woman wearing a jacket and carrying a handbag Atlanta felt a twinge of anxiety. This grew as Wharton introduced Delia LaCrosse, Roberto's niece, who was joining them for lunch.

"You might want to leave your car here and walk to the restaurant." She pointed toward the street behind them. "Broadway is busy. Parking can be difficult."

Wharton glanced at Atlanta with a raised eyebrow.

"We'd be happy to walk," she said.

Delia and Wharton led the way while Atlanta and Brett followed to a narrow restaurant boasting gourmet pastas. The hostess escorted them to a table for four and handed out menus.

Conversation centered on the City of Portland, weather, and good restaurants while they introduced themselves and placed orders.

When the waitress departed, Delia said, "I was alarmed when you wanted to talk about what happened to Roberto."

Wharton explained the deaths of his aunt and uncle.

"Last week Brett," Atlanta nodded in his direction, "ended up in emergency. They diagnosed serotonin syndrome which they said came from combining two anti-depressants."

"I'd never combine anti-depressants. I only take one," Brett added. "I've never even heard of the other one."

"You see why we're alarmed," Wharton leaned forward, placing his forearms on the table.

Delia frowned. "You think that's what happened to Roberto?"

"Why don't you tell us what happened?" Atlanta suggested.

"I can't say that I know." She glanced from Atlanta to Brett as if one of them had the explanation. "When I came back from grocery shopping and went upstairs to the apartment. I found him on the sofa violently ill and only partly conscious. I called 911 and they took him to the hospital."

"Did they tell you what caused it?" Wharton asked.

Delia beckoned to Atlanta. "They mentioned the term you used."

"Serotonin Syndrome?"

She nodded.

"What medicines does Roberto take?" Atlanta wondered if he also took anti-depressants.

"An anti-diabetes drug and an appetite suppressant. His doctors said his diabetes and heart problems would be reduced if he lost weight."

"But no anti-depressant?" Atlanta verified.

"No, in fact, they warned him about the danger of those with his medicine."

Atlanta met Wharton's eyes.

He lifted his eyebrows then turned back to Delia. "Have you received any information about what happened?" he asked. "Was it just his own medication?"

"The doctor said they wouldn't have all the blood test results until today." Delia appeared even more anxious.

Wharton frowned. "Will they give you that information?"

"I have his medical Power of Attorney." Delia turned to Brett. "What do you think is happening?"

"It appears someone is trying to eliminate the remaining members of Pistachio." Wharton answered for him.

"But why?" Delia's voice squeaked.

"Today's big question."

The waitress arrived with their meals changing the conversation topic. Once she had gone Wharton asked, "Do you know Marcella Damarios' family?"

"Not really. Roberto talked about them some. They used to live in Portland."

"They don't any longer?" Atlanta had the impression from Sunny and Philippe they still did.

"I don't know. I think her father died so I'm not sure if anyone is left."

"Would Roberto know?" Brett asked.

Delia shrugged. "He may."

Brett continued, "Do you think we could go with you to see him?"

She made a round of the faces before her. "It's on the other side of town."

"We have to make arrangements for a place to stay tonight." Wharton consulted Atlanta with a glance.

At this Delia perked up. "I have vacancies tonight at the B & B."

Atlanta nodded, figuring that would provide possibilities for other information. However, when she met Wharton's eyes they both looked at Brett. Unsure where the danger originated or how to avoid it she didn't know if it would be safe for him.

"What do you think?" Wharton asked.

Atlanta turned to Brett. "Are you able to be really careful?"

He grinned broadly.

Atlanta turned back to Wharton and shrugged her shoulders.

He turned to Delia. "We'd be happy to stay at your B & B if you have three rooms available."

"For tonight I do."

When they had finished eating and Wharton had paid the check they walked back to the inn where they filled out the paperwork for three rooms and moved their luggage in.

"We serve complimentary tea and dessert from 4:00 until 5:00."

That sounds good, Atlanta thought, hoping Wharton wouldn't make plans to miss it.

"I'll be going to the hospital at 2:00." Delia informed them.

Since more than an hour remained before time to leave, the group arranged to meet in the foyer at 1:45. Each retired to his assigned room. Atlanta found hers in the corner with a bay of windows overlooking the intersection on which the house sat. Its wing back chair and ottoman made a perfect spot for a nap. She set her cell phone alarm and sat down. When the alarm went off it startled her from dreams focusing on the groupies she had seen in the Pistachio videos. However, its logical essence had disappeared along with the images.

———————— ✦✦✦✦✦✦✦ ————————

Wharton found his room along the corridor next to Atlanta's with a connecting door that would transform it into a suite. Heavy green and gold drapes, a leather easy chair, a walnut desk and king size bed with wood-framed canopy produced a very masculine room. Pushing aside the drape he looked out on sunshine dodging leaves and casting shadows on the lawn. It raised his spirits.

He had caught the alarm in Atlanta's eyes when considering Brett's safety in a place so close to another who may have been targeted for death. Wharton didn't honestly know how to keep Brett safe. First he would have to identify the source of danger.

In his anxiety to get to the hospital he recognized his lack of patience with vacations. He always had his mind on some project, a frustration for his wife Linda. It might not endear him to Atlanta either. Here may be an opportunity to heal whatever breach now lay between them. That, too, he had been unable to identify. His powers of solving mysteries lay somewhere between minimal and nonexistent.

Opening a leather binder that lay on the desk, he checked the inn's amenities, noting free WIFI. He removed the IPad from his briefcase and took a seat at the desk. He went online to look up the two drugs Delia indicated her uncle took. The sulfonylurea anti-diabetes drugs were used for Type II diabetes where the pancreas still produced some insulin. The appetite suppressant worked by increasing norepinephrine, serotonin and dopamine in the brain. There was that word, serotonin. After reading cautions and warnings, possible side effects and drug interactions Wharton was convinced any disease was preferable to the medicine for it. He also noted both drugs warned against reaction with an MAOI anti-depressant.

That anti-depressant was turning up in all the deaths and attempts, yet not one of the victims took the drug. Were there other circumstances that produced those results? Or had the tests accurately diagnosed the murder weapon? How easy would it be to procure? Was it an available illegal drug? Or were prescriptions at fault?

So many questions and no answers. Wharton glanced at his watch, time to rally the troupes for the hospital trip. He knocked on Atlanta's door.

"Are you ready?" she asked when she opened it.

Hearing their voices, Brett opened the door to the room at right angles with Atlanta's. "Time to go?"

The three continued downstairs to the foyer which opened into an old-fashioned parlor furnished in antiques. A door behind the admissions desk was open displaying the inn's office.

Delia came out of it putting on her jacket. "I can navigate if you'd like to drive."

"Good idea." Wharton figured that would make it easier to locate the hospital later.

Legacy Good Samaritan was directly across the river from the Bed and Breakfast. They took the Burnside Bridge and traveled uphill to the Northwest section of Portland, an artsy quarter known as Nob Hill. The hospital sat at the edge of the restaurant and shopping area.

Having previously visited her uncle, Delia led the way through corridors and elevators to the room where he recuperated. Since it was visiting hours no one questioned their presence. Wharton figured that was dangerous, not that he could do anything about it.

Since he had never seen Roberto Lopez, Wharton had no idea if the tan-complexioned puffy-face of the man in bed was his normal appearance or the distortion of his misadventure. Since the medications he took were for losing weight and diabetes, it was fair to assume he had not been trim, although he did not look obese. His dark eyes were open as he watched the television screen on the ledge across from him.

Delia greeted him with a peck on the cheek. He smiled at her. When Brett stepped from behind her, Roberto stared at him with brows drawn together. His glance traveled over Wharton and Atlanta then returned to Brett.

"It's been a long time," Brett said when Roberto's face suddenly registered recognition.

"I'll be . . . Brett Hadleigh. What are you doing here?"

Brett grinned. "Checking up on you. Looks like you still don't know how to stay out of trouble."

Roberto grimaced.

"Don't feel bad I just got out of the hospital a few days ago."

"What happened to you?"

Brett glanced at Wharton and Atlanta as if for permission to explain. "Apparently a bad drug combination."

"Same as mine?" Roberto exchanged a glance with Delia who nodded.

"I don't think so. I take Prozac for depression and that's all, but I went into a serotonin syndrome I'm told."

"Isn't that what they said happened to me?" Roberto questioned Delia. She nodded.

Roberto appeared perplexed.

"When do you get out?" Brett asked.

"Probably tomorrow."

"That soon?" Delia sounded alarmed.

Roberto grinned. "You got a hot date?"

"Of course. What do you think?" Her laugh was hollow.

Wharton moved to the side of the bed. "Have you had any visitors recently?"

"Here?"

Wharton shook his head. "At home or anywhere else."

Roberto was thoughtful. "Not that I recall."

Stepping back from the bed, Wharton decided to let the others do the conversing. He was apt to interrogate the patient. Delia moved in, initiating a conversation about the old days and the band. Brett and Roberto exchanged memories.

Wharton approached Atlanta, standing to the side observing. "Did Brett say anything about a visitor before his adventure?"

She made a face. "He doesn't remember anything."

"Not even before?"

She shook her head. "At least not that he can identify as being that night. But," she added, "he's getting sensations that make him think he should remember something."

Noises in the corridor outside the room indicated visiting hours were over. The four said farewell to Roberto, indicating they would see him the next day. Wharton led the way back to the car for the return to the inn.

When they arrived, Delia announced she had a few things to do and then would be setting up tea in the parlor.

"How about a walk through the neighborhood?" Wharton suggested to Atlanta.

"As long as we're back in time for tea. I don't want to miss dessert."

Wharton glanced at Brett considering whether or not to invite him.

Brett shook his head. "I think I'll hang out here and read the paper."

Wharton turned to Atlanta.

"Let me put my handbag back in my room."

CHAPTER TWENTY-FIVE

Atlanta found Wharton in the foyer gazing out the window. Glancing through the double doors into the parlor she noted Brett in a big easy chair with the newspaper. "I just realized," she said, "if a bunch of people were all lined up behind newspapers you'd know they were old without seeing them. Young people don't read papers anymore."

Wharton frowned at her. "I read newspapers and I'm not old."

She rolled her eyes heavenward.

He opened the door and they stepped onto the porch. Traffic had picked up with cars returning home at the end of the day. People were walking their dogs.

"Do you want to window shop or investigate the neighborhood?"

"Put that way, I suppose we'd better investigate."

They descended to street level and turned away from the Broadway business district. Homes grew larger as they moved farther into the residential area. Some occupied nearly a half-block with wrought iron fencing and privacy shrubs.

"I love old houses." Atlanta pointed to one in sandstone with peaks, angles and bay windows.

"Would you really want to live in something that big?"

"I really would," she said. "But it'd be a lot to take care of even if I were a sweet young thing."

"And you're not?" Wharton turned a shocked expression to her.

Atlanta shot him a reproachful glance. "I'm not sure I ever was."

"You've always been that to me." He put his hand over his heart.

"How can such a hard-nosed attorney be so full of schmooze?"

He cast her a reproachful glance. "What do you mean when you say you don't care anymore if I care for you?"

She walked in silence considering how to explain, realizing he truly did not understand. "When you fell in love with Linda how did you feel about her interest in you?"

Wharton frowned. "What do you mean?"

"Were you indifferent about whether or not she cared about you?"

"Indifferent?" He scowled. "No way. I was anxious she like me, think well of me, want to see me. Why?"

"How would you have felt if she didn't?"

"Devastated," he huffed.

"I used to feel that way about you, but I don't anymore."

He stopped walking and turned to her. "Why not?"

That was the question was it not? "I was devastated, crushed. But I passed through that to indifference." She met his gaze defiantly.

"So you don't care about me anymore?"

She grimaced. "When I asked whether it concerned you if Linda cared about you, did I ask how much you cared about her?"

Wharton walked staring at the pavement as if making sure not to step on a crack. "No. You asked if I cared whether she cared for me."

"Right. Do you understand that's different?"

He sighed and took a few more steps. "I don't feel indifferent about you."

"Maybe I didn't devastate you."

He shot her a sharp look.

She turned away to gaze at a bush of late summer roses. "You walked away as if I didn't exist."

"I thought you understood."

"That your wife wouldn't let you talk to another woman?" Atlanta glanced at him sideways.

"No." He frowned. "It wouldn't work to talk to you."

"I didn't get the idea Linda was that insecure."

"She wasn't."

"What did you think I was going to do? Throw myself at you? Make a scene?" Atlanta walked carefully too, stepping over cracks.

"I'd never expect that of you." He sounded offended.

They continued in silence. Atlanta gazed at the beautiful old homes thinking how she had always wanted to live in a mansion. It was one of her childhood dreams. Probably an impractical one all things considered.

Finally Wharton said, "I don't believe I did think. I just reacted in the manner I felt appropriate. I took it for granted you'd understand." He turned to her. "What did you think?"

"That we'd go on being friends, talk sometimes, take an interest in each other's life. Just normal things friends do."

A breeze ruffling the trees showered them with golden leaves.

"The problem with being friends, I'd always be pressing you for more."

"And you don't think I could handle it?"

He turned to stare at her.

"You didn't have much faith in me," she scolded.

"I didn't have much faith in me," he mumbled.

"You realize that's selfishness." She watched him from the corner of her eye. "And ultimately selfishness is lack of love."

"Ouch!" He put his hand on his chest. "You know how to hurt a guy."

"When you truly love someone you set aside what you want and do what's best for the other person. I cared enough for you not to endanger your relationship with your wife."

"And I couldn't take enough interest in your wellbeing to just be friends?"

Silence reigned again. It did help Atlanta feel better having Wharton understand her feelings.

"So you thought I didn't love you and I took it for granted you loved me." Wharton sighed.

"We'd better turn back or we'll miss tea."

As they reversed direction to return to the inn, Atlanta wondered if the person who poisoned Roberto was part of the neighborhood.

"What address did you get for Damarios?" she asked Wharton.

He removed a slip of paper from his wallet and read off an address on Southeast Oak Street. "Have you seen it?"

She shook her head. "We should ask Delia when we get back."

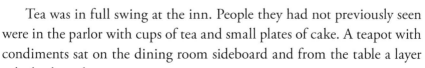

Tea was in full swing at the inn. People they had not previously seen were in the parlor with cups of tea and small plates of cake. A teapot with condiments sat on the dining room sideboard and from the table a layer cake beckoned.

Wharton scrutinized faces as Atlanta poured tea for him. An older couple, the right age but without the appearance of any interest in a seventies folk band, a young businessman, too young to even have heard of Pistachio and a couple from eastern Oregon doing a special presentation at one of the universities made up the group.

"Cake?" Atlanta asked him.

He flashed a big grin and she handed him a chocolate raspberry wedge.

Brett had not been in the parlor when they arrived, but came as Atlanta was pouring another cup of tea. She handed it to him, asking if he wanted cake.

He came to stand beside Wharton. "Do you think Roberto had the same problem I did?"

"There are enough parallels to make me uncomfortable. The culprit appears to be an MAOI anti-depressant. How would someone get hold of that?"

Brett shook his head. "I have a prescription for the one I take. I assume it would be necessary for that too."

"If you were trying to get hold of your medication without a prescription what would you do?"

"Ask someone I know who takes it."

"Ahhh," Wharton waved his fork. "I hadn't thought of that. You know someone who takes your medication?"

Brett lifted an eyebrow. "Several people. They're in my therapy group."

"Interesting," Wharton mumbled, his mouth full of cake.

"What's on your mind?" Brett placed his teacup on a nearby sideboard as Atlanta handed him a dessert plate.

"Finding someone who takes tranylcypromine sulfate."

"You might need the police to do that."

"You're right." Wharton made up his mind. Taking his plate and cup he headed to the porch. He sat at one of the small tables and took out his cell phone. When Lieutenant Sarkis answered, Wharton asked, "Could you find out who takes or has access to MAOI antidepressants? Particularly the one in that glass you took from Atlanta's house."

The lieutenant's voice mellowed. "Why do you want to know?"

"They've shown up in both Brett's and another band member's tests when they ended up in the hospital. If we found out who had access to it we might be able to find who spiked their blood."

"I don't know that I can do that, but I'll see."

Wharton returned his phone to his pocket and reentered the parlor. Atlanta and Brett stood together like a couple baby birds waiting for a worm.

Wharton explained the idea Brett triggered. "I imagine it's a controlled substance. There'd have to be records where it's dispensed."

Atlanta appeared skeptical. "I asked Delia about Oak Street. She says it runs from the Willamette River east. But it doesn't go all the way through. It runs in little sections parallel to Broadway about a mile and a half south, on the other side of I-84."

"We could take a trip out there tomorrow." Wharton noted the dissatisfaction in Atlanta's expression."Tonight it'll get dark too soon."

"Maybe it would be better in the dark, especially if lights are on. You might see inside."

"Or have a hard time finding it period," he huffed.

"Then what are we going to do tonight?" she asked with raise eyebrows. "You have any ideas?"

"I do," Brett put in. "Food."

Wharton looked at his watch. "Okay, let's go see what we can find."

Atlanta excused herself to freshen her makeup. Brett and Wharton took seats in the parlor to examine the Portland Magazine for dinner possibilities. They were still batting ideas around when she returned.

"There's a couple good seafood restaurants on the same side of town as the hospital," Wharton declared.

"And Danny's," Brett put in. "A steak house."

"You looking for a steak?" Wharton frowned at him.

"This is America isn't it? I thought you were famous for steak."

"Never thought about it like that."

"We can do Danny's right?" Atlanta verified.

Wharton ushered the group back to his Mercedes and they headed for the Northwest side of Portland. He would have enjoyed it more without Brett. Unfortunately, he grimaced, it was probably better under the circumstances with Brett.

CHAPTER TWENTY-SIX

Danny's menu allowed a wide choice of steaks one could customized with various sauces. In addition, it offered numerous accompaniments, almost too many for Atlanta to fix on one. She settled for a petite sirloin with a caramelized onion topping, garlic mashed potatoes and steamed fresh vegetables.

"Wine?" Wharton surveyed the table.

Atlanta nodded glancing apprehensively at Brett.

He shook his head. "Doctor's orders. I'll have water."

Wharton ordered a carafe of Cabernet Sauvignon and two glasses. Their waiter brought a basket of bread and dipping oil.

"I really think we need to look up the Damarios's address tonight," Atlanta challenged Wharton.

He sighed. "It wouldn't hurt to drive by if we can locate it in the dark." He turned to Brett. "Did you know her family?"

Brett shook his head. "I met her parents a few times when they attended performances. She had some teen-age siblings but they were usually off on their own or one of the crowd of kids hanging around then."

Wharton twirled his wine glass, staring at the burgundy liquid. "Do you think if you spent some time comparing notes with Roberto you could come up with memories of the night you were poisoned?"

Brett grimaced. "I wish I could remember."

Atlanta turned to Wharton. "Should we go to the hospital after dinner for visiting hours?"

"Did Delia say anything about going there tonight?"

"I heard her on the phone with someone, children I'd think. I believe she's babysitting."

Brett nodded. "It might be a good time to talk to Roberto."

Once they were back in the car, Wharton asked, "Do you remember where the hospital is?"

"If you head north you should run into it," Atlanta informed him.

They found the hospital and a parking place. Atlanta remembered Roberto's room number which they found without difficulty. He was sitting in the chair beside his bed watching television.

"Thanks for coming." His face lit with welcome when they entered the room. "This place gets pretty boring."

"Sounds like you'll be out tomorrow." Wharton found extra chairs in the closet and set them out for the others. He perched on the edge of the bed. "I'm surprised they kept Brett as long as they did."

Roberto's gaze travelled to Brett. "You don't know what happened to you either?"

Brett shook his head. "Sometimes I can almost grab a memory then it escapes."

"What were you doing the day it happened?" Atlanta asked Roberto.

"I don't remember anything special." He focused on the dark window.

"Delia said she'd been gone and came home to find you ill." Atlanta hoped to jog his memory.

"I was working on the computer. A couple guests arrived early and since the rooms were ready, I checked them in."

"Do you remember them?"

Roberto grimaced. "It seems as if several people were around then. Sandy, the cleaning lady, was polishing furniture in the parlor. I checked in an older couple. One of the guys who does the yard came to pick up a check. Some guy wanted to show me books, but I think he left because I was too busy."

"That ring any bells for you, Brett?" Wharton eyed him.

He shook his head.

Wharton turned back to Roberto. "Did you drink anything while these people were there, or eat anything?"

Roberto shrugged. "I could have. I usually carry a coffee cup around with me, but I don't remember specifically."

His memory allowed for some possibilities, Atlanta thought glancing at Brett. He was no help at all. At times she wasn't sure he wanted to be, especially where Ramona or Marcella were concerned. Atlanta wondered if any man had been such a fool over her. Would she have even wanted that? She wrinkled her nose.

Wharton sent a sharp glance her direction. She adjusted her expression. He still had a question in his eyes.

She turned to Brett. "Do you remember anyone coming to the house the night you ended up in the hospital?"

His eyes looked at her, but he was somewhere else. "Obviously someone must have."

"But you don't remember?"

"Not quite." He frowned as if working to recall.

"Were there any power struggles in the band?" Wharton asked.

Roberto and Brett exchanged a glance. Brett responded, "Preston and Annmarie began it. Their leadership was always taken for granted."

"What about after Marcella died?"

"The same," Roberto said. "The discussion then was whether or not to go on."

"So if there were no squabbles or contention for control probably there wasn't anything for someone to want revenge for," Wharton speculated.

Brett sighed. "Except what happened to Marcella and the end of the band."

Wharton raised an eyebrow. "But that wouldn't have had to be someone in the band."

Atlanta recalled her conversation with Sunny and Philippe. "Did you know Marcella before the band?"

Roberto turned to her. "We grew up in the same town, went to the same school. Right after high school we dated some but she was too much like a sister."

"But you were friends?"

Roberto nodded to Atlanta. "Yes, always friends. In fact she came to me sometimes when she had problems." He cast a concerned glance at Brett.

Brett appeared to be in a far off land.

"What sort of problems did she discuss with you?"

"Sometime after the band began she learned her grandfather had died in a mental institution. Her mother had mental problems too. I think Marcella was afraid she'd inherited them."

"Do you think she did?"

Roberto shook his head. "She dealt with some depression. Most musicians do, but she had both feet on the ground and lived in reality."

"So you wouldn't think that would have affected her?"

"Except she was afraid to get married and have children for fear they'd inherit mental illness. I told her the problems her mother had weren't inheritable. They were personality disorders from upbringing and attitude."

"Did she accept that?"

"She was working on it."

"Is that why she wouldn't marry Brett?"

"She did love him and wanted to marry him, but, yes, I think she was afraid to."

Atlanta glanced at Brett who had returned to the conversation wearing a puzzled expression.

Roberto also looked at Brett. "She never told you?"

Brett shook his head, lines between his eyes.

"She probably figured you'd talk her out of her fears and she wasn't ready to give them up."

"Why didn't you tell me?"

"It wasn't my place to tell you her confidences." Roberto met Brett's eyes and for a moment the two were locked in visual confrontation.

Wharton interrupted addressing Roberto. "I understand you're the silent partner in Stadium Music Company."

Roberto's eyebrows made a brief movement as if registering surprise. "That's right."

"Why silent?"

"At the time I invested with Preston others in the group hadn't made much money in music. My father had been a businessman and gave me a better understanding of how money works. I made better investments and had more money available. We were concerned the others would think I was doing something illegal."

"But you weren't?"

Roberto shook his head. "Just making good investments and being conscientious about handling money."

"Is that still a problem?"

Roberto gave Brett a mischievous grin, but said, "It appears they eventually caught on."

"But you've never said anything about your relationship to Stadium Music?"

"Not intentionally. It just never came up."

Wharton turned a raised eyebrow to Atlanta. She shrugged.

"How should we get there?" Wharton asked once they were back in the car.

Atlanta had her phone out. "This shows two alternatives. If you take either Burnside or Stark they go all the way out past I-205. Oak is a block off Stark."

"Okay," Wharton sighed. "How do I get to Burnside or Stark?"

"Turn left and go to 21st."

Wharton had no faith in what they would see, but then he had nothing better to do. Nightfall brought with it a bright cold moon. But it didn't provide enough light to make up for the night vision of which age had robbed him. Street signs were difficult. The GPS decided on Stark and although it curved, changing directions and names intermittently, it eventually got them to the area they sought.

The Damarios' house sat on a street of compact two-story homes, variations on the Cape Cod. Most were brick or had some brick trim, the one at the Damarios' address was no exception. Given it was a week night most were well lighted, some with porch lights on over small stoops. The house they sought was all dark and no cars were in the drive. Even in October it was easy to see the grass needed cutting.

"What do you think?" Wharton asked his companions.

"Maybe someone should ask the neighbors," Brett suggested.

Wharton parked in front of the house and got out. The one to the left was well lit and inviting. He rang the bell and waited. The door was opened by a young man in mid-teens who stared at Wharton blankly.

"Is your mother or father home?"

"Mom," the boy called, taking a step back.

An athletic young woman with fluffy brown hair gave Wharton a circumspect once over.

"I was looking for the family next door."

The woman sighed. "Ever since Estaban died no one has been there. I'm not sure the yard service even comes anymore."

"Did he live alone?"

"From time to time one of his kids would stay. At least I think they were his grown children. I never knew them."

"Do you have any idea how I might find any of them?"

She shook her head.

Wharton tried again. "Did he have any relatives in town?"

"I believe his family lives in Ashland." She raised her eyebrows as if hopeful she had provided enough answers.

Disappointed, Wharton thanked her and returned to the car.

"It doesn't sound like it would do any good to try again tomorrow," Atlanta commented after he explained the conversation.

"What we need to do is find the Damarios in Ashland," Brett suggested.

Recalling Ashland's location on the Oregon map, Wharton scowled. "That's a long way from here."

When they had returned to the inn, Brett announced he was tired and headed to his room.

"You want to sit for a while?" Wharton asked Atlanta beckoning to the parlor.

She shrugged, turning to the right. Several table and floor lamps produced a warm glow. No one was there.

"Maybe if I hunted I could come up with some tea. Are you up for that?"

"Sure."

In the kitchen Wharton found tea supplies had been set out earlier. A kettle rested on a hot plate with tea bags and hot chocolate packages nearby. The Keurig coffee maker also sat handy. He realized as he searched among the teabags he didn't know what kind Atlanta preferred. He chose the Earl Gray, filling cups with bag and hot water. Since he had seen no one else around he took the small milk pitcher, the sugar bowl, a couple spoons, put them on a plate then returned to the parlor.

Atlanta sat on the loveseat near a standing lamp, a pile of magazines in her lap. She beckoned to the coffee table in front of her when Wharton returned.

He set his supplies down noting how the lamp's golden glow lit the red in her hair. "What are you looking at?"

"Decorating magazines, I still have to finish my house."

An idea attacked Wharton. "Did you ever find out why your neighbor reacted every time Pistachio was mentioned?"

"No, but I'm suspicious. I asked Fredee about her since she works in Fredee's doctor's office." Atlanta sighed, setting down her magazine. "At one time she worked for a cleaning company with the contract for the coliseum in Spokane."

"A particular time?" Wharton wondered if Atlanta realized the possible significance.

"Right. When Pistachio performed there is my guess." She met his gaze. "What if she were there when Marcella died?"

Wharton grimaced. "Do you think we could find out?"

Atlanta shook her head. "She's real touchy about anything to do with Spokane, particularly relative to Pistachio."

"Isn't that suspicious?" Wharton stirred milk into his tea. "Maybe we should question her?"

"I've tried." Atlanta huffed, "without any luck."

"Maybe I should give it a try." Her expression made Wharton feel like a Supreme Court Judge banging his gavel. "You think I can't be tactful?"

"You'd be intimidating if you were a purring kitten."

"Thanks." Wharton scowled. "Where does that leave us?"

"Maybe Brett should try."

Wharton considered the idea. "That might work. We could arm his pen."

Laughing, Atlanta pointed to the kitchen where a light had gone on.

Wharton hadn't noticed anyone come down the stairs but realized the back of the house probably had another stairway. Delia entered the dining room carrying a stack of dessert plates. When she notice them she approached, "Good, you found the coffee and tea."

"Yes," Atlanta said, "thank you."

Another idea hit Wharton. "Would you happen to have any pictures of Pistachio?"

Delia drew her brows together. "I believe Roberto has albums and boxes of pictures in the bottom of that bookcase." She pointed to an area between the parlor and dining room where bookcases lined one wall.

"May we look at them?"

"Certainly, help yourself." Delia put her plates in the breakfront then came to where Wharton searched. "He often shows them to people who have questions about the group."

"Do many people ask?"

She smiled. "Only if they spend time talking with Roberto."

Wharton frowned. "No one has come with those questions asking for him?"

Delia shot him an alarmed glance. "I don't think so."

Wharton removed a stack of photo albums and a shoebox he took back to the parlor. Handing Atlanta an album, he said, "These will mean more to you than me."

"Would you like more water for your tea?" Delia came with a silver insulated pot from which she poured hot water into their cups.

For a time they sipped tea and paged through the albums. Wharton realized none of these people meant anything to him. "Brett should look at these."

"Why don't we have him do that in the morning?" Atlanta suggested. "Lots of these are of the group's early days."

"Do they mean anything to you?" He added, "For the present, I mean."

"I've seen versions of most of these before."

What was he hoping? Some picture would light up and blink, "Here I am, the one committing the crimes." Not likely.

CHAPTER TWENTY-SEVEN

Packing for the trip home Atlanta considered the pictures. In them she had seen something familiar, but familiar how?

When they arrived back at her house, Wharton asked to check the security video. She sighed, apprehensive of what might show up to invade their peace of mind.

Wharton charged back to her office as if he owned the place. She needed to let him know whose home it was. Brett followed looking like Atlanta felt.

The three sat in front of the computer. Wharton located the video for the time they were traveling. Nothing showed up on Friday except the newspaper delivery and mail. Saturday afternoon the camera from the side of the house picked up the people Atlanta remembered seeing before they went to Portland.

"Do you know them?" Wharton asked.

"They were looking for Drina, my neighbor." Atlanta studied the video with greater care. "Maybe they're interested in the restoration."

Wharton eyed Atlanta as if she was being naïve. She grimaced and he shrugged. "I suppose that's possible."

They continued to view the video. The camera at the front of the house picked up a woman at the front door who rang the bell. She waited, rang it again, tried looking in the side window then gave up and left.

Wharton reran the video. "Do you recognize her?"

Atlanta leaned close to the monitor for a better view. She didn't even look familiar. Atlanta shook her head.

He turned to Brett who also scrutinized the screen. "Not anyone I know."

On the same Saturday they saw the back of someone walking away from the house.

Wharton replayed the video several times. "Why do you think we see his back and never the front?"

"Maybe he came from a direction not picked up by the camera and only shows up when he is moving away within view of it." Brett suggested.

"What have we failed to cover with the cameras?"

"The north side," Atlanta responded. "No entrances there."

"Are there windows?"

She took a moment to think. "A couple, one large one in the living room that doesn't open and a small high one in the bathroom."

"Maybe he was trying to see if someone was home," Brett suggested.

"Why wouldn't he look in one of the accessible windows where he could actually see something?"

"Has he figured out the cameras?" Brett put in.

Wharton sighed. "I hope not."

"What would we do if that's the case?" Would all their effort be in vain?

"I'll check with Tsukimoto and see what he suggests."

Atlanta frowned. She didn't like the sound of that. She would have been happier had they actually seen someone, much as she didn't want that either.

"Okay." Wharton turned to her. "I think you need to talk to your friend and your neighbor. See what you can find out."

They continued viewing the Saturday video.

"Ramona," Atlanta identified the woman on the front step ringing the bell. "Well, she hasn't given up on you." She turned to Brett. "Did you tell her where I live?"

He cocked his head. "I might have." He shot Atlanta an accusatory glance. "I didn't know it was a secret."

"Everything is a secret from her." Atlanta snapped. So much for thinking they had gotten rid of her. She turned to Wharton. "What are you going to do?"

"Check on the surveillance equipment and talk to Lieutenant Sarkis."

When Wharton left Atlanta turned to Brett. "He didn't give you an assignment."

Brett grinned. "Do you have something you want me to do?"

"Stay out of trouble," she grumped then added, "and try to remember what happened to you. And," she took a deep breath, "avoid Ramona."

"You know I've been thinking about the person we only saw the back of. He's familiar for some reason."

Atlanta regarded Brett a moment. "What do you think would jog your memory?"

He shrugged. "Lunch?"

She laughed. "How about Barnes and Noble Café? I might run into my friends."

"Sure, I'm game.

Atlanta took her luggage upstairs where her bedroom looked put together again. No more glass lying around, the window and wall had been repaired. A new closet occupied the non-windowed wall. The sheetrock and taping were complete. All that remained was the actual decorating.

Lunchtime at Barnes and Noble had produced a crowd. The moment they stepped into the café they were assaulted by Fredee.

"There's that lovely man." She put her hand over her heart. "Where have you been? I've been pining away for you."

Brett laughed.

Sherry and Georgiana were there too, making room for Brett and Atlanta at the table.

"We've missed you," Georgiana beckoned Atlanta to a chair.

Sherry sat down beside her. "We wondered where you'd gone."

"Brett was sick then we made a trip to Portland." Atlanta realized she had opened door to more questions.

While Brett took the seat next to Fredee she asked him, "What were you doing in Portland?"

"We went to see an old friend."

"Just a get away," Atlanta added.

"Someone from the band?" Sherry eyed Brett.

"As it happened."

"What about that friend of yours?" Fredee turned to Atlanta.

She considered ignoring her but figured she would never get away with it anyway. "What about him?"

"Did he go too?"

"Shees you're nosy."

Fredee grinned maliciously. "No nosy, no find out anything."

"What have you guys been doing?" Atlanta tried redirecting the conversation. "Have you talked to my neighbor recently?"

Fredee cocked her head and considered. "Actually she was questioning me about you."

"What sort of questions?"

"If you'd been at the performance in Spokane where the singer died."

"What did you tell her?"

Fredee huffed, "I don't know if you were there or not."

Atlanta hadn't realized her friends might not know she attended that performance. "Did she say why she wanted to know?"

"Not really." Fredee grimaced. "I got the impression she wanted to know something in particular, but she didn't tell me what it was."

"Was she there that night?"

Fredee bobbed her head slowly. "You know I think she was. Maybe she was cleaning that night."

Atlanta raised her eyebrows. That would be interesting.

"She also wanted to know if you knew the woman who died." Fredee stared pointedly at Atlanta. "Did you?"

"I did." Atlanta nodded. "Sort of."

"What does that mean?" Sherry demanded.

Atlanta turned to her. "I was fifteen. How much do you know someone in a band with your cousin who is in her twenties when you're fifteen?"

Fredee grinned maliciously. "Depends how nosy you are."

Atlanta rolled her eyes.

"She also wanted to know if what's-her-name," Fredee waved her hand as if she could grab the name out of the air.

"Marcella?" Sherry put in.

"Right, Marcella, dated anyone in the band."

"She didn't know?" Georgiana looked puzzled.

"But it was in all the newspapers." Sherry added.

"Maybe she didn't read them."

Fredee had a point. It was time Atlanta visited her neighbor.

From Atlanta's house Wharton returned to his own, unloaded his luggage and got something to eat. While considering his next step he wondered if he should worry about the side of Atlanta's house not covered by surveillance cameras? A chat with Luke might help. Also figuring a session with Lieutenant Sarkis was in order he made that his first stop.

He found Davy squinting at his computer over the top of his spectacles with a frustrated expression. Wharton wondered if the lieutenant had vision problems, usually Wharton's difficulty. However, the lieutenant was too young to suffer from aging eyes.

He turned a frown on Wharton as he dropped into the visitor's chair. "What's on your mind?"

"Tranylcypromine Sulfate."

The lieutenant's eyebrows drew together. "Just a minute." He peered at his monitor with concentration then made a few key strokes. "Okay. What do you want to know?"

"Who takes it?"

"You know I can't tell you that."

"What can you do?"

The lieutenant sighed. "If you have a purchase point I may be able to find out who they sell to."

Wharton frowned. Who could he use to test? RJ would be his best bet. But he would need to find out where he purchased his drugs. "If I could eliminate R J Hamilton from having any contact with the drug then you should eliminate him from your suspect list."

Lieutenant Sarkis gave Wharton an incredulous double-take. "How do you figure?"

"Everyone who died had some contact with tranylcypromine sulfate. If RJ doesn't have access to it then he's not involved."

The lieutenant leaned back in his chair, studying Wharton. "That's a leap to conclusion."

"There is only one person associated with Pistachio whose death we can't connect to an MAOI with their medication, John Hanson. He died in a home for Alzheimer patients and was buried without an autopsy."

Lieutenant Sarkis put his feet on the floor and leaned toward Wharton. "If you can find where the drugs are purchased, let me know. We'll see where it gets us."

"What if the person is from another state?"

"What state?"

Wharton shrugged. "Oregon?"

"Get me the source and I'll see what I can do."

Wharton headed to Luke's business address while considering where they had gotten in their pursuit of RJ's innocence, not far. The only thing in RJ's favor were the victims that could not be laid at his feet, or could they? All of a sudden Wharton realized although he knew RJ was innocent he didn't know if RJ was safe from the law's persecution.

"Ah, Mr. Attorney-at-large," Luke greeted Wharton with a half bow. "How is surveillance going?"

"When we were gone over the weekend someone showed up on the video, but only from the back. Did we fail to cover something?"

Luke pressed his lips together. "Where do you think person was?"

"The north side where there are only a couple windows."

"No doors?"

Wharton nodded.

"You believe this is someone in your investigation?"

"I want to know whoever approaches Atlanta's house," Wharton huffed.

"I stop by and see video and house." Luke bobbed his head. "You might need camera that pans and tilts." He made hand motions to demonstrate.

"When can you do that?"

"Later . . . this afternoon?"

"Give me a call when you're headed there." Wharton turned to the door then back. "I'll warn Atlanta."

"Gotcha chief."

Atlanta wouldn't be happy about this either. What could he do to repair his relationship with her? Obviously he had blown it somewhere. It never occurred to him she would be devastated by what he figured was the most sensible approach to their relationship. Why did what made sense to a man never make sense to a woman?

"You know, God, it's hard not thinking you blew it when you made them." Wharton knew appealing to his Maker wasn't going to get him anywhere. God would never concede He made a mistake and Wharton knew better than to think He did. So, if the mistake was Wharton's then what was it? And what was he supposed to do about it?

Intellectually Wharton understood what Atlanta was saying but he couldn't relate to it emotionally. How could he be convinced she loved him, when in fact she had detached? And how could she believe he didn't love her when he thought about her continually? Obviously he assumed she loved him, because he loved her and since he didn't communicate she didn't know. What an idiot! Had he blown it for good?

Should he consult Kitty? Maybe it was time to invite himself over for dinner again. He grabbed his cell phone.

"Where have you been?" she asked.

"Portland."

She fired another question. "What were you doing there?"

"Looking for information." He could use Kitty's outlook on some other things, too. "Roberto Lopez lives there."

"Did you see him?"

"Invite me over for dinner and I'll tell you about it."

"Really, Wharton, what a mooch you are."

"And sister, dear, what an inquisitor you are."

"Five thirty sharp." She hung up.

CHAPTER TWENTY-EIGHT

As soon as Atlanta and Brett arrived home her cell phone announced a call from Wharton. Reluctantly she answered it.

"I'm bringing Luke Tsukimoto over to look at your surveillance set-up."

She sighed. "Okay."

Shortly he arrived with a cheerful Japanese man he introduced as master of surveillance. "We're going outside."

Brett, who was in the living room reading, joined them.

After some time outdoors the three returned, proceeding directly to Atlanta's study. She felt like a stranger in her own home. Wharton came and went as if he owned the place, paying her little regard. Did she resent his peremptory invasion or the fact he paid her no attention? She wanted to believe the former but feared it was the second. That was dangerous. Now was a good time to visit Drina.

Atlanta grabbed her rain jacket as insurance against the heavy overcast. It was good to get out. She felt stifled in a house full of men intent on their mission. Too much exposure to Wharton was affecting her equilibrium. She could live with his taking over the investigation, even Brett's safety, but he was on the verge of taking over her life. She had no intention of falling back into a painful romantic longing for the close relationship that constituted intimate friendship. In the blindness of being in love she had seen their friendship as more than it was. Realizing it never meant to him what it did to her had been a rude awakening. She didn't have to be shot twice to realize she had been hit. She needed to maintain her distance and keep her head on straight.

She rang Drina's bell then waited. It took so long Atlanta was on the point of returning home when the door opened.

197

Drina appeared distraught.

Figuring there might be a better time to ask her questions, Atlanta backed up a step. "I'm sorry. I didn't mean to disturb you."

"Come in." Drina opened the door wider.

"Are you sure? I can come another time."

"I'll put tea on."

Atlanta followed, chastising herself for not calling first. However, her neighbor was recovering, chatting about the weather as she placed cups, teabags, milk and sugar on the table in her kitchen. She motioned Atlanta to a chair and poured boiling water into the cups.

"Is there something I can do for you? I noticed you had company." Drina took the other chair.

"My friend and my cousin are working on the computer," Atlanta replied. "I feel like excess baggage."

Drina gave her a wan smile.

"I saw someone the other night I believe was looking for you."

Her companion frowned then nodded. "You mean Pansy?"

"I saw a man, a woman and a child on the sidewalk looking at the houses."

"She's the daughter of a friend I've known for years." Drina stared into her teacup, turning it around in her hands.

"You knew her parents?" Atlanta tried another assumption.

"Sort of." Drina shrugged.

Atlanta struggled for something to say. Consequently she said nothing, sipping her tea.

"I helped her mother out once."

Atlanta nodded, still groping for words. "My girlfriend Fredee said you were asking whether I knew someone."

A flash of alarm appeared in Drina's eyes, but she quickly recovered. "You said your cousin was part of a band."

"Pistachio." Atlanta forced a smile. "They were popular in the sixties."

Drina sighed. "What happened to them?"

"One of the lead singers died."

Atlanta watched but Drina registered no expression. "That's too bad," she said as if comforting a child. "Did you know the one who died?"

"Slightly."

Drina nodded. "Were you there when she died?"

"Yes, actually. Not with her, but at the performance."

"That's too bad," Drina murmured again.

Atlanta had answered Drina's questions but failed to even ask her own. Her cell phone played its tune and a glance at its face told her it was Wharton. She almost ignored it, but answered instead.

"Where are you?" he demanded.

Atlanta was offended. It wasn't like she was married to the man. "At the neighbors."

"I need your approval on some things."

She sighed. "Okay, I'll be there in a few minutes."

Atlanta explained to Drina while finishing her tea then returned to the house.

Wharton met her at the door, "We need to put up another camera on the north side of the house. Then we're going to change one of the others to pan and tilt. I think we may have missed some things."

Atlanta agreed. What else could she do? However, she was losing faith in the effectiveness of surveillance.

After finishing at Atlanta's house Wharton thanked Luke as they walked together toward the cars.

"Hope it makes the difference." Luke grinned. "Wouldn't want something to happen to your lady."

From there Wharton headed to Kitty and Aaron's house overlooking the sound. The water reflected the sky's dull gray. If he was inclined to depression his lack of success with his commission for RJ, his failed relationship with Atlanta, and the uncompromising gray would have sent him into the doldrums. He sighed. Somewhere was an answer and he would find it.

Kitty answered the door with her usual welcoming hospitality. Wharton noted the look of inquiry as she beckoned him to the family room after querying what he wanted to drink. He realized she had tuned into his dispirited mood.

"Aaron is showing a house," she explained handing him a glass of wine. She sat in the chair next to his. "He should be home in a little while."

They sipped wine in silence for a few minutes.

"So what's got your goat?" she asked with a gentleness belying her brash question.

"Failure . . . to put it bluntly."

She raised her eyebrows.

"We missed a spot at Atlanta's when we put in surveillance cameras. Someone was looking around the house we can't identify."

"I have the feeling your poor spirits are more than a camera that didn't work?"

Kitty's ability to see right through him frustrated Wharton. "Must be the weather."

"Give me a break, Wharton, when did the weather ever affect you?"

"I'm getting old," he sidestepped again.

Kitty rolled her eyes. "I don't believe you're admitting that. Must be a stall tactic."

What was the use? No matter what he said she would see through it. He needed to cough up his questions or forget the whole idea. "I just plain don't understand women."

Kitty waited without comment, indicating she expected him to go on.

"What does love mean to a woman?"

"That's a broad question."

This time he waited for her to continue.

"You mean what makes a woman feel loved?"

He nodded. "And don't give me the lecture on ways people feel loved. I've heard that spiel before."

"You don't believe it?" Kitty raised a skeptical eyebrow.

"I'm sure the theory has value. What I want to know is either more specific or more general."

Kitty harrumphed. "In male-female relationships a woman wants to feel she's the most important person in her man's life; that his life wouldn't be the same without her. She wants to know he cherishes the time he spends with her, isn't happy to be apart and thinks about her when they are necessarily apart."

"All the time?" Wharton's voice squeaked.

Kitty shot him a pitying glance. "That's how she feels. But, women also know intellectually that's impossible and in the end they really wouldn't want that. They need the illusion of it more than the reality."

"What does that mean?" he barked.

"What's this all about?"

He figured she would get around to that, which is why he was reluctant in the first place. He eyed his sister trying to determine the extent to which he could trust her. Much as she loved listening to gossip, she usually didn't spread it. His greatest concern was her use of the information to harass him. Heck, she harassed him anyway, might as well give her a good cause.

"You know I worked with Atlanta some time ago on a case?"

She nodded.

"What I didn't tell you was that I fell in love with her."

Kitty stared at Wharton, at a complete loss for words, making it almost worth telling her and getting harassed.

"It was before Linda was diagnosed with cancer." Wharton sighed. "We were both married and determined to honor our marriage vows."

"She was in love with you, too?" Kitty sounded like that was more than she could believe.

"That's what she said." Wharton also had his doubts.

Kitty frowned. "You don't think she was?"

"I believed she was until I saw her again recently. We've lost our spouses and are free to see each other. But she doesn't seem interested. Where did I go wrong?"

"Have you asked her?"

"She said she still cares for me but doesn't care anymore if I love her." He raised his hands in frustration. "What does that mean?"

Kitty stared at him with a faraway look in her eyes. He sipped his wine and waited.

"I think she doesn't trust you anymore." She cocked her head, eying him speculatively. "Somehow you've hurt or disappointed her."

"She said she expected we would go on being friends."

"And you went to work and ignored her."

Wharton shrugged. "What would you have done?"

"Give her a call once in a while to see how she was doing. Send her a birthday card. Harmless little things to let her know you still thought about her."

Scowling, Wharton crossed his arms over his chest. "Well, I didn't. Now what do I do?"

"Start over. Go back to the beginning. Win her love and trust again. She doesn't want to be hurt anymore. Obviously when you left her with no more communication she felt you no longer cared for her and she adjusted to that. She might believe you never cared and were just playing games with her."

With a deep sigh, Wharton leaned back in his chair and gazed at the ceiling.

Watching him Kitty added, "If you think it's worth it."

Did it make any difference if it was worth it? He had already realized he couldn't just get rid of the feelings he had for Atlanta. To do that would be painful. Giving up hope was always painful. Suddenly he saw the pain Atlanta had experienced. She had given up hope.

CHAPTER TWENTY-NINE

fter his trip to Kitty's Wharton made up his mind to do as she suggested. He would begin officially courting Atlanta. What did he have to lose? With this in mind he called her.

"How about dinner and a movie?" he asked the moment she answered.

She paused before giving him a hesitant, "Okay. When?"

"Tonight?" Why wait? Might as well set the plan in action. "I'll pick you up at 6:30."

"What about Brett?"

Wharton grimaced. He had forgotten. It was heck babysitting an old man. "Let's drop him off with Kitty and Aaron. I think they plan to be home tonight." He considered ordering flowers, but decided if he overdid it she might get suspicious, not that she wasn't already.

As he was considering his to-do list RJ called. "Would you have time for coffee?"

Sensing RJ's distress, Wharton asked, "Is something wrong?"

"Not necessarily. Lieutenant Sarkis called me this morning with a few questions."

"Really." Had something happened? "Sure. Starbucks or the bookstore?"

"The bookstore. I have to pick up a book anyway."

They set the time. Wharton arrived just as RJ parked his Camry. They chose their usual table and Wharton went for coffee.

"So what did he want to know" Wharton zoomed to the point as he handed RJ a cup and took a chair.

RJ sighed. "His questions seemed more like research than interrogation."

"That's a good sign. Maybe he's beginning to believe us." Wharton explained his trip to Portland and subsequent visit to the lieutenant. "Where do you get your prescriptions filled?"

"Safeway."

"Nowhere else?"

RJ shook his head. "What's this MAOI?" RJ fixed his gaze on Wharton."He asked me about that?"

"It's that antidepressant I told you about." Wharton took a deep breath. "It seems every one of the people who have died or gotten ill have had some trace of that in their blood tests."

"Even Annmarie?" RJ looked skeptical.

Wharton nodded. "According to the autopsy."

RJ frowned. "She didn't take any antidepressant."

"Except for Brett neither did any of the others." Wharton crossed his arms over his chest.

"Lieutenant Sarkis asked me a lot of questions about medications, the ones I take and the ones Annmarie took." RJ shot Wharton a crooked grin. "You must have sold him on your idea."

"It's about time I sold him on something," Wharton huffed. "You figure he's moving away from thinking you're guilty of Annmarie's death?"

"It seemed that way."

Wharton noticed Sunny and Philippe at the coffee counter. "Something just occurred to me. They're the only ones left in Pistachio who haven't had an attack."

"You're not suspicious of them?"

Wharton grimaced shaking his head. "I think it's more likely they haven't been hit YET. Let's see if there's a reason they wouldn't be when everyone else has been?" Wharton waved to the pair as they glanced around for seating. Sunny pointed to a larger table with four chairs and Wharton nodded. He and RJ picked up their cups and joined the other two.

"Atlanta and I just got back from a trip to Portland to see Roberto," Wharton announced as soon as they were seated.

"How was he?" Sunny asked.

"In the hospital."

Sunny and Philippe stared at Wharton skeptically.

"Apparently he had a similar incident to what other members of Pistachio experienced."

Philippe removed his hat and set it in his lap. "What happened?"

Wharton explained how they found Roberto. "He didn't seem to know what happened either." Wharton leaned forward. "Have either of you had any close calls, an unexplained illness?"

The two exchanged a glance then turned to Wharton shaking their heads.

"Have you had any strangers around your house?" RJ asked. "Anyone selling something door to door?"

Sunny shrugged. "You'd have to ask my wife. She handles that stuff."

"Why don't you ask her?"

Sunny bobbed his head then turned to Philippe who motioned to his ears. "If someone came I might not have heard the bell."

"Do either of you take antidepressants?"

"Never had a problem with depression," Sunny said.

"Not that bad anyway," Philippe added.

"Was there anyone associated with Pistachio you could say had that kind of problem?" Wharton kept pushing.

"Brett." Philippe offered.

"Besides him."

Sunny rocked his shoulders. "That problem could have surfaced much later than when we were together."

───────────── ✦✦✦✦✦✦ ─────────────

Atlanta had just finished tidying the kitchen when Wharton called. Although surprised by his request, since she had a few things to discuss with him she accepted. After doing so she realized that would leave Brett alone. He would have been perfectly happy but she didn't want him alone and she didn't want him to get in touch with Ramona. She felt fortunate they had avoided his ex-wife since they returned from Portland. She wasn't up for pushing their luck.

She found him in the living room seated on the wing back chair in a patch of sunlight shining through the leaded glass windows. "Wharton invited me out to dinner and a movie."

Brett smiled. "Sure. I enjoy Aaron and Kitty," he responded to her suggestion.

"I've been thinking about Marcella." She sat down on the sofa opposite him. "Yesterday while you guys were working on the cameras I went to see Drina. Fredee said she'd been asking about me and connecting it with the night Marcella died. I have this feeling she was there that night. She's touchy about too many things connected for it to be mere curiosity."

"Do you think she knew Marcella?"

Atlanta grimaced. "I doubt it, at least not before that night. She might have met her then if she was cleaning there."

"You still think all these deaths are connected to Marcella?" Brett sounded skeptical.

"I think they're connected to Pistachio and Marcella is connected to Pistachio."

Brett stared thoughtfully over Atlanta's shoulder. "I guess it's still important to find out why she died."

"But how?" Atlanta lifted her hands. "Who would know?"

"The doctor?"

"Was he young, old . . . ?"

"No one is a doctor terribly young. It takes too long to become one. And when you're young everyone looks old."

"Maybe he's still alive?"

"Forty-five and say thirty or forty." Brett cocked his head. "He could be in his seventies or eighties."

"Do you remember the name?"

He shook his head. "I might be able to look at the death certificate online."

"Really?" Atlanta was impressed. "I hadn't thought about that."

While Brett went to Atlanta's computer she sat at the dining room table and called the contractor, giving him her final instructions. She wondered what Wharton was up to with his invitation. Although it would be in her best interest to avoid him, she did appreciate company. Dinner and a movie would be fun. Plus she could run some of her questions past him.

Brett entered the dining room with a pleased look on his face. "I located the doctor's name. Donald Jalouski."

"Great." Atlanta figured that was progress. "Maybe we can find him?"

"There were a couple Jalouskis in the phone book, no Donald."

"His kids?"

Brett shrugged. "I'll keep working on it."

"I need to get ready. Wharton said he'd pick us up early enough to drop you at Kitty's on our way to dinner."

"In time for me to have dinner with them?" Brett lifted his eyebrows.

"Yes." Atlanta laughed. "I won't starve you."

At five o'clock Wharton arrived and they left for the Kentish home. Once Brett was safely deposited and they were back in Wharton's car he said, "I thought we'd go to a restaurant on the hill overlooking Tacoma."

Atlanta wasn't certain to which hill he referred until they arrived. "I've never been here before."

"One point for my side."

She shot him an inquisitive look.

"We can begin a memory."

If she wasn't mistaken he was actually blushing.

They were seated in a booth near windows with the city view. "I talked to Sunny and Philippe this afternoon. I thought they might know someone else in the group who took antidepressants."

"Did they?"

Wharton shook his head. "Also, they didn't seem to have had any strangers around or attempts made on their lives."

"Is that significant?" Apprehension attacked her. Were they due or were they passed over for some reason?

Wharton tempered his tone. "It's just curious that's all."

As he turned to his menu Atlanta studied his expression wondering if he thought Sunny and Philippe could be eliminating members of Pistachio.

"No, I don't suspect them," he answered her unspoken question.

Atlanta selected a seafood entree and accepted Wharton's choice of wine.

After placing their orders Wharton went on, "I talked to Lieutenant Sarkis about people who use that antidepressant. If I can give him a where they might buy it he thinks he could get names."

"How will you find that out?"

Wharton shook his head.

Their wine arrived. He lifted his glass, "To the loveliest lady in the restaurant."

Atlanta laughed fighting the blush she felt rising. "Brett gets his prescriptions in the UK."

"That's the trouble. It's not the people we know we'd want to find out about." Wharton took a pen from his pocket. "You got any paper?"

Atlanta removed a small notebook from her purse and handed it to him. "Who then?"

He tore off a sheet and handed it back. "It may not be the one committing the crimes who has the antidepressant, but someone from whom that person can get hold of it like Lucille Maginnis, Delia Lopez, RJ . . ."

"Me."

Scowling, Wharton ignored her. "What about John Hanson?"

She sighed. "Perhaps someone at the home where he stayed."

"Maybe I should give the home a call and see what they say about that drug."

The waiter arrived with their entrees, grilled salmon with apricot chutney and risotto.

"I have the feeling we're missing someone," Atlanta said perusing Wharton's list, "but I can't think who."

He studied her with concern. "Are you still worried about Brett?"

"I'm afraid we'll lose our edge of fear and get sloppy, then something else will happen."

"In the end you're going to have to leave it in God's hands."

Atlanta nodded. She knew that. "What movie are we going to see?"

"I thought we'd check out the latest romantic comedy."

She eyed him suspiciously wondering what he had up his sleeve. He only smiled.

CHAPTER THIRTY

Wharton felt like a school boy again, and not such a smart one either. Here he was trying to figure out what to do to win the girl. You'd think by this time he'd have that down to an art. Well, he didn't.

As usual she was lovely, like an autumn day full of color and motion. He had to concentrate not to lose the thread of conversation.

"Brett looked up the doctor who signed Marcella's death certificate." Undoubtedly he had a stupid look on his face for she went on, "You know, Marcella."

He nodded, his mind drifting. "Right, a long time ago." A vague feeling he had seen something or someone he should have recognized attacked him.

Atlanta frowned at him. "I still think something to do with her death may be the cause of all the problems." She sipped her wine eying him over the rim of her glass, "You act like you're not all here tonight,"

"I'm bedazzled by your loveliness." He placed his hand on his chest.

She stared as if she could see inside his head. "You sound like you've had too much to drink." She glanced at his wine glass. It was still half full. "Where have you been today?"

"Just what I told you."

She eyed him suspiciously. "You sound like it couldn't possibly have anything to do with Marcella."

His concentration kicked in again. "Did Brett find the doctor?"

"His name." She grimaced. "But he still has to find out if he's alive."

"What will you do if he is?"

"Try to see him of course." Atlanta rolled her eyes.

"I suppose it's worth a shot." He grimaced. "But what happened to her is a very long time ago."

"It might depend on what happened to her." Atlanta had a determined look in her eye.

Wharton raised an eyebrow. What was she driving at?

"My neighbor may have been there when Marcella died."

"You think she knows how she died?"

"I wouldn't go that far." Atlanta took a deep breath. "But she may know something helpful."

"Why don't you ask her?"

"Every time I get close something happens and I miss my chance." Atlanta shot him a reproachful glance. "Like you calling me back to the house yesterday."

Wharton made a face. "Sorry about that."

Atlanta gave him a fierce look. "You've become very bossy and presumptive."

He was taken back.

"You march through my house like you own the place."

That sucked the words right out of him. He stared at her trying to think of what he had done that was so offensive. Everything he did was for her and her cousin. The temptation to sulk attacked him. People were so unappreciative. However, that would get him nowhere. "What did I do?"

Atlanta gazed out the window as if reluctant to express her thought.

"Go ahead, hit me between the eyes."

"Yesterday you and Luke came and went, acting like I didn't even exist, much less own the house. You order me around like a teenager."

"You can't order teenagers around, they object."

"Exactly." Atlanta glared at him then laughed. "You have no clue."

"Now I'm the one who feels like an idiot."

"Good, it might temper some of your arrogant bossiness."

Wharton signaled the waitress. "How about dessert?"

"I'll share. I can't do a whole one."

"Blueberry cobbler?"

Atlanta smiled. "Absolutely."

When the waitress had served a blueberry cobbler with ice cream topping and two spoons, Wharton asked, "What are you doing to find the doctor?"

"Brett's calling people in the phone book with the same last name. It's not a common one."

"You might find something by just looking it up on the Internet." Wharton took a healthy scoop of cobbler and ice cream. "We need to look at those surveillance videos when we go home."

Atlanta groaned. "You're hopeless."

His expression questioned her. "I did it again?"

She nodded, licking the ice cream off her spoon.

Wharton raised his eyebrows. "You don't think we should look at them?"

"No." She sighed. "We should. But you shouldn't act like you live at my house and whatever you say goes."

"Marry me, then it would be my house too, save a lot of arguments."

"That's a crummy way to obtain property."

They both laughed.

After dinner and a delightful romantic comedy they headed to the Kentish home where they found Aaron sitting in the family room, but no Kitty and no Brett.

"They're in the study with the computer," Aaron informed them.

Wharton sat down beside Aaron while Atlanta headed in the direction of the study.

Approaching the room she heard excited voices. Although the door was open she knocked to warn of her presence.

"We found the doctor," Brett said when she entered.

Kitty swung her rolling chair around. "He's living in Seattle with his daughter and her family."

"He's in his eighties."

That was good news in spite of Wharton's misgivings. "Did you get an address or phone number?"

"An address. We can probably find a phone number, too."

"We should probably talk to him in person."

As Brett nodded Atlanta noted his apprehensive expression, wondering at the cause.

While Brett exited the internet Kitty and Atlanta discussed the movie she and Wharton had seen. After bidding farewell to the Kentishs Wharton returned Brett and Atlanta to her house.

"May I come in and check your surveillance video?" Wharton asked with painstaking politeness.

"Yes," Atlanta replied with a laugh. "Thank you for asking."

Brett gave the two of them a quizzical glance.

"Sit down and I'll teach you to check these videos," Wharton directed.

At his bidding Atlanta sat at her computer and activated it. Brett retrieved the video from the recorder and handed it to Wharton, who demonstrated how to call it up. Once it was running the guys each took a chair at Atlanta's side and focused on the monitor.

No activity appeared from the night before. During the day the newspaper was delivered, the neighbor's lawn service dropped off a brochure. Brett and Atlanta left and returned. Late in the afternoon a figure approached from the back of the house along the north side. The camera picked him up from the rear, staring at the house as if approving the reconstruction progress. Then briefly caught his face before he turned his back again.

"What do you think?" Wharton observed Atlanta's expression.

"I've seen that face before," she said, "but I don't know where."

"What about you?" Wharton addressed Brett.

He shook his head.

Wharton stared at the figure as if committing it to memory.

"Does he look familiar to you?" Atlanta asked him.

"I don't think so. But I've seen a lot of people lately in videos, in person, in pictures.

Atlanta stared at the Chagall print on the wall, considering faces in her recollection, especially in regard to Brett. No one came to mind, no matter how hard she worked to recall. From experience she knew it was better to let her subconscious work on the project while she did something else.

They continued with the video. According to the registered time approximately an hour after the man showed up a woman came to the front door and rang the bell. After waiting she rang the bell again then receiving no response left.

"How about her?" Wharton asked Atlanta.

She shook her head. The woman didn't even look familiar.

Wharton turned to Brett who did the same. After staring some moments at the monitor he put his palms on the desk and rose. "Time for me to get home."

Atlanta walked him to the door.

"I'll call you in the morning."

She found Brett in the living room when Wharton had gone and sat down across from him. "You looked worried about visiting the doctor."

"I overheard a conversation once between Annmarie and Preston regarding Marcella." Pain occupied Brett's expression. "Annmarie wondered if Marcella had a long term illness like cancer. They thought she had gained weight, although with cancer I think you lose not gain."

Atlanta nodded.

After another minute, he said, "They also suggested she may be pregnant."

Atlanta felt a prick of concern. "But you've said she wasn't."

"After that conversation I questioned her. She actually became angry with me for asking, said there was nothing wrong. She wasn't ill and she wasn't pregnant."

"And you believed her?"

"I didn't have any choice."

"Now you have second thoughts?" Atlanta noted Brett's wretched expression.

"I fear something was wrong I could have done something about and didn't take serious." His agonized gaze met Atlanta's. "It wasn't murder so something must have been wrong."

Her mind continued to the conclusion. "And you're afraid the doctor will tell us and . . ."

"I'll have to live with guilt for what I didn't do."

"You know it's not your responsibility. If she wouldn't tell you she needs to be responsible for her own illness and its consequences."

Brett grimaced. "But what if we could have prevented her death?"

Atlanta gazed at him with growing sympathy. "Do you think you're better off not knowing?"

He sighed. "No. It's haunted me all my life. Maybe if I knew the truth I could put it behind me."

"Shall we try to see that doctor tomorrow?"

"I think so."

CHAPTER THIRTY-ONE

When Wharton's radio alarm sounded a finale chord in the stillness of his bedroom, a moment of silence ensued. His eyes opened, looking for the source while the announcer informed him of the chord's origin. Although preferring to ignore the encouragement to rise, he figured it wouldn't be strategic.

Once he had showered, dressed and consumed a cup of coffee the day held greater promise. He had a list of locations to run by Lieutenant Sarkis, but first he needed to order flowers for Atlanta. Once that task was completed the sun, an unpredictable visitor, nearly blinded him as he headed into the port and across the waterways to Sarkis' office.

The lieutenant was staring at his doorway when Wharton entered. "What brings you here today?"

"I have some places to check." Wharton plunked himself down in the extra chair.

Lieutenant Sarkis grabbed a notepad. "Okay, shoot."

Wharton read off the list he and Atlanta had made.

The lieutenant bobbed his head. "I'll see what I can find out."

"You'll let me know?"

"If I find anything."

He left the detective's office in a funk. A thin layer of clouds had spread across the sky blocking the sun's rays and making him feel as if that was happening to his quest for Annmarie's assailant.

Suddenly he recalled the conversation with Atlanta. He still needed to check with the people at that home where John Hanson died. He looked it up on the internet and found a phone number.

"This is Nancy Johnson," the lady answered in a cheerful voice.

Wharton introduced himself, explaining their acquaintanceship and conversation.

"Oh, yes, I remember you, with all the questions about John's death and medication."

"I'm still on that tack. There's been a rash of deaths among his fellow band members in addition to some unsuccessful attempts."

"You're kidding." She sounded astonished. "I'm sorry. Obviously you're not. What can I do for you?"

"Every case in which we could determine the cause of death an MAOI antidepressant showed up. Have you ever come across that among your patients? Do any of them take that medication?"

"We don't have much call here for antidepressants. Most are dangerous with the other medications our patients take."

"Would it be possible for medical people to obtain antidepressants easier than other people?"

"Hmmm." She hesitated. "Some probably, especially if the person works with patients who use it. However, antidepressants are usually more specific to the individual taking them, particularly the radical ones. They wouldn't generally be available even to medical people. We'd be more apt to have the antidote."

Wharton sought for appropriate words to ask his question without raising an alarm or offending. "I got the feeling you weren't particularly satisfied with the cause of John Hanson's death."

"I'm not," she confessed, "but I don't know what I can do about it." She sighed. "Ah, just a minute. I do remember something. When they were cleaning his room they found a package addressed to Sunny Damasi."

"Really? What did they do with it?" Maybe there would be a break yet.

"We mailed it to him, yesterday, or the day before."

"So he may not have gotten it yet," Wharton mumbled to himself. "I appreciate your help," Wharton told her before ending the call. Maybe John Hanson would furnish them a clue yet. He needed to give Sunny a heads up.

As he considered his cell phone jingled at him. "Wharton Forde."

"Why the heck are you doing a credit check on me? Of all the hair-brained, irresponsible, idiotic, crackpot things to do. Don't you know what kind of problem that causes a person? Every time I apply for credit I have to explain why a lawyer wants my credit history." The female voice took a breath.

Wharton charged in. "And who are you?"

"Sylvia Nelson. I don't do or want to do any business in Washington State so what's the deal anyway. I couldn't find where I'd even done anything with you on the internet. You leave me alone and everything about me." She hung up.

"Whoa," Wharton mumbled, Preston Erving's daughter having a tantrum. During her tirade he recalled the credit check. He had forgotten her in the recent falderal. If he remembered correctly her credit was okay, but her debt load enormous, especially given she should have had an influx of money at Preston's death, which could have cleared her obligations.

Something in the back of his mind plagued him. Suddenly it flashed to the forefront. The woman in the video the day before, he knew who she was. He even knew her, Sylvia Erving Nelson. All the time they had discussed Sylvia his only recollection was of his annoying little girl cousin. Mentally he had locked her into that time frame, failing to recall her as an adult. She had been like a terrier always snipping at people. Although he could handle confrontation without a qualm, her the-world-is-unfair attitude made his hair shoot up in spikes.

Wharton, less convinced than Atlanta and Brett the source of problems lie in the distant past, figured someone in the present had something to gain. Here was a possibility.

After a moment's thought he looked up the number of Stadium Music. Lucille answered in her hesitant stutter.

Wharton identified himself. "I just had a nasty call from Sylvia Nelson." He could hear Lucille's intake of breath. "Have you heard from her recently?"

"S-s-she c-c-called a week or s-s-o ago."

"What did she want?" Wharton could guess.

"S-s-some question about a c-c-credit report."

"Ahhh. Did she tell you why it was such a problem?"

"It had to do with her j-j-job. Sh-sh-she has to have security c-clearances p-p- often and they ch-ch-check her credit."

"Okay. I probably got you in trouble. We did a check on her." Wharton paused then asked, "How are you?"

"F-f-fine." He could hear the smile in her voice. "How are you c-c-coming on the investigation?"

He sighed. "We're still at it."

"Thank you for t-taking an interest."

"You never believed the accident theory?"

"N-N-never, but I d-d-didn't know who to t-trust."

"By the way, do you know where Preston got his medications?"

"The drugstore on the c-corner north of here."

Considering the video, Wharton asked, "Have you seen Sylvia recently?"

"No. Just the ph-phone call."

"Have you any reason to believe she is in the area?"

"N-no."

Wharton hesitated uncertain whether to say anything about the video, but decided against it. "If you hear anything about her would you let me know? Especially if you learn where she was when her father died."

"C-certainly."

Brett got directions to Dr. Jalouski's residence while Atlanta fixed breakfast. It didn't appear difficult to find and the weather was cooperating.

As they put on coats the doorbell rang. Brett glanced at Atlanta and shrugged his eyebrows. She raced through possibilities wondering if it was one of the contractors. However, when she opened the door all she could see was a huge bouquet of brilliantly colored flowers.

"Atlanta Gabriel?" a voice from the flowers asked.

"Yes." She opened the door wider allowing them to enter.

"Where shall I put them?" asked the short chubby man who carried them.

She led him into the living room where she made room on the coffee table. "They're beautiful," she murmured, wondering to whom she owed thanks.

"They are indeed." He bobbed his head and left.

Brett stood looking at her with raised eyebrows. "So who are they from?"

Atlanta picked a tiny card off the plastic fork that held it and read: Flowers requesting forgiveness, Wharton. She frowned. What did that mean? As she locked the house she sorted through her memories of the night before wondering for what Wharton felt he needed forgiveness . . . and such a big bunch of it too.

They traveled I-5 northbound then took the bridge over the Duwamish and wound around the West Seattle hill with its exquisite view of the sound. The Jalouski house sat on a street of modest well cared for older residences with two cars in the driveway, a hopeful sign.

Brett had found a phone number and called while printing directions. "His daughter sounded as if any visitor for her father, especially if interested in the past, was welcome."

Atlanta sighed. "Since this concerns you more than me, I'll leave it to you to explain and ask questions."

They parked on the street then walked to the porch and rang the bell. The door was opened by a large jovial-faced woman with streaks of gray in her hair.

"I'm Brett Hadleigh. I called this morning."

"Oh, yes. You wanted to talk to Dad." She opened the door wider and stepped back. "I told him you were coming."

The woman, introducing herself as Pamela Jalouski, led them to a cozy room where a wall of windows provided the view of a park across the street. "He gets bored so company is welcome. He can't get around like he used to and finds the limitation difficult."

Sympathizing, Atlanta could deal with aches and pains, but confined to the house would be over the top.

Dr. Jalouski sat in a wing back chair with his back to the window reading a medical magazine. He had thinning gray hair and brilliant blue eyes, but looked as though he had shrunk from his former weight since his clothes hung loosely on him. He smiled with interest as his daughter-in-law introduced them.

The brightly colored room contained print easy chairs and a coordinating striped sofa. Brett and Atlanta sat together on the sofa.

"How can I help you?" Dr. Jalouski asked.

"We found that you're the doctor who signed Marcella Damarios' death certificate." Brett explained. "We wanted to ask a few questions about that."

The doctor frowned. "I'm not familiar with the name. When did she die?"

"1967." Atlanta put in.

Looking puzzled, Dr. Jalouski shook his head.

"I realize her name may not mean anything to you," Brett said. "She was the lead singer in our musical group and died suddenly at the Spokane Coliseum."

The doctor's eyes lit. "Ahhh," he said. "And who are you in relationship to her?"

"I was dating her at the time." Brett beckoned to Atlanta, "This is my cousin."

The doctor studied Brett as if he were somehow significant. "How well did you know her?"

"We'd been in the group for about two years and had been dating for about a year."

The doctor's gaze traveled out the window then returned to Brett. "Having intercourse?"

Atlanta glanced at Brett as he flushed and nodded.

"I see." Doctor Jalouski adjusted his position. "Why do you want to know now?"

Brett glanced at Atlanta. "We've always wanted to know."

"Recently," Atlanta explained, "there have been mysterious deaths among other members of the band and some near deaths."

The doctor frowned. "But these people must be in their sixties at least."

"But they shouldn't all die within a few months of each other."

"No, I suppose not." Dr. Jalouski searched Brett's expression. "Are you implying something?"

"Someone appears to be targeting them," Atlanta answered. "We wondered if it had anything to do with Marcella's death."

Brett continued, "We were never able to find out why she died."

"What did the death certificate say?"

"Unconstrained hemorrhage."

Doctor Jalouski nodded. "Yes, I suppose it did."

"That doesn't say much." Brett frowned. "Do you remember her?"

Dr. Jalouski spent a moment in thought before answering. "Yes, I do, a very odd case. I can tell you what caused her death but it may create more problems for you than it solves."

Brett glanced at Atlanta with a question in his eyes.

She nodded. "What else can we do? We have to know especially if it affects the here and now."

"In addition," the doctor continued, "what caused her death won't answer any other questions that follow."

What did that mean? Atlanta frowned. Apprehension gave her a prick.

"I think we need to know regardless." Brett appeared as apprehensive as Atlanta felt.

"Childbirth," the doctor said.

"What?" Atlanta frowned.

"She died in childbirth."

"But . . ." Brett stammered, "she wasn't pregnant."

"She couldn't die in childbirth if she wasn't pregnant," the doctor stated flatly lifting his eyebrows.

"You're sure?"

Dr. Jalouski nodded. "I examined the afterbirth."

"Did the baby die too?" Atlanta asked.

The doctor shook his head. "I never saw the baby. It wasn't there when I arrived."

Brett and Atlanta exchanged a glance. "How can that be?"

"I don't know." Dr. Jalouski sighed. "Perhaps someone took the baby away."

"Which probably means it was alive." Brett looked stunned.

"But then what happened to it?" Atlanta had difficulty accepting the report.

The doctor leaned his head against the back of his chair. "It grew up and is somewhere an adult with children of its own."

Atlanta watched as Brett attempted to assimilate the information.

"Would you be the father?" Dr. Jalouski returned his gaze to Brett.

"I suppose it's possible . . . I mean likely, if she really was pregnant."

"You honestly didn't know?"

Brett shook his head. "I suspected it once, but when I asked she denied it. If I were to say, she didn't know she was pregnant."

Atlanta turned to the doctor. "Is that possible?"

"It's happened before. A woman has her normal menstruation, gains weight she can't explain, but figures she's eating too much. Explains away the other symptoms. Refuses to confide in anyone because she is ashamed of the weight she gained and fearful of her symptoms. A combination of ignorance and denial."

"But to be far enough along to give birth," Atlanta tried to comprehend. "Surely the weight of the baby and its movement would have . . ."

The doctor raised his eyebrows. "Some babies are more active in the womb than others."

"But still . . ." Atlanta protested. She had two sons. She couldn't imagine not knowing she was pregnant.

"I can't explain it. As I said before I never saw her until she was already dead." Dr. Jalouski grimaced. "To be honest I've spent years haunted by that experience. I've never felt comfortable I handled it correctly. I was a young doctor in the audience and called backstage. They put pressure on me to sign the death certificate in a way that caused the least amount of problems. Her death was due to natural causes and there was no way for me to lay blame to anyone for negligence. I could see no reason why I should make more trouble than they already had from the situation. What has always haunted me was the baby. Like you said, in all probability it was alive. When preterm births and miscarriages happen, a baby can often be found in the garbage or somewhere. But nothing was ever found. I had the crew there make a search before I'd sign the certificate. It seems someone got the baby away before all the fuss, but I had no way to prove that either."

"You're saying that somewhere I may have a son or daughter." Brett's face had turned white.

"And no one at the time knew about it?" Atlanta asked.

Dr. Jalouski explained, "The only people permitted backstage at the time were the police, the paramedics and some officials of the program."

Anger made an appearance in Brett's expression. "Why didn't they allow the family back there?"

"I believe the officials were worried about lawsuits."

"It's hard to imagine them getting away with it." Brett's lips were pressed into a thin line.

"Things were different then." The doctor adopted a soothing tone. "People with enough pull could make things happen or not. Even now I'm not sure anything different would have resulted except a lot of unsolvable lawsuits."

"But if the baby lived . . ." Brett began.

"If the baby lived, it's probably still living."

Brett and Atlanta exchanged a glance. "Drina?"

CHAPTER THIRTY-TWO

When they arrived home Brett pleaded fatigue and went to his bedroom. Atlanta sat in her chair considering possibilities unable to draw a conclusion. She needed someone to bounce ideas off. Unsure of the wisdom she called Wharton.

He answered with surprise in his voice.

"Are you busy?"

"What did you have in mind?"

"Coffee at the bookstore."

"In an hour?"

She left Brett a note then got out her Cruiser and headed for Lakewood. Wharton arrived just ahead of her and together they searched for an empty table, locating one in the corner by the bookcases.

"So what's up?" he asked once they were settled.

Atlanta explained the Seattle trip and what Dr. Jalouski had to say.

"A baby?" Wharton shook his head. "That's incredible. It opens the door to numerous possibilities."

"An angry baby?" Atlanta widened her eyes. "Which would make sense if someone was taking out Brett, or thought someone else in the group was the father, but Annmarie?"

"In truth." Wharton frowned at his coffee. "If that's why Marcella died, except for the father, these deaths make no sense."

"Brett's devastated. He figures he's the father."

"Which makes him the cause of her death and his child's absent father." Wharton grimaced.

"But he asked Marcella if she was pregnant. She denied it." Atlanta lifted her hands. "What else could he have done?"

"What did the doctor say?"

"He admitted it's possible she didn't know. She could have lived in denial. It's hard for me to believe, but . . ." Atlanta shrugged. "There's something else. Both Brett and I think my neighbor knows something about it. She's acted strange ever since she met Brett."

Wharton admonished her with a look. "Which makes it even more important you get her to talk."

"But how? I'm not an attorney nor a detective."

He smiled. "But you're a sweet lady who is a particularly good listener."

She rolled her eyes. "I've already tried that and got nowhere."

"Hmmm. Maybe Brett needs to appeal to her. It's him she seems so interested in, right?"

"I'm not sure Brett would go for it." She grimaced. "Although more appears at stake than we thought."

"Would he tell you what he finds out?"

"That might depend on what it is. For years he's kept secrets regarding Marcella."

"We could activate his pen then listen to the results."

"That would be tempting." Atlanta laughed. "But he'd think we didn't trust him."

"We don't where women are concerned, right?"

She nodded. "Right."

"Have you seen any more of his ex?"

"No, thank heavens. Every time he gets a phone call I expect it's her."

"Is it strange she hasn't been around?"

Atlanta grimaced. She hadn't thought about that. "She's spent years leaving him alone – at least to my knowledge – then all of a sudden shows up here."

"Maybe that's suspicious." Wharton raised his eyebrows. "She wouldn't be taking that antidepressant?"

Atlanta stared at him. That hadn't occurred to her either.

"Should I give her name to the lieutenant?"

She sighed. "I'd have to figure out what it is now."

"Would Brett know?"

"Probably, but . . ." Atlanta grumbled, "he might be offended."

"We need to take our chances with offending people."

She gazed into the parking lot wondering if they would ever catch the culprit. At least the lieutenant was on alert now.

Absent-mindedly watching people make their way from parked cars into the store she noticed a lone dark-haired man staring at the café windows. "Wharton" She touched his hand, nodding toward the individual now moving toward the café's outside entrance. "Look at that guy."

"What about him?"

"Does he look familiar to you?"

Studying the figure, Wharton shook his head. "Why?"

"I'll swear I've seen him before but I can't place him."

Watching him enter the bookstore she recalled the large bouquet. "By the way, thank you for the flowers."

Wharton smiled. "You're welcome."

"For what do you need forgiveness?"

He looked into her eyes. "For allowing you to give up hope."

She frowned.

"I realized when you say you no longer care if I care for you it's because you've given up hope. I figured it was best to avoid each other. Not because I no longer cared, but . . ." He paused.

Atlanta waited for him to continue.

"It was a selfish thing, I suppose. Easier for me to not see you than exercise self-control. In addition being around you unable to have any real relationship would have been painful."

She raised her eyebrows and cocked her head. "And by a real relationship you mean . . .?"

Wharton had that oh-oh look on his face. Staring at his cup twisting it, he mumbled, "I'm not sure I can explain."

As the stranger Atlanta had observed came into the café she realized where she had seen him before. He was the Hispanic man who had interrupted her the first time she talked to Sunny and Philippe. The same man she saw at John Hanson's funeral.

Wharton watched the flash of recognition appear in Atlanta's expression. "So who is he?"

"Someone I saw here once." She sighed, shaking her head. "And at John Hanson's funeral."

"But you don't know who he is?"

"Probably doesn't mean anything." She shrugged.

"You know we can't afford to overlook anything . . . or anyone."

"But I don't know who he is," she protested, "or how I'd find out."

"Go ask him." Wharton grinned. "Ask him if he uses antidepressants."

She rolled her eyes.

"If you saw him here at least a couple times, maybe the baristas know who he is." Wharton signaled the young woman wiping tables near them. "Do you recognize the man standing at the end of the coffee line?"

She turned to look where he indicated. "I don't know him," she said, "but he comes in frequently. He talks to one of the other baristas who used to live in Oregon."

Wharton and Atlanta exchanged a glance.

The young woman went on. "I think he still lives there but is here temporarily."

"Which of the baristas talks to him?"

"She's not here today."

"Thanks for your help," Wharton dismissed her then turned to Atlanta. "What do you think?"

"We need to find out who he is."

Wharton took his cell phone, aimed it at the stranger and took his picture.

Atlanta scowled.

He examined his efforts. "Not very good, but it could help."

"What are you going to do with it?"

"Show it to Sarkis." Wharton downed the last of his coffee. "You want some assistance convincing Brett to help us . . . himself actually?"

Atlanta's gaze accused him of ulterior motives. Then she shrugged. "Oh, okay, join us for dinner."

Giving her a big smile, Wharton put his hand on hers. "I do love you."

She cast her glance heavenward and withdrew her hand. "You're incorrigible."

"Remember that." He gave her a pointed stare.

She laughed. "I'd better get home and see how Brett is fairing."

Wharton returned to his car feeling more light-hearted than he had in days, even weeks.

He mulled over their conversation. The idea Marcella had a child somewhere opened the possibility door, but not enough to convince him that was the cause of recent deaths. Would the child, now an adult – older adult at that – harbor so much anger and resentment he or she would resort to murder? And if so who would be the target? The father? That would make Brett the only sensible target. Unless whoever did not realize Brett was the most likely father. Even then it would make no sense to kill Annmarie.

To Wharton's way of thinking a fatherless child or even one who grew up with a father not his own would be more likely to search for the father than try to eliminate him. Even if disposing of a delinquent parent was the desired outcome, wouldn't he want that person to know how he felt about the delinquency? Try as he would Wharton could not make Marcella's baby the cause of murder.

If Brett and her family did not know Marcella had a baby who else could have? By the time he reached his house Wharton was no closer to having an answer than when he began.

Once home he attended to some paperwork. Setting the mystery aside he plunged into his task, amazed how quickly the afternoon disappeared making it time to leave for Atlanta's.

Drizzle began again as he crossed town. With the daylight savings reversal it was already growing dark. Atlanta's expression when she answered the door made him think things were not going that well. He raised his eyebrows. She shrugged, ushering him into the living room where Brett sat in the wing back chair.

He looked like he had shrunk. He had not looked that ill in the hospital after his overdose. Wharton had second thoughts about approaching him. On the other hand maybe that was what he needed.

"How's it going?" Wharton took the seat across from Brett.

He sighed.

"That bad?"

"Have you ever felt all the mistakes you've made in your life suddenly caught up with you?"

"Every other day," Wharton declared. "On the day in between I rush out and make a bunch more, figuring I've faced all my mistakes, only to realize the day after I was mistaken."

A smile flickered across Brett's face.

At least he wasn't dead yet, Wharton thought. "Atlanta told me about your visit to the doctor."

"I wish I'd known at the time."

Wharton leaned forward. "What would you have done?"

"Try to find the baby." Brett's tone accused Wharton of missing the obvious.

"Maybe we need to do that now."

Brett turned a skeptical eye on him. "How?"

Wharton grimaced. "There has to be a birth certificate somewhere. We know the date of birth, right?"

Brett sat up straighter. "And the place, at least the city."

"Even if they avoided mentioning the coliseum," Wharton reasoned, "they'd still probably admit to it being born in Spokane."

Atlanta appeared at the door. "Dinner is ready."

After filing into the dining room, saying grace, and passing the food around, Wharton suggested to Brett. "It's possible we can find public records on the internet. At least we can try." He turned to Atlanta. "We should take another look at your surveillance video, too."

She grimaced and nodded.

After tidying the kitchen Atlanta followed the guys to the study and the computer. She pulled a chair up beside them. "Have you found the birth certificate?"

"We need a date. Brett can't remember exactly."

She glanced at him with raised eyebrows. "Forty-five years ago. October?"

He frowned then shrugged.

"How about a date?"

"It was a Friday night as I recall. The 18th," Atlanta suddenly recollected the date that had for many years been imprinted in her mind.

"How can you get a birth certificate for a baby when you can't explain its birth?" Brett asked. "Who'd be listed as parents? How would the authorities know it wasn't a stolen baby who already had a birth certificate?"

Wharton sighed. "To my knowledge those things are handled by attorneys."

"Well, you're a lawyer," Atlanta challenged him.

"Let's see what we can find under birth certificates. It would still have to be registered."

For a time they sat in silence as Brett searched public records for the date.

"Why don't we look at anything from the 17th to the 20th," Wharton suggested.

Brett glanced at him. "How do we choose possibilities?"

"We want one not born in a hospital."

They carefully examined the information available for each of the births within the time frame, twenty-six of them. One birth certificate stood out. Wharton pointed to the signatures and explained, "This one has been altered due to an adoption. You won't be able to find the original."

"Do you think that's what happened to Marcella's baby?" Atlanta asked.

"It's a good possibility."

Brett squinted at the monitor. "What's the name on that certificate?"

"Esperanza Rosa Valazquez."

Atlanta frowned. "Hispanic?"

"Marcella was Hispanic," Brett said.

"If it's okay with you I'll take this information and consult a couple resources I have." Wharton said.

"Lieutenant Sarkis?" Atlanta asked.

"For one." Wharton nodded. "I know another lawyer who deals with adoption." He turned to Brett. "Marcella didn't have someone with her at that performance?"

Brett looked confused.

"A friend, a parent, someone who would have been backstage and helped her?"

"Her brother may have been there but not backstage. Probably flirting with the groupies, especially in the middle of the performance."

"That's right. It happened in the middle of the show." Wharton nodded to himself. Recalling his cell phone picture, he looked it up and handed the phone to Brett. "Does he look like anyone you know?"

Brett studied the phone grumbling, "I doubt I'd recognize my mother from this picture." He held it close then at arm's length, shaking his head.

Wharton glanced at Atlanta and she shrugged.

"Atlanta thinks Drina knows something about what happened at the Spokane Coliseum that night. Do you think you could get her to talk about it?"

Brett frowned at Atlanta. "What do you think she knows?"

"What if she were backstage when Marcella died?"

"I'm not sure what I could get her to say you can't." Brett stared at Atlanta as if he didn't see her.

"You could tell her what you know about Marcella and the baby. If she knew anything about it, she may talk to you."

Before he could raise an objection, Atlanta asked, "By the way, what is Ramona's last name now?"

Brett blinked and refocused, "Silvatrin."

"Is there anyone," Wharton put particular emphasis on the word "anyone", "who could have been the baby's father, or thought he was, besides you?"

Brett's gaze drifted to the dark window then back to Wharton. "You're asking the wrong person. That's something someone else might have known, but not me."

"Why don't we check that video," Atlanta suggested. She could see Brett becoming worn down from the questions and implications.

Wharton grabbed the disc from the recorder and loaded it onto the computer. They watched while it played the scene. However, although it picked up a number of people they were all ones with whom Atlanta was familiar and had appropriate reasons for being caught on video.

"Could we take another look at the one from the other day?" she asked.

As they watched the man who came from the rear of the house then appeared in the video, Atlanta wondered about the one she had seen at the bookstore. Could they be the same person?

"Get out your phone and compare your picture to the one on the video."

Wharton shot Atlanta a startled glance then did as she directed. After looking for a time at the photo and the computer screen he shook his head. "Inconclusive."

"But who is he?"

"That my dear." Wharton gave Atlanta an exaggerated smile. "I cannot tell you, however, she," he pointed to the woman who came later, "is Sylvia Erving Nelson."

Atlanta sent Wharton an astonished glance. "You're sure?"

He nodded.

Brett moved to get a closer look. "Would you have known her?" He addressed Atlanta.

She shook her head. "I never knew her."

Brett rose. "I'm tired. I think I'll go to bed."

Wharton watched him leave. "He looks like this has taken a toll."

"I almost wish I hadn't invited him to come." Atlanta cast a mournful glance after Brett.

"Don't start blaming yourself. This didn't start with him."

"But he might have been safer in England."

"Living safer often means not living at all." Wharton pushed his chair back from the desk.

"How about coffee?" Atlanta offered.

"Sounds good." He followed her into the kitchen where she examined the coffee maker.

"I think I'll make fresh."

While she fixed a pot of coffee Wharton took a seat in the breakfast nook. Recalling her earlier question, he asked, "So what does a real relationship mean to you?"

She frowned at him.

"I seem to recall ever since we met again you've been implying I don't know what that is."

She continued preparing coffee. Then she brought a couple cups to the table with milk, sugar and a plate of cookies.

"You've quit talking to me?" Wharton asked as he poured milk into his.

"I'm thinking." She sat across from him. "The word that comes to mind is connect."

"Connection?"

Atlanta shook her head. "That's too general. Lots of things and people have connections, but that's different than actually connecting."

Wharton frowned. It sounded like splitting hairs to him.

"You're the word man," she accused observing his frustration. "For anything to connect it must be two sided, right?"

He considered a moment then shrugged. "Technically, I suppose."

Atlanta scowled at him. "Technically, nothing. If both sides of something don't participate there is no connection, even if the two are so-called connected. Two people can be related but have no relationship. Two things can have a connection, but not be connected."

"I'm not sure what that has to do with the question."

"There are two sides to a real relationship. If both are not fully engaged then it's not genuine. It's like unrequited love. One person may be in love and the other see themselves as friends. Although there is a connection, they're not connected."

Wharton grimaced, working to follow her thinking. "Does that mean although I'm in love with you but you only want to be friends we don't have a real relationship."

"In the situation you describe, would those two be lovers or friends?"

He huffed. "It depends on which one you're talking to."

"But if you're an outside observer what would you say?"

Wharton stirred his coffee thinking. "I guess they'd be friends."

"Why?"

"Because the one in love would not be able to express that without the reciprocation of the other. But they could relate as friends, because the one in love would be able to go that far in his expression."

"So as lovers they'd not connect, but as friends they would?"

He nodded grudgingly.

"What part of that couple's relationship would you consider real?"

Wharton lifted his shoulders. "Their friendship?"

"Why?"

"Okay, okay, to that extent they're relating or connecting. So which of us is the one in love and which is the friend?"

Atlanta laughed. "That depends on who you talk to."

"I'm talking to you."

"If you're referring to our relationship, we both agree we're friends, right?"

Wharton bobbed his head. "Go on."

"At one point I thought both of us were in love, but when you walked away and wouldn't even be friends I realized love didn't mean the same thing to you as it did to me. So from my perspective, I was in love and for you we were just acquaintances. Now you say you're in love but I've had to accept the fact we weren't even friends anymore and have gotten over being in love."

"How do you get over being in love?"

"Face the fact what you believed in didn't exist and let go."

Wharton frowned. He didn't think he could do that.

"Every time you think about that person remind yourself what you thought was real wasn't. Eventually the other part of you gets the idea and moves on."

"Great," Wharton grumbled. "What am I supposed to do about that?"

"We can still be friends."

"What if I don't want to be friends?"

"Then we can go back to being acquaintances that spent a lot of time together once upon a time."

"But you could never be in love with me again?"

"I don't know." Atlanta's gaze drifted across the room.

Wharton figured he lost that battle hands down. "What about starting over, is that possible?"

"Anything's possible." She gave him a sympathetic smile.

His emotions revolted at the idea of pity. However, he had a second thought. Someone told him pity was a relative of love. Hope gave him a high five.

CHAPTER THIRTY-THREE

Since the receptionist said Lieutenant Sarkis would return momentarily Wharton took a chair in his office and waited. He fought the temptation to check out the lieutenant's computer. He was still arguing with himself when the lieutenant came through the door.

"To what do I owe the pleasure?" the lieutenant plunked himself down and twirled his chair to face Wharton.

"More questions and something to show you."

Lieutenant Sarkis leaned back eying Wharton.

"First of all here's a list of drug suppliers to check. Also would you check particularly for the names 'Valazquez' and 'Silvatrin'."

"Okay." The lieutenant accepted the note Wharton handed him. "How do you spell those names?"

Wharton sighed. "Try anything you think would work. I don't know."

"You have any first names?"

"Ramona for Silvatrin. Esperanza for the other one."

Wharton removed the cell phone from his pocket and brought up the picture from the bookstore. "Could you find out who this is?"

Accepting the phone, the lieutenant observed the photo, turning it then holding it at arm's length. "Not a great picture."

"Can't you blow it up, make it easier to see?"

The lieutenant shrugged. "What would I do if I could see it better?"

"Identify the individual."

"Do you believe he has a criminal record?"

Wharton hesitated. "That's putting it a little strong. I believe this person, whom Atlanta recognizes from the bookstore, may be showing up on her surveillance videos."

The lieutenant scowled, "At her house?"

Wharton nodded. "We've been looking for someone to connect to the deaths. This is the first stranger we've been able to tag who is actually hanging around the house. Maybe he's not a stranger, just someone they knew when they were younger, but don't recognize now."

Sarkis appeared skeptical. "I can run it through the computer, when there's someone with spare time to do that."

"I won't ask for more." Wharton stood. "You'll let me know?"

With a grimace the lieutenant nodded.

Wharton had questions for RJ and figured it wouldn't hurt to stop and see him. RJ's expression when he answered the door matched the gray gloom of morning.

"Buck up partner, we're making progress." Wharton encouraged him.

"Sorry, Wharton." RJ invited him in. "I know you're doing what you can."

"What's got you down?"

R J led the way to the kitchen where he poured a couple cups of coffee. "It seems nothing good ever happens. Life is all death and dying."

Depression, Wharton figured, although RJ did have a point. "I have some questions. Did you find those books Annmarie bought from the stranger?"

"I did." R J set his cup down. "I'll get them." When he returned he brought a stack of eight by eleven soft bound books with glossy photo covers. The books contained similar glossy pictures of interior decorating, more than a magazine but less than a hard bound book.

Leafing through them Wharton checked title pages, failing to recognize the publishers.

"What are you looking for?" RJ asked.

He wasn't sure. What would make a difference? "Something indicating the one distributing these is legitimate."

"But the books wouldn't necessarily be illicit."

"No." Wharton compared several of the title pages. "But if he is representing a publisher, designer, or writer I'd think it'd be the same for all the books."

"And they're not?"

Wharton grimaced. "They all have different publishers, writers and designers. I wonder what pitch he gave Annmarie."

"You think this might be the person who killed her?"

"I wouldn't go that far . . . yet, but it's certainly suspicious."

"How would he have done it? Books don't kill people or give them inappropriate medications." RJ looked frustrated.

Wharton shook his head. "What would Annmarie have done with someone selling things door to door?"

"You knew Annmarie," RJ smiled at the memory. "She'd invite him in, offer him coffee, make lunch. Who knows? If he had enough of a sob story she'd give him advice, offer to help."

"I wonder how an MAOI is administered." Wharton frowned. "Is it a pill? A capsule? A hard tablet? Something else?"

"One would assume it's a pill or capsule."

"Which means he'd have to put it in something she was drinking, or eating."

RJ sighed. "Which might not be that difficult."

Wharton grimaced. "I wonder if it has a taste."

"Given those who've been affected, not enough to say, 'oh yuk, what's that?'."

"Maybe he disguises it."

"With?"

"Vanilla or cinnamon." Something else occurred to Wharton. "When did you last see Sylvia Nelson?"

RJ stared at the window with narrowed eyes. "She was here for Preston's memorial."

"Did she come for Annmarie's?"

"Yes." He grimaced. "But I didn't see much of her. She had a man with her."

"Did she introduce him?"

RJ shook his head. "Sylvia was never easy-going or congenial, always hard-headed."

"Spoiled?"

"Oh, I wouldn't say that, just difficult. Some people are born difficult and she was one of them."

Wharton described her phone call. "I keep wondering what she did with the 100K from Preston's insurance. She's in debt with a large judgment against her."

"Annmarie said she had a huge fight with Preston the fall she came to visit before he died."

"How long before?"

"If I remember it was earlier than she usually came. Two or three months."

"Do you know why she came then or what the fight was about?"

"Money. Apparently she wanted him to support some idea she had and he wouldn't go for it."

"Was she here when he died?"

RJ shrugged, shaking his head. "Are you trying to connect her to their deaths?"

Wharton raised an eyebrow and met RJ's eyes. "You think that couldn't be the case?"

He sighed. "I really can't see Sylvia involved in something like that."

Wharton recalled another question for RJ. He took a slip of paper out of his pocket on which he had written the dates Preston died, Brett and Roberto were overdosed, and even when John Hanson died. "Do you know where you were or what you were doing on any of these dates?"

RJ scowled. "What's this?"

"I want to make sure you can't be accused of taking part in any of these incidents. Maybe we can back the police off."

RJ stared at Wharton. "I'll have to check my calendar."

"I'm not implying you had anything to do with them," Wharton assured him, "but if I can convince the police of your unavailability it might end their pursuit of you."

"I still want to know what happened to Annmarie."

"I know. But my first commitment was to get you off the hook."

When Atlanta descended the stairs dressed for the day she found Brett in the kitchen with a cup of left-over coffee. Recognizing his dispirited expression she debated how to deal with it.

"You should be happy at the prospect of having a daughter or son." She challenged him while brewing a fresh pot of coffee.

He cast her a startled glance. "I never thought about it like that."

"You can't bring Marcella back. You should have figured that out in the last forty years." Atlanta brought plates, silverware and napkins to the table. "Brett, you're not to blame for what happened to her, even if she died from childbirth and the baby was yours. You've mourned her loss. Now look at the positive side."

"Do you think we can find the child?"

"It's as possible as anything else these days." Atlanta set the table, bringing a plate of toast and the butter dish for Brett to finish. "Maybe that approach would work with Drina."

"It might, if there is anything to find out."

"At least you can give it a shot. I could call one of those contractors she gave me for the retaining wall." Atlanta set the pan of scrambled eggs on the table. "That might furnish an opening."

"Why don't you do that," Brett agreed. "We could invite her over. Then I could talk to her."

"By the way Wharton gave Lieutenant Sarkis both the birth certificate name and Silvatrin."

Brett narrowed his eyes. "Ramona was staying here with her third husband's son's family. His name is Silvatrin."

"Do you really think she could be behind this?"

"She's too flighty." Brett shook his head. "Plus she wouldn't have known . . . actually, I forgot. She would have known Annmarie, Preston and John."

"But it wouldn't help her to harm you."

They retreated into silence while finishing breakfast.

"But, you know, that doesn't mean her step-son couldn't have provided someone else with the medication. What's his name?"

Brett grimaced. "Charles, I believe."

As soon as Atlanta had cleaned the kitchen and put breakfast away, she called the contractors. One who was available agreed to come by before noon to give her a price on installing a retaining wall.

She spent some time considering her conversation with Wharton the night before. His frustration made her feel sad, but it was what it was. Sparing his feelings with an untruth would only make things difficult later. Had she been totally honest? Examining her emotions and the words she had used to explain them, she could find no other explanation than what she gave. It frustrated her that when other people were forced to live with the consequences of how they treated her she was the one who felt bad. Wharton made his choice at the time, now he needed to live with the consequences. No one ever wanted their consequences. They always want to blame someone else. Well, he could blame her if he wanted; it wasn't going to change anything. She still didn't feel she could trust him, although she truly enjoyed his company.

When the contractor arrived, Brett and Atlanta walked through the yard with him. He took measurements and made notes on a clipboard. He told Atlanta he would work out a price and give her a call back that afternoon.

"Well, that's that for the time being." Atlanta followed Brett into the living room. "By the way, did you look at those pictures of Roberto's?"

He nodded. "You know after looking at them and the videos then pictures from your surveillance cameras I have this feeling I should have realized something. It's just not quite in reach."

"A memory?"

Brett shrugged. "It feels more like a connect-the-dots issue."

Atlanta frowned. Why does one always remember what doesn't matter and forget what does?

Just after two o'clock the contractor called back with a price. Atlanta told him she needed to check with her neighbor who was sharing the expense before she made a decision. After which she called Drina, inviting her to join them for tea and explaining that she had talked to a contractor regarding the wall.

Drina arrived shortly after. Atlanta noted the slightly apprehensive expression with which she greeted them. Did she suspect something? Atlanta felt guilty as she invited her into the kitchen, but then they didn't have an evil motive.

Brett was seated at the table with a mug of tea. He made small talk while Atlanta fixed tea for herself and Drina. She brought the notes she had made from speaking with the contractor and they discussed arrangements for the wall.

"The price wasn't as bad as I expected," Atlanta said. "I think I can pay for the wall since it's on my property if you take care of removing the trees."

"Are you sure?" Drina asked. "I'm happy to pay my share of the wall."

"It sounds as if none of it will be on your property."

They agreed and Atlanta went ostensibly to call the contractor, removing herself to the dining room where it was still possible to hear Brett and Drina. She did call the contractor, agreeing to his price and plan but remained to eavesdrop.

"I just found out I may have a son or daughter," Brett began.

Drina made no comment, which made Atlanta wish she could see her expression. Her body language probably spoke when she didn't.

"You said you'd worked sometimes at the Spokane Coliseum?"

Again Atlanta could only imagine Drina's reaction.

"Did you hear about the death of the singer there?"

"When was that?" Alarm mingled with suspicion in her voice.

"Oh, a long time ago." Brett's tone was soothing. "Forty-five years. She died during a performance."

After a pause Drina asked, "Do you know what happened to her?"

"I just found out from the doctor she died in childbirth."

"The doctor?" Alarm was back in Drina's voice.

"Yes, the one who signed the death certificate?" A long pause ensued in which Atlanta wondered what was happening then Brett continued, "Do you know something about that?"

"You believe you're the father?" Drina's voice was barely audible.

"I wanted to marry her. No one told us at the time what happened. It was all hushed up."

"And you want to find the child?"

"If I could. The doctor said he didn't see the baby but presumed it lived."

After a time of silence Atlanta wondered if they had left the room or if her hearing had gone bad. Finally Drina said, "I was working there that night."

"Did you hear anything about what happened?" Brett maintained a chatty tone.

Atlanta was sorely tempted to return to the kitchen. However, figuring that might end the conversation she enlisted her self-discipline.

Drina spoke again although even softer. "I'd gone backstage to the ladies' room to make sure the supplies were okay and tidy up a bit."

Atlanta struggled to hear the conversation.

"She was there on the floor, holding the baby. I was so shocked it took me a minute to do anything. I stepped into the hall and told the other lady to call an ambulance. I got cloths and towels from the supply area and went back to keep her and the baby warm until the ambulance came."

"How was Marcella?"

"Well I thought she was okay. But when she passed the placenta she kept bleeding. I kept looking for the paramedics. I used string to clamp the cord and cut it. I've helped with births before. She was frightened and getting week from loss of blood. I don't know why the ambulance took so long. She was panicked about the baby, a sort of unreasonable panic so I agreed to take her away. I wrapped the baby and when I came back they wouldn't let me anywhere near the lady. The ambulance, and medics, and police were there."

"They didn't see the baby?" Brett sounded incredulous.

"I was careful to carry her so no one would see what I had. The lady had been so afraid of something happening to her."

"But surely . . ."

"They weren't paying any attention to me. I – I didn't think she'd die." Drina's voice squeaked on the last word.

"The baby was a girl?" Drina must have nodded for Brett went on, "So what happened to her?"

Atlanta decided it was time to return to the kitchen.

When she entered Drina was wiping tears from her eyes. "When they said the lady had died I didn't know what to do. I was scared to death. I didn't speak English very well then."

"Did you keep the baby?" Brett was so focused he didn't even glance at Atlanta.

"I tried to find out if anyone there was related to the mother, but they wouldn't let me talk to anyone. No one paid any attention to me. I overheard someone say she had a teen-age brother in the audience. I asked someone if she was married. The person said she wasn't. So I took the baby home and took care of her." Drina paused for a deep breath then went on. "The next day I read the newspaper. All it said was she died of natural causes, no mention of the baby or pregnancy. I was afraid to say anything for fear they'd think I was lying or had done something bad."

"Do you have any idea why she died?" Brett asked.

"The only thing I heard was that she bled to death." Drina lifted her shoulders. "I still don't know why the ambulance took so long or maybe it just seemed like a long time to me."

"Sometimes when the afterbirth comes a woman begins to hemorrhage," Atlanta put in. "It can go really fast."

"I felt so bad about it. I've felt so bad and guilty all my life." Drina wiped her eyes and patted her cheeks with the tissue.

"I'm sure it's not your fault," Atlanta assured her.

"Do you know anything about where the baby is now?" Brett asked.

Drina put her lips together and gazed apprehensively at him.

"Does she know who her parents are?" Atlanta asked.

With a shake of her head Drina said, "She believes they're both dead."

"Would she want to know her father?" Brett's voice was tenuous.

Drina gazed thoughtfully at both Brett and Atlanta. "I think she'd be very happy to know her true family. She's always wondered who her parents were, but I've never told her what I know. I didn't know anything about her father, and explaining what happened to her mother seemed such a tragedy I couldn't bring myself to tell her. I didn't know how to explain what happened."

"Did you raise her?" Brett asked.

"Oh, no. I kept her for a while, thinking someone would ask . . . there'd be something in the news . . . something. But there was never anything. I had a friend who desperately wanted children and couldn't have her own. She raised the baby, going through all the legal stuff to adopt her. But she and her husband are both dead now. I've known Pansy all the time she was growing up so she comes to see me sometimes."

"The woman who came the other day?"

Glancing apprehensively at Atlanta, Drina nodded. "She's married and has a son of her own, but otherwise no family. She treats me like we're family since I knew her adopted parents. We used to spend a lot of time together."

"Where does she live?" Brett ran his hand through his hair.

"Toward the mountains past Graham."

He smiled at Drina. "Thank you for telling me. I've spent my life wondering what happened that night."

241

"I'm sorry. I didn't know about your relationship. I was concerned when I learned who you are."

"It's not your fault. I'm sorry I didn't know she was pregnant." Brett sighed. "Do you think you could help us meet her?"

"She's a big girl now. I guess she can handle it." Drina smiled. "But I'd prefer to tell her what happened and prepare her first. She might not believe you otherwise.

Brett nodded. "I'm sure that would be wise."

"I can't guarantee how she'll feel about it," Drina cautioned.

"I realize that. You tell her and let me know if there is any problem, okay?"

Brett and Atlanta sat in stunned silence when Drina left.

CHAPTER THIRTY-FOUR

At loose ends when he left RJ, Wharton tried to recall what tasks he had assigned himself. Having checked with the lieutenant, RJ and Lucille, he considered who else might have helpful knowledge. A trip to Barnes & Noble wouldn't hurt. He would like a look at the guy Atlanta had seen. Maybe the barista who spoke with him would be there.

Once he had arrived and obtained coffee he searched for a table, locating one with a single chair in Sunny and Philippe's corner. He examined the patrons for the face they had seen the day before. Just as he concluded he was out of luck he noticed the man arriving at the café entrance. The man ordered a drink then looked for a table. A group of four left a couple small tables moved together. The man moved the tables apart and took a chair at one of them, well within Wharton's range of vision but outside his hearing.

Was this the man caught on Atlanta's video? Unfortunately most people fit into homogenous groups with individuals bearing amazing resemblance to one another. Wharton hesitated to draw a conclusion.

Considering his dilemma he noticed Sunny, one of the people he wanted to see, hunting for a place to sit. Wharton waved beckoning to an empty chair at a nearby table. Sunny approached bringing the extra chair.

"Where's your buddy?" Wharton asked.

"He'll be around, I expect." Sunny leaned back and unzipped his navy windbreaker. "What brings you here?"

"I thought I might catch a glimpse of the man Atlanta noticed the other day."

Sunny raise an eyebrow.

Wharton indicated the individual to whom he referred. "She thinks she should recognize him. I think he may be showing up on her surveillance video. Does he look familiar to you?"

Sunny studied the man. "Of course you realize all white people look alike."

Wharton laughed.

"Still," Sunny went on, "there's something vaguely familiar about him."

"Another question, did you receive something in the mail from the institution where John Hanson died?"

Sunny's face lit. "Yes, I did. Looked like a journal he was writing. I read some of it, but it didn't make sense, like rambling. There were a number of entries about someone visiting him. Although I got the feeling he wrote about it immediately after the visit, it still didn't make sense."

"Any idea who it was?"

Sunny shook his head. "I had the feeling whoever it was triggered memories of Marcella."

"But that wouldn't mean the person had anything to do with her."

"Right."

Ah, well, Wharton thought, it was worth a try. Maybe he needed to give the home another call.

"I asked my wife about strangers coming around. She said a guy came selling books one day, but she gave him the heave-ho. She has no use for door-to-door salesmen."

Wharton nodded toward the man at the table. "I'd like your wife to take a look at that guy."

"I don't know if I can work that out." Sunny grimaced. "It's not just getting Gladys here, but getting her here when that man is too."

Wharton leaned forward. "What's she doing right now?"

"Planning a party."

"Could she come by when she's done?"

"I can ask." Sunny took out his cell phone.

"We can let her know if our suspect departs."

While Sunny made the call Wharton watched the man converse with the barista wishing he was close enough to hear.

"She'll stop by when they're done," Sunny said, putting away his phone.

Smiling his thanks, Wharton noticed Philippe entering the café. He headed directly to the counter without even glancing their way, but came directly to their table once he had secured his coffee. They confiscated an additional chair and he joined them.

Wharton pointed out the stranger to Philippe and asked the same question he had of Sunny.

"Hmmm," Philippe murmured gazing at the man. "He does look familiar in a way."

"Did you ever know any of Marcella's family?"

"I wasn't paying attention to anything like that when she was around." Philippe flashed a roguish grin.

"I understood her siblings were a lot younger than her," Sunny added. He waved to a tall black woman in a royal blue pantsuit standing at the café entrance. When she approached he introduced her to Wharton. "This is my wife, Gladys."

Wharton had risen. "My pleasure." He secured another chair while Gladys greeted Philippe.

"So what's the big emergency?" she asked Sunny.

"Take a good look at the guy at the table by that pole." Sunny wagged his head in the man's direction. "Does he look familiar to you?"

"Why should he look familiar?" Gladys huffed.

"Does he look like the man who came selling books door-to-door?"

She frowned squinting at the man who was reading the paper. "You know I only saw that man for a minute while I figured out what he was doing and sent him on his way." She sighed. "I suppose he could be, but I wouldn't swear to it in court."

"Well, that's something. It still leaves the door open." Wharton was ready to grab hold of any thread.

"Do you think he could be a Damarios?" Philippe asked her.

"The same deal." She rocked her shoulders. "Maybe, maybe not."

As they finished their coffee Wharton wondered where this got him.

After some time Brett said in an awestruck voice, "I have a daughter."

"Well, that explains what happened to Marcella," Atlanta said. "I'm not sure how it relates to what's happening now. From what Drina says Marcella's daughter shouldn't know anything about the group."

Brett stared into the back yard from the window near him. "It destroys your theory about recent deaths relating to her."

Atlanta nodded. "But . . ." She didn't continue, feeling they had reached a dead end.

Brett's gaze returned to her face. "You might as well call Wharton."

Atlanta sighed. "What are you going to do?"

"Spend some time on the computer. Take a look at that birth certificate again."

Atlanta frowned, unsure his idea would produce any results, but at least it seemed innocuous. And he was right, she should call Wharton, although she despised the idea of becoming so dependent on him. It resembled when they worked on the lawsuit together. She didn't want to end up back there. Nonetheless, more was at stake than her emotions or pride. There was Brett and the safety of all those connected to Pistachio.

When Wharton answered his phone, Atlanta suggested they get together for a chat.

"Great. I'm at Barnes & Noble now. You can join me."

After informing Brett, she took her Cruiser and headed to the bookstore. As she glanced around for Wharton she noticed her girlfriends. Figuring the direct approach would be safer she headed to where they sat.

"Where's that lovely man," Freddie accosted her.

"Home with the computer," Atlanta patted her shoulder.

"You do keep him to yourself." Freddie complained with a reproving expression.

"Hope to keep him from running into that ex-wife of his."

"Oh," Georgiana interrupted. "I think we saw her here the other day."

"With another man." Freddie nodded smugly.

"Really?" Atlanta looked from one to the other.

"They looked pretty chummy." Freddie rubbed her hands together gleefully.

Georgiana wagged her head and rolled her eyes. "But she's right. They had their heads together over something."

"So have you made any discoveries on your mystery?" Sherry asked.

"We're still working on it," Wharton who stood behind Atlanta answered for her. "Have you anything to contribute?"

His direct approach appeared to intimidate them.

Turning to Atlanta, he asked, "What can I get you?"

"Coffee with cream."

He left to fetch beverages.

"What's going on with you two?" Sherry motioned toward the departing Wharton.

Atlanta shrugged. "We've been working on this mystery."

Freddie eyed her suspiciously, but before she could get a question off, Sherry spoke. "There was an article in the newspaper this morning about the dangers of combining medical prescriptions."

"Particular ones?"

Sherry lifted her shoulders. "Mostly those affecting the central nervous system."

Atlanta's mind went racing through events. Did her friends know what happened to Brett? And if they did how did they find out and who else knew?

"Didn't you say Wharton's aunt died of a combination of medications?" Sherry went on.

With a sigh of relief, Atlanta nodded. "But I'm not sure it was central nervous system drugs. She had high blood pressure and took medication to prevent a heart attack."

Wharton returned and they excused themselves, moving to a table near the windows.

"How's Brett doing?" Wharton asked once they were seated.

"The more he finds out about Marcella the more depressed he becomes." Atlanta grimaced.

"What has he found out now?"

"He has a daughter."

Wharton turned a wide-eyed gaze on Atlanta. "He knows that for certain?"

"My neighbor, the one you met, took care of the baby after Marcella died."

"Whoa." Wharton leaned back in his chair. "That's an amazing coincidence."

"I suppose it is," Atlanta agreed. "I'm getting used to crazy things lately, although it's not quite as crazy as it seems. Her husband is retired military. They were on assignment in Spokane and eventually here. A lot of retired military live here."

Wharton frowned at his coffee. "So where is this daughter now?"

"The woman with the man and child we saw on the surveillance video was Marcella's daughter." Atlanta watched his reaction.

Wharton raised an eyebrow. "Does she know Brett is her father?"

Atlanta shook her head. "She doesn't know she has any living parents. I think Drina had a great deal of guilt about Marcella."

"So it was actually natural causes then?"

"I'd say so. She'd probably be alive if she'd been willing to deal with what was happening to her and talk to someone about it."

"But it's not like these days when everyone and his neighbor has an illegitimate child."

Atlanta grimaced nodding. It was easy to forget "the old days" when having a child out of wedlock meant disaster to one's life and future.

"It made for a whole lot fewer illegitimate children and fractured angry kids." He sighed. "Maybe she was in denial because of what it would mean to her life."

"I suppose," Atlanta conceded, "but it's really hard to imagine. It's not like having a tumor that never moves."

Wharton frowned. "Is there a chance Brett will get to know his daughter?"

"That's a good question." Atlanta sighed. "He's still struggling with guilt over what happened to Marcella, afraid his daughter will resent him. But he is also excited to meet her."

"I should think the joy of finding her father may outweigh any antagonism she'd have. After all it wasn't his fault her mother died."

Atlanta nodded uncertainly.

"Do you see anything in what you've learned for what's happening now?"

She stirred her coffee, shaking her head and gazing at the mural above the coffee counter. What did cause what was happening now? Were they missing the obvious somewhere?

Wharton raised a questioning eyebrow. "I think I may be able to back the police off RJ. But it still won't answer what happened to Annmarie. He'll not let go until we find out?"

"Do you blame him?"

Wharton shook his head. "Do you think it's possible the person you recognize here is related to Marcella?"

She lifted her shoulders. "Brett should know but I can't get him to part with any information about Marcella."

"Still?" Wharton arched an eyebrow.

Atlanta nodded. "A sibling might have a motive for going after him, but why would he kill Preston, Annmarie and even John or Roberto?" She sighed. "I presume her family already has Marcella's royalties and none of them would get the other's no matter what."

Wharton grimaced. "I've never found it easy figuring out what motivates people."

"Which reminds me," Atlanta went on, "Ramona's step-son's last name is Silvatrin. Charles Silvatrin is a name you could try."

Wharton grabbed a napkin and a pen from his pocket and wrote down the name.

Looking up from the note he was making Wharton saw a woman approaching their table with an older man in tow. Barely taller than she, the man had thinning sandy hair and innocent brown eyes. At the same time Wharton noticed Atlanta's frown.

"Ramona," she grumbled under her breath.

Never having seen the infamous Ramona, he almost laughed as the orange-haired, over-made-up woman headed their way. His expectation for the Delilah who had snared Brett, continuing to pursue him while collecting husbands on the side had grown into an elderly siren with the prospect of being seductive. This woman looked like a feather-headed ditz with the sex appeal of a red hen. He watched her with fascination.

"This is Harry Matson." She waved a fluttery hand in the direction of her companion. "He helped me find a new car." She sounded like she had just landed the Sheik of Arabie.

Atlanta responded by introducing Wharton.

Ramona shot him a coquettish glance then turned back to Atlanta. "How's Brett?"

Atlanta narrowed her eyes. "Fine."

"I haven't been available lately," Ramona went on. "I thought he might have missed me."

Wharton watched Atlanta muster something to say. "What kind of car did you find?"

"A Lincoln." Ramona smiled broadly. "It's pink."

Wharton nodded wordlessly, noting a sputtering sound from Atlanta. Not daring to look at her lest he burst into laughter, he said, "Sounds great."

"We have to buy new floor mats," Ramona said. "Tell Brett hello for us." And they drifted toward the door.

"Atlanta Gabriel, I'm shocked." Wharton put his hand on his chest eying Atlanta with a scolding expression.

"I'm sorry," she sputtered then burst into laughter. "I'm thrilled she's found a new target."

Wharton frowned. "I do see what you mean about her not being the type to plan a complicated murder."

"And all things considered this is a complicated murder." Atlanta focused on Wharton raising her eyebrows. "We know it's murder, right?"

"We know it is." Wharton sighed. "We just have to convince Lieutenant Sarkis."

"The police already think Annmarie was murdered," she huffed. "Do they have any suspects besides RJ?"

"You know," Wharton grimaced. "I was so busy telling Sarkis what I thought I didn't think to ask."

Atlanta rolled her eyes and forced a smile. "Maybe you should do that."

"Okay, what do I need to find out? I have the names we thought were of interest." Wharton waved his napkin note. "What else?"

"You gave him your picture of the guy here?"

Wharton nodded. "I can ask if he has any info on that."

"It occurred to me with Roberto poisoned in Oregon just after Brett was here it's almost impossible for the guy we saw here at the bookstore to be the one."

"Why?"

She scowled. "You can't be in two places at one time."

"No, but to be in both Portland and Tacoma in one day is not impossible or even that difficult.

"But it's not just a matter of driving from one place to another," Atlanta insisted. "He has to have time to do the deed in both places."

"And what exactly do we figure the deed is?"

Atlanta sighed. "A door-to-door salesman who gets into someone's house to introduce bad drugs."

The jingle of Wharton's cell phone interrupted them.

"This is L-lucille M –"

"Lucille," Wharton recognized the voice. "What's up?"

"R-roberto c-called. He w-wants you to c-call him."

"Did he give you a phone number?"

Lucille recited the 503 number in her halting voice.

"Okay, I'll get hold of him. Thanks." Wharton looked at Atlanta with raised eyebrows, putting the number into his phone. "Roberto? This is Wharton Forde."

"I decided to take a drive out to Damarios' place. I got to wondering if anyone was living there. I ran into the neighbor who said a man and woman had been staying there for a couple days."

Wharton pictured the house he had driven by with Atlanta and Brett. "Did the neighbor know who they were?"

Roberto inhaled noisily. "He thought it could be one of Estaban's children."

"Marcella's siblings?"

"Right. She had a couple brothers and a sister who were a lot younger than her."

Wharton frowned. "You think it was a brother and sister?"

"No." Roberto sounded definite. "I got the impression he didn't know who the woman was but the man might be a brother."

"She might be his wife?"

"Possibly." He didn't sound convinced or even hopeful. "He said she was a redhead."

That didn't mean a whole lot. A woman's hair was one color one day and another the next. "They're not still there?"

"No."

"Would you know the names of her brothers or sister?"

"No. When we went to school together they were so much younger they were just little kids. I never knew them as adults. She was dead by then."

"Thanks, Roberto. I may call you back with more questions. If you think of anything else let me know."

When the phone call ended he gazed at Atlanta with raised eyebrows.

CHAPTER THIRTY-FIVE

When Wharton's alarm went off he thought he had set it wrong. It was as dark as the middle of the night. Turning over, he looked at the digital numbers. Holy cow, 7:30.

Once he was dressed and having breakfast, the day seemed brighter. A brisk breeze from the west had pushed the morning mist toward the mountains. Reviewing his plan for the day, he felt hopeful about results from the lieutenant on the picture he gave him.

When Wharton entered the lieutenant's office Sarkis was leaning back in his chair staring at the ceiling.

"Looks like you've got a big problem," he commented.

The lieutenant sighed, turning his chair to face his desk. "Actually I was considering this mystery of yours."

"Any conclusions?"

"I expect we can leave your uncle out of it, at least regarding the death of his wife."

Wharton raised his eyebrows. "You suspect him of other deaths?"

Sarkis scowled.

"Sorry, but the way you put it begs the question."

"It's more I think he may know something."

"Does that mean you're taking an active part in the investigation?" Suddenly an idea hit Wharton. "Or does it mean you've learned something?"

Eying Wharton, Lieutenant Sarkis asked, "Did something in particular bring you here this morning?"

"I thought maybe you had found out something about the picture I gave you."

The lieutenant shook his head. "I had it blown up, but nothing came of it."

"I wondered if you could check out the name Damarios. It's the last name of the singer who died forty-five years ago. We wondered if someone in her family may be causing these deaths."

"And why would they do that?" the lieutenant sounded as if Wharton's statement was preposterous. "Forty-five years? Isn't that a long time after the fact?"

Wharton shrugged. "It's Atlanta's premise the deaths connect to what happened to Marcella. I can't buy it myself. As you said it's a long time ago. But," he stopped to observe the lieutenant's reaction. "Nothing else seems plausible either. In addition," Wharton went on, "there's a guy showing up on Atlanta's surveillance videos. We can't eliminate the possibility he is a Damarios."

"You'd better not be taking matters into your own hands." The lieutenant had a warning glint in his eyes.

Wharton nodded, thinking that would be easier if the police got involved.

"I reread the files on your uncle and aunt's deaths. Plus I talked to the hospital in Portland regarding Lopez and St. Clare regarding Hadleigh." The lieutenant leaned back in his chair. "As you've implied a case could be made for use of that antidepressant. I'm going to request an autopsy on the death in Port Angeles."

That was good news. When Wharton left the lieutenant he headed to his office to check his mail and sign a couple papers for Kelley.

"Dad," she said, entering his office. "I checked on Uncle Preston's daughter Sylvia, the one who called you. She has a Facebook page."

"Did you learn anything?"

Kelley perched on the chair across from his desk. "Apparently her financial problems come from a romantic relationship she had with a con man who took her for a pile of money."

Wharton wrestled with the information. "Is she prosecuting him?"

"On Facebook. I don't know about court."

"She might get into more trouble for her Facebook page than any credit check," Wharton huffed. Amazing what stupid things people do and who they blame for their problems.

"She may have discovered that." Kelley grinned. "What I found was from a while ago. She's keeping a lower profile these days."

Wharton leaned back in his chair. "Was this in Pennsylvania where she lives?"

"I'm not sure. With Facebook you can't tell."

Something occurred to Wharton. "Does her Facebook page have a picture of her?"

Kelley rose. "Go to the internet and I'll show you." She came around his desk to stand behind him as he called up the internet. "Now go to facebook.com."

Wharton did as instructed. When he arrived at the sight, Kelley logged in. An assortment of faces and pictures appeared. She directed him to scroll down until they arrived at a message where she had him stop.

"There, that's her."

"A redhead?" He shot Kelley a surprised glance.

"At least in that picture."

"She's not always one?"

Kelley bit her lip, considering. "I think she might actually be a redhead. You don't remember her?"

"I'm not sure I paid enough attention the times I would have seen her." He lifted his shoulders. "Is there a way to find more about the judgment she has? Outside of calling her?" he added.

Kelley stood. "Give me some time, I'll check."

Wharton stared out the office window at a row of trees tossing their leaves into the breeze. He felt he had lost with the lieutenant. Something was afoot but he had no clue what had triggered the man's interest in the case. At least it was hopeful.

Atlanta and Brett spent the morning running errands. The grocery supply had dwindled and Brett needed more personal care supplies. She bought greeting cards and he picked up magazines. While shopping she mentally reviewed their progress regarding the Pistachio deaths. Who was the man at the bookstore? Was he connected to Pistachio? Like Wharton had said, why would anyone want to get rid of the group now? That could have made sense forty years ago, but not now. She wondered about the man with Ramona. But that seemed farfetched, too, absurd. Was it all just coincidence? Were they making something of nothing? Preston took antidepressants. He could have accidentally mixed them up with his other medications. The police had found nothing suspicious in his death to begin. And Annmarie, had she mistakenly taken some of RJ's medication? Such things happen. Supposedly John died of Alzheimer's. However, when she came to Brett she couldn't explain that away. And Roberto's misadventure fell in the same category.

After they got home, put away the groceries and had lunch Atlanta decided to take a walk. She missed her daily exercise and was feeling the lack of it. As she headed to the door her cell phone rang.

"Is there dance class tomorrow night?" It was Wharton.

"I imagine." Atlanta hadn't thought about dance class since the night of Brett's adventure. She wasn't sure she wanted to think about it now.

"How about we go? Bring Brett, we can all have a night out. I'm sure Kitty and Aaron will be there too."

It did sound inviting, especially if Brett came along so she didn't have to worry about him. "Let me check with him."

"You'll let me know?"

After agreeing, Atlanta continued her walk. The shorter days, the cold and rain made it difficult to find time for walking. When she was younger it didn't matter. However, darkness was intimidating now that her eyes no longer adjusted well. The cold and rain made it worse. Were those just excuses? She sighed.

The mist had lifted, leaving the water a glorious deep blue with little tufts of white. The sky was clear and although the breeze blew cold, the sun radiated warmth. She trekked down the hill to Lafayette Street and walked north as it headed toward Sunnyside Beach. It wasn't a beach day, but one could always dream. Brett's idea of the Italian Riviera flashed into her head. She could go for that. Unfortunately that picture instantly included Wharton. She found it frustrating that every dream reminded her of him. Was she falling back into his spell? She couldn't afford that. She had been happy and carefree before he came back. Could she return once the mystery was over?

Would it ever be over? Sometimes things go on forever. She almost felt she had made the whole thing up. But if the danger was real then somewhere was a real solution.

How had the perpetrator gotten Brett to take whatever drug caused the problem? He wasn't so naïve as to take anything someone gave him. Unless, she snorted, it was a woman. Was that possible? Ramona seemed occupied elsewhere. Atlanta couldn't believe she was actually involved. She was too busy being helpless. What other woman was there? Preston's wife Susan was dead, Annmarie was dead, Marcella was dead. Atlanta knew of no other woman connected.

Arriving at the beach, she stood for sometime gazing across the sound at McNeil Island, deep green against the sky's blue. She could imagine sitting on a sailboat drifting. "With Wharton" flashed into her mind. She shook her head. It was too cold for a sailboat, time to go home.

When she arrived she found Brett in the hall pacing the floor, clearly apprehensive. "Drina called. She has arranged for me to meet my daughter." He looked like he'd just been told he needed brain surgery.

Atlanta tried to comfort him. "She said she'd explain what happened when Marcella died."

"But that won't explain where I was . . . and wasn't." His voice was a whine.

"Give yourself a break, Brett," Atlanta scolded. "You take too much responsibility for something you knew nothing about."

He sighed. She could see he wanted to believe her, but his fears were too great.

The late afternoon sun had succeeded in warming the day beyond its seasonal temperature. Sunshine followed as they climbed the hill to Drina's small square house. She opened the door with a smile, assessing Brett with a glance and looking as if a great weight had been lifted from her shoulders. However, doubt still hovered in her eyes.

Atlanta noted each expression, thinking Drina was probably relieved to have been able to explain the night Marcella died to the baby she had cared for. However, she still doubted Brett's reception.

Drina led them from the tiny foyer into the compact living room. Seated on the sofa was the woman Atlanta had seen on the sidewalk outside her house conversing quietly with the man beside her.

The woman stared with undisguised interest at Brett whose discomfit Atlanta could feel. However she detected no hostility in the woman's gaze. The man flashed a quick smile as Drina introduced them.

"This is Panzi Lomas and her husband Frank." To the couple Drina said, "This is my neighbor, Atlanta Gabriel, and her cousin, Brett Hadleigh. Have a chair," she indicated those across from the sofa.

Atlanta sat in the chair farthest from the couple, allowing Brett the closer one. She wondered if he saw the resemblance to Marcella. Although she might not have recognized it after forty-five years if she had not just watched videos of the past, viewing Marcella at an age even younger than her daughter.

A glance at Brett told her he, too, was struck by the likeness, staring as if in a trance. She could only imagine what it might be to see a likeness of the person one had loved and cherished all his life, believing he would never see again.

However, Panzi stared with equal concentration at Brett. What had Drina told her? What had they told Drina? How much information could she have even given the woman?

An uncomfortable silence fell on the group. Drina turned to Atlanta.

"You explained to her?" Atlanta asked quietly.

Panzi took up the conversation. "She told me about my mother's death and how she found me. Also how she took care of me until I was adopted."

"Did she tell you about your father?" Atlanta asked.

"Only that she had met a man who thought he may be my father."

"I believe," Brett cleared his throat but still spoke hoarsely, "I'm your father."

Panzi's eyes returned to his face. "But you're not sure?" A trace of antagonism rose in her voice.

"Only your mother could be sure." He met her gaze. "But I don't believe there was anyone else in her life at the time."

"You were in the band with her?"

Brett nodded. "I loved your mother, loved her for over fifty years although she's been dead most of that time."

"But you didn't marry her?" It sounded like an accusation.

"Not my choice. I'd been asking her to marry me for months before she died."

"She didn't want to marry you?" Her voice implied something must be wrong with him then.

"According to another friend, a member of the band who had known her since high school, she was afraid to get married for fear of having children who were mentally ill." Atlanta related what Roberto had told them.

Panzi cast a concerned glance at Drina.

Atlanta went on. "There was no real reason for the fear. The illness he described isn't the sort to be inherited. It's a dysfunctional family issue."

Panzi's gaze returned to Brett. "Did you know she had that fear?"

He shook his head. "She wouldn't say why she wouldn't marry me."

"What about when she got pregnant?" Panzi narrowed her eyes.

Brett sighed. "As best we can determine she didn't know she was pregnant, or was so in denial about it she wouldn't face it."

Panzi frowned. "That seems a little far-fetched."

"I agree," Atlanta said. "Having had two sons I can hardly believe it possible. However, the doctor who signed her death certificate verified it could happen."

"If she was afraid of having a mentally deficient child she'd have a lot of reason to be in denial and protect herself from evidence to the contrary," Brett added.

"And you truly didn't know she was pregnant?" Her skepticism had not evaporated.

He shook his head. "I've found out a lot of things recently that If I'd known then . . ." he paused and swallowed. "I'd have done things differently. Maybe your mother would still be alive. Maybe we'd have been a family. If I'd known about you I'd have done everything I could to find you. I'd never have left you alone."

Panzi stared at him intently her dark eyes becoming watery.

"There was a time we questioned her about it, even suspected it, but she denied it absolutely. There was nothing I could do?" He lifted his hands. "Believe me a thousand times I've wish I could have prevented what happened." He clasped his hands together in his lap. "Then when recently we were told the cause of her death . . . if only I had known, pressed her harder, insisted, she might be alive. I cannot tell you how I regret my ignorance." His voice caught and he took a deep breath.

Panzi gave him a gentle smile. "I've always wondered about my birth mother." She sighed. "I've no reason to regret the parents who raised me.

They were wonderful and I'm grateful to them, but one still wonders about real parents, things you might have inherited."

"I didn't know your mother," Drina said. "I found her in the ladies' room and did what I could to help her, but I knew nothing about her."

"Did you know my mother?" Panzi addressed the question to Atlanta.

"I did, but she was a popular singer and I was a gawky teen-ager. I knew her mostly through Brett."

Panzi smiled at Atlanta.

"You look amazingly like your mother." Brett said.

"Do you have pictures of her?"

"We do." Atlanta suddenly realized the importance of things they had saved through the years. "And videos too."

"Really?"

"I understand your parents are deceased now?" Atlanta asked.

Panzi nodded. "They both passed away fairly young." She glanced at Drina. "Drina has been like an aunt and recently the only extended family I have. Frank has a couple brothers and his mother is still alive."

"But they live in the southwest," the man said.

Panzi nodded. "Where do you live?" She addressed Brett.

"England."

"Really?"

Atlanta could see the questions parade across Panzi's face. "We were raised there," she added. "My parents moved here when I was in grade school. Brett came over to attend graduate school, which is where he met your mother."

"Could I see the pictures and videos?"

"The pictures definitely." Brett glanced at Atlanta.

"I'm sure we can arrange for the videos too."

"They don't belong to me but to another member of the band."

As they were talking a boy about eleven entered from a room in the rear and took a seat between Panzi and her husband. Atlanta stared at him in disbelieving awe.

Panzi put her arm around the boy's shoulders. "This is my son Cory."

If there had been any doubt Brett was Panzi's father this boy cancelled that. He was definitely Brett's grandson. The resemblance was startling.

Atlanta glanced at Brett wondering if he saw what she did, but realized it might not be as easy for him. However, Drina also saw the likeness.

"There's no doubt Brett is your father," Drina said. "Cory looks just like him."

Panzi looked from Brett to her son and back then smiled. "Well, that answers one question. We could never figure out who he looked like. He didn't resemble any of Frank's family and mine is Hispanic. People think we adopted him." She laughed, turning to her son. "Meet your grandfather, Cory. You do look like a member of the family."

Cory stared at Brett with interest, a tentative smile on his face.

After spending some time getting better acquainted, Atlanta and Brett took their leave. Parting was awkward, for although they had discovered the closeness of their relationship they were still strangers. Atlanta figured that was okay. She had no idea what issues Panzi may need to work through, but she knew Brett had many.

Giving Panzi a brief hug and shaking hands with Cory and Frank, Altanta assured them she would work out a time for them to see the pictures and videos of Marcella and the band's performances.

As they walked down the hill to her house, Atlanta told Brett about Wharton's suggestion they go to dance class. He agreed it was a good idea.

"I'll talk to him then about arranging for Panzi to see the Pistachio videos."

When they reached the house she called Wharton's voicemail and left a message that they would meet him at dance class.

CHAPTER THIRTY-SIX

Before leaving his office Wharton checked his phone and found the message from Atlanta. Things were looking up. His courting plan progressed. He considered checking her surveillance video again but figured he didn't need the set-back. Somehow that annoyed her. Maybe after class he could bring up the topic.

Considering what he had learned from Kelley he wondered what he might find on Facebook. He never had an account; it wasn't his thing. But since Atlanta had been willing to deal with security cameras maybe he needed to buck up and give Facebook a try.

When he reached home he went immediately to his computer and set up a Facebook account without much difficulty. However, doing something with it was another problem entirely. After a couple hours he located a few people he knew and requested some friends. He wasn't sure how much good it would do, but no stake no take.

He did find Sylvia Nelson's site. Tempted to friend her he figured that wouldn't fly, not after her angry phone call. He took a careful look at her pictures, committing them to memory. He wanted to make certain if he saw her again he would at least recognize her. Was it possible she had been around when Preston or Annmarie died? Would it mean anything if she had been?

Wharton took his own car to dance class rather than accompany Kitty and Aaron. He would have preferred to take Atlanta but figured it better not to push too hard.

Steilacoom City Hall with lights ablaze had entered the Halloween spirit. Scarecrows stood guard at the entry and ghosts were floating in the foyer as the lilting notes of a waltz floated on the evening air. Entering he checked his watch wondering if he was late. Kitty, Aaron, Brett and Atlanta were already there.

Approaching the four he recalled his desire to ask Kitty about Sylvia. However, the instructor called the group to line up for the dance, announcing the Latin American series would begin with the rumba. Wharton claimed Atlanta, noting her gabby friend had arrived and was headed straight for Brett.

After explaining the relationship of the rumba to the waltz, Charlie encouraged the group to follow him in the steps. Wharton struggled with the syncopation while Atlanta laughed.

"I'm glad I provide so much amusement," he huffed.

She raised an eyebrow. "Lighten up Mr. Forde, the beat will come easier."

He sighed, forcing a smile. They managed to get through a couple pieces in more or less appropriate form before the instructors announced the break.

Kitty and Aaron joined them while Fredee trapped Brett in the corner, engaging him in a laughing conversation.

"Kelley found Sylvia Nelson on Facebook," Wharton informed Kitty.

She turned to him with raised eyebrows. "Did you learn anything?"

"Is she really a redhead?"

Kitty rolled her eyes. "I can't believe how little you know about your family."

Wharton grimaced. "I have to admit it's caused me some problems."

"Yes, she's a redhead, takes after Grandma Erving."

Resolving to save himself further scolding Wharton didn't admit he had no idea Grandma Erving was a redhead. He only remembered her with faded gray hair.

Kitty eyed him as if she could read his mind. She probably could, but he wasn't going to stick his neck out and admit to anything.

"I checked on her judgment. It's a loan on which she defaulted," Kitty informed him.

"With no collateral?"

"I'm not sure about that." Kitty frowned. "The default judgment was to a building contractor. Generally that means there'd have been some real estate involved."

"Any idea what happened?"

"I called the contractor's office. I'm not sure who dropped the ball, but it looks like Sylvia signed a loan for work to be done on property someone else owned, ending up with the debt and judgment."

"Who's the property owner?"

"A Dennis Harder." Kitty shrugged. "Looks like she got played for a sucker."

"No wonder she's so grumpy." Wharton sighed. "But that wouldn't mean anything as far as Pistachio is concerned."

The dancing instructors called the group back to the floor and they resumed the dance. When the class ended Wharton felt at least marginally competent at the rumba. He didn't figure he'd win any prizes but he could get through a piece of music.

"You up for dessert?" Kitty consulted him with raised eyebrows.

He glanced at Atlanta and Brett. "How about it?"

After all had agreed to the dessert place on Steilacoom Boulevard Wharton led the way to the small angular building. The cozy library atmosphere was enhanced by bouquets of yellow and orange chrysanthemums in jack-o-lantern vases reminding him that Halloween was only a few days away. Not exactly Valentine's Day but he might be able to find an appropriately romantic card for Atlanta. He put it on his mental to-do list.

The group claimed a table for four and grabbed an extra chair from another table. They discussed plans for handling trick-or-treaters while ordering tea and dessert. Wharton could foresee potential problems with Halloween night. He'd better put Atlanta on alert. However, he decided to wait until afterward, still hoping to check out her video.

Returning to their earlier discussion, Wharton asked Kitty, "Have you talked to Sylvia at all?"

"I haven't been able to get hold of her."

An idea hit him. "Maybe you should friend her on Facebook."

Kitty stared at him as if he had just sprouted big black ears and a long tail. He wouldn't have been surprised had she broken out singing, "M-i-c-k-e-y-M-o-u-s-e-." Instead she said, "Don't tell me, Wharton, you have a Facebook page."

"Okay, I won't." He flashed her a cheesy smile. "But I'd lay money you do."

Unwilling to admit to his page, Wharton explained. "Kelley showed me her page. Isn't there some way you can get more information if you're her friend?" He thought he had heard that.

"Did you try friending her?" Kitty cocked her head.

"She'd probably quit Facebook altogether if I did that."

Kitty rolled her eyes.

"Why don't you try your Ipad?" Aaron suggested.

She dug in her enormous handbag and removed her Ipad. After a few minutes of fingering it she said, "What did you want to know?"

"Whatever you can find. Particularly where she is now and where she was when Annmarie and Preston died."

Kitty drifted into total absorption in her apparatus.

"Do you think she was here when her father died?" Aaron asked.

"I actually wondered more if she were here when Annmarie died or when Brett was poisoned."

"You don't seriously think she had anything to do with those?" Kitty's attention was drawn from her instrument.

"She may have had more to gain than anyone else," Aaron put in.

"And like you said she was taken for a considerable sum of money recently."

Wharton glanced at Brett and Atlanta, following the conversation attentively.

"Here's a picture of her. It looks like the memorial for Annmarie." Kitty passed her Ipad to Wharton who studied it with concentration.

"Who do you think the guy beside her is?"

Kitty shrugged and shook her head.

"You who know so much about the family should have an idea," he accused. "Do you remember seeing her at Annmarie's memorial?"

Kitty crossed her arms and stared at her cheesecake. After a moment she shook her head. "Which is odd because I remember everyone else from the family."

Tempted to feel smug Wharton realized that information may have some actual significance. He examined the guy beside Sylvia again then handed the Ipad to Atlanta. "Does he look anything like the guy you saw at the bookstore?"

She studied the picture with her eyebrows drawn together. "I suppose it could be him. Maybe it's not Marcella he's connected to but someone in your family."

Wharton frowned, glancing at Kitty. "What do you think? Is there someone in the family I don't seem to know anything about who looks like him?"

As Atlanta handed back her Ipad Kitty scowled at Wharton. She found a few more pictures of Sylvia with the same guy, but it didn't help identify him.

When they had finished dessert, Wharton figured it was time to try the surveillance video idea on Atlanta. If it upset her there was no help for it. They still needed to check.

She sighed but invited him over. He followed her Cruiser and parked behind her garage.

The moon rode high in the sky as the wind wrestled with the trees on the ledge. The clear evening made it possible for Wharton to note the north side layout where the video had failed to pick up the stranger. Given there was less intricate landscaping it facilitated the pass through to the front much easier than going through the south where a patio garden occupied much of the space.

Atlanta turned on the lights and invited the guys to set up the video while she put away her coat and changed shoes. By the time she returned they had the tape ready to go.

"Something I realized when we came in tonight," Wharton said as she moved a chair in position, "the person we couldn't identify last time might not have realized there were cameras but just be taking the easy way around the house."

Atlanta shot him a look of hopeful skepticism.

They began the video. Again it was the usual identifiable people. Only one visitor made Wharton pause the play and seriously study the woman.

"Do either of you remember her?"

With a sheepish glance at Atlanta, Brett nodded. "The doorbell rang and without thinking I went to answer it."

"Who was it?" Wharton's tone was sharp.

Brett shrugged. "A woman looking for someone she thought might live here. I didn't know the name obviously. Atlanta wasn't home."

Atlanta looked worried and Wharton grumbled under his breath, leaning toward the screen and studying the image. "It looks like the Facebook picture of Sylvia Nelson."

"What would she be doing here?"

Wharton shook his head. "Makes no sense to me."

"Could you find out?" Brett asked

"I can try, but it's not that easy. She'd probably hang up if I called her." Atlanta looked apprehensive.

"I'll see what Kitty can do or Kelley."

"I've got tickets to the Broadway Center production of *Rita*. Would you be interested?" It was Wharton.

A jumble of pictures crossed Atlanta's mind. She would love to go. She hadn't been to the theater in a long time. Then she thought, what about Brett?

"I checked with Philippe. He'd be happy to spend some time with him."

It was worse than having a child, Atlanta thought with despair. "Tonight?"

"Too short notice?"

"No. If you can actually get Philippe to come."

"I have his number. I'll give him a call and get right back to you."

When she hung up, Atlanta asked Brett, "Would you mind spending time with Philippe while I go to the theater with Wharton?"

"That would be great."

When Wharton called again, Atlanta agreed to his plan, arranging for pick up at seven. While fixing a quick dinner she considered Wharton's interest in the stranger at the bookstore. Was that person actually a Damarios? And if he was, so what? What motive would he have to eliminate Pistachio?

When Brett joined her at the table she asked him, "Were any of Marcella's siblings at the performance the night she died?

Brett grimaced thoughtfully. "I'm not sure. She never talked about her family. I was usually otherwise engaged. When she died I was so devastated I lost all track of what was happening. What are you thinking?"

"More people may have been involved in what happened that night than any of us realized."

"You could ask Sunny or Philippe."

"Why don't you ask Philippe tonight when he comes?"

After dinner Atlanta spent time dressing for the occasion, delighted about something for which to dress up.

Wharton arrived in a sport coat and tie, looking every bit the elegant gentleman. He escorted her to his Mercedes with the awkwardness of a teen-ager making her feel like a twenty-year-old on a date. Silence ensued as he began the drive to downtown Tacoma. Then they both spoke at once.

"Thank . . ." Atlanta began.

"Did . . ." Wharton started, then stopped. "You first."

"Thank you for making arrangements for Brett."

"So Philippe arrived on schedule?"

"Yes. Something else," Atlanta recalled her promise to arrange for Panzi to see the videos. "Brett met his daughter yesterday."

"His daughter? You mean Marcella's baby?"

"Panzi Lomas. He also has a grandson who looks just like him."

"No lie?"

"It's truly amazing. She'd like to see the videos of Marcella and the band."

"I still have them so that shouldn't be a problem."

In downtown Tacoma they located parking then walked to the theater in the mild evening reminiscent of late summer. Their seats were on the aisle halfway to the stage. The lights dimmed and Atlanta became lost in the production until intermission suddenly brought her back to reality.

"Let's make a dash for the lobby. Maybe we can get coffee and cookies."

Atlanta followed Wharton to the glass enclosed lobby. He proceeded through the refreshment line, purchasing coffee and dark chocolate brownies covered with thick frosting. Standing by the windows they admired the view of downtown Tacoma. Above the city lights Mount Rainier was etched against the evening sky.

"Something occurred to me this afternoon," Atlanta said. "Could some of Marcella's family been present the night she died?"

"What are you thinking?"

"I don't know, nothing in particular. But they'd have been teenagers then. It would have had to be traumatic for them."

"You think one of them never got over it?"

She shrugged.

The lobby lights flashed alerting the crowd to resumption of the play. Wharton and Atlanta returned to their seats. When the production ended Wharton's question returned to plague her. Intuitively she felt somewhere was a reason for what was happening. But logically she couldn't make a case for it.

Walking back to the car, Wharton offered her his arm as the unevenness of the sidewalk caused her to wobble.

"I guess I don't go out often enough in my dress shoes."

"Maybe we can rectify that."

"We could get season tickets to the theater. I noticed they had a great lineup."

Wharton shot her a surprised glance.

"You're not that into the thespian scene?" Atlanta lifted an eyebrow and smiled.

"I'm just surprised by your suggestion, but I'm game." Wharton nodded to the coffee shop they had reached. "How about a cup of tea?"

They found a place to sit and Wharton went to order.

"No dessert," Atlanta cautioned. "The chocolate brownie was all my waistline can handle."

Wharton returned with two cups of tea.

After sipping hers, Atlanta said, "A picture just flashed into my head of the night backstage when Marcella died. Someone was trying to get into the ladies' room the police had to wrestle to keep out."

"A man or a woman?"

"A man but I don't know who it could be."

As he was stirring sugar into his tea Wharton's cell phone rang. He shot Atlanta a puzzled glance. "It's a little late for phone calls," He looked at the face of his instrument.

"Who is it?"

"Don't recognize the number." He put it to his ear. "This is Wharton. Philippe. What's up?"

Apprehension seized Atlanta.

Wharton looked at her with raised eyebrows as he listened. "What!"

After listening another couple minutes Wharton said, "We'll be right there."

Atlanta gave him an alarmed look.

"The guy we saw at Barnes and Noble is there with Brett and Philippe." As they returned to his car Wharton explained, "Philippe said not to worry they recognized him. Brett wanted him to call us while he keeps the guy busy."

"Busy how?" Atlanta figured Brett had kept him busy the time before. That was no comfort.

Wharton handed his phone to her. "While I drive you call Lieutenant Sarkis."

"Sarkis," the voice on the other end barked.

"This is Atlanta Gabriel. I'm with Wharton. Philippe called from my house to say the person showing up in our surveillance videos is at the house with Brett. We're afraid he's going to try to hurt Brett again."

"I'll meet you there."

Atlanta sat anxiously rigid as they made their way from the north end back to Steilacoom. Her mind raced through dangerous possibilities. She could not even form a specific worry to concentrate on. As they approached the house she noticed Lieutenant Sarkis' SUV across the street. Wharton slid his Mercedes in behind it and extinguished the lights.

The lieutenant got out of his truck and came back to the car. "What do you think is going on?"

Atlanta leaned across the seat. "I'm afraid that guy is back to finish Brett off."

"How did you find out he was here?"

"We left Brett's friend with him," Wharton explained. "He called."

"Can you call him back?"

Wharton got out his phone. "Philippe? What's going on?" He listened for a moment. "Out in front of the house. Where are you?" He gazed up at the second story. "Brett's okay? Keep your phone handy."

"So," Atlanta said to Wharton.

"Philippe is in the upstairs bedroom. Brett is in the living room with this guy."

"Is Brett okay?" That was the important issue.

Wharton turned to Atlanta. "Yeah, he's fine." He turned back to the lieutenant. "They're not sure what the guy has in mind. He's showing Brett some books."

Sarkis addressed Atlanta. "Is there a way into your house and upstairs without going through your living room?"

She thought for a moment. "If you came in the door from the backyard you could get to the stairs without being noticed. You'd have to be careful because a part of the stairs is visible from the living room."

The lieutenant pressed his lips together. "Okay. Forde you come with me. Atlanta you go in through the front door just as if you're getting home as normal. Give us time to get to the back door before you do that. Perhaps we can get upstairs while you're diverting them."

Atlanta swallowed her qualms and nodded. She waited while the two men climbed the stairs from the street and went around the outside of her house. Approaching her front door she prayed for assistance and calm. Using her key she unlocked the door and stepped into the foyer.

Lieutenant Sarkis and Wharton were in the back hall as she stepped through the French doors into the living room. Brett sat on the sofa with the individual Atlanta had seen at the bookstore. A collection of books were spread on the table in front of them. A cup and saucer sat on the end table and another at the edge of the tea table in front of the men. Both of them looked up at her with an expression of surprise.

"I didn't expect you home so soon," Brett said, determination in his expression.

"It's not soon," Atlanta huffed. "It's after eleven."

"Oh, I guess I lost track of time." Brett turned to his companion. "I didn't catch your name."

"Rick," the man said, giving Atlanta a concerned glance mixed with frustration. "I've stayed later than I should have." He gathered his books and placed them in the briefcase at his feet.

Atlanta gazed at the door wondering what to do. Was it alright for him leave? What could she do to keep him there?

Rick reached to pick up his teacup.

"I'll take those to the kitchen." Atlanta dropped her handbag on the credenza and quickly grabbed both cups and saucers, eliciting a look of alarm from Rick. When she stepped into the hall she noted the lieutenant on the stairs. He had his cell phone in one hand and with the other he gave her an okay sign. Taking the cups to the kitchen she realized they may contain evidence. So she put them in the cupboard to avoid having the proof accidentally or intentionally washed away.

When she returned to the hall, Brett and Rick were near the door.

"I'll stop by again when I'm in the neighborhood. You may decide in the meantime you're interested in one of the books. Or convince your lady here." Then he made a hasty retreat.

Atlanta went to the window in the living room and pulled aside the curtain. When they arrived she had given no attention to the cars on the street and now wondered if the man had one there. However, as she watched he crossed the street walking south to the corner and then turned up the hill. She continued watching for a time. A dark sedan came down the hill and turned north traveling in front of the house. Just as she was about to turn away she noted another sedan come down the hill from the same direction following the other car.

"What do you see?" Wharton stood beside her.

"Look at that car." She pointed to the first of the vehicles. "Do you remember seeing it before?"

Wharton stared with double lines between his eyes, but only shrugged and shook his head.

Atlanta turned back to the room.

"So have we got anything?" the lieutenant asked.

"I saved the cups." Atlanta said, "I didn't know how to keep him here."

"You didn't need to. I've got a tail on him."

Atlanta sighed with relief.

"Why don't you get those cups for me?" the lieutenant said.

She glanced at Brett. "Did you drink anything?"

He shook his head. "Do I look stupid?"

Atlanta returned to the kitchen where she retrieved the cups. One had been empty and the other two-thirds full of tea. She emptied its contents into a glass jar, put the lid on then carefully placed the cups into a plastic bag, making every effort not to leave or remove fingerprints.

"Was there anything in them?" The lieutenant had followed her.

She held up the jar. "This was in one of them, Brett's I presume."

The lieutenant accepted the bag. "You and your cousin stay put for tonight. I doubt he'll be back, but don't take any chances. I'll get this to the lab and see where his tail is."

"What will you do with him?" Although she appreciated the lieutenant's confidence she would rather have the guy completely out of circulation.

"It depends on what the lab finds." The lieutenant eyed her as if concerned she might have some harebrained scheme up her sleeve.

"What if it doesn't find anything?"

"Then there's not much I can do except keep an eye on the guy." His gaze held a warning. "You can't arrest a man for trying to sell books."

Although disappointed, she nodded. She had hoped at least the culprit would be unavailable to continue executing his plan. However, maybe they would find something in the liquid from the cup.

CHAPTER THIRTY-SEVEN

tlanta's eyes popped open. While getting oriented she glanced at the bedside clock. It was 1:00 a.m. She lay staring at her new bedroom skylight through which a ray of illumination streamed from the streetlight up the hill. What woke her? Straining her ears for unusual sounds, she heard nothing. She debated returning to sleep but figured it best to check on Brett.

As she set her foot on the floor a tapping noise alerted her senses with a stab of alarm. Standing perfectly still she concentrated to determine the source of the sound. All was quiet. Grabbing her cell phone, she stepped carefully out of the bedroom and to the rail on the petite landing. Looking over the edge, she felt her heart lurch in surprise when she saw someone there turning the knob of Brett's door. She backed away from the railing to think. Containing her alarm with anger, she looked again. Dressed in jeans and a dark shirt with a balaclava over his head he seemed unaware of her presence, intent on his purpose.

Courses of action raced through her brain like a video on fast forward. Unsuccessful at opening the door the man knocked softly. The impending danger propelled Atlanta into action. She opened her mouth and screamed as loud as she could while putting 911 into her phone. Turning on her the man threatened, waving a knife in the air.

Atlanta noticed Brett open his door, take a quick assessment of the situation and slam it shut again. She heard the lock snap. This drew the man's attention back to Brett's door. Atlanta took advantage of the moment, racing down the stairs, across the hall, and into the kitchen, while giving her name, address and intruder information to the 911 operator.

In the kitchen she grabbed a frying pan from the hanging rack and a butcher knife from the block on the counter then whirled around expecting the intruder to have followed her. However, no one was there. Grasping her weapons she returned to the hall, fearing the intruder had successfully accessed Brett's room.

Still in pajamas and slippers Atlanta moved quietly. The man was on his knees at Brett's door working to free the lock. With his back to her, he appeared consumed by the task. Heedless of the consequences, Atlanta lifted her frying pan and moved toward him. Suddenly he turned. Surprise flashed on his face. As he lifted his knife with a threatening gesture Atlanta managed to slam the pan down on his hand, releasing the knife from his grip. When he bent to pick it up again she whacked him on the head. Heedless, he continued scrambling to retrieve the knife. Preparing to strike him again she heard a noise at the front door sending a chill of fear through her. She stepped back. The trespasser's dilemma registered in his expression. He had also heard the sound at the front door.

Abandoning the knife he rose, scrambling toward the back entry. Atlanta raised her pan and followed. She heard the door behind her open. A rush of footsteps turned out to be Lieutenant Sarkis charging past. However, the intruder had successfully made it outside before the lieutenant reached the door. While he continued in pursuit Atlanta heard more footsteps. Making a quick turn she found Brett staring at her in awe.

Gradually his gaze of admiration turned into asmirk. "You're quite a crime fighter," he commented.

Atlanta's relief in seeing him safe turned to frustration. "Where did you come from?"

He opened his mouth and she could see the smart remark coming. However, he must have changed his mind. "I climbed out the window in the bedroom. When I came around the side of the house the lieutenant was there."

With a gesture of relief Atlanta set her pan on the hall credenza. "I called 911." She placed the knife beside it.

Brett considered her weapons with a look of amazement. "He was monitoring the surveillance car."

"Was this the guy here before?"

He made the maybe-maybe-not motion with his hand. "But what I do know is the man who came with the books is same guy."

"When you were overdosed?" Atlanta verified his comment.

He bobbed his head.

"Does that mean you're memory has returned?"

Lieutenant Sarkis reentered through the front door. Brett and Atlanta turned to him expectantly.

"Well?" Atlanta wanted to know the man had been apprehended and was on the way to jail.

The lieutenant grinned. "I sent him with the officers."

She let out a sigh of relief.

"That was quite a performance." Lieutenant Sarkis grinned. "Maybe I should put you on the payroll."

Atlanta rolled her eyes. She felt like collapsing. It had taken all of her emotional resources. Now she was drained. "What will they do with him?"

"He'll be booked and held on suspicion."

"But he could still be let go?" She wanted the intruder locked up and the key thrown away.

"It depends on what evidence we have to charge and convict him."

She opened her mouth as more questions rushed into her head.

Lieutenant Sarkis made a stop motion. "Give me a little time to get lab results and see what we have."

Sighing, Atlanta turned to Brett. "How did you get out the window?"

"With difficulty." His grin mimicked the lieutenant's.

"What made you think of doing that?"

"I wouldn't be much help stuck like a prisoner in that room." His expression said, why else, then he added, "I also saw the police car arrive."

"We had the guy under surveillance when he left here. I got a call from the surveillance team just before your emergency call came in." The lieutenant glanced at his watch.

Atlanta felt he hadn't told them everything, but her energy had escaped. She knew enough now to get a good night's sleep.

"I'll give you a call tomorrow when I have some results." With that he departed.

"Are you okay?" Brett asked when the lieutenant had gone.

"Are you?" Atlanta returned the question searching Brett's face.

"Better than I expected to be."

Wharton had a restless night. He kept seeing Brett overdosed. Whoever the person was he seemed intent on eliminating Brett, which may mean he would eliminate Atlanta also. The sooner he was locked up and out of circulation the better.

Even when morning came, the gray light of dawn bringing form and clarity to the furniture in his bedroom, he could not dispel his concern. A glance at the clock told him it was too early to call Atlanta. It was even too early to get hold of the lieutenant, leaving him to bat questions around in his mind. Who was this guy? And why was he eliminating Pistachio? Probably insanity. Nonetheless Wharton wanted answers. What did the guy think he was doing, even if it was a neurotic obsession?

He fixed a cup of coffee and took it to his study where he investigated insanity on the internet. When he had finished his research he figured almost everyone he knew was insane in some fashion or another, but he was no farther ahead relative to the intruder.

Just after eleven Atlanta called to tell him Lieutenant Sarkis was coming by at one. Wharton was welcome to join them.

He grabbed his keys, locked the house and headed for the freeway. Patches of blue sky indicated the sun was working its way through the heavy overcast. He felt that was happening to the mystery they pursued. Maybe they would get some answers now.

He arrived at a quarter to one and Brett opened the door for him.

"We had some excitement here after you left last night," Brett informed him with a crooked grin as they moved into the living room.

"What kind of excitement?"

Brett explained the return of the bookseller and his subsequent arrest. Wharton felt a pang of regret at having missed the action. "No one was hurt?"

"Atlanta whacked the intruder over the head with a frying pan, stunned him for a while."

"She what?" Wharton gaped.

Brett laughed. "She charged the intruder with an iron frying pan and a butcher knife."

Appearing at the door to the living room, she looked calm and composed, glancing from one of the men to the other. "I suppose Brett told you about our escapade last night."

"And your heroic stand?" Wharton was torn between open admiration and a smart remark. She gave him a warning look and he resisted the remark. "I'm proud of you."

She rolled her eyes. "I think he figured I was a harmless old lady."

"Oh how wrong he was." Wharton laughed.

"At least I don't think we have to worry about that guy anymore."

"You didn't find out who he is?"

She shook her head. "I'm hoping Lieutenant Sarkis has the answers when he comes."

As Brett and Wharton took seats on the sofa the doorbell rang. Atlanta answered it, ushering the lieutenant in. He brought a briefcase with him which he placed on the floor beside his chair.

Gazing at them over the edge of his spectacles, he verified, "Everyone is okay?"

"We've recovered from our adventure," Atlanta assured him, "but we're anxious to hear what you found out."

"Well, to begin the tea in the jar you gave me did contain tranylcypromine sulfate."

"So this was the same guy who tried to poison Brett." Atlanta sat on the edge of her chair regarding the lieutenant.

"And probably the one who killed Annmarie and Preston," Wharton added. "Who is he?"

"Enrique Pedro Damarios." The lieutenant sent a glance around the group. "Are you acquainted with him?"

Wharton watched Atlanta and Brett exchange a glance.

Brett cleared his throat. "He's probably Marcella's younger brother. But," he added, "it's been over forty years since I've seen him. He'd have been a teenager then."

"This is the woman who died?" the lieutenant clarified, opening his briefcase and taking out a pad of paper.

"Correct." Brett went on, "We've only recently found out what caused her death."

Lieutenant Sarkis stared at Brett a moment, but went on without asking about Marcella.

"Damarios had been treated for post traumatic stress disorder some time ago. He is currently being treated for a borderline personality disorder according to his medical records. When he was treated for PTSD he had a prescription for the tranylcypromine sulfate. They don't use that medication much anymore."

"Does that mean he used a left over prescription to poison people?" Atlanta asked.

"It appears that way."

"Whoa, that's a dangerous thought," Wharton commented.

Brett and Atlanta nodded their agreement.

"So then it's insanity?" Wharton jumped to the conclusion.

"Not specifically," the lieutenant hedged. "PTSD is a treatable mental problem. I'm not sure it exactly qualifies as insanity."

"But he must have been insane to kill all those people," Atlanta protested.

"We'll have to leave that to the psychiatrists." Sarkis sent a warning look around. "Once we've determined he's actually guilty."

"But it all fits, doesn't it?" Atlanta asked.

The lieutenant shrugged. "Apparently, but we can't jump to conclusions." He shot Wharton a meaningful look.

"But why?" Atlanta frowned. "Why would he kill them?"

Wharton looked to the lieutenant who was shaking his head. "All we have so far is the analysis on the things I took from here last night and his medical records. He's not been interrogated yet."

"Will they do that?"

"Since it's a mental case they'll be more careful. Use a psychiatrist rather than a detective."

"So you won't get to talk to him?" Atlanta thought that seemed unfair.

The lieutenant shrugged.

"But you'll let us know what you find out?" Wharton wanted to be sure they didn't get left out of the information loop. After all they had been through the least they could get was an explanation.

Lieutenant Sarkis nodded.

When the lieutenant had gone the three sat quietly absorbing the information.

Atlanta turned to Brett. "Are you sure Marcella never talked about her family?"

He sighed. "Her oldest sibling was at least eight years younger than her."

Atlanta frowned at him. "Could the guy trying to get into where she died that night be Enrique?"

Brett shrugged. "I guess it would make sense."

"Making sense isn't the issue," Wharton barked. "It's what actually happened we want to know." He turned to Atlanta. "If this was Marcella's brother what does Sylvia Nelson have to do with it?"

Atlanta and Brett looked like someone had cast a spell on them.

"The woman on the video of your surveillance system was Sylvia Nelson, Preston's daughter." Wharton waved his hand in the air. "What was she doing here?"

Brett ran his hand through his hair. "I wouldn't think she'd have known Enrique Damarios."

Atlanta rose and stood with her back to the fireplace. "She could have met him at one of the funerals."

"Meeting him is one thing," Wharton huffed. "It still wouldn't explain why she was here or why they would team up."

"Maybe she and Enrique had something going," Brett wiggled his eyebrows.

Wharton scowled at him. "That seems farfetched to me."

Atlanta shot him a you-poor-idiot look.

"Okay, so I'm not particularly perceptive where relationships are concerned. Still . . ."

"How do we find out?" She echoed his thoughts.

"I suppose the best way is to talk to Sylvia." He sighed. "She's not particularly pleased with me right now."

"Maybe you shouldn't be that pleased with her." Atlanta raised her eyebrows.

Wharton sent her a questioning glance.

"Well," Atlanta crossed her arms over her chest. "She's shown up here on my videos where I've had an intruder break in. She does have some explaining to do."

Wharton grimaced. "I guess I need to find out what I can."

CHAPTER THIRTY-EIGHT

Wharton debated his options for contacting Sylvia. Being straightforward, he figured a direct approach would be best, take her by surprise. However, she might refuse to see him, making it impossible. Something else, how did he go about finding her? A surprise wouldn't work if he couldn't find her. Lieutenant Sarkis popped into his mind. Would he help?

He called the lieutenant's cell pondering an approach.

"You forget something?"

"As a matter of fact. On Atlanta's surveillance video and in pictures of recent family events a woman shows up who has been in the company of this Damarios. I believe she's my cousin Sylvia Nelson. I need to know what she thinks she's doing. However, she's pretty disgusted with me. Would probably refuse to see me if I called. And I can't show up where she is if I don't know how to find her."

Silence ensued. The lieutenant asked, "What do you want me to do?"

"I think she's staying in Tacoma, perhaps at a hotel. Maybe, if one believes what one sees on Facebook, the one on the waterfront. Could you find out?"

"I'll see what I can do and get back to you."

Wharton ran his Saturday errands while waiting to hear from the lieutenant, his mind speculating on Sylvia. However there were too many possibilities and too little information. He had just put away the groceries when his phone announced the lieutenant's call.

"We'll do this together," Sarkis declared. "I'll meet you at the parking lot on the corner of McCarver and Ruston Way."

Ruston Way traffic was heavy as it wound along the waterfront where restaurants were scattered next to a paved walking trail. Wharton spotted the lieutenant's truck as he turned the corner and swung into the parking lot. Sarkis backed out, allowing Wharton to slide his car into the parking spot.

"Who is this Sylvia Nelson?" the lieutenant asked when Wharton got in.

"She's my uncle Preston Erving's daughter. He was a founding member of Pistachio."

"How come she won't talk to you?" Sarkis maneuvered his truck out of the lot and to the stoplight.

Wharton explained his credit check and Sylvia's phone call.

Pulling onto the hotel grounds, Davy told him, "We'll make this a social call, but you need to inform her I'm with the sheriff's office. I'm afraid if you do this alone we'll lose important information."

Wharton scowled. "Won't telling her you're the police keep us from getting any information?"

"We won't make a big deal about it unless it's necessary, but it needs to be legal."

They crossed through the lobby and took stairs to the second floor where Sarkis proceeded to a room at the end of the corridor. He turned to Wharton indicating he should knock.

The door opened so swiftly they were taken by surprise. The occupant appeared as surprised as they. However, her recovery was even quicker. Wharton could see the flash of recognition and anger race across her expression. He also anticipated her reaction as she stepped back and took hold of the door. The lieutenant moved fast making it impossible for her to close it.

"Sylvia, wait a minute," Wharton managed to get out.

She was scowling at the lieutenant and leaning on the door. But a six foot five lieutenant wasn't easy to push out of the way.

"We need to talk to you," Wharton continued.

"I don't want to talk to you. I told you to stay out of my life and leave me alone."

"Then what are you doing hanging around people I care about with someone who's threatening their lives?"

This made her pause. However, she resumed pushing the door. "I haven't been hanging around with anyone you know or who knows you."

"Enrique Damarios," the lieutenant said.

She stopped to stare at him. "Who are you?"

Lieutenant Sarkis reached into his pocket and produced his identification, flipping it open for her.

She eyed him a moment then turned back to Wharton. "Why are you doing this to me? What have I ever done to you?" Turning back to the lieutenant without allowing Wharton time for a response, she said, "Where's Rick?"

"He's been arrested for attempted murder."

"Murder! You're nuts!" she shrieked, glaring at Wharton. "This is all your fault."

In a deep restrained voice, Lieutenant Sarkis said, "What is all his fault?"

She opened her mouth, glancing from one to the other.

"Why don't we sit down and talk about it?"

With another snarling look at Wharton she took a step back. They took the move as an invitation to enter. She perched on the king size bed while the lieutenant took the chair at the desk and Wharton occupied the one in the corner.

The lieutenant repeated, "What is all his fault?"

"You said Rick had been arrested." Sylvia crossed her arms over her chest.

"How could that be Wharton's fault?"

The glance she shot Wharton said it should be perfectly obvious. "He had a credit check done on me. My employer reviewed my security clearance and decided there were problems. So they suspended me until they could redo the security check." She huffed, "I'm on a leave of absence until it's finished."

"How did you get to know Enrique Damarios?" Sarkis asked.

"I met him at Dad's memorial service."

"What was he doing there?" Wharton frowned.

She flung him a what-business-is-it-of-yours look.

"Did he know your father?" the lieutenant asked.

Her gaze returned to Davy with a frown. "I assume so."

"But you don't know?"

She shrugged. "Why would he go if he didn't know him?"

That was the point, Wharton figured. "Did you return to Pennsylvania after the memorial?"

"I still had a job then." Her gaze knifed him again.

"You also came for Aunt Annmarie's memorial?"

"Did you see Damarios then?" The lieutenant asked.

She nodded. "I had this awful judgment. That's what made my credit a problem. I ended up with debt for work done on property I was supposed to be a part owner in, however . . ."

"You got left holding the bag."

She scowled at Wharton. "He was a conman."

"I know." Wharton nodded. "I understand."

"Did Damarios offer to help you?" the lieutenant asked.

She shook her head. "But we talked about people taking advantage and how bad things happened. We had a lot in common."

Wharton sighed. He wasn't sure that was the case, but undoubtedly Enrique made it appear so. "Did he want you to help him?"

"He wanted to find someone who was a friend of his sister who died."

The lieutenant leaned forward. "Did he tell you about his sister?"

"Only that someone had killed her a long time ago at a concert. He was trying to find the one who did it."

"What did he want you to do?"

"Go to a house and see if a man was there who he described to me."

"Did you?"

She nodded. "The man answered the door. So I told him."

The lieutenant exchanged a glance with Wharton. "Did he go see this man?"

"I thought that's where he was last night. He said he would come today." She glanced at Wharton then back at the lieutenant. "Is he really in jail?"

"He tried to kill that man and threatened his cousin. He didn't tell you that he was trying to kill him?"

"It was the second time he had tried to kill him," Wharton added. "He almost succeeded the first time."

"But he didn't," Sylvia clarified. "So he's only in for attempted murder?"

"We believe he killed your father and Aunt Annmarie and perhaps another man."

"But why?" Sylvia's voice rose. "He seemed so kind and understanding."

"He may be all those things in his right mind," the lieutenant explained, "but he has a mental condition."

"What will they do to him?"

"He'll have a psychiatric evaluation before any decisions are made." The lieutenant rose. "You're going to need to stay available for questioning."

She sighed, nodding.

"Did you find out what you wanted to know?" the lieutenant asked Wharton as they headed back to his truck.

Wharton lifted his shoulders. "Do you think she was involved in what Damarios was doing?"

"I'd guess she didn't know what he was doing. She was probably as involved as he could get her without telling her what he was up to."

"So you wouldn't be looking to prosecute her?"

The lieutenant shook his head. "But we need to keep her available for information. She may be the key to getting him convicted." He grinned at Wharton. "I'm not sure we got you off her hot seat."

Wharton sighed. "I can live with that. I just want all this death nonsense to end."

"Good morning," Kitty said in her cheerful realtor's voice.

Wharton consulted his watch. It was early, even for her. "What's up?"

"Tomorrow is Halloween."

"So?" He wasn't aware it was a big holiday on her calendar.

She rushed on with enthusiasm. "I thought you might want to join us handing out trick-or-treats."

On the point of accusing her of finagling to get the latest gossip, he realized a get-together could serve to his advantage. "How about a party?"

"What did you have in mind?" She sounded suspicious.

"I need to tie up some loose ends. Get a few people together."

Suspicion elevated to skepticism. "Like who?"

"Atlanta and Brett, Atlanta's neighbor."

"Why her?" Kitty snapped.

"She knows Brett's daughter." Wharton continued, "Also cousin Sylvia and some friends of Brett's."

"You actually mean a party." Kitty sounded surprised.

"I can do it at my place if you don't . . ."

"No, no," she interrupted him. "We can do a party. Invite who you want. We can put together some snacks and drinks. You bring the candy."

"And the videos."

"Videos?" She was back to suspicion.

"We'll need to watch the Pistachio videos RJ has."

"And hand out candy." Kitty verified.

"Right."

When they had agreed on the arrangements Wharton warmed a cup of coffee, then called Atlanta and explained the get-together.

"Thanks, Wharton. That'll be great."

Although he would like to have taken credit and the points it might earn him, he felt he needed to be honest. "You'll have to thank Kitty. I'd never have thought of it without her."

After explaining Wharton's call to Brett Atlanta suggested, "Why don't we go to the bookstore and see if we can run into Sunny and Philippe?"

"Are you going to talk to Drina?" Brett sounded apprehensive.

Atlanta nodded. "I'd better do that now."

Drina answered on the first ring as if waiting for the call.

"Panzi wanted to see the Pistachio videos. We're all invited to a Halloween party where they'll be showing those." Atlanta read off Kitty and Aaron's address then explained the best way to get there.

"I'll let Panzi know." Drina sounded excited. "She'll be happy to hear."

The beautiful late fall days of the past week had disappeared leaving behind a heavy overcast portending rain, right on track for late October. Barnes & Noble was warm and inviting with the usual hum of activity coming from the café.

Sunny and Philippe occupied their usual corner. Atlanta noted her girlfriends were there too.

When they had obtained beverages, Atlanta suggested, "Why don't you invite Sunny & Philippe to Kentish's? I'll go face my friends." She grimaced, unsure she was ready for the third degree.

The three sat together, ostensibly chatting, absorbed by their conversation. They gave every evidence of surprise when Atlanta greeted them. However, she knew them better than that.

"We heard they arrested someone for Preston and Annmarie Erving's deaths."

"Where did you hear that?" Atlanta couldn't believe the news got out that quick.

They glanced at each other guiltily. Fredee's eyes strayed to the corner where Sunny and Philippe sat. They had quizzed Brett's friends. Obviously Philippe knew what had happened. Maybe Atlanta could avoid the third degree.

Fredee covered her stray glance by a frontal attack. "So where's your friend?"

Atlanta decided to play dumb. "You're all here, aren't you?"

Fredee rolled her eyes.

So much for avoiding the third degree, it was time for the offensive. "You questioned Philippe?"

Ignoring her Sherry accused, "You didn't tell us Brett had been in the hospital."

"We were trying to keep him safe."

"From us?" Fredee's voice squeaked.

Atlanta cast her gaze heavenward and shook her head.

"So what are you hiding now?" Sherry raised her eyebrows.

"Nothing official has been done. They still have to do a psychological evaluation."

"So you don't know if he's the one?" Sherry summarized.

"He's the one, we just don't know why."

"Okay, back to your friend, you know, the big guy you've been going around with lately." Fredee waved her hands descriptively.

"What about him?"

"Are you two . . .?" Fredee rocked her shoulders.

"No."

The three stared at her with varying degrees of disbelief. However, no one challenged her. She had to wonder a little at their reticence, but figured that beat the alternative. She could not have answered the question if she wanted to, nor was she sure she would ever be able to.

CHAPTER THIRTY-NINE

Wharton had said to arrive at Kitty's around six o'clock. That was when trick-or-treaters began parading through the neighborhood. For reasons she could not have explained Atlanta was anxious to see how Panzi felt about the videos. Although she tried to imagine what it would be like for her, it was impossible. She could not relate.

Brett wandered in a daze. Atlanta could sympathize, but not relate to him either. She left him to his thoughts since she figured it would take time to process what had happened. Amazed and intrigued by the boy who looked so much like him, she felt that must mean a lot to Brett. But perhaps it was Panzi, his daughter, so resembling Marcella that had him locked in a trance. It crossed Atlanta's mind perhaps Brett would want to take up permanent residence in this area where he could be near them.

She was tempted to envy him. Though he had lost the love of his life, the dream he cherished, he had some recompense. Something to hold on to that gave his dream substance and reality. Everything wasn't illusory.

Several cars occupied the driveway when they reached the Kentish home. One was Wharton's Mercedes from which he was unloading a cooler. Jack-o-lanterns sat on the front stairs and a scarecrow stood at attention near the garage. On the door hung a large floral wreath in bright fall colors.

Atlanta sighed with relief to think they were finally free from the danger hanging over their heads. She could once again enjoy these scenes and the thought of a gathering with friends for the sheer pleasure of it.

Pulling into the driveway behind them was Drina with Panzi, Frank and Cory. Philippe, Sunny and his wife parked along the curb. They all approached the house in a flurry of greetings and questions.

Aaron opened the door holding out a basket of candy. "You need to get one before the kids take them all."

They were ushered into the living room and invited to help themselves at a table of hors d'oeuvres in the adjacent dining room. There were wine coolers, soda and coffee in the kitchen. Atlanta took a glass of white wine and some quesadilla-style snacks then retired to a seat on the brick ledge near the fireplace. Wharton sat next to her munching on a petite sandwich of deli meat and cheese.

"Did you meet Brett's daughter?"

Wharton nodded. "She's what the enigmatic Marcella looked like?"

"Look closely at the videos, the resemblance is amazing."

"I wonder what would have happened if Brett had met her without knowing she was his daughter."

Atlanta smiled. "Do you ever see people who remind you of your wife?"

He was thoughtful. "I used to once in a while right after she passed away. I figured my brain was playing tricks on me."

"I believe that's what he would think after so many years." Atlanta lifted her shoulders. "Especially since Brett never knew she was pregnant."

"What about Enrique Damarios? What would he have done with Panzi?"

Atlanta shook her head. "Did you talk to Sylvia? I see she's here."

Wharton sighed. "I took the lieutenant with me, or rather he took me with him, and we questioned her. I don't think she knew what Damarios was doing. That may be in our favor when it comes to her being a witness. Only a psychiatrist can guess what Damarios thought he was doing. It seems he may have been getting revenge on the ones he believed caused his sister's death. Given the PSTD he may have been fighting another battle entirely."

"Do you really believe that?" Atlanta cocked her head.

"No." He grimaced. "Regardless of his mental state and the diagnosis I think he was fighting the battle for his sister's life, or against who he believed caused her death. He'll probably be declared mentally incompetent and committed to an institution."

"And your cousin?" Atlanta noted her talking with Aaron. "Do you think she'll forgive you for interfering in her life?"

"She's smart enough. Eventually she'll see the light." He grinned. "She's here tonight. That's hopeful. I'm not sure she'd ever have gotten involved with Damarios if she hadn't gotten into trouble with that con guy. She needs to learn how to tell the good guys from the bad."

"She's not just rebellious and interested in bad guys?"

"I don't think so." He shrugged his eyebrows. "I think she got sidetracked. She may stay for a while with Kitty. The lieutenant wants her to be available for questioning and she's on a leave of absence from work. Kitty can get her straightened out if anyone can."

Atlanta laughed.

"You don't believe me?" He pinned her with a gaze from beneath his heavy eyebrows. "She gave it to me straight where you're concerned."

"In what way?"

"She hit me square between the eyes with the fact I blew it after the law suit by not doing little things to make sure you knew I still thought about you. She scolded me for going back to work and acting as if nothing had happened. I realized from what she said you had given up hope."

Atlanta bit her lip. The emotional traitor inside was on the point of sending tears to her eyes.

"That's right isn't it?"

Not trusting her voice she nodded.

"I'm sorry. I really am." He looked across the room and then back at her. "Could you forgive me enough for us to start over?"

Atlanta took a tissue from her pocket and blew her nose. Then she smiled. "We could get season tickets to the theatre."

Wharton laughed, putting his arm around her shoulders. "That's a deal."

Printed in the United States
By Bookmasters